Colors of Deceit

Colors of Deceit

Valerie Massey Goree

Parson Place Press
Mobile, Alabama

Colors of Deceit by Valerie Massey Goree

Copyright © 2014 by Valerie Massey Goree
All rights reserved.

Cover art by Valerie Massey Goree
Cover design by Just Ink Digital Design

ISBN: 978-0-9888528-6-0

Library of Congress Control Number: 2014908963

Dedication

To my grandchildren, a blessing like no other.

Acknowledgements

A special thanks to my American Christian Fiction Writers online critique group for your insight, comments, suggestions, and support.

I appreciate the information provided by Captain Carol Twiss, a criminal investigator with the Kerr County Sheriff's Office, and Sergeant Mary Krebs from the Kerrville Police Department. Any errors in police procedures are mine.

Liberties

Hanson Ridge, Brooder, Carl's Diner, Camp Alpha, the antique store Use it Again, Sam, and the churches mentioned are fictitious places. However, The OST Restaurant is real. If you visit Bandera, stop by for a delicious meal and admire the photographs of John Wayne.

> "Who shall separate us from the love of Christ? Shall tribulation, or distress, or persecution, or famine, or nakedness, or peril, or sword?" (Romans 8:35 KJV)

FAMILY TREE
VIRGINIA SUMMERLAND-HAYES

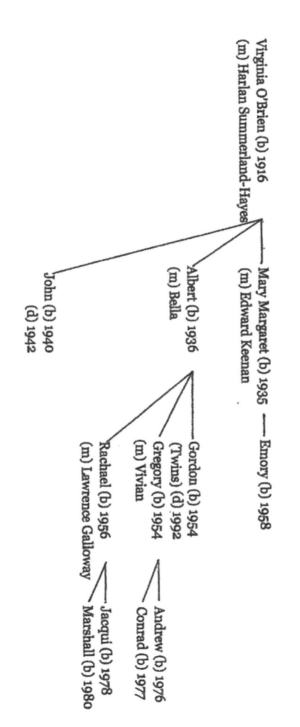

Virginia O'Brien (b) 1916
(m) Harlan Summerland-Hayes

Mary Margaret (b) 1935 —— Emory (b) 1958
(m) Edward Keenan

Albert (b) 1936
(m) Bella

John (b) 1940
(d) 1942

Gordon (b) 1954
(Twins) (d) 1992
Gregory (b) 1954
(m) Vivian

Rachael (b) 1956
(m) Lawrence Galloway

Andrew (b) 1976
Conrad (b) 1977

Jacqui (b) 1978
Marshall (b) 1980

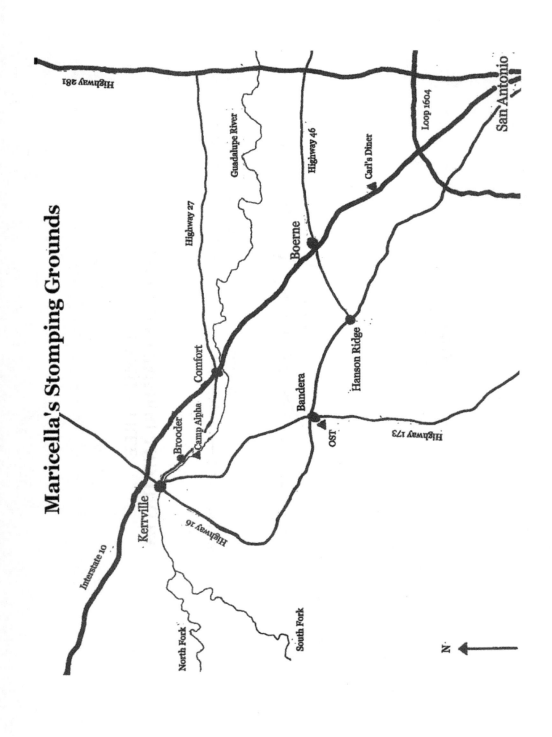

CHAPTER ONE

The front door stood ajar. Not a good sign.

I eased it open. "Teresa? It's Maricella. I've brought a baby gift from my neighbors. Are you all right?" My daughter-in-law wasn't expecting a visit from me. Why would she leave the door open?

Crossing the living room in quick steps, I peered down the long, narrow hall. Teresa, eight months pregnant, lay with her back to me looking like a mound of rumpled clothes.

"Teresa!" I dropped my purse and the gift bag as I hurried to her side and knelt.

A groan escaped from under the veil of black hair that had fallen over her face. She clutched her belly.

I finger-combed the hair aside and touched her cheek. "Are you in labor? Is the baby on his way?"

Her eyelids fluttered. She pointed to the master bedroom at the end of the hall. "There's a man . . ."

Floorboards squeaked. Light flickered in the bedroom doorway at the same time Teresa's words registered. There was someone in the house. Creepy-crawly fingers of fear tickled my scalp.

On my feet again, I hesitated. Should I stay with Teresa or call for help?

A figure emerged from the bedroom, filling the hall with menace. He carried something tucked under one arm.

"What are you doing?" Anger edged Teresa's words as she raised her head. "No, don't take that."

In the gloom I couldn't tell what he held.

With the grace of an athlete, he bounded over Teresa. She caught a hold of his boot which threw him off-balance. He dropped the object and hopped twice.

Momentum already established, he careened into me, sending me staggering backward until I collided with the wall and slithered to the floor.

In the distance the kitchen door banged shut and footsteps clipped across the back porch.

Crawling to Teresa, I asked, "Are you hurt?"

"He hit me." She rubbed her jaw. "The baby. I fell and—"

"You need professional help." I scrambled up, located the phone in the living room and dialed 9-1-1. Once I knew the ambulance and law enforcement officers were on their way, I returned to Teresa.

"I . . . I want to get up but my back aches, and I'm having contractions. They might be Braxton Hicks again, but—"

"Let's not take any chances. I know it's uncomfortable on the floor, but you better stay there until the paramedics check you out. I don't want to deliver my grandson here in the middle of the hall."

A brief grin momentarily brightened her drawn face.

I slipped into the bedroom and yanked a pillow off the bed. After placing it under Teresa's head, I sat next to her. "There, that should help a little."

"*Gracias*, Chella. Why—"

The front door opened. Ambulance already? We'd heard no sirens.

"Teresa, I'm home. Mama, I saw your car outside. This is a nice surprise." Mike, my oldest son.

"We're in the hall. Be prepared—"

When he turned the corner, his welcoming tone vanished. "What in the world?" His large frame blocked the light for a second, then he dropped to his knees beside Teresa. "What happened? Are you in labor?"

Teresa eased out a tight smile. "Not exactly." She stilled the hand Mike rubbed on her belly by clasping his fingers.

Sirens echoed through the neighborhood. I stood and slipped behind Mike with my hands on his bowed shoulders. "Take it easy, son. Teresa's been attacked."

"What?"

"The ambulance is here. I'll go meet them." I opened the front door as two paramedics climbed the porch steps.

After directing them to the hall, I waited at the door for the officer who'd also arrived.

With the paramedics working on Teresa in the confined space, I answered the deputy's questions in the living room. The Kerr County Sheriff's Department served the small community of Brooder, ten miles south east of Kerrville.

Deputy Wilson, a young man I'd guess to be in his late twenties, opened his small notebook. "Can you describe the intruder, ma'am?"

I'd already explained to him what I'd seen and heard when first entering the house. "He was tall. My husband and sons are all over six foot, and this guy was at least that. And slim. No extra weight for sure."

"What about hair color, clothing, identifying marks?"

The intruder's silhouette at the end of the hall lurked behind my eyelids. "He had curly hair, sticking out of a baseball cap. And he was in black. Even his hands."

"Are you saying he was African-American?"

The man's face flashed in my mind as I relived the wall-slam. "No, no. He wore a black turtleneck T-shirt, black jeans, and black gloves. His hair was brown. He was Anglo." Bobbing curls had revealed a pale cheek. "Very Anglo. And the baseball cap was blue."

"He was Caucasian?"

"Yeah. With lots of curly hair."

"Anything else?" Wilson glanced up as Mike joined me on the sofa.

"Um, not about his appearance, but as he ran by a strong whiff of epoxy followed him." I wrinkled my nose at the memory and shrugged. "Don't know where it came from, or if it's important."

"I'll add it to your statement. Do you live in Brooder?"

"No. We live in Hanson Ridge, about forty miles south of Kerrville. I stopped by to deliver a gift."

"I've driven through Hanson Ridge." Wilson closed his notebook. "Thank you, Mrs. McDonough." His buzz-cut light brown hair gave him a military air.

We all turned as a paramedic rolled a gurney into the house and down the hall. Wilson excused himself and entered the kitchen. Mike's tight lips and furrowed brow plucked at my heart as he leaned forward on the sofa.

I rested my head on his shoulder and held his hand. "Is Teresa okay, and the baby? Is he on his way?"

Mike's fingers tightened. "The paramedics are evaluating her condition. Too early to tell about the baby."

His panic-strained voice hung in the air.

"Did Teresa tell you what happened, why the man attacked her?"

Eyes fixed on the activity in the hall, Mike released my hand. "No. They're giving her oxygen right now. The deputy said he'd question her at the hospital." He sprang to his feet as if he'd made up his mind that second. "I'm going with her." He turned, his worried blue eyes beseeching me. "Mama, can you come, too?"

"Of course, *mijo*. I'll follow in my car."

Mike left the house with Teresa and the paramedics. Wilson returned to the living room, writing in his notebook.

I wasn't sure about protocol. "Can I leave, too, or does a family member have to stay?"

"You're free to go, ma'am. I'll lock up when I've concluded my investigation. I understand you need to be with your family. If I have any more questions, I'll address them when I visit with your daughter-in-law."

"Thank you." I grabbed my purse from the spot where I'd dropped it and headed to my car.

Anxiety added weight to my right foot as I raced along the winding, two-lane country road to Kerrville.

Slow down. No sense getting a speeding ticket to add to the drama.

Two lanes expanded into four. Friday afternoon traffic multiplied, but nothing like I'd face if Mike and Teresa still lived in San Antonio. They'd recently moved to the Hill County north west of San Antonio. What a welcome they'd received. Here a week and Teresa had been attacked and on her way to the ER.

Well-placed signs led me to the hospital. The receptionist in the ER listened to my frantic pleas concerning Teresa, and then told me to have a seat in the waiting area. After eons, which I'm sure was really only minutes, Mike pushed through the double doors.

We met in the middle of the room where he wrapped me in a bear hug. I could barely get my arms around him, but my mother-pats covered as much of his back as I could reach.

"What did the doctor say?" I patted a few more times. "How's the baby?"

His arms relaxed and he cleared his throat, but the action failed to squash the anxiety in his voice. "They're monitoring the fetal heart beat. Teresa's bruised, no broken bones, but . . . but she's in shock and the baby . . . Mama, I'm so worried."

"I'm sure you are. Is there any danger of—?" I couldn't complete the question.

"We don't know." His voice quavered in a sob.

The concern in Mike's words constricted my throat. I hadn't heard my twenty-four-year-old firstborn cry for many years.

We comforted each other until the receptionist tapped on the glass partition.

She pointed to the doors. "You can both go in. The deputies have arrived and need to question your wife."

Mike led me through the triage area. I crinkled my nose against the sharp odors of alcohol and antiseptic. Ignoring moans and beeps from behind green curtains, we arrived at last in Teresa's room. She rested on the raised bed, her baby bump prominent under the covers. Protruding wires connected various parts of her anatomy to monitors and machines. She had one arm crooked covering her eyes. Her long black hair cascaded down the pillow.

A chill swept my body, and I rubbed my arms through my light jacket.

Teresa lowered her arm, eyes widening in greeting. "I'm glad you came too, Chella."

I moved to the bed. "Teresa, *mija*. This is not a good way to get bed rest." I hugged her as best I could and kissed her forehead.

As I straightened, I noticed the swelling on her left jaw line. "Ouch."

She jutted her chin in my direction. "He landed a good one."

I gratefully perched on the chair Mike scooted behind me. He brought in another chair and sat next to me.

Teresa maneuvered in the bed and clutched at her belly. "Ooh."

"What's wrong?" Mike jumped up.

"Nothing. He's making his presence known. It's a good sign because he hasn't moved much since the attack."

The monitors beeped and blinked. My heart thudded. *Relax. You have to be the calm one.*

I tugged at my son's arm. "Sit, Mike."

He poised on the edge of his chair as if ready to go into battle at a moment's notice.

Two deputies stopped at the door, Wilson and a younger female with short auburn hair and striking green eyes.

A sorry-to-bother-you bend to his shoulders, Wilson stepped in. "The doctor said we can question you now, Mrs. McDonough. Are you feeling up to it?"

"Sure." Teresa's voice seemed as rigid as the pole holding her IV.

"I'm Scott Wilson and this is Vanessa Irving. She's going to record your answers."

Deputy Irving entered the room and withdrew a small recorder from the pocket of her dark blue shirt. She punched a button, named the participants, and indicated the date and time. "We're ready."

At the foot of the bed, Wilson consulted his notes. "Right, Mrs. McDonough. To begin, please tell me how the man gained entrance to your house."

Teresa focused on the young woman beside her. "We moved in about a week ago. I was unpacking the last of our boxes when someone knocked at the back door. I didn't think anything of it, because people from church have been stopping by all week. Some walk through the neighborhood, and the back door is more convenient."

"Which church?" Wilson asked.

"Eagle Crest Community Church." She smoothed the sheet over her belly and paused a moment. "A young man stood there with a plastic storage container full of cookies and asked where I wanted it. I was not concerned because people have been super generous." Plucking at the tape holding her IV in place, Teresa scrunched up her nose. "I told him to place it on the counter, which he did, but instead of leaving, he asked if he could see the rest of the house. Before I could reply, he entered the living room, opened the front door, then headed down the hall."

"I should have been there." Mike wrung his hands. "I didn't have to go to the church office today. I'm sorry, honey."

"Please, sir, let your wife finish." Wilson tapped his pen on his notebook.

Mike mouthed, "Sorry," and held Teresa's hand.

"Where was I?" Teresa intertwined her fingers with Mike's. "Right. I followed the man down the hall and asked what he was doing. He didn't respond, but peeked in the baby's room and the spare room. I told him if he didn't leave right away I'd call the cops. My threat didn't bother him. He entered our bedroom and came out carrying the jewelry box that was given to me at the pounding last Saturday. Remember it, Maricella?"

"It's an antique, right?" Oops. Wilson's brow crinkled as he shot me an impatient glance.

"Yes, and I wasn't about to let him—"

"Wait, wait." Irving paused the recorder. "What in the world is a pounding?" Her wide eyes underscored her confusion. "Am I missing something here?"

Suppressing a giggle, I recalled a similar reaction when Teresa invited Tom and me to the pounding, and I'd asked what they were going to be pounded with and why.

Wilson surprised me by answering his colleague. "It's a country custom from the old days to welcome newcomers to a church with a pound of flour, or sugar, or other food items. But these days parishioners bring groceries, or baked goods, or housewarming gifts."

Irving's eyebrows rose an inch. "Really? Never heard of it."

"That's because you're from the heathen town of—" Wilson turned and found three pairs of eyes focused on him. A flush tinged his tan with pink. "Sorry, folks." He rubbed his chin. "Irving, turn on the recorder, please."

He waited for her to punch the button. Irving's green eyes sparked as she fiddled with the hair covering her ear. She appeared to be annoyed with Wilson.

"Now, Mrs. McDonough, you were telling us about the jewelry box."

"I wasn't about to let the man steal all my jewelry."

"Valuable items?"

"A few. Such as a diamond necklace I inherited from *Abuelita*, my grandmother. Some pieces from Mike. Others with sentimental value."

"Wonder why he didn't try to remove the items from the box?" Wilson shrugged. "What happened next?"

"The man just stood there. So I snatched a chunky bookend from the hall table and threw it at him. He ducked and it landed on the floor. He . . . he came right at me. I yelled at him, asking why he wanted the jewelry box. But he said nothing. Then I heard a car in the driveway, and by his expression I'm sure he heard it, too."

"That must have been me." I couldn't help the interruption. "If only I'd arrived ten minutes earlier."

Straightening in the bed, Teresa turned to me. "Coming when you did may have saved my life."

Wilson cleared his throat, his irritation undeniable.

Teresa continued. "I wasn't about to let him get away without trying to identify him. I knew there'd be no fingerprints because of his gloves, and he wore a baseball cap low on his forehead." She folded her arms on top of her baby bump and raised her eyebrows in defiance. "I reached for his cap."

"Teresa!" Mike shouted.

Wilson rolled his eyes.

"You should have let him have the jewelry box, Honey. We can replace jewelry, my love. I can't . . ." Mike feathered his fingers across her cheek and jaw.

Teresa clasped his hand and raised it to her lips. "I know, *mi amor*. But I didn't like the idea of him coming into our house and taking my jewelry and the gift, part of such a warm welcome to our new life in Brooder."

I observed the interaction between my son and his wife and thanked God she'd come into our lives. Teresa had been a tower of strength to me when I'd faced the death of a childhood friend the previous year.

Mike stood and paced to the door and back. He ran a hand through his mop of thick brown hair. He looked so much like his father. I could tell he hated the fact he hadn't been home to protect his wife and unborn child.

"Come, son." I patted the chair. "Sit." He alighted next to me. "Sorry, Deputy Wilson. This isn't easy for us. We can't let Teresa describe what happened without reacting. Do you want us to leave?"

"No. We'll transcribe what we need for her statement. Y'all can stay, but please keep your comments to a minimum. Now, Mrs. McDonough, did he strike you?"

Touching her jaw, Teresa nodded. "When I raised my hand to his cap he blocked my action and punched me."

Mike squirmed and muttered under his breath.

"I stumbled back and hit my head against the wall." Rubbing the affected area, she flinched. "Ooh, I have a nice lump there. Anyway, I slid to the floor. Thank the Lord I landed on my side and not on the baby, but I don't remember anything else until Maricella came in."

The smile she sent me thanked me for more than simply showing up when I did. Her gaze then shifted to Mike.

"Mike, I'm real thirsty. Please see if I can have something to drink."

"Of course." He marched out of the room, intent on his mission.

"Will you be much longer, deputy?" I scooted to edge of my chair. "Teresa needs her rest."

"No, ma'am. One more question. Physical description. What can you tell us?"

Lines of determination still etched on his face, Mike returned with a cup of water that Teresa eagerly sipped. Her description of the intruder matched mine, with the added detail that he might be a little older than Mike.

"That's it for now, Mrs. McDonough." Wilson and Irving shared a glance. He slipped his notebook into his shirt pocket, and she turned off the recorder.

Mike rolled his shoulders. "Thank you, deputies. In all the confusion, I didn't notice. Did the guy steal the jewelry box?"

"No, and it appeared to be full when I checked. You will have to inventory the contents, Mrs. McDonough. He took nothing else. According to your mother's statement, he left the house empty-handed." Wilson stopped at the door. "I wondered why he returned to the master bedroom when he heard the car. Seems he was trying to escape out a window, but he could only open it a couple of inches."

"It's an old house. Some of the wooden frames are warped," Mike said.

Wilson nodded. "One more thing, Mrs. McDonough. You were correct. No fingerprints on the jewelry box. An officer will stop by the house and retrieve the container of cookies. We're questioning the neighbors." He gave a half salute. "We'll be in touch."

The deputies' exit from the room allowed some of the anxiety to ease from Teresa's face. She placed her empty cup on the side table and, gathering her hair together, twisted it into a knot on top of her head. "I lost my clip in the chaos."

"I'll see if I have an extra one." I searched through the spacious compartments of my purse. I often wore my hair in a similar fashion. In fact, Teresa and I were sometimes mistaken for mother and daughter. We both had shoulder length black hair, chocolate brown eyes, and olive-toned skin, our Hispanic heritage very evident.

"Here you are." I handed her a tortoiseshell plastic claw clip which she clamped into her hair.

"*Gracias.*"

Elbows propped on his blue jean-clad knees, Mike stared at Teresa.

Unaccustomed to seeing him in jeans on a work day, I had to remember he no longer belonged to the corporate world. As a youth minister, he could wear casual clothes whenever he wanted.

The past year had brought great changes to all our lives. Mike and Teresa had agreed to forsake the fast-paced life associated with a lucrative career in technology. After long deliberations and hours of prayer, they joined the ministry with a church in the small town of Brooder. I worked part-time as a physical therapist for the Bandera Independent School District. *Abuelita* would need time to play with her grandson.

Grandson.

I shook off the reminiscing. "Since no one's said anything about the baby, I assume he's okay?"

"*Sí*. At first Dr. Goldman, the ER doc, said that because I was in shock they were concerned with his heart rate, but see there." Teresa pointed to one of the monitors. "That's his little heartbeat right there."

We all watched the line blip up and down, rapid and consistent.

"It looks strong to me. Has the doctor said anything about the other . . . you know, the cysts?"

When Teresa had a routine sonogram at twenty-eight weeks, two arachnoid cysts were detected between the baby's skull and brain. The doctor had explained that the cerebrospinal fluid-filled sacs could be absorbed or could grow larger as the baby developed.

Teresa shook her head.

"We told the ER staff when we arrived. They were going to do a sonogram anyway." Straightening Teresa's IV line, Mike's eyes grew weary. "They will compare her previous sonograms and look for any changes in the cysts, which means at least an overnight stay."

"Even without waiting for them to compare sonograms, an overnight stay is a good idea. Or even longer. You might not agree, Teresa, but after a fall and the shock, you never know what might develop later. How's your blood sugar?" She had been diagnosed with gestational diabetes at twenty-one weeks and had to monitor her blood glucose levels four times a day.

"It's within normal limits, but you don't have to convince me. I'm tired and sore and—" Teresa clutched her belly. "Ooh. He's kicking like he wants out."

Mike stood and rubbed Teresa's stomach. "It's too early, son. Go to sleep, and let your mama rest." He turned to me. "Speaking of mothers, Mama, do you have to go home? Can you stay? I don't—"

"Sure. I'll stay as long as you need me. Barbara can take care of Brutus." Our neighbor often pet-sat. She'd take good care of my four-legged baby.

"What about your job?"

"Don't you know? It's Spring Break."

"Of course. Great. And Daddy?"

"He's in Houston at the National Medical Sales Conference. It ends at noon tomorrow." I checked my watch. "He's almost through with today's presentation. I'll call him in fifteen or twenty minutes. So, you see I'm free to stay." As one of the main speakers to fellow medical equipment salesmen, Tom would not be able to leave before the conference concluded.

With relief evident in his slump, Mike sat again. "Thanks, Mama."

I stretched my arm around his shoulders. "You take care of your wife and baby, and don't worry about anything at the house for now. Okay?"

Resting in my embrace, he nodded.

"Chella, the house." Covering her eyes, Teresa moaned. "It's such a mess. Boxes and—"

"No problem. I understand. I've done my share of moving."

A petite nurse waltzed into the room and announced Dr. Goldman had contacted Teresa's doctors in San Antonio—her ob-gyn, Dr. Quinn, and the pediatric neurosurgeon, Dr. Conway. "Dr. Goldman and Dr. Conway are comparing the sonograms electronically. I'm processing your admitting paperwork, and we'll have a room assignment shortly. I'll be back in a jiff."

We stared at each other after she left, subdued now with the hospital stay confirmed. The beeping monitors punctuated the silence until Dr. Goldman entered.

The stocky, gray-haired man stood in the middle of the room and all eyes focused on him. "Dr. Conway and I have compared the sonograms, and we have a little good news." He peered at Teresa over his glasses, then back at the file. "One of the cysts has decreased in size, but the other one is about the same. I recommend a follow-up visit with her next week. But all things considered, your son appears healthy and none the worse for your fall, Mrs. McDonough."

He closed the file. "But we'll keep you overnight for observation. Your blood pressure's a little high, and with the diabetes and the stress the baby's been through, it's advisable. Your room is ready, but before they take you, do you have any questions?" He removed his glasses and slipped them into the pocket of his white coat.

Questions? I had a thousand and didn't wait for Mike and Teresa to voice theirs. "The cyst that's decreasing in size, is there a chance it could go away completely?"

"Yes. The cerebrospinal fluid could be totally absorbed and—"

"Why would one be absorbed and not the other?" Teresa asked.

"I don't know. This is not my area of expertise. Dr. Conway will be able to provide more information when you see her next week."

Mike placed his hand on Teresa's stomach. "And you're sure the baby suffered no ill effects?"

"Not as far as we can tell."

"Praise the Lord. The baby's okay." Mike raised his eyes heavenward.

"Amen," Teresa whispered.

"You'll also need to make an appointment with Dr. Quinn. Are you going to have the baby in San Antonio or here in Kerrville?"

Teresa squeezed Mike's hand. "We'd like to stay with Dr. Quinn in San Antonio, and then find a local pediatrician later."

"I understand. Dr. Quinn informed me she has contacted an associate here in Kerrville—Dr. Fletcher. She will examine you tomorrow before you can be discharged." Dr. Goldman nodded, checked the monitors, and hastened out of the room.

I placed my hand over my heart. "We'll take all the good news—"

The fetal monitor squawked.

We froze.

Lights flashed and alarm bells blared. The line on the fetal heart monitor flattened.

Teresa screamed, "No! What's happening?" She grabbed her belly and groaned.

Mike headed to the door to call for help as three nurses and the doctor raced in.

"You two have to leave, please," said a nurse.

"Get her to surgery! Stat!" yelled the doctor.

CHAPTER TWO

Mike and I clung to each other in the waiting room. Time took on the quality of molasses. The seconds seemed to be dripping off a Salvador Dali clock. What was happening in Teresa's room? A troop of celebrities could have sauntered by and we wouldn't have noticed. With eyes fixed on the double doors we waited, surrounded by mumbled voices from the TV in the corner, sniffles from a grieving family next to us, and the squeal of a distant siren zooming closer.

Dr. Goldman pushed through the doors and they swished closed behind him. We rushed to meet him.

He held up a manila folder as if to ward off our assault. "Now, now, folks. Calm down. Mother and baby are fine."

"What about the surgery?"

"I know you're concerned, Mr. McDonough. Come on back, and I'll explain in private."

With Mike's arm around my shoulders, we followed Dr. Goldman back to Teresa's room.

Dark, sunken eyes dominated her drawn face.

Mike kissed her forehead and held her hand to his chest. "My love."

Dropping into a chair, I slid my purse to the floor and my heart fell with it.

Dr. Goldman's glasses balanced on the bridge of his nose. "I've already explained to Mrs. McDonough that uterine contractions probably caused the baby's heart rate to fluctuate. Studies show high levels of stress—and she has definitely experienced stress—can release hormones that trigger contractions."

He opened the folder and consulted his notes. "But my examination shows no sign of dilation, or the leaking of amniotic fluids. Baby's heart rate is reassuring, and according to the sonogram his position is good. So, all in all, I'm satisfied we're not looking at preterm labor and won't administer any medication at this time."

"So our baby is okay?" Mike's anxious eyes followed the doctor as he examined the monitors again.

"Yes. He needs to wait, by my estimation about four more weeks."

Holding up four fingers, Teresa waved them in front of her bump. "Four weeks, *mi bebé*. I can make it if you can."

Chuckles of relief spilled out. I clasped my hands, while Mike rolled his eyes and grinned.

"I'm satisfied with baby's condition." Dr. Goldman snapped the file closed. "Your room is ready. Any more questions?"

We had none, and he exited the room.

One glance at Teresa and I knew it was time to go. Exhaustion pulled her pasty skin taut across her face. Eyelids half closed, uneven breathing. She needed rest.

"I'm leaving now, Teresa." I kissed her cheek. "See you tomorrow."

Mike stepped out with me. "Mama . . ." His six-foot-two frame crumbled before my eyes.

I drew him back to the chairs outside Teresa's room and held him while emotions sent shock waves of turmoil through his body.

After a draining minute, he straightened and drew in a gulp of air. "Whew. I thought we were going to lose her. Lose them."

"But we didn't, *mijo*. Go back to her. I'll call Daddy. Have you called your brother?"

"No. Haven't had time."

"I will. Now give me the house keys. I'll stay at your place, close by in case you need me. You go take care of your wife."

He wriggled a set of keys from his pocket, twisted one off and placed it in my hand. "Thanks for staying, Mama. I might spend the night here with Teresa."

"Good idea. Love you." I kissed his cheek and escaped outside. Late afternoon traffic sounds echoed around me. The sun's decline behind the hills chilled the mid-March air. I shivered and zipped my jacket.

Relief and anger churned in my stomach. Running to the edge of the half-empty parking lot, I clung to the sturdy trunk of a large oak covered in newborn leaves. What was wrong with me? I knew I couldn't call Tom, my husband, at this moment. If he heard me right now he'd be worried sick. Conflicting emotions tightened my throat. My voice squeaked out, "Is this their reward, God?"

As I circled the tree, I swiped tears away with my sleeve. Sucking in air, I folded my arms and rested against the bark. I had to figure out what was wrong before I called Tom, before I climbed behind the wheel.

Events of the past couple of hours had dealt a severe blow to my nascent faith. Although I'd attended church services with my husband for over twenty years, I'd only recently accepted Jesus as my Savior and committed to serve Him. I'd heard enough scripture to know a Christian's life wouldn't be problem-free, but I had a hard time understanding and accepting Mike and Teresa's current situation. They gave up a career to serve in the ministry. For this?

So much had happened since making that decision. Almost to the day of accepting the position, Teresa had been diagnosed with diabetes. Two weeks later, the coup de grâce—discovering their unborn son's arachnoid cysts. He might require surgery after birth, which could result in brain damage.

I cringed. My first grandchild. Raising my eyes to the heavens, I stared at stringy clouds through the lacy branches. "Lord, why an innocent child?"

Checking off mental items on my list of complaints, I kept up the tirade as I kicked twigs and pieces of bark on the gravel. I stomped when I recalled the final straw. They had recently been told by the church leadership that Mike's position, and therefore the salary, wouldn't be full-time, as originally agreed. Although given the opportunity to reject the offer, Mike had accepted anyway. Would the job still include medical insurance? Good thing he could develop a home-based computer business to supplement their income. What about the attack on Teresa and the scare in the ER?

"I know the problem with the baby's heartbeat was a false alarm, God, but how can you treat your servants this way?"

An elderly couple approached a car near the tree. I turned away from their curious stares and waited until they drove off. The brief respite allowed me a moment to calm down.

A blue jay squawked in the branches above and swooped to a patch of weeds at the far end of the lot. The bird's raucous noise reminded me of my recent grumbling to God. I knew I had a long way to go and years of study ahead, but I needed a solution right now. If Tom were here he'd tell me to pray. I was still learning how to pray. Praying *anytime, anyplace* was new to me.

"Okay, God. Please forgive my previous rants. I don't understand what's happening to Mike and Teresa. Why are so many trials hitting them all at once?"

I stood under the tree and tried to clear all negative thoughts from my mind and soul. Tiny oak leaves stirred in the breeze, then all was quiet for a brief second.

God didn't answer my prayer in that second, but my jumbled emotions calmed, and the tightness eased around my chest.

Minutes later, I dialed Tom's number and told him all that had transpired.

"When my conference concludes tomorrow, I'll drive straight to Kerrville. Hold on, sweetheart, you caught me as I entered the hotel. Let me open my door." He mumbled, then came back on the phone. "How are you holding up?"

My cheeks heated as I recalled my mental argument with God, and I let out an embarrassed chuckle. "Better now. There was a moment . . . when I had to stop and pray."

Tom's brief silence caught me off guard, but his reply sent ripples to my heart. "I'm proud of you, Chella."

We ended the call with a short prayer. I wiped the tears off my cheeks and punched in the contact number I had for José, our youngest son, and left a message. He was on a plane, traveling to El Salvador for a Spring Break mission trip with a group from the church he attended in San Antonio. A definite change from his usual Spring Break exploits. He'd be able to call us sometime later in the day.

After calling Barbara Bailey, my neighbor, I climbed in the car. Not knowing what Teresa had in the way of groceries, I stopped at a Chinese restaurant for a take-out container of my favorite General Joe's chicken and vegetables, then purchased toiletries at a drug store. Brooder straddled the river southeast of Kerrville, and Mike and Teresa's house nestled in an old tree-lined neighborhood three blocks off the main road.

Streetlights twinkled as I turned onto Kirkwood Drive. Residual tickles of unease from my earlier visit played in my stomach. Mike and Teresa's vehicles lined the gravel driveway. I parked on the street, and carried my sack and food container up the side steps. White railings, columns, and gingerbread scrollwork graced the wide porch, a perfect framework for the hanging plants and rocking chairs. I rearranged the chairs and little side table, then shook my head and moved them back the way they were. *Not your house. Don't be an interfering mother-in-law*. I shrugged, unlocked the door and entered the ranch-style house.

In my traumatic arrival earlier in the day, I'd overlooked the redecorating progress Mike and Teresa had made since Tom and I last visited. Living room and dining room walls had been painted in muted shades of peach and cream, covering the dreadful gray that previously gave the room a battleship atmosphere. Sofa and armchairs grouped around the coffee table; dining table and chairs ready for company; art work arranged, and photographs displayed on the mantel.

The house had been a shambles when Tom and I participated in the pounding the church folks gave them the previous Saturday afternoon, two days after they'd moved to Brooder.

Daniel Ward, pastor of the church Tom and I attended in Hanson Ridge, knew of the custom when I inquired. But our church, established a brief six years ago, with most of the congregation made up of transplanted city folk, had no such tradition.

The antique jewelry box the thief attempted to steal had been one of Teresa's housewarming gifts.

After tossing my purse on the sofa, I carried my food to the kitchen. "Uh-oh, now I see what you mean, Teresa."

Cardboard boxes stacked two and three high filled a corner of the large kitchen.

Unpacked items covered the table, and crumpled newspaper littered the floor.

The open container of cookies beckoned from the counter. "Hmm. Chocolate chip."

My voice echoed in the cavernous kitchen. Frequently on my own, I often voiced my thoughts out loud. Tom teased me about my quirk, but it's how I coped with hours, sometimes days, of being in a house by myself.

I poked a cookie. It was as hard as a dinosaur egg. *He* must have been planning this robbery for a while and had the cookies ready, waiting his opportunity. Waiting for . . . Teresa to be alone.

Alone.

I dashed back to the living room, made sure I'd locked the front door, and then searched for the jewelry box. Not in the living room or dining room. In the hall I found the bookend Teresa had thrown, but no jewelry box. Had the deputies taken it after all? I kept searching, and finally found it in the guest bathroom.

The exquisite dark wooden box, about the size of a small, dome-shaped breadbox with short, sculpted legs, had small intricate roses carved on all four sides and a brass latch. I carried it to the kitchen and cleared a space at the table. After wiping off traces of fingerprint powder from the box and washing my hands, I opened my Chinese take-out. Pungent aromas hit my nostrils, awakening my taste buds.

Munching on chicken, vegetables, and noodles, I pondered over why the intruder hadn't removed the jewelry instead of attempting to steal the whole box. When I turned it around, I noticed a crack along the base at the back and fresh wood exposed where a large sliver had been removed.

"Have these been here a long time or are they a result of the scuffle?" I'd have to ask Teresa.

I lifted the latch. Teresa's diamond necklace, the James Avery charm bracelet I'd given her, and emerald earrings, an anniversary gift from Mike, and other items twinkled on the rose-pink satin lining. Teresa would have to inventory the contents when she came home.

The open box measured about eight inches high, not including the lid and legs, but the interior compartment sank down a mere four inches into the satin.

"That's odd."

I pushed my near-empty food container aside, and carefully removed the jewelry so I could examine the box more closely. Knocking through the satin onto the base produced a dull thud.

"Interesting. Maybe there's a hidden compartment under the lining."

I'd have to tell Teresa to check it out, or better yet, ask the family who gave it to her if they knew the history of the antique. A secret compartment might explain the attempted theft.

Mike called to report on Teresa. She slept fitfully, so he'd decided to spend the night at the hospital.

Although emotionally exhausted, sleep evaded me. After taking the gift bag I'd dropped earlier to the master bedroom, I unpacked the rest of the boxes, stacking the items on the large kitchen table. Empty boxes and newspaper scraps joined others on the screened-in back porch.

When satisfied with the state of the kitchen, I located sheets and made up the bed in the guest bedroom. Wide awake, I peeked in the nursery. The assembled changing table stood along one wall, but the crib lay in pieces in the corner. The baby bed would have to wait for Tom or Mike. Assembling wooden structures with tiny nuts and bolts exceeded my handywoman skills. My forte lay in easing muscles and joints. I closed the door and murmured a prayer for my future grandson.

Tom must have felt his ears burning because he called five minutes later. We'd been married twenty-five years, and he'd worked for medical supply companies most of that time. Although I was resigned to his traveling and being away from home, every once in a while it would be nice to have him around for a crisis.

But he offered what support he could over the air waves, and we ended our conversation with a prayer.

The CD by Ednita Nazario ended, and I swayed in salsa dance steps to the living room, her last tune still pulsing through my body. When I turned off the CD player, I spied the antique box on the coffee table where I'd left it. Sinking into the sofa, I held the box at arm's length.

"What secrets are you hiding? Money? A love letter?"

A splinter from the exposed fresh wood pricked my finger. I plucked it out, then examined the gash in the fine, dark wood. It ruined the surface. A fuzzy image of a little girl holding a smashed wooden box floated into my mind, lingered for a brief second, and then vanished. My insides felt as if I'd dropped a thousand feet on a carnival ride, then swooped up the other side. I clutched my middle.

"What was that all about?"

When the sensation eased, I studied the box again. Could it be repaired? Where was the missing piece of wood? I searched the hall where the box had fallen during the altercation. Wedged behind the hall table I found the sliver. It fit perfectly over the raw wood and could be glued back on. Norm Harrison could do it. When Teresa came home I'd offer to take the jewelry box to our neighbor who restored furniture, specializing in antiques. He'd do it right.

The little girl sailed into my mind again. This time she sobbed, and held the broken box up to a man and pleaded, "Can you fix it, *Papi*?" She disappeared as my stomach twisted in a frenzy of pain.

"Ooh." Setting the box on the sofa, I doubled over. "What on earth is happening to me?"

The pain eased, but the conviction I had to have the jewelry box repaired surged through my heart and brain. Teresa must agree to let me take it to Norm. She had to.

Later, while sipping a glass of iced tea, I examined the box further and discovered the securely attached satin lining had no openings. I wouldn't remove it without asking Teresa's permission. There must be another way to get at the hidden compartment.

I picked up the box, turned it over, and thumped the base in several spots. Each thump produced a different tone. Did change in resonance indicate something lay concealed inside? Then I examined the sides. Three roses decorated each end, seven along the back, while the front had six, with the brass latch plate taking the place of the seventh.

Pushing, prodding, and poking the roses produced nothing but a sore finger. I held the box to my chest and slumped into the sofa. The little girl didn't reappear in my thoughts, but the day's events assaulted me all at once. My energy level hit zero. Better rescue Teresa's jewelry from the mess on the kitchen table before retiring for the night.

After replacing the items, I set the box on the coffee table, turned off the lights, and shuffled to the bathroom for a quick shower.

Snuggled under the quilt in a borrowed nightgown, I tossed and turned. In the half asleep stage of early dreaming, the little girl swirled before me. About five years old, black hair in braids, a piece of the box in her tiny hands. "Please, *Papi*! Can you fix it? I didn't mean to break it."

"No, *mija*. It is too broken. I cannot."

"But *Mami* is so angry at me!"

"*Sí*, Maricella. You should not have played with her favorite jewelry box."

I bolted upright at the stone cold memory. I had dropped my mother's jewelry box and it had shattered into a thousand pieces. She never forgave me, I don't believe, for destroying the one item she had from her mother, a precious heirloom.

Hugging my knees, I wept for the little girl who would never have her jewelry box repaired. After I drained my body's supply of tears, I slid under the covers, hoping sleep would ease the memories of a past that I never wanted to relive.

Streetlight filtering through the blinds and town noises punctuating the night intruded on my sorrow.

Our nearest neighbors in Hanson Ridge were almost a mile away. Since we seldom heard anything at night except occasional barking dogs, and the only light visible glowed from millions of stars, these intrusions kept sleep at bay.

I climbed out of bed and meandered to the kitchen for a drink of water. Illumination entering from outside guided my way. I reached for the cabinet above the sink. A faint clicking sound caught my attention. My breath froze in my throat.

I stood still, fingers clutching the cabinet handle.

Squeaking. Scraping. Were the sounds coming from the kitchen? No, the back porch. I lowered my tingling arm, and backed into the middle of the kitchen.

The counter which housed the sink ran along the back wall. The door leading to the screened-in porch stood three yards from me. My eyes were riveted on the knob.

It turned.

CHAPTER THREE

I stifled a scream and backed out of the kitchen. Had the intruder returned?

My heels hit an armchair with a thump and I stumbled, knocking my shins on the coffee table. Ouch! The jewelry box wobbled.

Jewelry box. He'd come back for it.

I snatched up the antique and dashed down the hall to my bedroom. The open closet beckoned. Too obvious for a hiding place. Turning, I caught my toe in the quilt. I tossed the cover back on the bed and stuffed the box in the jumbled messy folds of the patchwork fabric.

No telephone in the guest bedroom. I removed my cell phone from my purse and tiptoed down the hall to the kitchen.

The door knob rattled. Muted cursing seeped through the closed door. I hurried to the bedroom, dialed 9-1-1, and reported the attempted break-in. The dispatcher advised me to stay on the line and lock myself in, but the door had no lock. Besides, I refused to be a passive victim.

In the hall, I picked up the bookend Teresa had thrown at her assailant. With slow deliberation I edged to the kitchen entryway.

The silver beam of a flashlight wavered back and forth. A man searched the kitchen. His exclamations indicated he assumed he was alone.

Flattened against the wall I waited, listening to my heart thud while jolts of fear twisted my gut into a tight knot. The man switched on the light above the stove. I peeked into the kitchen. Dressed in blue jeans, a long-sleeved denim shirt and black gloves, he had dark brown, curly hair trapped under a blue baseball cap. It must be the same intruder. While he examined the items I'd unpacked on the table, I etched his profile into my brain.

He muttered, returned to the stove and extinguished the light. The glow from his flashlight bounced around the room. I slid into the shadows. The bookend weighted my arm down. He tramped to the doorway. The strong, biting whiff of epoxy accompanied him again. I raised the bookend. As he entered the hall, I lowered my arms with all the force my five-and-a-half-foot, one-hundred-thirty-pound frame could deliver.

A wasted effort. He blocked the full force of my blow with his forearm. His hands encircled my throat and white spots danced before my eyes as I struggled for air.

◆ ◆ ◆

"Ma'am, are you sure you don't need to go to the hospital?" Deputy Rayburn, an investigator from the Kerr County Sheriff's Department, sat on the sofa next to me and opened her notepad. About my age, mid-forties, amply-proportioned, with short blonde hair and gray eyes, her stare penetrated my bravado.

"I'm sure, thank you." The paramedics had examined my throat, taken my blood pressure, and shone a pen light into my eyes. "The ambulance can leave. I assure you I'm okay." I tucked my legs beneath me in the large armchair and snuggled inside Teresa's robe.

Deputy Rayburn flipped through pages of her notepad. "I read my colleague's report of the earlier break-in. Do you think it was the same man?"

"I'm pretty sure it was. He'd changed clothes, but the hair, hat, body build—they were all the same. And Teresa described him as tall, older than my son, and Caucasian. So was this guy."

"Your description matches the one your daughter-in-law gave the deputies earlier. Even the cap. And you're sure nothing has been taken?"

"As sure as I can be since this is not my house. I checked each room before going to bed. I kind of remember what I saw."

"Then obviously he didn't find the jewelry box?"

"No. When I regained consciousness and knew he was no longer in the house, that's the first thing I checked." I rubbed my neck and winced.

"Mrs. McDonough—"

"I'm fine. Don't worry about me."

The back door creaked open and my heart skipped a beat. Had he returned?

A deputy entered the living room. Blood whooshed back into my brain.

He joined Rayburn on the sofa, his black pants blending with the black leather. "I sealed the cookie container in an evidence bag, like you said."

"Thank you." Rayburn stood. "Ma'am, I need to complete my investigation. Do you have another place to spend the night?"

I hadn't thought that far ahead. But once the deputies left I'd be on my own again, and the intruder might return. He'd already attempted to take the jewelry box twice. Would his third try succeed?

"I'll go to a motel in Kerrville. Tomorrow, my son can install deadbolts on the doors, but for now—"

"Good idea. Deputy Vargas can escort you out of Brooder." Rayburn slid the notebook into the pocket of her shirt.

In the kitchen I found a green cloth grocery bag, a perfect size for the jewelry box. Jeans and T-shirt pulled on, robe and nightgown returned to Teresa's bedroom, toiletries gathered from the bathroom, and with the antique concealed in the grocery bag, I exited the house. I nodded to Deputy Rayburn and slid into my car, jittery fingers scarcely able to guide the key into the ignition.

Vargas followed me to Kerrville, where I stopped at the first decent motel I found. Once settled in the room, I tugged off my boots, threw back the spread and lay on the bed. I turned off the bedside lamp, but menacing images advanced from the darkness and hands slithered around my neck.

Light on. Wasting electricity, I know, but I couldn't rid myself of *his* hulking form above me. I'd woken in a heap on the hall floor, the nightgown barely covering my body. I lay still, listening, and when the silence indicated I was alone, I shuffled to the bedroom. The jewelry box lay where I'd hidden it. Sirens spurred me to action. I threw on Teresa's robe and examined the other rooms. Nothing seemed to be missing, although items were scattered about.

I shivered at the recollection and tucked the spread around my shoulders. What was so important about Teresa's jewelry? Did the intruder know she had a valuable necklace? Or was it the box itself? The green grocery bag sat next to my purse on the dresser. I stared at the cloth as if I could discover the box's secrets through the cotton and wood. The letters on the bag swirled and twisted. My eyelids fluttered, my head bobbed. Exhaustion eventually resulted in sleep.

Hours later, noises from the hall woke me. After getting dressed, I wedged my purse on top of the jewelry box, and then carried the grocery bag down to the lobby for the continental breakfast.

Mike called as I drained my coffee mug. I cleared the table and listened to his report on Teresa's condition.

"We've been told she's to be discharged later today. Can you bring her a change of clothes, please?"

"Um, I'm not at your house. I'm . . . I'm having breakfast in Kerrville." How much should I tell Mike? I'd spent years lying to my family, and vowed after accepting the Lord as Savior I'd never lie again. But did I have to tell him everything? I had raging personal battles with *the whole truth* part.

But Mike rescued me. "No problem, Mama. We don't expect you to drive all the way back to Brooder. Come straight to the hospital when you're finished. By the way, Don Petrie, a friend from church visited last night. I gave him the keys to my SUV so he can bring it to us."

On the way to the hospital, I stopped at a discount store in the mall and purchased a maternity dress for Teresa, undergarments and two turtleneck tops for myself. A ring of bruises circled my neck. I wanted to hide them while out in public. In a hospital restroom I changed clothes, choosing the new bronze top, and then rode the elevator to Teresa's floor. The jewelry box, hidden under my jacket, lay safe in its green bag. With all the interest shown in it, I chose to keep it close.

Teresa sat in bed. Her cheeks had a touch of pink and her eyes sparkled, a definite improvement over my last image of her. However, her left jaw, mottled purple and swollen, was a stark reminder of her encounter with the intruder.

"*Holá*, Chella!"

"Good morning, Teresa!" We hugged. "Where's Mike?"

"The nurse told us Dr. Fletcher, the local ob-gyn, will be here in an hour. Mike's gone to the cafeteria for breakfast. He wants to be back in time to visit with the doctor."

"I see. Sorry I wasn't home to get a change of clothes, but I purchased this dress for you." I handed the canary yellow garment to her, then scooted a chair closer and sat, depositing the bag at my feet.

"You didn't have to do that, but thank you. I love the color." She fingered the soft fabric. "I'm curious, what else is in the bag? It looks heavy."

Mike entered, humming. "Hi, Mama. Thought I'd bring my breakfast up here in case Dr. Fletcher comes early."

He stooped to kiss my cheek, his whiskers pricking my skin, then sat and opened his carry-out container.

"What's in the bag?" Teresa asked again.

I licked my lips. *The whole truth. Don't hold back.*

"It's your jewelry box."

"My antique? But why?"

With a hand on Mike's arm, I kept my voice even. "Now, don't get upset, but the man came back last night and—"

"Mama, no." He dropped his breakfast taco into the Styrofoam container. "Are you okay?"

"Maricella, what happened?"

In a reassuring tone, I described the events of the night. I stuck to my resolution and lowered the turtleneck to reveal the ring of bruises.

"My jewelry and that box have caused too much trouble."

"Mama, why didn't you have the ambulance take you to the hospital?"

"Because I was fine once I regained consciousness. I wasn't out very long and couldn't see the need for all the fuss."

"Chella, you're hard-headed. Tom's right, as usual."

I blinked at Teresa, then at Mike. "The paramedics checked me out. I'm fine.

Now can we move on, please?"

Mike's blue eyes conveyed his displeasure as he bit into his egg and potato taco. Teresa shook her head and relaxed against the pillows.

"Okay, enough about me. Back to the jewelry box. Teresa, I have a theory about this antique."

I described my investigation into a secret compartment, and told them my idea of having Norm Harrison, my neighbor, repair the box. Visions of my five-year-old self with my mother's smashed box flitted through my mind for a second. Inwardly wiping the screen clean, I examined my peach-tinted nails. "He may also know how to open it."

Teresa rubbed her abdomen and shifted her legs. "Ooh, the little guy is anxious for me to get up and walk around. He's playing touch football in here." She breathed deeply and exhaled, then rubbed her belly. "I like your idea. Take the jewelry box to Mr. Harrison, please."

"It's beautiful." After removing the jacket that concealed the box, I slid it out of the bag. "Why don't you make sure everything is here?" I set the box on the bed.

"Good idea." Teresa opened the domed lid and sorted through the items. "Doesn't look like anything's missing. I see all the important pieces."

"That's good. Who gave it to you?"

"Allen and Sammie Howard. They own an antique store here in Kerrville, but live and worship in Brooder." The contents of a small bottle of orange juice disappeared down Mike's throat in one gulp.

After latching the lid, I slipped the box back into the grocery bag. "I'd like to ask them about its history, if you don't mind."

Mike wiped his mouth with a napkin and gathered his trash together. "If you're here Sunday, you can talk to them at church."

"Good idea. But I'll have to go home for a change of clothes. All I have is another new turtleneck top."

"I have an ankle-length black skirt you can borrow. Will that work?"

Teresa was a little taller than me but we wore the same size. "Sure. *Gracias*. And Daddy will be here later this afternoon. I'm sure he won't mind spending the night."

"Great. He can help me assemble the baby's crib."

Teresa moaned. "We may need it pretty quick. Junior's telling me he's ready."

A tall, statuesque nurse, wearing bright turquoise scrubs bustled in. "Dr. Fletcher is on her way, Mrs. McDonough."

"I'll step outside." Placing my jacket in the bag, I lugged it out of the room.

Once in the hall, I sauntered past the nurses' station, located the glass-walled waiting room and chose a chair in the corner. I removed the box and attempted a variety of prodding and poking to open the secret compartment. Nothing worked. With the box in my lap, I peeked at the TV monitor mounted on the wall. An elderly man passed the waiting room and glanced in. He did a double-take, then stopped, turned, and entered. He sat opposite me and picked up a magazine.

I slid the jewelry box back into the green bag.

A quivering voice from across the room interrupted me. "That's a mighty fine box you have there."

My grip tightened. After all, it still concealed Teresa's jewelry. I stared at the man. At least in his late seventies, balding and black, he couldn't be the intruder. Tall and thin, yes, but my intruder had been much younger and Anglo. Perhaps he had a special interest in antique jewelry boxes.

I relaxed. "Yes, it's unique." I scrunched the bag down and traced a carved rose with my finger.

"Do you mind if I ask where you got it?"

"It was a gift."

"Is that right?" His head wobbled on his slender neck as he nodded. "A gift. Can I see it?" He held out his hand.

His gnarled, twisted fingers revealed years of arthritis pain. But caution overrode any pity I felt for him.

"Sorry, I have to go." I straightened the bag and stood. "I see my daughter-in-law's doctor." I hurried after a dark-haired woman in a pink lab coat and entered

Teresa's room with her.

The doctor nodded to Mike and Teresa, and stuck her hands into the pockets of her long coat.

"Good morning, Mr. and Mrs. McDonough. I'm Dr. Fletcher, and I'm afraid I have bad news."

CHAPTER FOUR

"No, no, I can't believe Dr. Conway's dead." Teresa sobbed on Mike's shoulder.

Feeling as helpless as a butterfly in a tornado, I stood beside the bed, twisting my hands. A small box of tissues lay on the side table. I yanked out a handful and held them out to her. Teresa accepted them and slumped against the pillows.

"*Gracias.*" She wiped her eyes and blew her nose.

"What a shock." Mike maneuvered the two chairs we'd previously used closer to the bed. We sat and faced Teresa.

"She had two young children. I wonder if they were in the car with her." Teresa's eyes misted again. "The accident report may be in today's San Antonio newspaper."

Mike bolted upright. "I'll go get one."

"It can wait. Let's say a prayer for her family."

Teresa always knew the right time to pray. She'd beseeched the heavens on my behalf many times. I stood next to Mike, and the three of us held hands. Teresa began the prayer, and Mike added his words of supplication. I closed with my infantile plea for wisdom to know how to support my children in their time of grief.

The Christian walk was relatively new to me. Even after months of talking to God like a father, prayer didn't come naturally. I stuttered and spluttered, and opened my eyes at the conclusion like my soul had gone through a scouring car wash.

I kissed each hand before releasing them "Does Dr. Conway have a partner in her practice?"

"Yeah, but Conway's thorough knowledge of our baby's condition gave us confidence." Mike propped his elbows on his knees and buried his face in his hands. "I can't believe she's gone."

Rubbing his back, I leaned closer. "*Mijo*, I'm sorry."

For a while, the only sounds in the room were from the monitors and an occasional sniff from Teresa.

I broke the tension. "In all the drama, I missed the part where Dr. Fletcher said you could go home."

"As soon as they bring the paperwork. In fact, I should dress now."

Teresa's IV and monitor leads had been removed. Mike lowered the bed rail, and held out a hand to his wife, when a timid knock sounded on the door.

"Come in," Teresa called.

The door cracked. A baldheaded man stuck his head in the opening. "Hi, Teresa, Mike. Hope we're not intruding."

"No. Come in. Mama, remember Hank and Ruth Trenton from church? He's our pastor."

"Sure. We met at the pounding."

"Of course." Mike hiked a shoulder.

We shook hands, and they moved to the bed to greet Teresa. The couple appeared to be in their fifties, a little older than Tom and me. Ruth Ann had shoulder-length blonde hair, dimples creasing plump cheeks, and brown eyes sweetened by her smile. A gray mustache bobbled above Hank's upper lip as he talked. His barrel chest gave his voice a deep resonance.

"We want you to know this is not how newcomers are usually treated in Brooder. Our community is pretty safe." Hank eyed Teresa's swollen jaw. "Did the deputies catch the guy?"

Mike shared the information Deputy Wilson had provided, and his rendition of events included my run-in with the intruder.

"I apologize again. Hope this doesn't give you the wrong impression of our little town." Hank nodded to me, then turned to Mike. "By the way, I met Don Petrie in the parking lot. He brought your vehicle." Hank handed Mike a set of keys.

Ruth Ann produced a square envelope from her purse. "Here's a little something to cheer you, Teresa, dear. And, if you're up to it, we'd like y'all to come for lunch tomorrow." She glanced at me. "And you, too, Mrs. McDonough."

"Thank you. Please call me Maricella. My husband will be here by then."

"He's welcome, too." Ruth Ann stepped toward the door. Hank followed.

I volunteered to bring dessert.

"Dessert? Sure thing. We won't stay any longer. See y'all tomorrow." She closed the door behind them.

"That was a nice surprise. How did they know I was here?" Teresa opened the envelope and slid out a booklet. "It's a collection of lullabies."

"I called them last night." Mike took the book Teresa handed him and flipped through it. "Interesting. I don't know any of them."

"You'll soon learn." I patted Mike's shoulder. "I'll leave now so you can dress, Teresa. On the way home I'll purchase groceries for tonight's supper and tomorrow's dessert. Mike, do you feel like firing up the grill?"

"Sure. Dad can help."

"Great, and I'll stop by a hardware store for two deadbolt locks. No more uninvited guests." No sense taking any chances.

"And Maricella, you and Tom must stay with us tonight. No motel, okay?"

"If it's all right with Tom. See you later. I love you."

I rode the elevator down, and made my way through the parking lot. The faster I walked, the harder the jewelry box bumped against my leg. What a nuisance. Surely it would be safe in the trunk. I popped it open and wedged the box next to two milk crate containers I used to hold my groceries in place.

My phone rang as I slid into the car. Joey calling from El Salvador. After the initial shock of Teresa's situation wore off, his excitement bubbled through the phone.

"Mama, we'll be teaching Bible classes every day, but guess what else we'll be doing?" His miniscule pause gave me no time to answer. "My group is going to build a house, and, you won't believe this, we're going to repair a hall to be used for a school. Isn't that fantastic?"

My heart warmed to hear my twenty-one-year-old son so enthusiastic over something other than his car, for a change. "It certainly is."

Joey's excitement lingered as I made my purchases. Since I had a vague idea of what the kids had in the pantry, I loaded the cart with everything from charcoal to mayonnaise, and added a few make-up items. Once I'd located all the ingredients for my famous apricot and ice-cream torte, I headed to the checkout.

Outside the store, newspaper vending machines reminded me I wanted to read about Dr. Conway's accident. I dug four quarters out of my purse and retrieved a San Antonio paper. As I maneuvered my cart through the crowded parking lot, Tom called.

"The conference ended early, sweetheart. I'll be in Kerrville about three-thirty."

"I'm on my way to Mike's now."

After discussing Teresa's health, I slipped the phone into my pocket and scanned the lot. Where had I parked? In the next row I spied my silver Chevy Impala. A man lingered by the back passenger window. The rattling cart wheels announced my approach. He moved away from the car and glanced at me, then squeezed between the vehicles and disappeared around the corner of the store.

Tall, elderly, and black. Was it the same man from the hospital waiting room? Too far away to tell.

I popped the trunk. The jewelry box lay next to my milk crates. I emptied the grocery cart as fast as I could, and drove down the road, watching for a car following me. Nothing suspicious. I then made my way to Brooder, parked outside the kids' house, and unloaded the groceries.

Half expecting the intruder or the old man, I hid the jewelry box under the bed, and placed a heavy frying pan by each door.

Groceries stored away, I prepared my marinade for the *carne asada*, and set the thin steak slices in the refrigerator. Then I assembled the ingredients for the dessert. The wooden meat mallet from the utensil drawer served to crush the Vanilla Wafers in a zip-top plastic bag. With each whack I released pent up anxiety and anger. If the intruder had returned at that moment he would have ended up on the floor.

Whack. Whack. "Ooh, that felt good."

The toasting sliced almonds filled the kitchen with a nutty aroma. I mixed the cookie crumbs with almond flavoring and the toasted almonds, then I layered the dessert. Cookie crumbs, half-inch slices of vanilla ice-cream, topped with apricot preserves. All repeated, to end with cookie crumbs and almonds.

I opened the small freezer and made room for the nine-by-eleven inch dish. Closing the door, I studied the old avocado-green eyesore. The kids had given up a new condo with stainless steel appliances. This antiquated piece would have to fit in their freezer.

"I'm so proud of your decision, Mike and Teresa. I don't understand it, but I'm proud."

While in a cleaning mode, I removed all remnants of the black fingerprint powder from the night's investigation. I also straightened the rooms as best I could. In the master bedroom, last on my list, I arranged knick-knacks on Teresa's dresser and gazed out the window. Three young children played tag in the yard across the street. Teresa had informed me their mother was five months pregnant. A future playmate for my grandson. There were several other families in the area with young children. I knew there was a young boy in the house next door. A four-year-old who had a severe hearing loss. All in all—the recent attack notwithstanding—a pleasant neighborhood in which to raise a family.

On my way to the kitchen to prepare a sandwich, Deputy Rayburn called.

"Sorry to say, Mrs. McDonough, but we found no evidence to identify the assailant in the house. And we garnered nothing useful from the cookies or the container."

I pressed the speaker icon and set the phone on the kitchen table. "Nothing. What's going to happen now?"

"We're following a lead from a neighbor."

"What kind of lead?" I slapped Mayo on whole-wheat bread and added cheese and ham.

"Rather not say at this time, ma'am, but we'll get back to you and your family. How's your daughter-in-law?"

"Her jaw is bruised, but everything else seems fine. She's coming home shortly." I cut the sandwich in half. "There is something I need to tell you. Don't know if it's important." I related the incident with the black man at the hospital and in the grocery store parking lot, and supplied a brief description.

"Without a name or other means of identifying him, there's not much I can do. But I will ask around."

I settled at the kitchen table and, while munching my ham and cheese sandwich, searched in vain through the San Antonio newspaper for a report on Dr. Conway's accident. With each bite and turn of a page, my arm grew heavier and my eyelids drooped. My tea consumed and most of the sandwich eaten, I pushed back from the table. Frying pans ready at each door, I collapsed onto the bed to catch up on my sleep.

Carved roses swirling in a baby's crib filtered through my dream. Pounding on the front door woke me. I checked my watch. Three o'clock. Must be Tom, because Mike had another key. I hurried to the door, nudged the skillet out of the way, and almost had the lock turned when tingles like ant feet prickled my neck.

I peeked through the peep hole.

It wasn't Tom.

An elderly couple stood there. They looked harmless enough, and something about them seemed familiar.

Opening the door halfway, I raised my eyebrows inquiringly.

"Hi. Are Mike and Teresa home?" asked the man.

"No. I'm Mike's mother. Can I help you?"

"There you go. Thought I recognized you. We met at the pounding. We're Allen and Sammie Howard."

I invited them into the living room where they sat on the sofa, and I gave a brief account of Teresa's situation.

"How terrible! But she and the baby are fine, right?" Sammie fiddled with strands of gray hair escaping the knot at the base of her neck.

"Yes. A little bruised, but they should be home within the hour. Would you like tea or coffee?"

"No, thanks. Considering the circumstances, we won't stay." Allen stood and extracted a business card from his wallet. "Tell them we stopped by and give them our regards."

I almost dropped the card when I read the gold and black writing. *Use It Again, Sam: Quality Antiques. Proprietors Allen and Samantha Howard.* They had given Teresa the jewelry box.

"I . . . have a question for you. I'll be right back." I ran down the hall to the bedroom and unearthed the box from under the bed.

After removing the jewelry box from the bag, I hurried back to the living room. "If I'm not mistaken, you gave this to Teresa." I placed it on the coffee table and sat in the armchair.

Allen peered at me through his thick glasses. Bushy reddish eyebrows quirked above the dark frames. "Yes. Why?" He joined his wife on the sofa.

Should I tell them a man had been after it? *The whole truth.* I expanded my original description of Teresa's attack and added the intruder's second visit.

"How awful! And you're sure he was after this jewelry box?" Picking up the antique, Allen examined the sides.

"Yes, or the jewelry in it."

He prodded and poked the roses.

Eyes glued to his hands, I said, "I think it has secret compartments."

"More than likely. I've seen a half dozen of these over the years." Allen turned it over. "Usually the mechanism to open them is in the carved design. But I can't trigger this one."

Curiosity nibbled. "Where did you get it?"

He handed the box to Sammie, and they stared at each other. "If I remember right, Sam, this was part of the estate sale we attended a couple of weeks ago." He attempted to flatten his thatch of graying red hair.

After studying the box for a moment, she set it back on the table, then rummaged in her purse.

She extracted a pocket calendar and flipped through pages, then tapped one. "Yes. The Summerland-Hayes sale, February 23. We acquired many of their pieces."

"A local family?" My antennae for more information bristled.

"Been in the county for generations." Allen's brown eyes focused on a spot behind me, and he nodded as if acknowledging people he knew from the past.

"I'd like to jot down a bit of information." Bolting from the chair, I asked, "Can you stay a little longer?"

I was halfway down the hall before they answered in the affirmative. The guest bedroom also served as Mike's home office. I snagged a pen off the desk, slid a sheet of paper from his printer, and returned to the living room.

"Okay, the Summerland— What was their name again?"

"Summerland-Hayes–with a hyphen," Sammie said.

I wrote and chuckled.

"What's so funny?" She frowned.

"I remember something my *tia*, my aunt used to say. When I lived with her in San Antonio after . . . after my parents died, she cleaned houses for several rich families for a while. She'd say people with hyphenated names usually had twice as much money, were twice the snobs, and had twice as many skeletons in their closets."

Sammie and Allen glanced at each other, then she picked up the jewelry box. "The Summerland-Hayes family sure have their share of skeletons. Dozens of them." She caressed the carved roses. "It wouldn't surprise me if every item from that sale had a skeleton attached to it."

Goosebumps erupted on my arms. Whatever did she mean by that?

CHAPTER FIVE

"Any more dirty dishes?" Tom placed the last saucepan in the cabinet.

"Nope." Wiping the counter, I wrung out the cloth and hung it over the faucet.

A second later he sidled behind me and slid his arms around my waist. "Good." His kisses traveled from my hairline down my cheek to the top of my turtleneck. Hints of barbecue smoke overpowered faint traces of his spicy McGraw cologne.

"Tom, quit. The kids are in the living room."

"They won't be for long. I heard Teresa say she was ready for bed."

I turned, laced my fingers behind Tom's neck, and planted a kiss on his smiling lips. "I love you too, dearest, but I need to talk to Teresa and Mike before they go to bed."

Arm in arm we entered the living room. Teresa relaxed on the sofa, her head in Mike's lap. He toyed with tendrils of her hair.

"Hey, Mama, Daddy. Thanks for all your help."

"Yes, Chella, your *carne asada* is the best, and Tom, I don't think Mike could have assembled the baby bed without you." Teresa swung her jean-clad legs down, and sat up with Mike's help.

We'd had a busy afternoon and evening. Mike and Teresa arrived ten minutes before Tom. After she opened the gift I'd brought from the Baileys—a delicate, pale blue and white crocheted blanket—none of us allowed Teresa to do anything but supervise. We found homes for all the items I'd unpacked, installed deadbolts, prepared supper, and then ate outside under the Live Oaks, sure the intruder wouldn't dare face two large, formidable men. Later in the evening, once the crib had been assembled, Mike helped Teresa organize the nursery while Tom and I loaded his van with all the flattened cardboard boxes and newspaper.

Now Tom and I sat in armchairs with the antique jewelry box on a side table between us. Teresa had already removed the contents.

I fingered the carved roses. "While Norm is repairing the box, I'd like to learn its history and, with your permission, Teresa, see if I can open the secret compartment."

"Sure. What family did you say it belonged to?" Teresa rested against the sofa and rubbed her abdomen.

"The Howards bought it from the Summerland-Hayes estate."

"Hmm," Tom grunted, "I've heard that name before." He scratched his head. "But I can't remember where."

After thirty minutes we were all ready for bed. When I entered the room after my shower, Tom sat in bed, leaning against the headboard, his tank top exposing shoulders and chest still in great shape. I dumped my dirty clothes in his suitcase and stepped to the bed, straightening the scooped neckline of the borrowed nightgown.

"Maricella, what in the world!"

Tom's words caught me by surprise. I stopped. "What?"

He jumped out of bed and seized my shoulders, the citrusy scent of his shampoo lingered from his shower. "What happened to your neck?"

My hands flew to the exposed bruises. "Didn't I tell you?"

"No!" He dropped his hands and paced to the door and back, his pajama pant legs thwacking against each other in his haste. "You said you'd never lie to me again. I . . . I'm disappointed." He sat on the edge of the bed, his head bowed.

Rooted to the carpet, I couldn't move. I hadn't lied. I'd forgotten to tell him about the intruder's attempted strangulation. Hadn't I?

I sat next to him and gripped his arm. "Tom, I didn't lie or deliberately leave out the part where he hurt me. I promise." His head sunk lower. "Tom, you have to believe me. By the time you arrived, my neck didn't bother me, and I was so excited to see you and the kids—"

Smarting from his reaction, I tramped around the bed. "I haven't lied to you—to anyone for that matter—since I made the vow at my parents' graves." I slid under the covers.

Tom climbed in next to me and enveloped me in his arms. "Sweetheart, forgive me for being hasty in misjudging you."

◆ ◆ ◆

Pastor Trenton's sermon focused on the story of Job. Hank's booming voice seemed too big for the quaint, old stone building. He needed no microphone. His words sailed past the furthest pew to the woods beyond, searching for souls seeking truth. Job's calamites caught my attention. Did God test His servants today?

At the conclusion of the service, we followed the line of parishioners outside. Pastor Trenton greeted everyone at the door. I had questions about Job but wouldn't take up Hank's time at the moment. Tom and I could study the book in depth later.

In the mottled shade of the budding pecan trees, the Howards introduced me to their youngest son, Warren. He ran the antique store while they traveled and acquired items from various locations in the South West.

"I believe you're interested in the Summerland-Hayes estate." Warren, several years my junior, one-handedly slipped on his sunglasses and adjusted a charcoal cowboy hat atop his head of riotous red curls. His left arm, in a cast from elbow to fingers, hung in a gray sling. Short and stocky, he'd inherited his father's build and coloring. Freckles vied for space on his round face.

"Yes, I am. What happened to your arm?"

He raised the cast. "Oh, this?" Lowering it to his chest, he said, "Interrupted a break-in at our warehouse behind the store two weeks ago. Broke both bones in my forearm during the scuffle."

"Ooh, painful way to stop a robbery. Was anything stolen?"

"Nope. I heard noises out back. When I investigated, two guys in stocking masks roughed me up. As far as we could tell, they didn't take anything. Weirdest thing. We store recent purchases out there before we display 'em in the store."

"I see."

Tom appeared in the crowd behind Warren, and I knew I had limited time. "Items from the Summerland-Hayes estate sale?"

Warren scratched under the cast at his wrist. "Yeah, come to think of it, some of their stuff was in there."

Aha. "Like the jewelry box your parents gave Teresa?"

"No, no. Mother had it at the house. As soon as she laid eyes on the box she said she wanted it for a special gift."

"I'm fascinated by the jewelry box. What can you tell me about it or the family who originally owned it?"

He rubbed his chin. "I have the inventory from the sale at the store. I'll check on the box for you. Come by during the week. As for the family, believe me, I know a lot about them. Ask anyone in Kerrville and you'll hear enough tales to fill a book."

My ears perked and my heart fluttered. Here come the skeletons.

Warren stuck his thumb in a belt loop of his blue jeans. "One family member died accidentally. At least, that's what the newspapers reported. Another one left the country under suspicious circumstances, and—"

"Pardon me." Tom moved to my side, nodding to Warren. "The Trentons are leaving. It's time to go."

"Okay." Just when the family skeletons were about to be revealed. "Thanks for the information, Warren. We have to leave, but I'd like to stop by your store and continue this conversation."

He doffed his hat. "Anytime."

Tom and I walked to my car. We'd left his company van at the kids' house, packed and ready for our trip home right after lunch. The jewelry box rested in the green grocery bag, wedged safely next to the milk crates in the Chevy's trunk.

"What was that all about?" Tom fastened his seat belt over his tan twill slacks. No blue jeans for him.

Shaking off heavy thoughts of men breaking into the Howard's warehouse on a possible hunt for the jewelry box, I answered, "Guess I'm curious." I backed the car out and turned onto the road.

"Chella, are you going to investigate the mystery surrounding this box?"

I stopped at the intersection, made a fuss of checking both ways, twice, and drove through. "I might."

"Remember your last investigation?"

How could I forget? I'd endangered Teresa's and my life when I'd searched for the murderer of my childhood friend. I tugged at my peach turtleneck top, and banished visions of the haunting escapade. "But we survived."

Tom folded his arms and stared out the windshield. "Why the fascination with this box?"

Negotiating a hairpin turn, I ignored his question, the same one I'd been grappling with since hearing the Summerland-Hayes name.

"Chella, what is your interest in this family?"

I had no answer for Tom since I had none for myself. "I don't know. The family has a wild history. Guess I'm inquisitive. That's all." But the question lay heavy on my heart. My answer to Tom didn't satisfy.

We rode in silence for a couple of miles.

"I suppose there's no dissuading you. Please be careful."

Once I parked outside the Trenton's house, I turned to him. "I will, Tom. This time there're no dead bodies on our property." I slipped the keys into my purse and opened the door. "I'll keep you apprised of my whereabouts every step of the way. Promise."

"Okay, sweetheart." His words agreed, but his blue eyes betrayed his reservations.

We entered the Trenton's home. Aromas of baking bread and roasting meat swirled around us. My taste buds worked overtime as Hank directed us to the large shaded deck overlooking the Guadalupe River where he introduced us to the other guests.

"This is our daughter."

A petite version of Ruth Ann shifted her position in a lawn chair. Almost as pregnant as Teresa, she held out her hand. "I'm Leah Howard."

We shook hands and followed Hank to the railing. "And this good-for-nothing—"

"Dad!" Leah hollered.

"This young man is our son-in-law, A. J."

Hank patted A. J.'s shoulder. His grin softened his words.

When A. J. turned, his kinship to Warren was unmistakable. They had to be brothers. He stood a good six inches taller, but the red curls and freckles were a dead giveaway.

After shaking hands, we sat in comfortable chairs grouped around glass-topped tables. Mike and Teresa, who had returned home to retrieve my dessert from their freezer, joined us minutes later. On their heels entered a couple close to the Trenton's age, straight off the pages of *Texas Monthly Magazine*. I'd caught a glimpse of them on the church grounds. He wore a ten-gallon straw Stetson, western cut gray jacket, blue jeans held up by a broad belt on which sat a silver buckle in the shape of Texas, and fancy boots. Her gracious smile complemented her diminutive size. Bouffant blonde hair, elegant two-piece scarlet suit, and heeled tan boots completed her ensemble.

The tiny woman waved a multi-ringed hand in our direction. "Howdy, folks. We're the Ballards, Lexi and Buck."

"Hi, y'all." Removing his hat, Buck stretched his arms wide and did a three-sixty. "It's soooo good to be back in Texas."

Lexi and Buck shook hands all around before sitting at our table. Hank, grinning in the background, entered the house.

"Your daddy and I were at university together, A. J., many, many years ago. Tell me about your family. I see you're about to add to it." Buck's Texas twang resounded through the oaks.

"Yeah, this one's due in May. Quite a surprise." Resting his arm across the back of Leah's chair, A. J. caressed her neck.

"Those three you hear down there are ours." Leah pointed to the yard. "Micah, ten, Lane eight, and Sadie is five."

"Are you in the antique business with your folks?" Shedding his jacket, Buck draped it on the back of his chair.

"You've got to be kidding. Not interested in old things at all." A. J.'s smile diluted his feigned disgust. "I'm a middle school principal in San Antonio."

Ruth Ann's call to come in for the blessing interrupted the conversation. She produced a feast of roast pork loin, rice pilaf, vegetable medley, homemade apple sauce, and fresh bread. My dessert scored major points, too.

Relaxing on the deck after clearing away the dishes, the Howard children entertained themselves with games, toys, and books from a large chest Hank had brought outside. Leah discussed pregnancy with Teresa. I appreciated the fact she didn't dwell on disasters and war stories. Two of her children were born at Methodist Hospital—the one Teresa chose—and Leah showered praises on the facility. Buck plied us with questions about our lives, and A. J.'s description of student pranks kept us roaring with laughter until the Howards packed their minivan for their return to San Antonio.

After they left, Hank tapped Buck's shoulder. "Now, ol' buddy, are you ready to hear our plans?"

"You betcha! That's why we're here!" Buck scooted his chair back and crossed one booted foot over his knee.

Hank's eyes glowed with anticipation as he adjusted his baseball cap. "You know there are summer camps all along the Guadalupe River and its tributaries."

"Oh, yeah. Used to come here every year with my Boy Scout group from Dallas. The highlight of my summer. That's one reason we bought a retirement spread down here."

"Boy Scouts, Girl Scouts, YMCA groups, and many private organizations have utilized the camps for generations. But due to the financial situation in the country, a large number of camps are facing bankruptcy."

"A shame. A cryin' shame."

"Durban Street Bible Church in Houston works with large groups of inner-city youth, troubled teens, and foster families. They've leased one of the camps, saving it from foreclosure."

Tom and I had heard a bare-boned outline of the story before. I concentrated on the details while eyeing the Ballards for a reaction. She twirled her rings and tsk-tsked. His face distorted with sadness or beamed with pleasure at each piece of news.

"So, exactly how will the church here in Brooder fit into the plans?" The furrows on Buck's tanned face deepened.

"That's where Mike and Teresa come in." Gesturing to them, Hank continued. "Mike will serve as youth minister for our small group of young people, but also for the kids scheduled to attend our Camp Alpha. We named it Alpha, because we hope and pray their experiences here will be a new beginning for many of them."

Tom, sitting next to Mike, thumped him on the back. "We're proud of you, son, and you, Teresa."

I smiled in agreement as my heart expanded in gratitude. What a career choice. To work in the ministry required one level of commitment, but to include troubled youth demanded an extra measure of courage or faith, or was it naïveté?

"Eagle Crest Community Church here and Durban Street in Houston have worked on this partnership for close on a year." Hank's voice reverberated with passion. "We're going to utilize the camp facilities year-round. Durban Street plans to send groups of young people for extended stays of six to eight weeks, for intense outdoor therapy. Many of these kids know little more than the concrete and steel of the big city. They have never been to the country, or to a camp. Never been fishing, canoeing, or hiking either."

"We know firsthand what life is like for kids in big cities. Our years in Detroit were eye-openers. Weren't they, Buck?" Lexi's eyes brimmed with tears.

"Sure thing, honey. We were involved in several deserving projects up there, but we're awful glad to be back in Texas. Keep talkin'."

"The Houston church will supply academic teachers and counselors, and the children will attend Eagle Crest Community Church on Sundays."

"When do you anticipate opening the camp?" Buck asked.

"The first group of kids will arrive in three-to-four weeks." Scratching his bald head, Hank slipped the cap back on. "We're almost ready, but the mess hall needs some repairs."

"I like what I'm hearin'. I'm gonna be in touch with our foundation in a day or two. See how we can help."

"Appreciate that, Buck." Hank and his friend shook hands. "There are other preparations under way."

Mike glanced at the group. "Before the kids arrive, I'll be working with the teachers and counselors on curriculum and procedures."

"While camp is in session, Mike will provide Bible teaching, a solid role model, and will interact with the kids during the day. Among the many qualifications Mike and Teresa have, they're both fluent in Spanish." Hank cleared his throat. "This is such an exciting venture for us. We prayed for the right couple to come our way, and we believe God provided."

Adjusting her maroon maternity dress over her knees, Teresa shifted in the chair. "God answered our prayers, too." She clutched her belly. "Ooh, but I may not be able to help right away. I don't think this baby's going to wait a month."

"Do you need to go home and rest?" Mike asked.

"*Sí*. I'm sorry. Feels like he's wrestling Hulk Hogan in here."

"You don't have to apologize, honey." Mike helped her up.

"We're gonna stay a while." Extending a hand in farewell, Buck stood and waved. "Nice to meet all y'all. Hope to see ya again. We haven't chosen a place to worship yet. Who knows? We may come to Eagle Crest."

Lexi waved from her seat.

Tom and I followed Mike and Teresa into the house. I collected my now clean dish from the kitchen counter, and as I turned into the living room, spied an antique hall tree. I touched the delicately carved wood framing the mirror.

"It was my grandmother's." Ruth Ann stood next to me, her head scarcely reaching my shoulder. "I love antiques, but can't afford to buy many."

"I don't know much about them. I . . . I don't have anything from my grandmother or mother. Except a patchwork quilt."

Ruth Ann placed one arm around my waist and smoothed her floral print skirt with the other. "I love 'em, but memories are equally important. You have those, don't you?"

I knew she meant well, but conjuring up memories of my past gave me a headache. My mother's smashed jewelry box lay at my five-year-old feet.

Inwardly, I cringed, but managed a smile, and lassoed the conversation back to antiques as we headed to the front door. "Teresa has her first antique. The Howards gave her a beautiful jewelry box."

"The one the intruder tried to steal?"

"Right. It came from the Summerland-Hayes estate." I took a chance. "Do you know the family?"

She slouched against the doorframe. "Did you say Summerland-Hayes?"

"Yes." I stopped and held her arm. "Are you all right?"

Ruth Ann's pale face screamed distress. "Fine. Fine." She fanned her face with her hand. "I haven't heard that name in a long time."

Bones jangled. Closet doors squeaked open. Skeletons hovered within reach.

Breathe. Breathe.

"What do you know about them?"

Once on the sidewalk, she said, "I attended school with Gordon and Gregory, the twins. They were a year younger, but we were good friends. I dated Gordon, but then I met Hank."

"What happened to Gordon?"

She slowed her pace. "He found another girl, but she called off the wedding at the last minute. Poor Gordon. I don't think he ever got over her."

"Where is he now?"

With head bowed Ruth Ann stopped. "He's dead, God rest his soul."

"He must be the one that Warren Howard mentioned who died in a car accident."

Her head popped up and blood infused her face, her skin turning as red as the tomatoes she'd served at lunch. She beckoned me to bend closer while she whispered, "The newspapers reported a car wreck, but . . ." She glanced around as if expecting someone to listen in on the conversation. When she looked back at me her eyes widened to saucer-size. "I know for sure that Gordon was murdered."

CHAPTER SIX

Obviously Ruth Ann had no actual proof Gordon had been murdered. The Kerrville police had listened to her theories, but ruled his death accidental. In less than five minutes, I'd be home to document her accusations.

I pulled into the garage while Tom parked his company van at the side of the house. Brutus, my tan Chihuahua mix, bounded out of the pet door, his little body twisting in half as he wagged his greeting.

"Hey, poochy! Did you miss us?" His exuberant wiggles and licks answered my question.

"Pop the trunk. I'll get your things," Tom said. He would be occupied for thirty minutes or more, unpacking, showering, dressing, before he'd need the office to compile and e-mail his reports.

"Thanks." I carried Brutus to the office, opened my laptop, and waited for the Internet connection.

Gordon's accident occurred in October 1992. I Googled his name and sure enough, several stories popped up. I skimmed all except the one about his accident, which I read in earnest. Allegedly, he'd been driving home from San Antonio on Interstate 10. About eight miles from the Kerrville exit, his car careened off the road into a ravine. Alcohol fumes were detected in the car, but his blood work revealed he'd been sober. His body had been thrown from the Mercedes 380 SL convertible, the article continued, indicating he'd not been wearing his seat belt.

I printed the account of the accident. At the bottom of the page, I itemized the details which convinced Ruth Ann that Gordon had not been driving. She and Hank kept up their friendship with him. Ruth Ann knew Gordon to be fanatical about safety and that he always drove with his seat belt on. He never touched alcohol after enduring his father's battle with alcoholism. Also, his vision was impaired to the point he couldn't drive at night.

According to Ruth Ann, Gordon would never have set out from San Antonio for a sixty-five mile drive in the middle of the night. There were no witnesses, but the car's dashboard clock stopped at three a.m. He never told anyone in his family about his eye problem, but worked around it by spending the night in the city if he had to, or by hiring a driver. Above all, Ruth Ann insisted that Gordon's poor eyesight was the one piece of evidence proving he hadn't been driving.

"Hey," Tom entered the office and stood behind me. "Whatcha doing?"

I knew I couldn't hide the facts from him. Deception had almost destroyed my marriage, and I wouldn't resort to it again.

Expecting his resistance or outright disapproval, I kept my tone light. "Checking on a member of the family who owned Teresa's box." I closed my laptop and vacated the office chair. "The desk is all yours. Let me know when you're ready for supper."

Tom folded his arms across his broad chest and frowned. "So, you've started already. I suppose e-investigating can't hurt." He cocked his head. "Wish I could be sure that's all you'll do."

"I won't make any promises."

With a harrumph, Tom settled at his desktop computer. I planted a kiss on his forehead, massaged his shoulders for a second, then took my printed pages to the bedroom. Tom had set the green grocery bag and my personal items on the bed. I placed the jewelry box on my dresser, and lay the folded story of Gordon's accident beside it.

"Mr. Gordon Summerland-Hayes, did the person who caused your accident hide evidence in here?"

With my hands on the domed lid, I studied the framed photographs above my dresser. My eyes lingered on the one of my parents holding me as an infant. Since the incident with my mother's jewelry box had been so forcefully reintroduced into my consciousness, my childhood had been frequently in my thoughts.

Until I married Tom, I had no family. My parents passed away when I was fifteen. How I longed for family spilling out of every room, photographs too numerous to display, and names filling generations on a family tree. But there's just me.

A guttural sob erupted, and I slid to the floor. If only I had a jewelry box passed down to my mother from her mother. Something I could cherish and save, then pass on, filled with memories and love and . . .

Teresa's antique box balanced on the edge of my dresser. I nudged it back and blinked away warm tears. Family. So important. Yet some people were willing to sell family treasures like this box.

I knelt and opened it. "I'm going to find out your history. Like it or not."

Settling back on my heels, I heaved a sigh. So, that's the answer. My interest in the Summerland-Hayes family was linked to the loss of my own family. Could it be that simple?

♦ ♦ ♦

The threatened early-morning storm never materialized. Charcoal clouds scattered and streaks of blue sky emerged.

"I'm going to take advantage of the fair weather and spend the day mowing." Tom scrounged in the utility drawer for keys to the shed and his riding lawn mower, then kissed me on the cheek.

Early spring rains had turned the field grass green and spiky overnight. The back forty did look like it needed a haircut. "Okay. I'm going to take the jewelry box to Norm. See you later."

Dressed in blue jeans and khaki work shirt, Tom whistled on his way out the back door, headed toward the shed at the end of the cleared field where he housed his John Deere. The sun hadn't yet taken the edge off the morning chill. I threw on my jacket, zipped it up to hide the fading bruises on my neck, then leashed Brutus. With the box snug in its green bag, we set out down the driveway. The dog trotted ahead, straining at the end of the retractable leash. Once on the road, however, I reined him in. Little traffic made it to our cul-de-sac, but I kept Brutus close as I power-walked the half mile to Norm's house.

I latched Norm's manual gate behind me, and crunched down the caliche driveway to his garage workshop. Norm, a widower in his late seventies, stood about my height but weighed next to nothing. How he lifted the larger pieces of furniture he worked on, I couldn't imagine.

Brutus tugged at the end of his leash and barked. Norm waved a chisel at me. I entered the workshop and watched him work. Whiffs of wood polish and restoring oils swirled in the air. Norm's thatch of white hair bobbed with each body movement. Strong hands wielded hammer and chisel. Sinewy arms, exposed by his cream T-shirt, tensed and relaxed.

When he stopped working, he straightened slowly as if waiting for each vertebra to clink into place. "Hi, neighbor." He removed an unlit cigar from his mouth and squinted at it. "Although I don't light 'em any more, I can't work without one to chomp on."

I knew he'd stopped smoking the cigars six months ago. "Glad to hear it." I hated the smell of cigars.

"What brings you by, Mrs. Mac?" Norm placed his cigar in an empty mug on the work bench, and tugged a bandana from his pocket. He removed his glasses and wiped his brow. Skin like fine leather stretched over his sharp features. Years of working outdoors gave him a year-round tan. Pale gray eyes twinkled from beneath shaggy brows.

"I have an antique jewelry box in need of repair." My heart tightened for a beat or two. If Norm had been available, could he have repaired my mother's box? With a shake of my head, I attached Brutus's leash to a hook on the bench, and hauled the box out of the green bag.

Norm ran a hand over the jewelry box and whistled between his teeth. "Ah, yes. English walnut. I'll hazard a guess and say late eighteen-hundreds." He turned it over. "I see the damage. Do you have the piece of wood?"

"It's inside."

He opened the box and lifted out the sliver. He held it over the scar in back. "Yeah. No problem. And I'll fix this crack too."

"One more thing. I know there's a secret compartment. Any idea how to open it?"

With the box at eye level, Norm turned it until he viewed all sides. "Usually depressing the carved figures and twisting one of the legs simultaneously will do the trick. Let's give it a try."

He placed the box on the bench, and prodded and twisted in several combinations.

My eyes followed his every move. "You have to be a contortionist. Need any help?"

"Uh-uh. One person has to do it. The twist has to coincide—"

Brutus stretched the leash out to the door and barked. We glanced down the drive. A man closed the gate and walked toward the workshop.

"Must be a customer. Excuse me, Mrs. Mac." Norm stepped to the entrance.

Tugging Brutus behind me, I returned to the jewelry box, my fingers itching to attempt another combination. Brutus's barking had alerted Norm's dogs in the fenced area directly behind the workshop. The commotion obliterated Norm's conversation.

He pointed to various pieces of furniture around the workshop. The man nodded and came inside. I stopped manipulating the box, and scrutinized the new customer, a young black man. He seemed awfully young to be interested in the type of restoration Norm specialized in. Brutus's barking changed to a low growl when the man neared me.

After the customer admired various items Norm pointed out, he focused on my box. The nape of my neck tingled. What was it about this box?

Intent on impressing a new client, Norm moved to the trunk he'd been working on when I arrived. "And I also remove old paint and restore the original finish."

The man peeked in the trunk, but his eyes wandered back to my box. I shoved it into the green bag. His dark eyes shot to my face. He stood on the other side of the bench, but menace seeping from his eyes burned mine. I yanked the bag off the table and backed up to the wall. Brutus snarled and lunged.

"What the—?" Norm stopped mid-explanation of another restoration technique, and stared from me to the man. "You're not interested in my work. You—"

"Shut up, old man." The customer shoved Norm and moved around the bench.

Norm stumbled over a scrap of wood.

What could I do? The man loomed between me and the entrance. He could dispatch Brutus with one kick.

Norm's dogs let loose a peel of howling. I inched to the door leading to the backyard, restraining Brutus with one hand and clutching the bag in the other.

"Hey, mister. I don't know what you're after." I hoped it wasn't the jewelry box. "But—"

"I want that jewelry box."

"Tough. You're not going to get it." I transferred the leash to my other hand and grabbed the door handle. "Behind this door are two of the biggest, meanest dogs you've ever seen. Hear them?" I nudged my head sideways.

The man glared at me then at Norm, now standing next to the bench.

"That right? You gots big dogs?"

Norm pointed to Brutus. "Those barks aren't from miniatures like him."

Indecision shadowed the man's face, then he shook his head. "Naw. You bluffin'. Give me the box."

He and I were about the same size, but I knew I'd be no match for his youthful strength.

"Last chance to leave. I'll count to three, then I'm going to open this door. One. Two."

With a smirk on his face, he advanced.

"Three." I opened the door.

Trixie, the German shepherd, bounded in first. She ran to Norm and sat. So much for ferocious hounds. But then Sylvester, the Rottweiler mix entered. He sized up the situation and bared his teeth.

The young man had already backed out of the garage and now fled down the driveway with Sylvester and Trixie on his heels. Brutus barked support like a cheerleader.

Somehow the man managed to enter his car in one piece. He drove off before

Norm and I reached the gate. I glimpsed the car's color, but not the make or model to give to the sheriff.

The dogs responded to Norm's call and returned to him. He rewarded each with a pat. "Good kids." Wagging tails acknowledged they knew they'd done good. Norm closed the gate. "Great thinking on your part, Mrs. Mac. But why would that man want your box?"

After describing our eventful weekend in Kerrville, I reeled in Brutus's leash. "This makes the third person abnormally interested in the box. It must hold something special or incriminating. But how did he know I'd be here with it? I suppose Mike or Teresa could have mentioned I'd be bringing it to you."

Norm scratched his head. "Interesting. Could they all be after the same thing?"

"Don't know, but I need to open it. Whatever is hidden inside must be of great value."

"I'm in the middle of a big project right now. I could start on the box next week. Leave it and—"

"If it's all the same, Norm, I'll take it home and bring it back when you have time."

"Sure." He chuckled. "Don't blame you."

"Maybe I'll open it before then."

Norm opened the gate and scanned the street. "Don't see his car lurking anywhere. Do you want me to follow you home anyway"?

"Naw. I'll be fine. Thanks."

I followed Brutus down the road. My cell phone rang and jolted me out of reliving the scene in the garage.

"Hi, Mike."

"Mama, we have two doctor appointments in San Antonio tomorrow. Dr. Quinn, the ob-gyn at ten o'clock, and the new neurosurgeon, Dr. Janiskowski, at noon. She and Dr. Conway were partners."

During our conversation, Mike said Dr. Conway had been alone when the eighteen-wheeler hit her car head-on. When I offered to accompany them, he declined.

The box bumped my hip and reminded me. "Mike, did you or Teresa tell anyone I would be taking the jewelry box to Norm?" I described the incident in the garage.

"Mama, Teresa was right. Her box has caused nothing but trouble. Sure you're okay?"

"Yes, but who'd you tell?"

"Sunday evening Don and Jean Petrie invited their neighbors and a group from church to their house. We told them the story of the jewelry box—had to explain Teresa's bruised jaw to those who didn't know—and how you were going to have the box repaired and open it."

"I see."

"Sorry, Mama. Do you think the man came from Kerrville?"

"Who else would know I wanted to take the box to Norm?" The man's face loomed before me. "I hate to sound . . . racial or anything, but were any of the guests black?"

"Yeah. One."

"A young man?" My interest perked.

"No. A guy about your age." He inhaled sharply. "Mama, I didn't mean—"

Chuckling, I squinted as the sun peeked through the mesquite trees at the side of the road. "I know what you mean. But back to the man."

"A little older than you and Daddy."

"Oh." Couldn't have been today's intruder. "Never mind." My theory blew up in smoke, but it had to be a man from Kerrville or Brooder.

We chatted about the past weekend while Brutus led the way. When Mike hung up, I slid the phone into my pocket and pondered this new information. All of a sudden, gravel scrunched behind me. I turned. A car crept along, barely making any noise on the rough pavement.

I increased my pace. About thirty yards to our gate. Call Tom? The roar of the tractor filled the air. Even if he had his phone, he wouldn't hear it ring.

The old, dark blue Honda Civic inched toward me. I darted off the narrow lane, and tramped over dried grass stumps, my heart thumping with each step. Brutus trotted ahead, as if we played a game. The car drew alongside me.

"You gots nowhere to go, lady. Give me the box." It was the same man.

Twenty yards. I ran.

He sped up and veered off the pavement. His Honda cut between me and my path to the gate. I tried to skirt his car, but he opened the door leaving me no exit. With a snarl, he wrenched the grocery bag from my hand and shoved my shoulder hard.

I lost my balance and toppled to the ground.

CHAPTER SEVEN

The grocery bag had been in the man's possession for a fleeting five seconds when Norm's canines bounded all over us. Sylvester sunk his teeth into the thief's leg, and Trixie covered my neck and hands in loving licks.

"You'd better get out of here, quick," yelled Norm as he scurried down the road. "Sylvester's kinda hungry."

Panicked brown eyes beseeched me. I shoved Trixie aside, clutched the bag to my side and called off Sylvester, never thinking he'd obey. But he did.

The man jumped into his car, slammed the door and muttered, "This ain't worth it. He can steal the stupid box."

When Norm reached me, he helped me stand. "Are you all right?"

I brushed dust and dried grass off my jeans. "Yeah. I landed on a clump of grass. How'd you know he came back?"

"Sylvester ran to the gate and barked. I recognized the car and suspected the guy was following you. Once I opened the gate, Sylvester raced to the rescue."

"Thank you, friend. I owe you."

♦ ♦ ♦

"Wish I could have seen the man's face." Tom chomped on his sandwich, calmer now that I'd reassured him a dozen times that I was fine.

"No, you don't. It wasn't pretty." A skittish breeze blew across the back porch and threatened to blow my napkin away. "But it was kind of funny."

"He wasn't injured?"

"Nope. Scared to death, but no blood. His thick jeans prevented Sylvester's teeth from doing any damage." Brutus lapped up the crumbs I brushed off my lap.

The serene view of valleys and hills covered in new lime-green leaves and dark deciduous foliage couldn't completely erase the rescue scene from my mind.

"Chella," Tom's voice became pensive. "I know you love Brutus, but have you thought about us getting a bigger dog, you know, a Sylvester type?"

Picking up my petite but ferocious dog, I stared into his doe brown eyes. He'd protect me any way he could. "I have, but I can't handle a big dog. If you were home more—"

Tom covered my hand with his. "Sweetheart, do you know what I did one time when I was stuck in a hotel room during a tornado warning in Odessa?"

His rhetorical question needed no answer, so I waited.

"I calculated how much of our married life I've spent on the road, away from you."

My attention caught, I raised my eyes to his. "Interesting diversion. How much?"

"One third, including all the long-term training sessions."

My eyebrows shot up. "That's a lot."

"You should know. But our lives may change in the next few weeks."

"How?"

"There's a promotion—"

"Tom!" I pulled my hand away.

"I haven't said anything because I didn't want to get your hopes up, but Kurt is retiring and I'm in line for his job as the Regional Manager."

Releasing Brutus, I sprang up and sat in Tom's lap, sliding an arm around his shoulders. "When will you know?"

"In two, three weeks."

I nuzzled his cheek. "Does this mean you'll be home more?"

"Yeah."

"Ooh, if you're home more often, I'll have to think of all the chores I want done around here."

"Hmm." Tom bounced his knees up and down. "I may have to reconsider the job."

I held onto his neck. "You should finish mowing before you have to leave on Wednesday."

With an exaggerated salute, he said, "Yes, ma'am. Any more orders?"

I eased out of his lap and stacked our plates. "Not right now, but I'll make a list. A looong list."

Tom followed me inside, stopping in the bathroom to brush his teeth. I loaded the dishwasher and mulled over the news. I'd survived the empty-nest syndrome when Joey moved out, but could I survive having my husband home more frequently? I'd done my share of complaining about his absences over the years, but I was accustomed to making decisions, and doing what I wanted, when I wanted. Could I adjust to his constant presence?

Lost in thought, I bent over the sink to rinse a plate. Tom planted a kiss on the nape of my neck, sending a shiver down my body. I could probably adjust.

"Be back in two or three hours. I didn't mow much this morning." Baseball cap and work gloves in hand, he left the house.

Since only four of our nine acres were cleared, it would take Tom most of the afternoon to complete the weed-eating and mow the field behind the house. I hunted for an empty notebook in the office and began an Internet search on the Summerland-Hayes family.

A variety of stories popped up. I concentrated on articles featuring the twins, Gregory and Gordon. They were members of the family attached to the jewelry box. Their parents were Albert and Bella Summerland-Hayes. The next entry about Gordon's death mentioned a cousin, Emory Keenan. Same family. I read on.

Emory Keenan's mother was Mary Margaret Summerland-Hayes. I assumed Mary Margaret and Albert were siblings. Emory, born four years after the twins, worked in one of the family businesses in Kerrville until his disappearance in 1993. The author of the article asserted Emory embezzled funds from the company and skipped the country.

Bones rattled in my mind. Another skeleton?

Without knowing the names of Mary Margaret and Albert's parents, I could read forever to find another relevant article. Therefore, I followed a new line of inquiry.

From The *Kerrville Daily Times* I'd purchased earlier, I located a Web site and logged on. They had a month's back issues available. I opened several files, but nothing about the family caught my attention. Then I remembered Sammie

Howard mentioned the estate sale date as late February. I opened the earliest issues online, and sure enough in the second one, I read the announcement of the Summerland-Hayes estate sale. Gregory Summerland-Hayes and Rachael Galloway sponsored the sale. Rachael must be another relative. Which Summerland-Hayes was her parent?

My eyes crossed. I closed the Web site and reviewed my notes. Too many gaps. I'd have to visit Warren Howard, or another Kerrville resident who knew the family and could fill in the missing names.

I made a pitcher of iced tea, knowing Tom would guzzle glasses of it when he came in. Brutus, ignored since lunch, dumped his favorite chew toy, a red rubber bone, at my feet. I threw it down the hall, and he chased after it, tail and ears pointed skyward.

When he failed to return with it, as per rules of our game, I moseyed down the hall to find out why. Brutus pawed at the toy wedged next to a carved leg of the hall table. I pulled it out and threw it into our bedroom, then followed the dog.

The antique jewelry box sat on the corner of my dresser. I checked my watch. Three o'clock. I had enough time for a few combinations. With the box in hand, I slid to the floor. Push and twist. Push and twist. Over and over I tried, until my left index finger and thumb were numb.

I switched hands. The second combination worked and a drawer clicked open in the back.

Brutus nudged me with his red toy. I shooed him away, wanting to savor the moment. The hairs on my arms prickled under goose bumps as my chest constricted. What would I find? How long had it been hidden away?

Turning the box around, I slid the drawer open an inch. Then two. Three. Until it revealed a stack of yellowed envelopes. A sweet, spicy scent whispered around me. I sniffed the hint of exotic perfume.

My fingers itched to touch the contents, but I felt like an eavesdropper spying on a very private moment. Then I thought of the intruder from Brooder, the man in the parking lot, and the man from Norm's workshop. If they were after these letters, I needed to find out why.

Hand trembling, I slid them out. Eight envelopes. The larger one displayed the letters *V C* in fancy calligraphy. I peeked inside. Empty. Two envelopes had the name Esther Stiles on them. The rest were addressed to Esther Stiles, with a military postmark, dated either 1942 or 1943. The return address had been torn from all five.

"Whew. They're old. They can't have anything to do with Gordon's accident. He wasn't even born yet."

I arranged the dated envelopes chronologically. Then I opened the two addressed to Esther. They were dated 1940. I read them first.

March 12, 1940
Dear Ginny,

In your last letter you said Harlan nearly found out. How? Don't leave me in the dark and all. Are you safe? If you want me to stop writing, just say so. Watch what you say and do, or you'll plow up snakes. I wish I'd never taken this here job in Tennessee, especially now you tell me you're going to have another baby. When's it due? I plan on being back in Texas by October. I heard of a big new company in San Antonio that will need workers. Can I come see you then?

I have a job right now. Don't have much time to do nothing but work, eat and sleep. Remember David? He's the feller I wrote about last time. Well, he off and married his girl, Darlene. I'm real lonely. Wish I was in Kerrville with you. That's all my news. Hope to see you soon.
I love you,
Frankie

So many questions. First of all, Frankie's word choice sounded a little odd. Were Ginny and Frankie lovers? And who was Harlan, and if the letter was for Ginny why was the envelope addressed to Esther Stiles? Was anyone mentioned in the letter related to Gordon?

I opened the second envelope. Another single sheet in the same handwriting.

May 17, 1940
Dearest Ginny,

He's arrived! Congratulations! How can you say he looks like me? I've heard all babies look alike. You sounded so happy in your last letter, but I worry when you get too excited. You know how you are. You say things you shouldn't.

We've kept the secret this long, Ginny, don't spoil it now. Is Harlan at all concerned about the baby, or were you kidding me?

The job here is hard, but I'm grateful to have it. Mr. Woodward laid off four men last week. Don't know what I'll do if I'm laid off. I see David and Darlene almost every week. But I don't know what she sees in him. If dumb was dirt, he'd cover about an acre.

Hope to see you October. Sorry I wasn't there for the birthing. Keep safe. Gotta go. I'm all wore out.
Love,
Frankie

Was the baby Frankie's? I assumed Harlan was Ginny's husband and Frankie the absent lover. Were Harlan and Ginny part of the Summerland-Hayes family? I wish Frankie's last name had been mentioned. More Internet searches coming up.

As I opened the first envelope with a military postmark, a lump knotted in my throat. This had been mailed by a soldier during the Second World War. In awe, I withdrew the folded paper. Although mailed to Esther Stiles, the letter was also addressed to Ginny.

August 4, 1942
Dear Ginny,

Bad news. I'm shipping out in two weeks and won't be able to visit you before then. Basic training was tough, but I've gone through worse. Fighting neighborhood kids taught me some moves. I may not be built like a tank, but

I can handle myself.

Wish I could see Johnny one more time. Thanks for the photograph of the kids. Johnny sure is a cute little tyke. You were right, he does look like me. He doesn't resemble his brother and sister at all. Does Harlan suspect? He treats you right, doesn't he? I know you have a good reason to stay with him, but you must know I don't like him much. He thinks the sun comes up just to hear him crow. Sorry, Ginny, but that's how I feel.

If I survive this war and make my way back to Texas, I want to take you and the kids to San Antonio. It's a great city. Even if you've been there with him, I want to take you.

Write me, Ginny. I'll need your love and support now more than ever.
Love,
Frankie

Obviously, Frankie joined the military and served overseas. Johnny would have been two years old. It sounded like Frankie worked in San Antonio before joining the army. But again, why were the letters addressed to Esther?

Pins and needles attacked my crossed ankles, sending shards of pain up my calves. I eased to a stand and carried my trove of letters to the kitchen table.

The next letter, when opened, contained a pressed flower, leaves now brown and petals translucent and silvery. I carefully let the fragile memento slide onto another envelope, and unfolded the sheet of paper.

November 20, 1942
My Dearest Ginny,

My heart aches for you. When I heard about Johnny's death I wanted to come and hold you, but couldn't. Even if I wasn't on the other side of the world in this God forsaken place, I know I couldn't come to you because if I was there it would cause you more problems. I'm fit to be tied. I hope Elizabeth has helped you.

Don't feel you have to keep our secret for my sake. If you have to reveal it, I'll support you any way I can. Don't know when I'll be stateside again, but you know I'll do whatever you want me to.

Can Esther still deliver my letters? I guess I'll keep writing you through her as long as I hear back from you. I can't tell you anything about where we are or what we're doing. Only, it's not pretty. In all my years, and I know they're not many, I haven't seen anything like this. Lost plenty of guys in my platoon. Been places you wouldn't believe. One day I can tell you. Right now, I'm plum tuckered out. Write when you can.

Love,

Frankie

Oh, poor Ginny and Frankie. And Harlan. To lose a child so young. And Frankie to be away from home, on the other side of the world. Where did he serve? Obviously, his letters weren't specific. And Elizabeth. Elizabeth Summerland-Hayes? Another visit to Kerrville seemed imminent. But at least Frankie provided a clue as to Esther's identity.

I slid the flower back into the letter and folded it, then opened the next one.

December 18, 1942

Ginny Dear,

How are you? You didn't say much about yourself in your last letter. How are the kids handling Johnny's passing? And what you said about Harlan made me madder than a wild dog. Harlan is as yellow as mustard but without the bite. If I was there I'd let him have a piece of my mind. I'm not the same shy, skinny kid you last saw. Don't think I can't do it, because I will. Let me know if you want me to confront him.

Why did Elizabeth abandon you? Did she give you any reason? Doesn't she know you need her now more than ever? I hope she finds happiness in Houston, but as far as I'm concerned she's out of our lives forever.

I wish I was there to comfort you, Ginny, my dear. Don't worry about me. I have good guys around me, and I'm keeping my head down. Learning to live with sand in everything.

I'll understand if you don't write for a while. You've got a lot going on. But remember me so far away. Knowing that you're thinking about me makes all the difference.
Love,
Frankie

What had Harlan done? Skinny kid? Did I have the wrong idea about Frankie? Sand. Desert. Frankie in North Africa? I gathered clue words from the letters and stored them in a memory file labeled *Frankie*.

The diminishing roar of the tractor indicated Tom turned toward the shed. He'd come inside once he'd stored all the equipment he'd used. Time enough to read the last two letters. Almost a year had passed.

September 7, 1943
My Dear Ginny,

Now don't get all anxious and everything. I've been wounded and I'm writing from a hospital ship. It's not that serious, but for now I can't walk. Got a bullet and shrapnel in my left leg. My unit was hit, and some of us may not make it back over there to join them.

Not sure where I'll go when I recover, but one thing's for sure. When I get back to Texas, the first thing I want to do is see you and the kids, and visit John's grave.

And I think it's time we told Harlan the truth. I've had my share of close calls over here, and I don't want to meet my Maker with this big lie on my conscience. Think about it. I won't do anything without you knowing.

Haven't heard from you in a while. Might be because we've been moving around constantly. Hope your letters catch up to me once I'm in a hospital somewhere. Remember when you read this that I'm sure to be up and about by then, fit as a Tennessee fiddle. Did I ever tell you I learned to play one when I worked there? Fiddle players there are as common as cornbread.

Got to go. They're collecting the letters. Please consider telling Harlan. This is real important to me.

Love,

Frankie

P.S. Happy Birthday

Did Frankie ever make it back to Texas and confront Harlan? One more letter. Would it reveal the answer?

December 2, 1943

Dear Ginny,

Haven't heard from you for a long time. I made it to the hospital, and there were no letters waiting for me and none have come since I've been here. Just a few more days, the doc says, and I'll be shipping out again. Can't say where I'm going but it's not back with my original unit. That makes me sad. But no sense having a conniption fit over it. No one here's going to listen to the likes of me. The wounds are healing, and I have a limp, but I can still run and carry a weapon. Every able-bodied soldier is being shipped out, even those like me with a little hitch in our get-along.

I suppose you didn't agree with my suggestion of telling Harlan the truth. That's OK, I understand. But I miss your letters, Ginny. Don't you know what they mean to me? They keep me going, they give me hope, they make it possible for me to do what I have to do to stay alive over here. I'll need them more than ever now I'm returning to the front lines.

When I get home—if I get home, I won't talk to Harlan because I know it will affect your marriage and maybe your future with him. You said you sorted out your problems and things are good between you. I won't mess with that. But please write, Ginny. Please. Receiving a letter from you is like opening a packet of sunshine in a very dark cave.

Love,

Frankie

Ginny and Harlan *were* married and Frankie might have been her lover. My suspicions were correct. One skeleton found for sure. But which of the three men interested in the jewelry box wanted to silence the Ginny-Frankie-lover skeleton? They couldn't all be after the letters. What difference would the contents make some seventy years later?

I picked up the box and turned it over. There had to be another secret compartment.

CHAPTER EIGHT

Tom's boss called late Monday afternoon to reschedule his Midland-Odessa trip. We'd anticipated another day together, but now Tom rambled around the bedroom, packing for three days in West Texas.

During supper, I showed him the letters, and discussed my plan to visit Warren Howard to gather more details on the Summerland-Hayes family.

"This is more than computer research, Chella." His eyes raked over me.

After a moment's thought, I shared with Tom my need to investigate the box's original owners, especially now that I'd found the letters.

"Someone, somewhere knows Frankie and Ginny. Maybe that person would like their letters." A sip of iced tea soothed my tight throat.

Tom's blue eyes softened, and he leaned across the table. "Remember you have family. You have me. Don't endanger yourself."

With a nod I acknowledged his words and finished the meal in silence.

MedTech Supply Company required Tom to demonstrate and sell medical equipment and to provide workshops to hospital staff. He adjourned to the office to download reports and worksheets for his trip. I attempted more Internet research on my laptop, but my efforts proved fruitless.

We spent the rest of the evening in Bible study, a practice we began after my acceptance of the Lord.

Early the next morning, Tom closed his suitcase and I accompanied him to the van. "Just promise me one thing, Chella. When you go to Kerrville, be careful." Tom's concern furrowed his brow.

I melted into his embrace. "I will, my love."

While dressing for my trip to Kerrville, I decided too much interest had been shown in the jewelry box. I wrapped it in a towel, and traipsed down the hill to store it in Tom's tractor shed. An intruder wouldn't search out here. The shed wasn't even visible from the driveway or the house.

Confident in my decision, I locked the shed, and ran back to the house for my purse and notebook. My cell phone rang as I entered the kitchen. Warren Howard.

"Hi, Warren. I'm on my way to Kerrville. Do you mind if I stop by and pick your brain about the Summerland-Hayes family?"

"Not at all. But the reason I'm calling is I found out something interesting from Connie, my employee. She said a week ago a man asked about items from the Summerland-Hayes estate sale. When I told her about the problems the jewelry box has caused, she became real upset. Connie told the man that my mother intended to give the box to the new youth director's pregnant wife."

"Can she describe the man?"

"There were other customers in the store. All she can remember is he was tall, and good looking."

"Too bad. A description for the sheriff might help apprehend a suspect." I sidled to the window and watched a deer in the field grazing on tender shoots.

"Yeah, but there's another problem. My mother never met a stranger. I wouldn't be surprised if by now half of Kerrville's citizens know about the jewelry box and who has it."

"And I told her on Sunday I'd be taking it to my neighbor for repair."

He whistled. "Hate to say this about my own mother, but your news is spreading." Warren paused before speaking. "A customer just entered, but before I go, there's one last thing."

"I'm listening."

"An elderly man who knew Teresa had the box came in when I opened this morning. He asked me to give you his phone number."

"Why? How does he know Teresa or me?"

"Sorry, didn't inquire, but Mother—"

The strange events from the past couple of days swirled through my mind. "What did he look like?"

"He was tall, slender. African-American."

An elderly black man. It must be the man from the hospital waiting room and the grocery store parking lot.

"His name's Franklin Jackson."

Franklin. Could he be Frankie?

I swallowed and sank into a chair. "Why does he want me to call him?" I think I knew the answer.

"He said there may be an important document hidden in the box. That's all. He said he didn't intend to alarm you the other day. Whatever that means."

A document. Not letters. He must not know Ginny kept his letters. But if he knew of a document, then he might also know how to open the secret compartment concealing it.

"Okay, Warren. What's Mr. Jackson's phone number?"

I wrote it down in my notebook and told Warren I'd be in Kerrville later. In the office, I located a protective brown mailer, then removed the letters from their resting place in my Bible, and slid them into the envelope. Frankie would have to answer a bunch of questions before I'd hand over his letters.

Another skeleton hovered. If Ginny was a Summerland-Hayes, then having a black lover in the 1940's would be cause for a humongous scandal if discovered. Rattle, rattle.

I sat at the kitchen table, dialed the number, and scratched Brutus's head while I waited. Franklin answered after six rings.

"Mr. Jackson, this is . . . I'm Mrs. McDonough. I have the jewelry box."

Silence.

"Mr. Jackson?"

"Yes. Yes, ma'am." The elder voice I remembered from the hospital. "Thank you for calling. Did the man from the store tell you why I need to talk to you?"

"He did."

"Have you opened the box? I believe it's kinda tricky."

"I have and I found—"

"Oh, good." His breath huffed in and out. "Please, Mrs. McDonough, can I have the envelope? It's real important to me."

Should I tell him what I'd found over the phone?

"I can come to your house to pick it up." The tone of his voice rose.

"No. No, Mr. Jackson. I'll be in Kerrville later today. I'll meet you."

"I'm not home right now. On my way to San Antonio, down the road apiece, close to Bandera. Figured I'd travel the back way."

Bandera. Had he been on his way to see me? "Bandera sounds good. The Old Spanish Trail Restaurant, on Main Street."

"I know it. Ten minutes?"

"Make it fifteen."

Many of my questions were about to be answered. I drove to Bandera and parked across from the restaurant. The OST, one of our favorite eateries, had a legendary daily buffet where patrons sat at hand carved tables and benches surrounded by a collection of John Wayne photographs.

I found Mr. Jackson sipping coffee at a corner table. He stood as I approached and stretched out his gnarled hand.

"Thank you, Mrs. McDonough. I sure do appreciate you meeting me and all."

I shook his rough hand, surprised at its strength. After ordering coffee, I appraised the man. Tiny tufts of gray hair sprouted on the sides of his head. His dark watery eyes held a gentleness and sincerity, immediately and inexplicably touching my soul.

The waitress brought my coffee and refilled his mug. I added sweetener, and took a sip.

"Can . . . can I see it, ma'am?" He adjusted a hearing aid in his left ear. "Can't hardly hear nothin' in all this commotion."

Placing my mug down, I looked him square in the eyes. "Mr. Jackson, there's more than one—"

His sparse eyebrows shot up. "More than one certificate?"

"What? I didn't find a certificate."

"But . . . but what did you find?"

"There's an empty envelope in here with the letters *V. C.* on it."

"Oh, no! What could have happened to it? It should have been in there. She wrote the letters *V. C.* on an envelope. Stands for Virginia's Certificate." He leaned back, then shot forward like he'd been catapulted. "But you said you found more than one. More than one what?"

"Letters."

"Letters?"

"To Ginny from Frankie."

"Oooh." The word extended as a smile crinkled his cheeks. "She kept 'em."

"There are seven. But before I give them to you, will you answer my questions, please? Who is Ginny? And the baby, Johnny?"

His eyes misted, and he nodded, but I wasn't sure his spirit remained in the restaurant with me anymore. I gave him time. His jaw muscles worked as his lips protruded then puckered. Quiet mutterings emerged from his mouth as he rubbed his hands together, making the sound of paper against paper.

After a minute or so, he dipped his head to the side. "My Ginny. Virginia. She was my big sister—"

"Sister!" An unexpected relationship.

"My half-sister. We had the same mother. Different fathers."

The letters took on a whole new meaning. I blushed at my original assumption.

"And Johnny was her third child. He was special 'cause she thought she couldn't have no more after the problems with the last one." He chuckled. "Ginny always teased me, said Johnny looked like me."

"She said that in one of the letters. But why are Ginny's letters in a jewelry box from the Summerland-Hayes estate?"

After draining his mug, Frankie pushed it aside. "Don't you know? She married Harlan. Harlan Summerland-Hayes."

I frowned. Instead of clarifying my questions, the knowledge muddied the waters.

"I know what you're thinking." Frankie's head bobbed. "The certificate details information that could be harmful to her descendants. That's why I want it. The document should have been in there. She said she kept it there. I told you we had different fathers. My father was black like me, but Ginny's dad was a red-headed

Irishman. We had another sister too. Elizabeth."

"You mention her in a letter."

"Uh-huh. Elizabeth has light skin like Ginny. See, our mother was black, lighter than me, but Elizabeth and Ginny had the same father and passed for white. Back in the 1930s, if you could *pass*, you didn't do nothin' to mess with that. Elizabeth moved to Houston right after Johnny died, and we didn't hear from her much."

"Let me get this straight. The secret you talk about in the letters is Ginny's heritage."

Frankie nodded.

"I see. You're not going to believe—" But Frankie could live without knowing what I'd originally thought. "Did you ever confront Harlan about being his brother-in-law?"

"Naw. When I was discharged after the war, I came back here, but Ginny wouldn't see me. I suppose she didn't want to risk losing what she had." He stared at his empty coffee mug. "I don't blame her. Harlan was kinda crusty, so I never talked to him. In fact, I never met him. Of course, I knew a lot about him. I left things the way they were, 'cause once you let the cat out of the bag, it's a whole lotta trouble to get it back in." A sad smile tweaked his cheeks for a second. "I moved to Tennessee, got married . . ." Now he grinned. "I have three fine children."

I studied his face, alight with thoughts of his family, but when a shadow clouded his eyes, I asked, "What information is on this certificate? Why are you searching for it after all this time?"

Frankie clasped his hands together and flexed his finger joints. "I thought the jewelry box had been destroyed in the fire right before Ginny's death. But then I read about the estate sale. I've kinda kept up with reading about the Summerland-Hayes family 'cause of Ginny." He traced an imaginary line on the table with a crooked, arthritic finger. "When I found her box listed, you could have knocked me over with a feather. I figured her document was still in there."

"Is it a birth certificate?"

"Not exactly." Frankie fiddled with the top button of his blue plaid shirt. "See, when her mother married her father, she was already, um, in the family way. Cora, Ginny's mother, made her husband write out their names and the date of their wedding. Then later when Virginia and Elizabeth were born, they added their names and birth dates to the page."

"Like a marriage certificate and birth certificate all in one?" I fidgeted with the discarded sweetener packet.

"There you go. Signed by Cora and Peter, her husband, and the local priest. The priest insisted the race of each party be listed—"

"Now I get it."

"And that's why I want the certificate. Ginny kept the secret of her mixed parentage until the day she died. I don't want her personal information to fall into the wrong hands. Her children never knew. And I don't want her grandchildren and great-grandchildren to find out."

"But why did she keep the piece of paper if it was so incriminating?"

Frankie stretched out his legs. "It's hard to explain. Back then people weren't given birth certificates like we are today. You could register a birth at your church or you could go to the court house. Mr. Peter O'Brien didn't want to do either. Cora didn't trust him and came up with this idea."

"Adding the births to the marriage certificate?"

"Uh-huh. Cora wanted proof she was married before giving birth. She wanted to make sure her children had a legitimate name."

"I can see why Cora would keep the document, but after Virginia married Harlan, she—Virginia—no longer needed it. Why did she tell you she kept it?"

"There's one more little twist. Peter O'Brien left Cora when Elizabeth was three years old. He sailed back to Ireland. Had to fulfill his family obligations when he became Earl of something. Full of nonsense, he was. Cora held onto the document hoping one day to cash in on Peter's fortune. Nothing ever came of that fantasy. Later, she met another man . . . and I was born." Frankie's gaze dropped to the table. "After Virginia married Harlan, she had plenty of money, but she told me she was going to keep it anyway. In the end, it was probably more nostalgic than anything."

"And no one ever found out about her mother?"

With a shrug, Frankie said, "I don't think so."

I touched the brown envelope under my purse on the seat next to me. "Before I hand over the letters, a few more questions. How did you know my daughter-in-law had the box and ended up in the hospital?"

Wiping a hand over his face he tried to hide his sheepish expression. "Ooh, wish you hadn't asked that. I'm not proud of what I did when I found the jewelry box listed with the sale items. I went to the store, the one on Water Street—"

"*Use It Again, Sam?*"

"Right, and behind the counter was a sweet old lady with a ten gallon mouth. Talked non-stop. She had Ginny's box on the counter and was fixin' to wrap it in gift paper. I wanted to buy it, but she said she was giving it to the new minister's wife." He pointed a less than straight finger at me. "It took a bit of digging, but I found an article in the newspaper about your son's new position with a church in Brooder."

Frankie's words matched Warren's description of his mother's wagging tongue.

"But how did you know Teresa was in the hospital?"

"The friends I'm staying with live next door to a young Kerr County deputy. He blabbed about escorting a woman to a Kerrville motel after a break-in over a silly jewelry box. I figured the break-in had to be connected to Virginia's box. I weaseled more information from him, found the motel and followed you."

"You did?"

Lowering his head, he whispered, "Sorry."

Not much I could do about it now. All things considered, Frankie appeared to be the least dangerous of the horde clambering for the box. "One more question. Who is Esther Stiles?"

A grin broke over Frankie's face. "That woman's meaner than a skillet full of rattlesnakes. Don't want to cross her. She was a longtime servant in the Summerland-Hayes house. Ginny paid her to deliver the letters I mailed to her."

The fog obscuring the Summerland-Hayes family lifted wisp by wisp. I handed the envelope to Frankie. "I'm sorry about the certificate, but the jewelry box may have more than one secret compartment."

His gnarled, shaking fingers latched onto the envelope. "Ginny never said. All I know is she told me she kept it in the secret drawer in the front of her jewelry box. In case anything happened to her and I needed it. But you say it wasn't there and no one has revealed her secret." He hiked a boney shoulder. "She must have destroyed the paper before she died."

I slung my purse strap over my shoulder, and patted Frankie's hand. "The box might have another compartment. If I discover anything else of hers, I'll give you a call."

Frankie hugged the envelope to his thin chest. "Thank you, Mrs. McDonough. These letters mean the world to me. A connection. And I can smell her perfume. Oh, Lordy, this is a bonus I never dreamed of."

"Please call me Maricella." I stood and scooted in my chair. "I need to go now."

He followed me to the cash register and whipped out his wallet. "My treat, Maricella. And you call me Frankie."

"Thank you, Frankie."

He paid the cashier, and we stepped outside, lingering on the sidewalk.

Frankie adjusted his hearing aid. "Don't need the volume up so high now." His smile crinkled his leathery cheeks. Dark eyes sought mine. "About calling. I'm staying with friends in Kerrville. Beginning of April sometime I'm moving back to Memphis to live with my middle son, Leon." He pointed to a parked pickup across the street. "Usually, I drive myself, but when I need to visit San Antonio, like today, my friend's grandson is my chauffeur. Even if you don't find anything else of Ginny's, please keep in touch."

I extended my hand. "I will, Frankie." My fingers closed over his swollen joints. "How's the arthritis?"

"Ooh, not good. Some mornings I scarce can button my shirt. I take medication, but nothing works for long."

I gently rubbed his hand. "Take it easy, Frankie." I waved and walked to my car.

After buckling my seatbelt, I watched Frankie's progress down the sidewalk. He had a slight limp. A war injury? In spite of his age, he easily climbed into the passenger seat of a two-toned gray Ford truck. The young driver backed out and drove down Main Street.

As they passed me, I recalled what Frankie said about Ginny's jewelry box. She'd hidden the certificate in the front drawer of her box.

The letters I found came from a drawer in the back.

That meant the jewelry box did have another concealed compartment.

CHAPTER NINE

Armed with my notebook and a brain full of questions, I approached the Howards' antique store in Kerrville. *Use It Again, Sam* sat in a row of stores on Water Street. Live oaks shaded diagonal parking slots, and I pulled into one several doors down. The pristine storefront was painted maroon with gold trim. Three ornate, stained-glass panels hung in the windows.

I pushed open the heavy oak door, and entered to a jangling bell.

A short brunette dusting a roll top desk near the window abandoned her task and hurried to greet me. "Welcome to *Use It Again, Sam*. Anything in particular you interested in today, ma'am?"

"You must be Connie. I'm Maricella McDonough. I've come to see Warren."

Her fair skin blushed hot pink and her hazel eyes grew as round as the buttons on her blouse. "You're the lady with the box. I apologize for any problems I caused." She bowed her head and backed away. "I'll tell War . . . Mr. Howard you're here."

She bumped into a high table. The lamp displayed on it tottered, but she steadied it while inhaling a quick breath. With arms by her sides, she took brisk, deliberate steps to a door at the back of the store. Wood polish tinged the air. Surrounded by these ancient items, I wondered what secrets they harbored.

Warren and Connie emerged seconds later. He wore blue jeans, a crisp white shirt and brown boots. His arm still rested in a sling. They meandered through the furniture toward me, Connie a step or two behind Warren. She cast fleeting glances his way, and I could see her heart in those eyes. At times when I'm introduced to a couple I think, yeah, they look like Mr. and Mrs. To me, Warren and Connie looked like they belonged together. At least Connie and I thought so.

"Maricella." Warren and I shook hands. "Did you meet with Mr. Jackson?"

I described the meeting and the letters I'd found, but I didn't divulge Ginny's secret. "Do you have time now to fill in the gaps on the Summerland-Hayes family tree?"

I'd already diagrammed a rudimentary tree with the information I possessed. If I couldn't make one for me, I could at least make one for the owners of the box.

"Sure thing. We're not busy. Come back to the office. Connie can manage the store for a while. Right, Con?"

Nodding, Connie gazed up at Warren. "Yes, Mr. Howard."

Warren guided me back to his office and offered coffee, which I declined. I settled on the sofa upholstered in muted tan, red, and blue striped chintz, and placed my notebook on my lap. A cool breeze drifted through the open door leading to the alley. The windowless walls were covered in old movie posters.

He poured himself a mug of coffee before easing into a huge brown leather chair behind his desk. "Since our chat on Sunday I've researched the name. I'm a genealogy buff—kinda goes along with selling antiques—and I already have a lot of info on the Summerland-Hayes family. I can provide a firsthand account of the ones I grew up with. All in all, I think you'll get what you came for." He blew on his coffee and took a sip.

"Great. Let's begin."

"The first mention of the hyphenated name Summerland-Hayes is from the 1890s when Albert Summerland married Ann Hayes here in Kerr County. She came from a wealthy family back east and they insisted he adopt her name. Not a common practice at the time, but Ann's family wouldn't take no for an answer."

I held up my pen to halt his narration. "My neighbor, Norm, the man who's going to repair the jewelry box, concluded it was made in the late eighteen hundreds."

Scuffling and scraping from the courtyard punctuated our words.

"Ann probably brought it with her." Warren tilted his chair back and pointed to the door. "Guys are working out there. If it gets too noisy we can close the door. Anyway, Albert branched out into a variety of businesses—cattle, farming, banking. Seems he had a golden touch. Everything he dabbled in succeeded."

After a couple of sips of coffee, he continued. "You may have noticed the family name on buildings and businesses in town. There's a park along the river named after them."

"To tell the truth, I've not visited Kerrville much until now. The Summerland-Hayes name is new to me."

Cradling his mug in one large hand, he said, "They had six or seven kids, the records aren't clear, but only two survived to adulthood. John and Edward. I didn't follow Edward's family as he moved to South Africa. John married Mary Louise and their son Harlan—"

"He's mentioned in the letters I found."

Warren frowned. "You don't say?"

"Go on." I shouldn't have said anything about details revealed in the letters.

"John and Mary Louise had the one child, Harlan. He married Virginia O'Brien, and they had three children, Mary Margaret, Albert, and John. John died as an infant, and the other two passed away recently."

I kept my knowledge of Virginia and baby John to myself for now. "I know Mary Margaret had a son, Emory. Emory Keenan who disappeared."

Warren arched one eyebrow.

"I read the story on the Internet."

"Yeah? Don't believe everything you read. Emory—but I'm jumping ahead. Albert and his wife Bella had three children. The twins, Gordon and Gregory . . . Do you know about Gordon's accident?"

"A little. I read the Internet articles."

"Don't believe those reports either. People who knew him well don't believe it was an accident." He shrugged. "Their other child is Rachael Galloway."

Turning a page, I consulted my notes. "I read the announcement of the estate sale. Gregory and Rachael sponsored it."

"You're right. The fourth generation of Summerland-Hayes."

"And their children?"

"Gregory and his wife Vivian have two sons, Andrew and Conrad. Rachael and Lawrence Galloway have a daughter, Jacqui, and a son, Marshall. Marshall moved to Oregon years ago, and Jacqui is in New York. A stage actress or something. Conrad and I are friends. He doesn't believe Emory embezzled money."

I scribbled away. "Does anyone know where he went?"

"Conrad thinks Mexico, but no one's heard from him in years. He's been gone—"

"Since 1993."

Warren stood and poured more coffee into his mug. "The Summerland-Hayes family owned thousands of acres in Kerr County, and had a hand in many profitable businesses over the years."

A truck lumbered down the alley. Warren closed the door, shutting out the noise and the sunlight.

My eyes took a second to adjust. "Um, in all your research and your acquaintance with the family, has there ever been any scandal involving Virginia, Harlan's wife?" I had to ask about her.

"Not that I know of." Warren settled in his chair and rocked.

"One more question, Warren. Why did Gregory and Rachael sell the estate?"

"Money. Over the years one bad investment after another led to financial problems. Gordon was the one who held the others in check. Once he died, Gregory and Lawrence, Rachael's husband, ran the businesses into the ground." He placed his coffee mug on the desk and consulted a yellow legal pad.

"In 1993 there was a fire at the big house. Destroyed furnishings and severely damaged half a dozen rooms. No one from the family lived in the old house after the fire. I think they want to get rid of it all. They have a hundred acres left, up on the Guadalupe River, outside of town."

I nibbled the end of my pen and studied the family tree taking shape in front of me. This was fun. Maybe I should make one for our grandson, using Tom's ancestors. I hiked a shoulder and returned to the task at hand. "Rachael and Gregory couldn't be the ones after the jewelry box. It's been in their possession all this time."

"Not necessarily. As you can imagine, over the years different members of the family accumulated a lot of furniture. They placed old pieces in the attic of the big house, and other items were kept in storage. I overheard Rachael tell Gregory to be sure and pay the storage bill after the sale concluded. The jewelry box could have been hidden away for years."

So my suspects could include anyone from the family. I checked my list of questions and found one more to ask.

"Do you know anything about Virginia's family?"

Adjusting the sling, he studied the legal pad again. "Nope. My research focused on the male line of the family. But you can check the Kerr Regional History Center. It's also on Water Street, down several blocks from here."

"Thanks, Warren. This has been helpful. I still don't know who broke into Mike and Teresa's house. I know for sure it wasn't Mr. Jackson."

"I've been thinking about him all morning. How would he know of a secret compartment in a jewelry box from the Summerland-Hayes estate?"

"Um . . . because he knew Virginia."

He rubbed his chin. "I see, and . . ."

"It's his story to tell. I can't say anything else for now."

"Okaaay."

As I studied my notes, images of the intruder and the bogus customer at Norm's workshop danced across the page. The young man from the workshop had yelled as he fled the dogs for the second time, *This ain't worth it. He can steal the stupid box.* Then apparently he wasn't after it for himself. But the intruder at Mike's house, a tall Anglo man . . .

"Do you personally know Andrew, Marshall, and Conrad?"

"Yeah. We're all close in age. Attended the same school. I haven't seen or heard much about Marshall for a long time, but Conrad, Andrew, and I were close. That is until Andrew's divorce. His wife had an affair and that really messed him up. He quit coming to church and began drinking again. Lost custody." A deep sigh halted Warren's words. "His wife and son live here in Kerrville, but he moved to Austin when he was promoted last year. He's changed so much. Too bad. I miss him. He helped me through a tough time." Warren's smile had a sad edge to it. "But Conrad and I still hang out."

After a pause to let this all sink in, I continued with my train of thought. "Are any of these men tall and thin?"

Warren chuckled. "They all are. You can tell they're related." He attempted to smooth his shock of red curls.

All tall and thin. Could one of the Summerland-Hayes men be my intruder? "Can you describe them to me?"

A faint knock sounded. Warren held up a hand. "Just a minute." He called, "Come in."

Connie poked her head around the door. "Sorry to bother you, Mr. Howard. A customer has a question I—"

She couldn't finish her sentence. A man forced her into the office. She stumbled and sprawled at my feet.

"What the—?" Warren rose.

Dropping my notebook, I reached for Connie on the floor. "Are you okay?"

"Everyone, be still," the man yelled and slammed the door shut with his foot.

We all stared at him. Tall. Shaggy gray hair and beard. Dark glasses. Boots, jeans, tan shirt. Cowboy hat. Black gloves. But his weird gray facial hair contrasted with his youthful body. A brown leather knife sheath hung off his belt.

Warren eased from behind the desk. "Look mister, there's nothing in here. No money—"

"I said, be still." The man's deep voice sounded strange as he loomed over Warren. "Don't want money. Now back up and sit."

Warren stood his ground. "What do you want then?"

Connie stifled a sob. The sound was enough to distract the man. Warren lunged for a paperweight on the corner of his desk.

The man detected his move. "No, you don't." He threw a punch, hitting Warren square in the jaw. Warren staggered backward, struggling to balance with one arm in a sling. But he remained upright and wielded the paperweight at his foe again. Too late. Another blow to his chin sent him reeling. His head struck the corner of the desk, and with a thud he fell to the floor.

The intruder slid a long hunting knife from its sheath.

My mouth gaped. Blood tha-thumped in my head. What *did* he want? I shot a quick glance at the door to the alley. No noise. The workers must have left. My purse had fallen to the floor. I couldn't reach my cell without the man noticing.

I focused on Warren. All I could see were his twisted legs, his boots at awkward angles.

Connie struggled up and cuddled next to me on the sofa. Now the man faced us, the knife a menacing extension of his arm. His false beard flapped on his left jaw line and his gray wig hung askew.

He righted his hat and adjusted the hair, then patted the whiskers in place. "You," he pointed to me. "Tie her up." He pulled Connie off the sofa.

I hiked my shoulders and willed the quiver from my voice. "With what?" I wasn't going to make it easy on him. If he wanted Connie tied up he'd have to provide the rope.

Hauling her over to a small table along the wall, he picked up a roll of ugly gray duct tape. With an eerie smirk, he said, "Use this." The blade hovered close to her jugular.

Although he'd punched out Warren, every fiber in my being revolted at the prospect of doing his bidding.

"What . . . what if I refuse?" I stood, my knees knocking loud enough to be heard in the next store. "What if I walk out of here?" I inched to the main door.

With his arm around Connie's throat, he aimed the knife at her ribs. "You do, lady, and she's a goner." His voice fluctuated as if he tried to disguise it.

Connie gasped.

Ignoring my wobbly leg muscles, I held out my hand for the tape. "Okay. You win."

He released Connie, and thrust her to me. I caught her in my arms and whispered, "I'm sorry."

The fear in her eyes multiplied the cold knots cavorting in my gut.

"Sit her in that chair." He pointed to a straight-backed wooden chair by the table. "Tape her arms behind it."

I did as he requested, trying to make the tape as loose as possible.

"Now, tape her legs together, and tape around the chair."

Again, I followed his instructions.

"Good. Give me the tape."

I threw it to him and stood by the sofa. I had no idea what he planned next, but I wanted to be close to the door.

After sheathing his knife, he tore off a length of tape and slapped it over Connie's mouth. "There. That'll keep you quiet." He then checked on Warren. "And he's not waking up anytime soon."

"Is . . . is he all right? Can I tend to him?"

"Nope." Turning, he grinned, which looked ridiculous, surrounded by artificial gray hair and beard. "Now, it's just you and me."

Instinctively, I stepped backward and collided with the sofa. I landed on the edge. "What . . . what do you want with me?"

"What's your name?" As if to emphasize the seriousness of his question, he brandished the blade again.

I couldn't take my eyes off the weapon, but my brain shouted, *What*? at the unexpected question. Since he'd gone to all this trouble to get me alone, I figured he knew me.

A lump the size of Everest grated down my arid throat as I swallowed. "Why do you want to know?" I picked up my purse and clutched it like a lifeline.

He stomped toward me.

Tha-thump. Tha-thump. Blood pounded in my head like a bass drum.

Leaning over me, he prodded my shoulder. "I'm asking the questions."

As I glared into his face, I tried to scrutinize every feature, while willing my lungs to gather oxygen. Connie's whimpering in the background added fuel to my frantic hold on survival.

With a grunt, he straightened and yanked my purse from my grasp. "I need to make sure." He opened my billfold and located my driver's license. "Aha. Maricella McDonough. 507 Valley View Lane, Hanson Ridge. Perfect." After returning the billfold to my purse, he smoothed his fake whiskers. "Now, I know you have—"

"Warren, are you back here?"

We both froze at the faint voice coming from the store.

Clomp, clomp, clomp.

The man clamped his huge hand over my mouth. He hissed in my ear, "Not a word. Hear me, or your neck'll snap like a Popsicle stick."

His words weren't the only thing draining blood from my head and sending bile snaking up my throat. The ice cold tip of sharp steel poked at the base of my neck.

"Knock, knock. Hey, bro. I've come to take you to lunch."

The door opened and in stepped A. J.

CHAPTER TEN

With a knife to my throat and a sweaty glove over my mouth, I stared at A. J. standing at the office door. He seemed to digest the scene in one glance—the assailant beside me near the sofa, Connie secured to the chair, and Warren's legs protruding from the side of his desk.

A. J. closed the door. With hands out front in a calming gesture, he said, "Don't hurt her. I . . . I know the combination to the safe. I can get you—"

"Shut up. I don't want money." The man removed his hand from my mouth and slid his arm around my waist. "Get away from the door."

A. J. moved closer to the desk. "Can I see to my brother? Please?"

"No." He twisted me one way then the other, searching over my shoulder. "Where's the tape?" The roll lay on the floor by the table. He shoved me forward as he transferred the knife to Connie's throat. "Get it."

Rubbing my neck, I let out a breath of relief when my fingers felt not a drop of blood. I picked up the roll and offered it to the man.

He hovered near Connie and jutted his chin in A. J.'s direction. "Tape his hands behind his back."

I pointed to A. J. "Him?"

"Who else?"

With my eyes on A. J., I tripped over the corner of the carpet and dropped the tape. It rolled across the hardwood floor, past A. J., under Warren's desk. The action took all of five seconds, but it slow-motioned for eons as the man's cursing turned the air multicolored.

"You stupid, dumb—"

"I'll get it."

"No, I'll get it."

Next thing I knew, the man squeezed around Connie's chair and collided with A. J. I flattened against the wall. The men struggled in the confined space. The blade glinted first above them, then beside them. Grunting, huffing. They crashed to the floor, arms and legs tangled. The intruder was on top, then A. J. flipped him over. They twisted and turned, flipping again. Who had the knife? Where—?

A ragged wail. Then the struggling ceased. Blood oozed onto the blue and brown carpet.

They lay still for a moment.

Then the man staggered to his feet, bloody knife in his gloved hand. "I . . . I didn't mean . . . What have I done?" Now his voice sounded different. Younger.

In the commotion, the wig had shifted on his head. He righted it, snatched his cowboy hat off the floor and dashed out the back door.

A. J.'s pale blue shirt rapidly turned scarlet. I fell next to him. "A. J." I tore off my jacket, wadded it and pressed it to the slash in his abdomen.

His eyes fluttered. "I . . . I . . ."

"Hush. Can you hold this?" I placed his hand on the jacket.

He nodded, eyes glazed.

Stay alert. Ignore the blood.

I dialed 9-1-1 from the phone on Warren's desk. After I requested assistance, the operator remained on the line, directing my ministrations to A. J. I spied a pair of scissors on the table, and quickly cut Connie's tape. She checked on Warren while I resumed tending to A. J.

Warren regained consciousness when the ambulance and police arrived. Besides a huge goose egg knot to the back of his head, he came through the ordeal unscathed.

Although shaken, Connie's concern for Warren kept her focused.

A. J. lost consciousness while the paramedics worked on him. Warren accompanied him to the hospital.

Drained and shaking like a nervous Chihuahua, I led Connie to comfortable padded oak chairs in the store where we answered the police officer's questions.

No, neither of us knew the man or recognized him. Yes, he wore a disguise.

What did he want? He'd told Connie he wanted to purchase a confiturier. She had to ask Warren if they had one in the warehouse.

I related how he'd asked my name, and found my driver's license. Certainly his questions had been interrupted by A. J.'s arrival.

What did A. J. do? Did he go after the tape or the man? The scene blurred in my mind. I couldn't say for sure.

With a flourish, young Officer Owen closed his notepad. "Y'all need to go to the police station and see a sketch artist, and then you can sign your typed statements."

When we nodded, Owen stood to converse with the officers emerging from Warren's office.

"Can I go with you to the police station?" Connie's voice sounded quivery.

"Sure." I gave her a reassuring pat on the arm. "Soon as they tell us we can leave."

In the last hour, I had little time to dwell on anything but staunching A. J.'s bleeding, calming Connie, and answering questions. Now, melting into the chair, the enormity of what had happened stormed over me like a monsoon.

My breaths shortened, and a shudder rippled through my body. I closed my eyes. The tape. Did I drop it on purpose? Was all this my fault? *Please, God, heal A. J. and Warren.*

"Mrs. McDonough." Officer Owen's voice roused me.

"Yes, sir?"

"Y'all can go now. The techs are still working in the office. We'll take your fingerprints at the station."

I explained mine were already on file with the Bandera Sheriff's Department because my friend's daughter was found murdered on our property last year.

Officer Owen raised his eyebrows. "Okie dokie, then, but Miss Callahan, you need to have yours done. That is, unless yours are on file too?"

Wide-eyed, Connie shook her head. "No . . . no, sir."

Owen ushered us out of the store.

Once in my car, I willed my hands to stop shaking as I turned the steering wheel.

Connie snapped the seatbelt, her face pale and drawn.

To put her at ease, I asked, "Are you from the area?"

She cracked a brief smile. "No, ma'am. I've been here about three years."

"Do you enjoy working at the store?"

"Yes." Connie blushed and turned away.

Aha, I was right. A little detour to take our minds in a different direction. "Is Warren married?" I turned onto Sidney Baker Street.

"Huh?" She fiddled with the seat belt. "No. His . . . his wife died a while back."

"I see." After parking in front of the police station, I switched off the engine. "Don't give up. I think he likes you, too. And right now he could do with a friend."

◆ ◆ ◆

By mid-afternoon I had Connie back at *Use It Again, Sam* to collect her car. Allen and Samantha Howard were closing the store as I parked.

She wiped her eyes and said, "Warren called us as soon as they arrived at the hospital. We were in Junction on a shopping trip and just got in. A. J.'s still in surgery."

Allen ushered her to the car. "Let's go, Sam."

After they drove away, I searched for a restaurant. I hadn't eaten since breakfast. Although the anguish of the situation sat heavy on my heart, my head pounded, and I needed something to combat the acid churning in my gut before driving home. Pleasant weather encouraged me to have my meal on the outdoor patio when I found The Cypress Grille on the next corner. I needed all the positive, life-affirming elements I could get at the moment.

Phone calls interrupted my soup and salad. Joey from San Salvador—hall renovations progressing; Gospel shared; his soul touched. And Mike—good news from doctors. The remaining cyst had decreased, and the baby was shifting position to prepare for birth. Dr. Quinn doubted Teresa would make it to her April due date.

I'd managed to keep A. J.'s situation out of my mind while talking to Joey. With Mike, I had to concentrate harder to focus on his concerns. "It's good you and Daddy assembled the crib already."

"Yeah. Looks like I'm going to be a papa sooner than I . . ." His voice caught and his next words mumbled into silence.

"Mike, you're ready. You may not believe it, but you are. We've seen you grow and mature over the years. You were always a great kid, but Teresa brings out the best in you. You'll make a wonderful father. You and Teresa have an unshakable faith. It's shamed me on more than one occasion."

"Mama, stop."

"I love you."

"Love you, too, Mama. Have to go. Teresa's ready to leave."

Then Tom called from Midland. I hadn't told Mike about A. J. because I didn't want him to worry. He'd find out soon enough when he and Teresa were safely home. But in keeping my promise for truthfulness to Tom, I described the incident in Warren's office. He ranted and raved with concern, but in the end, he admitted I had no control over the situation. His lengthy prayer for A. J. and his family touched my battered soul, and when we ended the call, I stared into my half empty glass of tea.

In the whole struggle I'd not prayed one word. Why? Would my faith ever be strong enough to sustain me in the midst of a crisis?

I closed my eyes and prayed for the Howards and the Trentons.

Traffic sounds drifted through my consciousness, and I opened my eyes. People ate and drank. Laughed and talked. Cars cruised by. Babies cried. How could life continue as if nothing out of the ordinary had happened? Gazing up into the cloud-studded sky, I blinked away tears. Enough.

Searching through the contact numbers on my phone, I called Warren but wasn't surprised when he didn't answer. I left a message asking him to please let me know about A. J.'s condition. I felt responsible.

I pushed aside my half-eaten meal and headed back to the car, my mind a whirl of knives, cowboy hats, and silly wigs. In the distance, a group of teenage girls jostled each other, creating a cacophony of squeals and yells. A tall man veered around the bunch. Hands in the pockets of his jeans, dark brown curls sticking out the back and sides of a blue baseball cap.

My heart lurched as I quickened my pace. Near the Howards' antique store, he raised his head but was too far away to recognize as the intruder. Gold embroidery flashed on the front of his cap. I marched faster. Hands out of his pockets now, he held onto his cap, and ran across the street, disappearing around the corner.

I stopped at my car, panting. Was he the intruder, headed to the antique store to inquire about the jewelry box? Was it Marshall, Conrad, or Andrew? Knowing the box lay safely hidden beside Tom's John Deere offered me a crumb of consolation. I opened the car and slid inside, but suddenly my blood turned to ice. What if the man in the blue baseball cap had no connection to the situation, but the man who stabbed A. J.—what if *he* came after the jewelry box? Money wasn't his objective, nor did he demand anything from Connie or Warren. He wanted to know my name. And now he did. He also knew where I lived.

Hey, Norm, want to loan me Sylvester?

I rubbed my eyes and shook my head as if the action would dislodge the crazy notions jostling my brain.

Okay, it's a jewelry box. It contained Frankie's letters. There's nothing in there worth killing over.

No. There can't be. I shuddered and frowned at the people parading along the sidewalk, the sunlight filtering through the branches, birds flitting about.

No one's after Teresa's box.

When I'd calmed my frenzied thoughts, I drove toward Brooder, stopping to buy a bouquet of flowers for Teresa. After a tiring day of doctor visits and the long ride home, fresh flowers would be a welcome sight for her. And I needed to tell Mike about A. J. in person.

Since Mike and Teresa married, I resisted the urge to visit them. Daily. Or at least once a week. I was an only child, and every new person added to my family expanded my heart. Even if I didn't have a dynasty like the Summerland-Hayes,

I cherished every member of my family. I had no desire to intrude or take advantage of the special bond Teresa and I had, but a bunch of fresh flowers? It wasn't as if I planned to stay the night again. And I had sad news to deliver.

As I climbed the side steps and clomped on the wooden porch to their front door, I scrounged in my purse for the set of house keys Mike had given me.

I reached for the knob and stopped dead. On the hunter green door, white spray-painted words pierced my soul: GO HOME MEXICANS.

CHAPTER ELEVEN

"A. J.'s out of surgery and in the ICU. He lost a lot of blood." Mike sank onto the sofa.

I grimaced at the memory of my blood-soaked gray jacket lying next to A. J. as the paramedics tore open his shirt.

"He went into cardiac arrest several times." Mike wiped a hand across his brow. "Whew. It's been pretty tough. His wife Leah and the kids arrived from San Antonio. I offered what support I could, but with the Howards and Trentons all at the hospital, I thought—"

"I'm sure they appreciated that you were there." Teresa cuddled next to him.

Silence filled the living room.

The fragile hold we have on life hit me again.

After a moment, Mike said, "I stopped at the hardware store on the way home and bought a can of paint for the door."

"I'll help. The sooner it's painted the better." I stood and moved to the door.

Teresa remained inside while Mike and I painted over the graffiti. The color Mike purchased matched almost perfectly.

"This is not fair, *mijo*. It's not right." I handed Mike the paint can lid.

"I know, Mama." After closing the can, he collected the brushes. "You've been through stuff like this. I remember stories you told about when you first moved to San Antonio from Eagle Pass."

Carefully opening the freshly touched-up front door, I entered the house ahead of Mike. "This is different. You and Teresa are here to work in the church for the Lord."

Teresa, sitting at the kitchen table, motioned for us to join her. "Chella, the church leaders warned us that some people in this tight-knit community were against newcomers, especially people of color. We're not happy about the situation, but we'll deal with it."

Mike eased into the chair next to her, and I sat opposite.

"You never mentioned anything before."

"We didn't want you and Dad to worry."

With my chin propped on my hand, I frowned. "Do you know who painted those words on your door?"

Mike glanced sideways at Teresa and shrugged. "We've heard rumors, but we're keeping open minds and open hearts."

I shook my head. "How can you be so calm about it? Are you going to contact the police?"

"No need to involve the authorities. Mama, I'm sure it's only a handful of people who object to Teresa and me being here, working for the church. For the most part, the families of Brooder have welcomed us."

I gazed from one to the other. They'd handled the racial graffiti much more maturely than I had. I'd been outraged and ready to find the culprit and draw up battle plans. No one messed with my kids.

"We'll be okay, Mama. The Lord has plans for us here."

"*Sí*, Chella. He'll use this for His glory." Teresa rested her head on Mikes' shoulder. "Do you want to stay for supper?"

Stretching my arms above my head, I yawned. "Sorry about that. No, thanks. I must leave before it gets much darker." I pushed away from the table. "Stay seated, Teresa. Rest while you can."

Mike walked me to the door and planted a kiss on my forehead.

"Thanks for the flowers. Be careful, Mama."

"I will. Call when you have news about A. J."

With a heavy, troubled heart, I drove home. Mike and Teresa had accepted the racial slur in stride, with grace, but it cut me deeply. Taking the twists and turns of the road, I tried to analyze why it affected me so. Mike had been right. I'd had my share of cultural clashes when I left Eagle Pass—a town well over ninety percent Hispanic—to live in San Antonio. But this attack on them hurt me in a different way. It wasn't until I reached the driveway and viewed the hills beyond our property that it struck me. This was part of their *Job* story. Teresa's diabetes, their baby's cysts and possible brain damage, the break-ins and attack, the racial tension—all testing their faith.

But the problem wasn't with their faith. It was strong. My faith wavered and waned.

I opened the garage and grinned at Brutus's wriggling body squirming through the pet door. No matter what kind of mood I was in when I came home, he always made life brighter.

With him tucked in my arms, I punched the alarm code and located the keys to Tom's shed. I wanted to retrieve the jewelry box before the sun set since we had no electricity down there. On the return trip to the house, Brutus darted hither and yon, yapping in excitement. If only humans could be so resilient.

After supper, I prodded wooden roses and twisted legs on the box until I knew I'd tried every combination. No new hidden drawer popped open.

Tom called as I lay in bed trying to read *Brink of Death* by Brandilyn Collins. Although emotionally drained, my mind wouldn't stop twirling. I told Tom about the graffiti. His outrage matched mine, but he offered insight into the plight of Job.

"Satan is alive and well today, sweetheart. The Apostle Peter tells us in First Peter chapter five, verse eight, that our enemy, Satan, prowls around like a roaring lion seeking someone to devour."

"Kinda graphic." I sucked in a breath. "But it's not fair. What can I do? I need to protect my kids."

"A natural reaction. And you can. Remember when Mike and José were babies and you'd watch out for them like a grizzly protecting her cubs? Now you can do the same thing."

"Go to Brooder and find the vandal and confront him? I will, you know."

"Yes, Chella, I know you would, but that's not what I mean. Protect your kids by being a spiritual mama bear."

"That's funny." Staring at my closed book, I snickered. "I can see me in a furry costume waving a Bible around . . ." My voice trailed. Embarrassment replaced humor. Of course, he meant a spiritual bear.

"Sorry, Tom."

"It's okay, love. You've come a long way spiritually. Don't beat yourself up. And no bear costumes, please." He chuckled, then his voice sobered. "You protect your kids by praying."

"I can do that."

"Exactly. But then you have to protect yourself, too."

I shifted against the pillows. "What do you mean?"

"The roaring lion can and will come after you, too. As a new Christian, you're fresh meat, so to speak. You have to wear the armor of God."

"Armor of God?"

"Read Ephesians chapter six. Paul admonishes us to arm ourselves against the devil. When I get home, we'll study verses eleven through eighteen where Paul discusses the armor of God and how we need to be vigilant in prayer."

I glanced around the bedroom at photographs of the boys in grade school, Tom in his Boy Scout uniform, my parents holding me as an infant. All precious to me. "Let's pray now."

Tom opened his heart. My feeble words followed.

After saying good night, I tried to assimilate Tom's words of encouragement. He always listened to my questions and doubts, and offered a scripture or words of his own to help me. But this Christian walk was no easy road. One minute I was on a peak with everything rosy, then the next, I tumbled down into a deep, dark valley. Did every Christian experience these bipolar swings, or was it just me?

◆ ◆ ◆

Norm's phone call woke me.

"Mrs. Mac, you're in luck. I have time to work on your jewelry box today. The order of exotic wood to complete my other project has been delayed."

I wanted the box repaired, all drawers and compartments opened, and to get it safely back to Teresa. "Give me twenty minutes. Oh, by the way, there's another drawer in front."

Brutus and I made the trip in my car this time—I wasn't taking any chances. I parked at Norm's gate and took Brutus on his leash along with the box in its bag to the workshop. Sylvester barked, straining at the end of a leash near the garage entrance.

An unlit cigar bobbled in the corner of Norm's mouth as he glanced up. "Thought I'd keep him out here for a while."

"Good idea." I opened the bag and removed the box.

Sylvester and Brutus circled as far as they could on their tethers, sniffing the air around each other. I kept my baby close, securing him to the bench.

Stepping to the counter along the wall, Norm removed his cigar. "See what else I've got?" He pointed to a stack of lumber.

A shotgun stood amidst the wood. "Norm!"

"Until that guy came here the other day I never dreamed anyone might steal my pieces." He gestured around the workshop. "Some of this stuff, the furniture especially, is quite valuable, you know."

"I'm sure. But a shotgun?"

"I lock the workshop at night, and the dogs should scare off most would-be thieves during the day. But if need be, I have a backup plan."

"Let's hope you never have to use it, you crazy old man."

He rested his arm around my shoulders and chuckled. "Let's see if we can open the other drawer, you crazy young lady."

We prodded roses and twisted legs, stopping when Sylvester and Brutus barked. A car parked next to mine—a dark blue Honda Civic.

Ant-like prickles marched around my scalp, sending tingling shivers down my neck. "Is it the same car?" I nibbled a thumb nail.

Norm adjusted his glasses and reached for his shotgun. "Stay here, Mrs. Mac." He kept the weapon behind his back and stopped at the entrance.

But the customer who climbed out of the car and opened the gate wasn't the young man from before. This black man, at least my age, had inches and pounds on the other visitor.

He advanced up the driveway with measured steps, his eyes fixed on Sylvester.

I joined Norm at the entrance, and whispered, "It's not the same man."

"Could be a coincidence he has a dark blue car."

"Maybe. Please put your shotgun away."

A second's hesitation, then he said, "Okay." Norm returned the weapon to the corner stack of lumber, and stopped at the bench where I'd left the jewelry box.

The man halted about five yards from Sylvester. Although over six foot tall and at least two hundred pounds, he seemed to eye the dog with apprehension.

"Can you, um, restrain your dog, please?" His quavering voice belied his intimidating physique.

"Sylvester, sit." To my surprise, the dog sat and quit barking. Reassured by the Sylvester's protective stance, my apprehension eased.

Out of the corner of my eye, I glimpsed Norm hovering by the bench. I guessed he wanted to keep close to the shotgun while he toyed with my jewelry box.

"How can we help you, sir?" Arms folded, I stared at the light-skinned man.

Hands stuck in the pockets of his khaki slacks, he squinted at me. "I watched you come here. You're the lady with the jewelry box, right?"

A chill snaked down my spine. Did everyone in Texas want this box? Norm's shotgun now seemed like a good idea.

I backed up and hoped Norm had heard the question. "Why do you want to know?"

The man attempted to take a step, but stopped when Sylvester growled. "Please, I don't mean you any harm. I . . . I need that jewelry box. I promised."

"Norm." I peered over my shoulder. "He wants to know if we have a jewelry box."

"Ma'am, I'll pay for it."

I inched further inside. "Why do you want it?"

"It . . . there might be an important item in it."

"Like what?"

His wary gaze lingered on Sylvester. "A . . . a . . . Have you found anything in it?"

"I have. Letters, but I gave them to their owner."

"Letters. I'm not interested in letters." He took a step as if he wanted to follow me but hesitated. Sylvester stayed by my side, deterring his passage.

"That's all I found—"

"Are you sure?"

"Of course." By this time I stood inside the workshop, close to the bench.

The man hung his head. "I was sure she said—"

"Mrs. Mac, come see."

I turned. Norm had opened the front drawer. I wasn't about to let the man discover this new development before we had a chance to examine the drawer's contents.

"Norm." I stepped in front of the bench. "The customer is leaving. Let's escort him out."

Norm got the message. He unhooked Sylvester's leash and moved closer to the man, eyeing him up and down. "Sorry we couldn't help you, sir."

The man tromped down the drive, his shoulders bowed.

When we reached the gate, I opened it, allowing him to exit. At first, his presence had unnerved me, but his subdued demeanor now posed no threat. However, I was intrigued by his interest in the contents of the jewelry box. "If I find anything else in the box, sir, I'll give the information to Warren Howard from the antique store in Kerrville. Do you know which one I mean?" I was sure he did. How else did he know who had the box? He was probably also the man who heard Mike tell the story of the box at the Petrie's home.

"I do, and . . . and I'm sorry. I shouldn't have hired that kid to steal the box. I should have come in person. It was wrong of me." He opened his car door. "Again, I'm sorry."

So the young man who'd visited previously had come at this man's behest. One piece of the puzzle solved. How many more were there?

After his car had disappeared down the road, Norm and I hastened back to the workshop, Sylvester charging ahead of us.

"How did you open it?"

"Depressed a rose with each thumb and twisted both front legs. The drawer opened an inch and I nearly blurted out—"

"I know. You almost gave it away. Let's see what's in there."

Norm eased the front drawer open. This one was narrower than the one in back. A white linen handkerchief lay folded inside. I lifted it out. It exuded the same spicy perfume as the letters. I turned it over. The initials *E S* were embroidered in red, with green stems and leaves intertwined. Unfolding the linen revealed a curl of dark brown hair tied with a thin blue ribbon, and an oval gold locket on a delicate chain.

My heart twisted and a knot tightened in my gut. I swallowed. Another necklace. I fingered the half-heart pieces I wore all the time, a constant reminder of my friend, Eva, who'd been murdered the previous year.

"Open it." Norm tapped my arm.

The oval locket, covered in filigree leaves and flowers of gold, clicked open to expose two sepia photographs—one of a toddler, and one of a man and a woman. Could this be what today's intruder wanted?

I closed the locket and placed it and the hair back in the handkerchief. "I'm going to show this to my friend at the antique store. He knows the family and may recognize these people."

"Sure thing. Quite the excitement maker, this box." Norm closed the drawer. "I can work on it all day, and I'll be sure to lock it up in the house at night in case anyone else gets a hankering for it."

"Thanks, Norm. I better go now. Keep safe." I handled the handkerchief like fragile crystal, and led Brutus down the driveway.

Before opening my car door, I scanned the road for the dark blue car. Clear. Frankie and the man today had been after the jewelry box. The Anglo intruder who'd attempted to take the box from Teresa still lurked out there. Did he want the locket? And what about the man who'd stabbed A. J.? Was he also interested in the box?

Once home, I examined the treasure again with my notebook open. Who could E. S. be? Why would her handkerchief be in Virginia's jewelry box, and who were the people in the photographs?

I reviewed my notes, and Frankie's description of Esther Stiles popped out. The handkerchief might belong to her.

Curiosity nibbled at me. I'd assumed the photographs in the locket were Virginia and Harlan, and one of their children. But why was the locket wrapped in Esther's handkerchief?

I carefully pried the pictures out of the locket. The adults were identified as Virginia and Harlan, taken in 1934, but the baby wasn't Mary Margaret or Albert or John. It was Stephen, dated 1941.

Stephen. Who was Stephen? Did Virginia have another child? I thumbed through my notebook for Frankie's number.

But before I found it, Mike called.

"Mama, I'm sorry to tell you. Hank called." His voice cracked. "A. J. died an hour ago. He never regained consciousness."

CHAPTER TWELVE

Clutching the locket, I slumped to the floor. "No, no."

Tears flowed, and my shoulders heaved. I'd known A. J. such a short time, but he was a father, a husband. He was a son and brother. And, to save his life, I'd tried to staunch his flow of blood with my own hands.

The locket slid from my fist. I covered my face and wailed.

"Dear God, why? Why?"

Brutus licked my arm. My whines turned to inward pleas. *Dear God, be with Leah and the children. Allen and Samantha. Hank and Ruth Ann. Warren.*

I'm not sure how long I sat on the floor, but when I did get up, I knew I couldn't concentrate on any task. The peaceful scene from the back door drew me outside. I wandered over our acreage until the afternoon sun broke through the clouds. As I neared the back porch, Brutus, who'd forsaken his task of following me, wagged his tail.

"You hungry, boy? Let's go inside."

I poured food into his bowl, and then made myself a mug of tea.

Spent and heart-sore, I gathered the locket, handkerchief, and lock of hair into a zip-top plastic bag and closed my notebook. Although still grieving, I continued to work on my own little mystery. First, I called Frankie. When I told him the name Stephen had been written on the back of the child's photograph in the locket, his surprise exceeded mine. We arranged a time to meet the next day.

To supplement my part-time salary from the school district, I wrote a monthly article for the *Texas Physical & Occupational Therapy Journal*. I tromped to the office. It took a while for my brain to switch gears, but hours later, I had three articles outlined and one three-fourths complete.

When Tom traveled out of town, I seldom cooked. I thawed a container of chicken enchiladas, and added a fresh salad.

After working on my articles a while longer, I read the scriptures Tom suggested. The armor of God described in Ephesians chapter six provided a mental picture to carry with me. In recalling how Mike and Teresa handled their decision to move from San Antonio and the subsequent trials blocking their way, I could see how they had been girded with God's armor. Girded. An interesting, strong word.

Settling in bed with my novel, I read page after page, until my eyelids fluttered. Lights off, alarm on, Brutus asleep in the living room, I lay in bed with visions of sepia photographs pasted around my bed, and breastplates, shields and helmets floating in the mist, out of reach.

A blaring siren jolted me from my dream. The house alarm. I sat up in the cave-black room, heart thumping, hoping the sound would dissolve with my dream. But it didn't.

I slid out of bed and fumbled for the baseball bat I kept nearby. My door was closed—to keep Brutus out. I inched toward it. The staccato alarm drowned any other sounds. I opened the door and turned on the hall light.

The house phone rang. The alarm company. I wrenched the phone from its base. *Yes, I'm okay. No, I don't know if there's someone in the house.*

I crept down the hall with the bat in one hand and the cordless phone in the other. Brutus slunk past me to my bedroom. No time to comfort him. Now would be the perfect time to have a Sylvester dog.

Office clear.

Guest bedroom clear.

Joey's old room, living room, dining room, kitchen.

No one in the house but me. I checked all the doors. Locked. The windows. One in the office at the back of the house was unlocked but not open. Tom could have forgotten to lock it since it was hard to reach behind the desk. I locked it, then silenced the alarm. My running commentary on the phone let the alarm company rep know I was safe. I told him not to send a deputy sheriff. It would take at least fifteen minutes to drive from the Bandera Sheriff's Department. And then what could he do? Tell me what I already knew—no sign of an intruder in the house.

I flipped on all the outside flood lights. Peeking through various windows, I scanned the land directly surrounding the house and noticed nothing suspicious. In the morning I'd check the flower bed outside the office window. If an attempt had been made to open it, there'd be evidence.

The relatively new alarm system had gone off before without cause, but this was the first time I'd been alone in the house.

Whatever the reason, for sure I wouldn't be going back to sleep anytime soon. After rescuing Brutus from under the bed and making a mug of hot tea, I turned on the computer, and to take my mind off the scare, set to work on another article for the T. P. & O. T. Journal.

By morning, with settled nerves and a calm Brutus, I completed the second article. I fixed a vegetable omelet, and then dressed in blue jeans and white T-shirt. The bruises on my neck had faded, and I no longer needed the turtleneck tops. I disliked them anyway. Too confining.

Brutus and I ventured outside to check the perimeter. Tom had planted deer resistant shrubs around the house. Red and blue salvia, Texas sage, lantana, rock roses, and gold canyon daisies thrived under his care.

Branches of sage close to the office windows were disturbed, but I couldn't see footprints in the mulch. I pushed aside the silvery gray-green branches and found a stump of wood that looked like a piece of oak. It could have fallen off the nearby large live oak tree during the night and hit the window, setting off the alarm.

Not an intruder. A broken branch. I threw the stump and Brutus chased it.

I giggled. "It's bigger than you, silly pooch."

He gnawed and pawed at it while I returned to the kitchen. Frankie and I had arranged to meet at ten o'clock.

I set out for Kerrville with the baggie and my notebook, planning to be home by the time Tom returned in the late afternoon. I rounded the bend in the driveway, finger on the gate remote, and right in the middle of the white caliche sat a blue blob. Easing up on it, I rolled to a halt. It was a royal blue baseball cap.

Could it belong to the intruder who broke into Mike's house last week? Had the same man tried to open the office window? Car doors locked and windows closed, I glanced about. Was I alone? Thick, scrubby Texas cedars lined the drive. Nothing caught my eye, not even a squawking mocking bird.

Taking care, I opened the door and picked up the cap using a stick. The cap had a gold lightning bolt zapping through the letters *R J* like I'd seen on the intruder's cap before the man seized my throat. I threw the cap into the backseat like it was contaminated. Without knowing the identity of the intruder, I couldn't prove to whom it belonged. But I'd keep it. Just in case . . .

The drive to Kerrville took forty-five minutes. I had a hard time concentrating on the road as thoughts of A. J. and his family floated into my heart and mind at every turn.

Frankie and I met at Billy Jean's Restaurant on Junction Highway. Departmentalizing my thoughts became a priority. Concentrate on the contents of the jewelry box.

Over coffee, Frankie examined the curl of hair and the locket. "Yeah, this looks like Johnny's hair color, and the locket was Ginny's. A wedding gift from Harlan." He popped it open. "See." A twisted finger pointed to the adults. "Taken on their honeymoon at Niagara Falls. She told me they went there."

Frankie studied the photo of the toddler, holding the locket in various positions to catch the best light. He raised sad eyes to me. "That's Johnny." When conversation from the couple in the booth behind him escalated, he adjusted his hearing aid.

I gave him a reassuring smile. "But why is the name Stephen written on the back?"

With a crinkled brow and watery eyes, he hiked his shoulders. "Don't know. Are you sure it was Stephen?"

Easing the locket from his trembling hands, I used the knife from the table and popped out the photograph. "See for yourself." The tiny photo lay in my hand.

He picked up the quarter-sized picture and turned it over. "It's Johnny, but why would Ginny write . . ?" Sinking into the booth, he pounded his chest. "No. No."

His wail drew the attention of customers behind us.

"Frankie, what's the matter?" I slid next to him and placed my arm around his bony shoulders.

In his large hand, he clutched the picture to his chest and rocked back and forth. I patted his shoulder, sensing pain and sorrow ebb from his body. He relaxed. I waited.

"Esther Stiles had a son named Stephen." Frankie's feathery voice barely made it to my ears.

I leaned closer. "Why would his name be on the back of Johnny's picture?"

Frankie shrugged and shook his head.

My mind raced. What could this mean? Was the photo mislabeled, or had something more sinister happened here? I glanced at my companion. His eyes dulled, and he seemed to shrink two sizes.

"Frankie, Frankie," I said. "I need you to help me. What do you think happened?" I continued to rub his slumped shoulders.

He straightened and handed me the photo. "I . . . I'm not sure, but I hope I'm wrong." A glimmer of spunk returned to his eyes. "I can find out. I need to find out."

"How?" I returned to my side of the booth, and inserted the photograph back into the locket.

"After we talked the other day when you gave me Ginny's letters, I did some digging. Esther Stiles is in a nursing home here in Kerrville. In fact, around the corner from this restaurant."

"She is?"

He paused, then nudged his chin at the locket now lying near the embroidered *E S* on the handkerchief. "We need to pay her a visit. She can explain this. Esther's the only one who can."

I checked my watch before folding the linen around the curl of hair and the locket. "Are you free to go now?"

With a shrug, he pushed his coffee mug aside. "Uh-huh. When I first found out she was alive, I wanted to visit her, but couldn't. Too many old memories, but that." He pointed to my purse where I'd stored the plastic bag. "I gotta ask her about that. I couldn't see her by myself, but with your help, I can face her. She makes a hornet look cuddly. Scares me to death."

"She sounds like an interesting person. Let's go visit her."

We eased out of the booth and made our way to the exit.

A menu lay on the counter at the cash register. Billy Jean's. *B J*. I was sure I'd seen *R J* on the blue baseball cap, but I could have been mistaken.

I had to give it a shot. As I paid for our coffee, I asked, "Do you have baseball caps with your restaurant's initials?"

The cashier shook her head. "No, ma'am, but we do have T-shirts. Would you like one?"

"No, thank you. I was interested in a cap." Taking my change, I ushered Frankie to the door, and we left the restaurant.

I followed his truck to the River Oaks Senior Living Community on River Drive. We entered the foyer and a wave of nostalgia washed over me. The last time I'd been in a nursing facility I'd collected my friend Eva's things after her death. Coffee churned in the pit of my stomach. I clutched my middle as we signed in.

We found Esther in a wheelchair outside her room. Short gray curls covered her head, but by considering her clear, toffee-brown face, I'd never have guessed she was in her eighties. She used her feet to propel the wheelchair forward a pace or two. Her bowed back indicated osteoporosis or scoliosis that can worsen with age. She kept her gaze glued to the floor.

At our approach, she raised her head. Her misty brown eyes focused on me, then moved to Frankie. Her feet stilled, and she drew her hands into her lap, fiddling with a crocheted lap rug over her knees. The brown eyes wavered and her gray brows rose slowly.

"Hi, Esther." Frankie stretched out his hand.

She ignored the gesture.

By shuffling her feet, Esther turned the wheelchair.

I stepped around her chair and stooped to face her. She looked at me without raising her head and quickly averted her eyes.

"Hi, Mrs. Stiles. My name's Maricella. We need your help. Can we go to the lobby?" I remained stooped, hoping to catch her eye again.

She turned her head and pointed down the hall.

"Is it okay if I push your chair?"

She nodded, and I moved behind her. We found the lobby vacant and positioned Esther's chair so we could both see her face.

Frankie rubbed his chin, then said, "Esther, it's Frankie, Ginny's brother. Do you remember me?"

With eyes closed, Esther shifted in her chair. I studied her face. Memories seemed to flit across it like a movie screen. Her mouth twitched into a smile, then a smirk, her eyes fluttered, and her jaw muscles tensed.

But when she opened her eyes and beamed, her words surprised us. "Where's my baby? Did you bring him to visit?" She pointed down the hall. "I'm having an art show next week. Want to come?"

Mouth agape, Frankie glared at her then at me. "What's going on?"

I stood and motioned for him to join me at the door. "I don't think we're going to get anything out of her. Could be dementia, Alzheimer's, or plain senility."

Frankie stomped his foot. "We're too late."

Out of the corner of my eye, I noticed a smirk cross Esther's face. Was she role-playing for our benefit?

"I have an idea. Let's take her back to her room."

We wheeled Esther down the hall but found an aide cleaning her room.

Esther's work-hardened hands lay in her lap. I touched them. "We'll come back another day, okay? And we'll bring you a treat."

She raised her head a fraction. "Okay. I like chocolate and almonds. Not Hershey's Kisses but the bar."

After a quick wave, we walked down the hall to sign out.

In the parking lot Frankie grabbed my arm. "Okay, what's your plan?"

"I've worked with enough elderly patients to recognize true symptoms of Alzheimer's or dementia. First of all, the way Esther responded to you when she first saw you was too real for her not to have recognized you."

When we arrived at my car, I turned. "And her request for a treat was too specific. I think she was faking it. She knew you. Her eyes gave it away. Let's come back another day. Visit her in her room and show her the photograph from the locket."

"I want to find out about the picture, but I can't come back here again." Frankie bowed his head. "It's too depressing. My wife, Viola, had a stroke and was in a home like this for a year before she passed."

I linked my arm through his and rested my head on his shoulder. "I understand, Frankie. My childhood friend, Eva, also died in one. Not good memories."

Shadows of loved ones bonded us together as we stood in the parking lot.

A breeze tickled the infant leaves of a pecan tree above us. Frankie sighed, and I stepped away.

"I'll come back another day—before you leave for Tennessee."

He kissed my forehead. "Thank you, Maricella."

With my parents dead, I missed the older generation. Frankie filled the grandfather gap well. Maybe I could manufacture a family tree out of people I'd like to be related to. Frankie would have a place of honor. That thought reminded me of my idea to compose a list of ancestors for our grandbaby.

We climbed into our vehicles, and he drove off. I answered a phone call from Tom, who was stuck in a line of traffic leaving Odessa. I didn't tell him about the house alarm from the night before. Better do that face to face when he arrived home.

But when I hung up, I glanced in the back seat at the blue baseball cap. How could it have ended up in our driveway?

The road we lived on ended in a cul-de-sac. The Bailey's and Norm's properties were next to us, with the Bullock's house, and the Dos Sierra Ranch occupying the other side of the road. The cap could have belonged to a ranch hand, but they usually wore cowboy hats.

After a half-hearted shrug, I started the car. Other than taking the cap to the sheriff and asking for DNA testing—not that they would do anything like that—

the cap was useless to me.

Unless . . . unless someone who knew Conrad, Marshall, and Andrew recognized it. And Warren was the one person I knew who might. This was not the time to bother him with trivial concerns, but I turned right on Junction Highway and headed back to the antique store anyway.

I parked across the street. The crime scene tape had been removed, but a black wreath centered on the door above the stained glass was a reminder I didn't need. Opening the door, I chewed on my bottom lip, and for a brief second almost abandoned my silly errand. Still, I'd come this far . . .

Connie, dressed in a tailored pale yellow top and pants, stood at the counter with a young couple. Scanning the store, I saw no sign of Warren. I really hadn't expected to.

Holding the cap tightly in my fingers, I swung it back and forth, impatient for Connie to conclude her sale. When the customers walked out with a pair of brass table lamps, she joined me, a smile popping her cheeks into round apples.

"Hello, Mrs. McDonough. How are you today?"

"Okay, and you?"

A crease formed between her eyes, and a slight shiver traveled down her body. "I still have nightmares."

I patted her shoulder. "I'm sure. Call me Maricella. I know the family is in mourning, but is Warren here by any chance?"

"No, he's out with his folks making funeral arrangements. He'll be back this afternoon." She laced her fingers behind her back and swayed on her high-heeled shoes.

Something about her behavior caught my attention. "Connie, what is it?"

"This might be inappropriate, but in all that's happened since . . . since that man came in here, Warren has been very concerned about me. He calls me. He stopped by my apartment last night and brought me a card and a little bunch of flowers." A flush infused her face, clashing with the yellow top.

Baseball cap forgotten for the moment, I said, "That's interesting. He seems like a nice guy. I'm glad for you, but I'm sorry I can't stay. Please tell him I stopped by."

"Will do." She spied the cap in my hand. "Why do you have Conrad's cap?"

I slid to a halt, almost knocking over a vase. "What did you say?"

She pointed to my hand. "Isn't that Conrad's cap?"

Holding it up, I examined the gold logo. "I don't know who it belongs to. But you know for sure it's Conrad's?"

"Not exactly, but he works for Rick Jennings Electrical, and all their employees wear these caps."

All their employees. More than one. Not necessarily Conrad's cap. But he had a connection to the jewelry box. What other employee fit that description?

"Thanks, Connie. I'll see you later. Please ask Warren to call me."

After I left the store, I called Mike. When he didn't answer, I assumed they were still at the real estate office in San Antonio signing the final papers for the sale of their condo.

The Cypress Grille on the next corner was too convenient to ignore. I stopped there for lunch, sitting inside this time as all the patio tables were occupied. Sipping the last of my iced tea, my cell phone rang. Mike.

"Mama, now don't get upset. I didn't call you earlier because we wanted to be sure. Teresa's in labor. We're at the Methodist Hospital in San Antonio."

CHAPTER THIRTEEN

How plans can change in the blink of an eye. No cheesecake for dessert. Baseball cap forgotten. I stopped for gas at a convenience store and drove to San Antonio.

Mike had phoned Teresa's parents in Santa Fe, New Mexico. I'd called Tom who was on the road, and also his mother, Julia, in Dallas. The baby would arrive about three weeks early. With the arachnoid cyst and Teresa's diabetes complicating matters, everyone in the family anticipated his birth with some degree of anxiety.

At the hospital, Mike joined me in the waiting room. He reported Teresa had back pain during the night, and her contractions had begun while concluding their real estate transaction. They scheduled an emergency visit with her ob-gyn, Dr. Quinn, who recommended they stay in San Antonio and proceed to the hospital. Teresa had now been in labor five hours, with contractions occurring at inconsistent intervals.

I entered her room and tried to console her. She asked questions about my experiences. I reassured her every delivery was unique, and seldom followed the steps outlined in the pregnancy books. Mike's delivery had taken all of five hours, unusual since he was my first, but then José arrived after a twelve-hour labor.

Twirling the identity band on her wrist, Teresa's voice became serious. "Chella, something I've wanted to ask you, but it never seemed appropriate before. Now might be a good time since we're talking about such personal things. Why . . . why did you and Tom only have two children? Mike and I want at least four, if God blesses us that way."

Her question carried me back many years. Memories of sitting in Tom's lap as newlyweds discussing how we wanted to fill the other chairs around the dining table with little McDonoughs surfaced. I swallowed the lump of sadness.

"We . . . we also wanted lots of children. Especially since we both had no siblings. But after Joey, I had terrible pain and with a diagnosis of endometriosis, the doctor recommended a hysterectomy." I shrugged. "I guess I should have gotten a second opinion, but I was young and accepted the doctor's word."

With a gasp, she clutched the railings and huffed in and out as a contraction rippled through her. "Whew, that one lasted longer than the others. If they keep coming like that, I may rethink this business of having lots of babies."

I wiped her forehead and bit my tongue on the words: *you ain't seen nothin' yet, girl.*

The door swung open and Mike entered with a can of soda. "Did I miss anything important?"

We both said, "Nope," and settled in to wait for the next contraction.

Teresa couldn't be still. She paced the room, returned to the bed, sat in the easy chair, walked some more. Her agitated movements infected us, too. Mike looked at me with pleading eyes.

"I'm going to step out for a bit. Mike, why don't you sing to Teresa?" Mike had a strong baritone but could reduce it to soothing notes.

"I'd like that." Teresa lay on the bed and arranged the sheet around her legs.

Sitting in the waiting room again, I flipped through a magazine and admired a picture of a basketful of yellow lab puppies.

"Oh, no. Brutus."

I dialed my neighbor, Barbara Bailey, and asked her to take care of my four-legged baby again. How could I have forgotten him?

During my next visit to her room, signs of fatigue shadowed Teresa's face. Breathing exercises could help to a point. I stayed for an hour, observed a nurse administer her blood glucose level check, and then rode the elevator down to wait for Tom. The cool March evening air chilled me as I stepped outside, but I didn't have long to wait.

Tom jogged to the entrance and enveloped me in a bear hug. We embraced for a moment before entering through the automatic doors.

"So, he's on his way?"

"Yeah. But for someone who was in such a hurry, he sure is taking his time now."

In the waiting room Mike joined us. Although Teresa's contractions were closer together, and we were allowed to visit her. Tom didn't stay long. Back in the waiting room we alternated between idle chatter and periods of silence. Mike refused our offer of supper. He vowed if Teresa couldn't eat a meal, neither would he.

When he returned to Teresa, Tom and I found the cafeteria. We munched on chicken cacciatore and spoke in whispers between bites. We agreed to stay at the hospital instead of risking the long drive home, wanting to be close in case . . .

Eight hours. A long time when you're sitting in the waiting room. A longer time when you're experiencing the excruciating contractions that seem to have no end.

Back in the waiting room. Shivering. Tom's jacket around my shoulders, his warm chest beneath my cheek, his arm around me. Twelve hours. Relentless contractions, but no baby yet. Considering a Caesarian Section.

Sleep. Dreams. Blue baseball caps.

Movement. "Wake up, Chella." Tom's gentle nudge.

"Mama, the baby's on his way. Teresa wants to see you both."

Tom and I followed Mike into Teresa's room. Her black hair lay in tired damp strands on the pillow. Exhaustion circled her eyes, but she smiled.

Clasping her hand, I brushed a lock of hair off her cheek. "What is it, *mija*?"

"I want my family to pray with me."

We held hands and prayed for Teresa's strength and the baby's safe arrival. Another contraction crashed through her abdomen like a tsunami. Tom and I left the room.

Sixteen hours. I paced. Tom dozed.

Then Mike burst in. "He's here." If he beamed any wider, it would have split his cheeks. "Born at three-thirty-eight. Six pounds, three ounces, nineteen inches long. But because of the cyst and being at least three weeks premature, he has to stay in the Neonatal Intensive Care Unit for a few days."

Dwarfed by my husband and son, I stood with them in the waiting room, our arms wrapped around each other.

"Thank you, Lord, for the safe arrival of our baby." Tom echoed the words on my heart. "Bless Teresa with rest and the doctors with skill to take care of his medical needs."

With a mammoth sigh, Mike sunk into a chair. "You guys can see Teresa in a little while, but they won't let you see the baby. You might as well go home once you've visited Teresa."

"Sure. We'll do whatever you need. Is she all right?"

He beamed. "She's great. Lasted as long as she could without drugs. She wants to stay with him, but they won't let her for now."

"Any name picked out?" Tom asked.

"We're working on it. We have his middle name, but . . ." Mike dropped his head into his hands. "I can't think straight. I didn't know she'd have so much pain."

I moved to the chair next to him and drew him into my arms. "It's okay, son." I didn't want to say anymore, not knowing Teresa's state of mind for sure, but I was confident she'd say the pain was worth it.

Kneeling in front of us, Tom laid a hand on Mike's bowed head and the other on my shoulder. "Father God, thank you for our son's compassionate heart. Bless him as he begins his journey of fatherhood."

We huddled in the calm early morning silence, exhausted bodies forgotten.

◆ ◆ ◆

Tom and I woke at nine o'clock to the ringing house phone. No one used that number much anymore. It was Tom's mother.

By his responses, I knew that Mike had called her with the news. Tom spoke at length, and then handed the phone to me. "She wants to know about the cyst. You can explain it better than I can."

Plumping the pillows behind me, I took the cordless receiver and prepared for a marathon conversation. We'd previously shared all the information we had with Julia, but she didn't seem to understand. I explained again how the fluid-filled cyst was between the baby's skull and brain. One had been absorbed, but the other was still there. That was one reason the baby had to stay in the NICU.

"Have you seen him?"

"No, we weren't allowed to." I squinted at the clock. He was only six hours old. "Perhaps we can see him when we visit today."

"I'm planning on driving down tomorrow, if that's convenient. And I'll stay in a motel."

"No, Julia. You can stay with us." We always played this game. It was as if she needed my personal invitation every visit.

"All right. That's so sweet."

"Call when you're close to San Antonio, because by Saturday, Teresa may already be home."

"I will. How's her face? Mike told me a man hit her when he tried to steal her jewelry box."

"She's fine now." I explained that I'd taken the damaged box to be repaired, which reminded me to ask Norm if it was ready.

"So bizarre, for someone to steal such a small thing. Do you know why?"

"The box has secret compartments, and I've found interesting items inside linked to the family who originally owned it."

"You don't say. Do you know who they are?"

"The Summerland-Hayes from Kerrville."

Silence.

"Julia, are you there?"

"Yes. I . . . I had the TV on and don't think I heard you. Say the name again."

I repeated it.

"What a silly name."

The discussion reminded me again of my desire. "Um, Julia, while you're here, can you help me compose a family tree? I already have information for

Doug's side, but not for you." I didn't even know her maiden name. Strange that Tom had never told me.

She paused. When she spoke, her tone held a note of tension. "Sure. I'll jot them down for you. I. . . I have to go, but let me talk to Tom again."

I raised my eyebrows at Tom and handed the receiver to him. Sliding out of bed, I heard Tom mutter a few words, and then hang up.

While showering, I rehashed the conversation with my mother-in-law. She was coming to see her great-grandson. Good. She'd be staying with us. Not exactly good.

She offered to stay in a motel, but, of course, I couldn't let her do that. We had a guest room. She was family. But her visits filled me with anxiety. I never felt like I measured up to her expectation of the proper wife for her son. Nothing overt was ever said or done, but subtle little comments and looks of disapproval over the years grated down my confidence. Letters addressed only to Tom. Phone calls to his cell phone or the house number, never to my cell. Hints dropped that using traditional Mexican ingredients weren't healthy.

Little of this occurred while Tom's father had been alive. But since his death in a road-side accident fifteen years ago, Julia's attitude had taken a marked change in direction. Tom seemed oblivious, and I couldn't find the words to enlighten him.

My parents-in-law had been good to us over the years, and I wasn't about to encroach on Tom's bond with his mother. But I did regret not having a closer relationship with her. My mother was murdered right in front of me when I was fifteen. I had long desired a mother figure. But Julia wasn't it.

What had I gleaned from the situation? I wanted to be the kind of mother-in-law my sons' wives wanted to be around. They would never dread my visits.

After dressing, I fixed breakfast. Tom joined me at the kitchen table.

"So, Mama's coming Saturday."

"Uh-huh."

The knife scraped over his toast as he slathered a glob of jelly. "You know I don't keep secrets from you, sweetheart."

I gulped. What now? What had Julia told him? "Right. Tom, what's up?" Bacon crunched as I stabbed it with my fork.

"Mama said the strangest thing."

With a mouth full, all I could do was raise my eyebrows.

"She told me to stop you from meddling in the affairs of that family who owned the jewelry box."

Bacon bits slid down my throat. "Why?"

"She didn't say, and your guess is as good as mine. But she said I needed to keep a better eye on you." Tom exaggerated a glare at me over the table, then chuckled. "What is she up to?"

"I don't know, but you can eye me all you want. Later. Right now we need to visit the kids and our new grandson."

"Amen."

We cleaned up the kitchen, and pampered Brutus before leaving for the hospital. Since Tom drove hundreds of miles for his job, I did most of the driving when he was home. On the way to the hospital, he called our contact number for Joey to tell him he had a nephew, and then he called Norm to ask about the jewelry box. Norm said he had an emergency job to do for a friend and would work on the box next week, which suited me fine. He assured us the box would be kept under lock and key until then.

With welcome balloons and flowers in hand, we entered Teresa's new room. She still had dark fatigue circles under her eyes, but her wide smile proclaimed her joy.

"*Holá, abuelos!*"

"And we are thrilled grandparents, *mija*." I hugged her. "How is the new mama this morning?"

While Tom arranged the balloons in the corner, I deposited the flowers on the side table.

"A little tired, but thankful it's over. I fed him this morning. He's exquisitely beautiful. Have you seen him?"

"No. We came straight here." I chose the chair close to the bed.

Tom sat next to me and asked, "Where's Mike?"

"Getting a coffee refill."

"Did he ever go home?" I shrugged out of my light jacket.

"No." Teresa chuckled. "Ever since Dr. Quinn told us the baby had shifted, we've traveled with our hospital bag in the car. Mike had a change of clothes in there, and used my shower this morning."

"Any word—?"

Mike's entrance curtailed my question. He greeted us, then stood beside Teresa's bed.

"What's up?" With anxious eyes on him, she moved his hand to her lips.

His taut face portrayed more than lack of sleep. "I met Dr. Janiskowski in the hall. She's on her way here with information about our baby's condition."

"What kind of information?" Teresa's words ended in a whisper of anxiety.

"Better let her tell us. It's complicated."

I didn't like Mike's flat tone. "Son, what have you heard?"

"Wait for the doctor, Mama."

A sudden chill slithered down my body. I threw my jacket around my shoulders. Teresa clung to Mike as Dr. Janiskowski entered the silent room.

"Do you want us to leave?" I asked.

"No, stay, please."

Mike introduced us to the neurosurgeon.

I slid to the edge of the chair and focused on the rotund woman about my age, with short salt-and-pepper hair.

She fiddled with the stethoscope around her neck as if searching for the right words. "Good morning, McDonough family. I have good news and bad news. I reviewed the MRI done on the baby. Compared to information from the Kerrville hospital, it now looks like the cyst is growing."

"Oh, no." Teresa's voice was barely audible as she nestled closer in Mike's embrace.

"Right now it's not causing any major problems. But we've confirmed that it is a simple cyst. That means it is wrapped in arachnoid cells only. This is good news. The preemie will have to remain in the NICU two or three more days. We'll monitor his lungs, motor functions, reactions to stimuli. Keep checking the cyst for growth or change."

"When can we take him home?" Mike asked.

"Too early to say. All depends on his weight gain, the cyst, and his adjustment to his new environment."

"And . . . and what about the cyst?" Teresa raised her head from Mike's chest to fasten her tear-filled gaze on the doctor.

Dr. Janiskowski moved to the foot of the bed and rested her hands on the rail. "Unless it absorbs in the next week or so—which I must say I doubt will happen—he'll need surgery to implant a shunt which will drain fluid away from the brain. The date of surgery will depend on his weight gain, but I'd guess in three to four weeks."

Teresa patted Mike's arm. "Remember Dr. Conway explained all this might happen."

"I know, but . . . but it's all much more real now. We're talking about our little baby."

The doctor straightened and addressed Teresa and Mike. "I know this is hard to swallow, but surgery will most likely be necessary. You have to be prepared. Until then, any more questions?"

I hadn't understood half of what she said. All I wanted at that moment was to see our grandson. "When . . . when can we see him?"

A smile dimpled her round cheeks for a second. "Now. One at a time. However, you can't stay long." With a curt nod, she said, "Okay, Mike, Teresa, I'll be in touch." After glancing at each of us, she left the room.

We sighed in communal resignation. She'd provided a tentative plan for the baby's future. NICU for now. Surgery in the near future.

Mike turned to us and said, "Why don't you two go see him now?"

"Good idea." Taking Tom's hand, I stood. "Be back in a bit."

Tom and I left the room and flagged a passing nurse for directions to the NICU. Anticipation captured my voice. We walked hand in hand, silently.

Colors of Deceit

I entered first, gowned and masked. There were other tiny babies in incubators, many with tubes and wires attached to various parts of their bodies. I mentally prepared myself to see our baby like that, but he only had heart and temperature monitors taped to his little chest. He wore a little blue cap, and a diaper. I studied my grandson. He reminded me of Mike—the shape of his face, the long fingers. But Mike had more flesh on his little bones. My heart flip-flopped as I gazed at the tiny body, so perfect and precious. I longed to hold him, and if I felt the ache in my empty arms, I imagined what a huge void Teresa experienced.

Before I left, a nurse assured me I could hold him at my next visit. Instead of waiting for Tom, I followed signs to the vending machines. Although well passed lunch time, we'd made no plans to eat yet, and my parched throat objected.

In an alcove, I found the machines and contemplated which soda to purchase. A man joined me, standing close enough to give me the creeps. In an attempt to get out of his way, I slid sideways. But he clamped a gloved hand over my mouth, an arm around my middle, and hauled me into a nearby closet.

CHAPTER FOURTEEN

Although I couldn't see my assailant in the coal-black interior of the closet, when he released me, I hissed, "What do you want?"

"Shut up. Any more noise and I'll silence you for good."

Was it the same voice I'd heard at Mike's house? I couldn't put my finger on it, but something about the voice sounded familiar.

"I'm whispering. Tell me what you want."

He turned on a cell phone and removed his gloves. The light shed an ethereal glow over shelves of towels and sheets, and outlined his tall frame. A baseball cap covered his head, and I'm sure a mass of curls protruded from under it. With his head bowed over the device, I couldn't see his face. His thumbs worked overtime. He must be texting. Did my fate depend on a text message?

While technology kept him occupied, I felt around for a weapon. Nothing but soft bedding. My purse. And cell phone.

I slid my hand into the voluminous interior and sought my phone. My car keys jingled.

"What're you doing?" He drew closer.

"Nothing."

He yanked the purse out of my hand. "No you don't." The heavy tote thumped onto the floor.

Propped against the wall, I folded my arms to ease the tightness in my chest. What now? He stopped texting again to mutter a string of choice words, but kept the phone open, allowing the bluish light to illuminate my tiny prison.

He slipped his gloves back on. "Now, I'll tell you why I brought you here. You've got a jewelry box I want. If you don't give it to me, I promise I'll hurt you or someone in your family." His tone rose and fell as if he deliberately altered it.

The jewelry box again. Was it cursed?

"Who are you?"

"Ha-ha. I'm not stupid. I won't tell you, but I know where you live." He shoved the phone into his pocket and inched closer to my face. "And I know you have a new grandson."

I gulped and slid along the wall until I collided with a shelf. "Okay. I believe you. But let me tell you what I know about that troublesome jewelry box." I waited for a response, but when none came, I gave him superficial details about the items I'd found in the drawers.

"You're too young to have anything to do with World War II letters, or photographs from the 1940s." I paused but he didn't comment. "So, why do you want the box, Conrad?" I took a chance.

"Huh? I'm not . . ."

If he wasn't Conrad, he could have been hired by Conrad. Like the man at Norm's workshop who'd hired the young customer. Or this guy could be lying.

"Conrad. I know you're Conrad." Had I just sealed my fate?

"I'm not Conrad. My name's— No, no. Wait a bit, you said you'd found letters and photographs. Is that all?"

I nodded.

"I asked you, is that all?"

Of course, he couldn't see me nod. "Yes. That's all. Now can I go, please? My husband's going to wonder where I am."

"Wait. I've gottta think."

"If you tell me who you are, then I can let you know if I find anything else in the box."

I thought this might convince him to let me go, but next thing I knew, his face was inches from mine, his breath hot and garlicky.

"So there's another drawer? Huh?"

Stunned into silence, I backed into the shelf, sending towels tumbling to the floor.

"Is there?"

"I . . . I don't know. It's so small, I doubt it. I was trying to get you to let me go."

He walked away.

A sliver of light flashed in front of me. He slid out of the opening, and the door closed behind him. I kept my eyes on the spot where I'd seen the light, and shuffled toward it. I stumbled over an obstacle on the floor. Fumbling for it with trembling fingers, I picked up my purse and headed for the door.

It opened into the alcove. I blinked, straining to see my assailant, but vending machines were the lone occupants. I leaned against the solid bulk of one. Who was that? What had he expected me to find in a secret drawer?

The jewelry box. I should burn it. Take out an ad in the newspaper. No. Video the fire and post it on YouTube. Maybe then whoever was after it would leave me alone.

With uncertainty swirling in my mind, I hurried to the maternity ward and found Tom pacing outside Teresa's room.

"Did you get lost?"

I shook my head, tumbled into his arms, and spilled out what had happened. I left out the part about the man's threats and his knowledge of the jewelry box. If Tom knew those details, he'd insist I stop my research. By not telling him everything, I knew I stood on shaky ground—ready to slip down the proverbial slippery slope that led to deception. But I couldn't tell him. I couldn't stop the research. I had to discover who was after the box. Somehow in my mind, this box was connected to my mother's, and in solving the mystery, I could allow the incident from my childhood to rest in peace.

Tom threatened to call the cops or at least alert hospital security.

"Don't bother, please. I don't want to add any more drama to Mike and Teresa's situation. The man is long gone, I'm sure, and it was dark. I can't describe him."

With his hands on my shoulders, he stared at me, his eyes searching my face. "Please, Tom. Let it be."

After a while, he drew me to his chest. "Chella, you're the most stubborn woman I know." He rested his chin on the top on my head, his arms shielding me in a protective embrace. "You know I want to tear this hospital apart to find the jerk."

"I know, but I'm okay." Once I stepped back, I noticed the lines of concern on his brow. "Please, Tom. Let's forget it. We need to give one hundred percent of our attention to the kids right now. Can you imagine what they're going through?"

Tom fisted his hand. "I'm mad as—but you're right. We won't tell them about your adventure in the closet."

Mike met us outside Teresa's room. "There you are. We have a favor to ask. Teresa's parents are arriving at two-thirty. Will you pick them up at the airport?"

"Sure," Tom said. "Then bring them here to see Teresa and the baby?"

"Right. You'll have to take my SUV. Ernesto and Alma are coming of course, but they're also bringing Rosie and Lucia." Mike referred to Teresa's two sisters.

"We can do that, *mijo*. Do you want us to take them to Kerrville later?"

"Yes, Mama. If you don't mind. They can use Teresa's car while they're visiting, and you and I can trade vehicles later."

"Don't worry about it. You know we'll be back tomorrow to see our grandson." We approached the room. "Have you chosen a name?"

Teresa, sitting in the easy chair, smiled as we entered. "We have a name—or rather names."

"Please sit while we tell you." Mike waited for Tom to scoot chairs next to Teresa, and then he sat on the bed. "We've given a lot of thought to naming our son. We didn't want to use family names—"

"Papa's feelings will be hurt since he didn't have a son to pass his name to," Teresa said.

"But we want to honor both sides of the family. So, for middle names we have Raul, to honor you, Mama, and Teresa's heritage, and Douglas, to honor your Scottish heritage, Daddy. And for a first name, we found one in the Bible."

"You can't go wrong there." Tom grinned.

"Our baby's name is Nathaniel Raul Douglas McDonough."

"I know it's a mouthful, but we'll call him Nate." Teresa relaxed against Mike.

"Nate. I like it. Good. Strong." I beamed at our kids.

"It means gift of God. Nathaniel." Tom, ever the fount of Biblical knowledge.

"We know, Dad. And he is." After rubbing his chin, Mike cleared his throat. "Um, there's one more thing. Hank called. The funeral for A. J. is tomorrow. Two o'clock in Brooder. We plan to attend."

"I'll be discharged in the morning." Tears pooled in Teresa's eyes.

With his arm around me, Tom squeezed my shoulder. "We'll be there, too. Right, sweetheart?"

Sadness washed over me as I nodded.

An aid entered, carrying Teresa's lunch tray.

"It's time we headed to the airport." Tom rose. "We can stop for lunch on the way."

Searching in my purse, I fished out my car keys and handed them to Mike.

We traded information about where the vehicles were parked, then Tom and I set out for a restaurant.

I know I ate something, but the food had little taste. The gloom of A. J.'s funeral and my ordeal in the closet clouded the fleeting joy of seeing Nate for the first time.

On the way to the airport, Joey called. Tom gave him details of Nate's birth and the situation with the cyst. Joey's obvious excitement about his nephew's arrival matched the satisfaction he derived from building the houses in San Salvador. We thrilled at his change in perspective.

By the time we'd negotiated highways hampered by construction, we didn't have long to wait at the airport for the Rangel family.

Teresa's parents, Ernesto and Alma, were a decade older than Tom and me. She was almost as tall as Tom, with Ernesto an inch or two shorter. His close-cropped black hair sprinkled with gray matched his mustache and goatee. Smile crinkles lined his dark eyes.

Alma's matronly figure, often bedecked in bright colors, used to intimidate me. But after our first meeting, I learned to cherish the heart of gold buried beneath her flounces and necklaces. Her round face, surrounded by black curls, beamed with pleasure.

"Maricella. *Abuelita*. Good to see you. And you Tom." She hugged us, latched onto my arm and marched toward the baggage claim area. "How are you, grandma?"

"I'm fine. Where are the girls?"

"They sat at the back of the plane. Could not be seen with *Mami y Papi*." She clucked her tongue. "Two handsome men, oyee, sat back there. What am I going to do with my girls? Wish they would find husbands like Teresa's Mike. Too bad your José is too young."

I could argue with her logic, but I'd learned years ago to stay out of my sons' romantic lives.

At the luggage carousel, Alma Rose and Lucia joined us. Teresa, the middle sister, looked like Rosie, the oldest. Both tall, with classical angular features, their undeniable beauty came from Alma's side of the family. Lucia, the youngest, had highlighted her hair, and although attractive with an oval face and rounded features, looked more like a cousin than a sister to Rosie and Teresa.

"So, Tom, what is our grandson's name?" Ernesto lugged the last suitcase off the carousel.

Tom raised his eyebrows. "We'll let the kids tell you. Come, the car's this way."

We swarmed out of the terminal and piled the luggage and six people into Mike's SUV. Excited chatter filled the drive to the hospital. Tom and I sat in the waiting room while Teresa visited with her family. At one time, the nurse had to admonish them to quiet down. Then they took turns visiting Nate.

I'm not sure when Mike and Teresa told them the baby's name, but when Ernesto came out of the room on his way to the NICU, his shoulders sagged, and his lips quivered.

Mike joined us minutes later. "That was tough. I'm glad I won't have to do it again." Air in the chair cushion whooshed out as he sat next to me.

"Explaining your choice of names?" I asked.

He slipped his wedding ring up and down to his knuckle. "Yeah. Teresa received the brunt of their disapproval, but she consoled them, and added when

Rosie marries she can name a son Ernesto."

"What did Ernesto say to that?" After closing the magazine he'd been flipping through, Tom slipped his reading glasses into his pocket.

"Nothing, but I think it's the first grandson thing." With a yawn, Mike stood. "He'll get over it in time. They're about ready to leave. I'm spending the night again because Teresa's being discharged tomorrow. No sense me going home now, just to come back in the morning."

We followed Mike into the room, kissed Teresa goodbye, and then herded the Rangels back to the vehicle. Stories of the jewelry box and its contents, plus the assorted problems it had brought, filled the hour-and-a-half drive to Kerrville.

Alma insisted on a stop at the grocery store in Kerrville before heading to Brooder. We crammed the grocery bags into the SUV and set off for the last ten miles. As I drove up to the house, my eyes darted to the front door. No spray painted slurs greeted us. What a relief!

The Rangels loved the house, the greening lawn, and large trees. Luggage and groceries inside, I figured Alma would find everything she needed. For now, Ernesto and Alma would use the master bedroom, and the sisters would share the guest room. Once Teresa came home, different sleeping arrangements would be needed. I remembered the sofa opened to a full sized bed, and figured the girls would use it.

Tom and I left the family unpacking. As I entered Kerrville, a truck with a Rick Jennings Electrical emblem on the side barreled past us. A crazy notion burst into my head.

"Hey, Tom. Want to do some investigating with me?"

He gave me a wide-eyed stare. "Sure. What do you have in mind?"

I told him all I knew about the blue baseball cap. "Let's find this electrical company, and see if we can meet Conrad." My excitement gave me courage. "What if Conrad is the man who dragged me into the closet this morning?"

"You . . . you mean the incident could be connected to the jewelry box?" Tom's words held a hint of uncertainty.

"It could be."

After a heavy pause, Tom thumped his knee. "Okay, I'm game. Anything to resolve the mystery. But let me make inquiries. If it is Conrad, then he's seen you, but he doesn't know me. And I don't want you in harm's way again."

"Fine. The address on the truck indicated they are on Peterson Drive. Here it is." I turned left. "And there's the building. On the right."

I parked in front of the single-story white and tan metal building and switched off the engine.

Tom entered the double glass doors.

Anxious minutes crawled by. I turned on the radio, drumming my fingers in time to the beat. What was taking so long? I opened the door and paced on the sidewalk.

When Tom joined me, his frown meant bad news.

"What?"

"I spoke with Rick Jennings himself. He said Conrad didn't show up for work today."

"Then he could be the guy—"

"No, Chella. He couldn't have been the man who accosted you in the hospital today."

I rested against the car. "Why not?"

"He was in a wreck. Leg's in a cast and he walks with crutches."

"Crutches? But . . . but it had to be him. Who else could it be? I have to— I'm going to ask one more question." I darted to the door and jerked it open.

Tom's voice trailed behind me. "Chella—"

The young receptionist glanced up at my entrance. "Can I help you ma'am." Tom entered behind me. "Oh, you're back."

"I'm sorry to bother you. I know my husband already inquired about Conrad Summerland-Hayes."

Fiddling with the row of earrings in her left lobe, she nodded. "He goes by Conrad Hayes around here."

"I know but, I mean . . ." I turned and searched the office walls. A photograph-lined hall peeled off to the right. "Are those pictures of employees?"

"Yes, ma'am. Employee of the year. Conrad has a picture there."

"Great." Without hesitation, I pulled Tom to the hall and searched the captions under each eight by ten framed glossy.

"I don't see him." I didn't recognize the intruder from Mike's house in any of the pictures.

"Here's Conrad Hayes." Tom pointed to a smiling tanned face with a hairline receded into short blond curls.

"That's not the man who broke into the house."

But, if Conrad wasn't the intruder, then who could it be? Someone else wearing his cap?

CHAPTER FIFTEEN

Once home, I paced the office. After the fifth turn, I threw my hands up in the air. I felt like shouting from the hilltops, "Would the people who are after the antique jewelry box please step forward?"

If Conrad Summerland-Hayes wasn't after the box, then who was? I searched my notebook and the family tree I'd developed for another possible suspect.

Gregory and Rachael could have removed the jewelry box from the estate sale at any time. It couldn't be either of them. What about Emory? Sure, no one in the family had heard from him in ages, but the box could conceal evidence of his guilt. Or innocence.

Then there were Conrad's brother, Andrew, and his cousin, Marshall. Where had they moved to, according to Warren? I flipped pages and found the notation. Marshall to Oregon, Andrew to Austin. Could either of them be my intruder? And what about Jacqui? Could she have hired someone? No. The man in the closet seemed to have a personal interest in the contents of a secret drawer.

I needed to find photographs of the Summerland-Hayes boys. Warren mentioned they were about the same age, went to school together. Aha! A high school yearbook. Next time I visited Kerrville, I'd ask Warren if he had his.

With a plan in mind, I cleaned the house from stem to stern in preparation for my mother-in-law's visit. When I climbed into bed, exhaustion brought sleep minutes after I kissed Tom good night. Sweet dreams of babies refreshed my soul.

Tom treated me to breakfast in bed, a Saturday morning luxury. Relaxing against the pillows, I almost forgot about the rogue antique jewelry box and my mother-in-law's imminent arrival. And we had a funeral to attend. When my cell phone rang, Tom removed it from its charger and handed it to me. Alma Rangel invited us to lunch.

Colors of Deceit

After we cleaned up the kitchen, I drove Mike's SUV to Kerrville. Having seen the items Teresa had received from baby showers, I knew she needed smaller diapers for Nate. Before heading to Brooder, I stopped at Wal-Mart to purchase a few packages. Tom remained in the car.

In the parking lot, I passed a van from River Oaks Senior Living Community. I wondered which residents had come to the store. While hunting for the baby department, I spied two women in wheelchairs examining a rack of blouses. The black lady with a head of gray curls caught my eye.

I sneaked up behind another rack of clothes and peered over the top. It was Esther Stiles.

She and her companion chatted away, extolling the virtues of cotton versus polyester.

"I don't like that there synthetic stuff. Sticks to my skin."

"You so right, Esther. Come. I want to look at the shoes."

"What size you wear?" Esther turned her chair.

"Think it's an eight. How about you?"

"Oh, Lordy. I need a nine. Extra wide."

The two wheelchairs slipped through the racks and disappeared down the aisle.

"So much for senility, Esther Stiles."

After paying for the diapers, I dashed to the car and told Tom what I'd overheard.

"Before we go to Mike's, I want to stop by the nursing home. I have an idea." I peeked in my purse. The plastic bag containing the handkerchief lay squished at the bottom. "That woman knows more than she let on the other day."

"Let's do it, Mrs. Sherlock."

I chuckled and drove to the nursing home on River Drive. Investigating with Tom was fun. He kept watch in the lobby while I signed in and sauntered to Esther's room. Her roommate dozed on the bed by the window. I crept into the gloom and examined Esther's area. Small photographs stood in frames on a dresser, but a large one dominated the wall above her bed. It showed three generations, with a much younger Esther seated in front, a man and woman behind her, and a grade school aged boy next to her.

The man behind her looked vaguely familiar. I leaned closer, but couldn't recognize him in the dim room. I searched for a light switch and nearly jumped a foot off the floor when a hand tapped my arm.

"What you doing?"

It was Esther's roommate. How did she climb out of bed without me hearing her?

"Who is this?" I pointed to the photograph.

"That's Esther's son, and some other people."

Esther's son. Why did he look familiar? "What's his name?"

The roommate, a frail slip of a woman with white wispy hair sticking out around her face like a halo, gazed at me, eyes wide and vacant. "Who? I don't know anybody's name. Who are you?"

Tom's figure darkened the doorway as he entered. "We better go, Chella. They're back."

"Okay, but I want to talk to Esther. Let's wait in the hall."

In a few minutes Esther glided down the hall in her wheelchair, holding a white plastic bag on her lap. I turned to face Tom so she wouldn't see me, but once she wheeled into her room, I followed.

"Hi, Esther. Remember me? I'm Frankie's friend. I saw you at Wal-Mart."

She spun the chair around and stared at me, her dark eyes wide. When recognition dawned, she dropped her head, muttering incoherently.

"I heard you and your friend talking in the store. Forget the act, Esther. You know exactly what's going on, and I need answers. Please."

She hiked her rounded shoulders and pursed her lips. "So, you got me. What do you want to know?"

I pointed to the photograph above her bed. "Who are these people?"

"That's my family, taken in the late '60s."

Anticipation heated my blood as I stared at the picture. "What are their names?"

My gaze shifted to the dresser. A headshot of a man swam before my eyes. "Who's this?" The shape of his head and his broad shoulders reminded me of the man who'd visited Norm's workshop.

"Make up your mind." Esther focused on the last photograph I pointed to. "That's my son, Stephen."

"Stephen?"

"That's what I said."

"Stephen, but that's the name . . ." Lockets and handkerchiefs and sepia photographs whirled through my mind. What did it mean?

"That's all I'm gonna say. I'm tired. I'm gonna nap. You want more answers, you bring Frankie back."

"But I want to show—"

"Leave now, or I'll call for help. Bring Frankie back and I'll talk. I'll only talk if Frankie comes with you." Esther moved her chair close to the bed, then applied the brakes. She pulled herself upright.

"I'll hold you to that, Esther. Frankie and I'll be back. You can count on it."

Stepping into the hall, I looped my arm through Tom's.

"I overheard part of your conversation. I take it you'll be back with Frankie."

"Uh-huh. Esther has the key to one of the mysteries of the jewelry box. Wish I could—ooh, I have an idea." I handed him the keys. "You drive. I need to call Frankie."

Hesitant at first, Frankie agreed to meet me at the nursing home on Sunday. I told him Esther was lucid and ready to talk.

We arrived at the house minutes before Mike and Teresa. Rich, spicy aromas of garlic, peppers, and meat surrounded us as we entered. Alma prepared a feast of green enchiladas, a New Mexican specialty which featured stacked tortillas instead of individually rolled, smothered in a sauce made from green, not red chilies. We celebrated Teresa's homecoming, albeit subdued because Nate had to remain in the NICU. He had developed jaundice, and combined with his other health issues, the staff had cautioned Mike and Teresa that he needed rest and quiet. We agreed to limit our visits.

Ernesto and Alma owned a real estate business in Santa Fe. Rosie worked for them, too. Alma and Lucia planned on staying at least through Nate's surgery, while Ernesto and Rosie had to return home within a day or two.

The tenuous situation with Nate and his upcoming surgery had everyone elated one minute and blue the next. But the close family bond infused the house with hope.

During a private conversation with Alma and me, Teresa informed us of her decision not to breastfeed Nate. She had considered it, but not knowing how long he would be in the hospital and his imminent surgery had influenced her decision. She also had to consider her university courses. The last semester of her senior year. Not a good time to quit, but Nate's early arrival had curtailed her Internet studies. We both assured her that she had to do what she felt was right for her situation. At least, she would have her mother and sister to help with the baby when he did come home.

I envied them. Not that I couldn't help, too, but I feared I'd be in the way.

◆ ◆ ◆

Tom, Mike, and I attended A. J.'s funeral later that afternoon. He'd grown up in the community and friends spoke of his antics as a boy. Colleagues from the school district in San Antonio attested to his strong character and leadership traits. Warren spoke of childhood spats and squabbles, but the admiration for his big brother shone through his words.

Many attendees left the church sniffling. The ride to the nearby cemetery took a scant five minutes. Standing with Tom, I searched the crowd, and my heart filled with the love and support shown the Howard and Trenton families. Butch and Lexi Ballard kept close to Hank and Ruth Ann.

Mike led the group in prayer. I bowed my head as his words lilted heavenward on the breeze.

The man in front of me turned sideways and sneezed. He whispered, "Pardon me."

My ears tingled. Did every strange man sound like the intruder?

With my head bowed, I stared at the ground. His boots filled the scene. A shiver slithered down my spine. I'd seen those boots before. Dark brown toe guard over tan leather.

Lord, please forgive me. I heard not a word of Mike's prayer. This was the man who stabbed A. J.

I slowly raised my head. Brown jeans. White shirt. Cowboy hat. All straw cowboy hats looked alike, but I willed him to turn around, I had to see his face. Then Mike ended the prayer.

People shuffled and moved.

Tom said, "Let's go home, Mariella."

I reached forward but the man vaporized. Or at least that's how it seemed. He disappeared into the crowd. I told Tom, and we scanned the people coming and going, but to no avail.

Later, when talking to Warren, I mentioned my suspicions. Skeptical at my suggestion, he said he could name everyone who'd attended the funeral. No one there would have dressed in disguise and entered his office with a knife.

Even so, I was certain the man had heard Tom address me by name, and that's why he'd vanished.

Warren gave us details of the police investigation into A. J.'s murder. They had no solid leads.

I still had my nagging suspicion the man was connected to the dratted jewelry box. I asked Warren if he had a high school yearbook. He knew his mother kept them all, and would locate the appropriate edition and bring it to church the next day—I'd already told Tom we'd be worshipping in Brooder.

Connie, at Warren's side throughout the conversation, beamed when he held her hand and joined his parents and Leah.

We left late-afternoon to meet Julia in San Antonio. She insisted on seeing her great-grandson. I liked driving my Chevy Impala again. Thanks, Mike, but you can have your big SUV.

By the time we entered the hospital parking lot, a spaghetti bowl of knots took up residence in my stomach. I could never compete with Julia. Always perfection.

I checked my blouse. Rats! I'd spilled chili on the aqua top. I tugged the gray jacket closed and buttoned it.

Julia eased out of her pale gold Mercury Grand Marquis, looking as fresh as if she'd driven across town, not two-hundred-seventy miles from Dallas. Tall and slender, her elegant cream pantsuit fit her like it was custom made. Pearls at her laced neckline, platinum hair in a chignon, not a strand dared to be out of place. Julia had worn her hair this way since our boys were babies. When we'd told Julia and Doug we were going to make them grandparents—and granted we made them young grandparents—Julia had said, "I'm going to grow my hair long. I don't want to be one of those grandmothers with short, curly, gray hair."

And she wasn't. Her hair hasn't been short or gray since.

We greeted each other. I was never sure of the sentiment behind her hugs. But she draped an arm around my shoulders and I glanced up at her—in her lofty company I resented being a mere five-foot six—and she smiled. We headed to the elevator.

Lowering her head a fraction, Julia asked, "So, what color is he?"

I frowned. Had I heard her correctly? "You mean his hair? We haven't seen it. He's wearing a little cap, but Mike says it's dark brown."

"You know what I mean, his overall color."

The elevator doors opened. "We're here. Why don't you see for yourself?"

Julia took the first turn. Tom sat and thumbed through a magazine while I stood by the window, staring at the gray clouds cavorting across the blue sky. What did she mean, what color was he? His skin color? Surely, she knew newborns' skin color darkened with age. But what difference did it make?

That was Julia. I could never guess what was on her mind and it was pointless to share my concerns with Tom. He'd say, "That's my mother. You know what she's like."

Tom gowned up next. Julia stood with me at the window. "I thought we'd be able to see a bump or something where the cyst is."

"We've been told his little head and face may swell from an accumulation of fluid. It's a waiting game." I folded my arms and squinted at Julia's facial reflection in the window.

We played a waiting game of our own, conversing about safe topics until Tom returned.

When I visited Nate, I teared up at the puffiness on the left side of his face. Was Julia satisfied with his color? I wanted to scrutinize his tiny body, caress every little finger and toe, but couldn't stay long under the observant eye of the nurse. We decided it was too late to drive back to Brooder for Julia to see Mike and Teresa. Surely, they'd had more than enough excitement for one day.

Tom rode home with Julia. They needed mother-son time, but I worried about what new critical darts were being aimed my way. I stopped at the grocery store and made a quick purchase of foods I knew Julia liked.

Her room was perfect, the meal delicious, and the view from the back porch, as always, serene. We sat out there after supper. Julia appeared relaxed in her spotless and wrinkle-free, cream pantsuit. Brutus nestled on my lap, burying his face in the crook of my arm as if he knew that Julia didn't like dogs. The undercurrents of tension seemed to wash right over Tom. Surrounded by his favorite women, he grinned like a boy in a toy store.

Julia, a retired accountant, regaled us with exploits of her travels with friends, and after Tom filled her in on his promotion prospects, I discussed the articles I'd written. As usual, my accomplishments failed to interest her.

When Tom stepped inside, I asked, "Do you have that list of names for the family tree?"

She slapped a hand over her chest. "Oh, dear. I'm sorry I forgot it. There are too many to recall offhand. I'll mail the list as soon as I get back home."

I had to be satisfied with her response.

The next morning Julia insisted she take her car to Brooder, too. She didn't like to be beholden and wanted her independence. She followed Tom and me, the backseat of her car bulging with gifts for the baby. I was surprised to see Teresa at church, but she claimed to be feeling fine and, with her mother and sister helping at home, had rested well.

Julia held out her arms to greet Mike. "My number one grandson. Good to see you, honey."

I cringed. Poor Joey, as number two grandson, I was glad he didn't hear those words again.

At least, her greeting of Teresa seemed genuine and heartfelt that Nate wasn't home.

We sat in the row behind Mike and Teresa. Julia, Tom, then me. I'm ashamed to admit I couldn't focus on Hank's sermon. I'd seen Warren sitting across the aisle from us. He mouthed he had the yearbook. All I could think about was checking the photographs and not disappointing my mother-in-law. What a combination!

At the conclusion of the service, I did everything but run over people in my rush to meet Warren outside. He and Connie stood near a magnolia tree. She waved as I approached.

I hastened to them. "Hi, you two!"

Warren doffed his cowboy hat. "Howdy, Maricella. The book's in the truck. I'll go get it."

"Hi!" Connie's greeting begged further inquiry.

"How are you?"

Her round face turned pink. "Great, thanks. He's taking me out to lunch today." She bit her bottom lip.

"That's good."

Warren joined us carrying a stained maroon yearbook. "You wanted to see pictures of Marshall, Conrad, and Andrew, right?"

"Uh-huh." I told him about seeing Conrad's photo at Rick Jennings Electrical, but I wanted to be sure.

He gave the book to Connie, who balanced it as he flipped pages back and forth. "Here's Marshall."

I studied his picture. "No, that's not him. I know these were taken years ago, but the face is too narrow. Hair wrong color; too much red."

He turned a couple of pages. "Next, here's Conrad."

A younger version of the photo at Rick's Electrical, this one with more hair and a shade darker, took up half a page.

"Last one." Three or four pages flipped with his index finger. "Andrew."

Dark brown curls haloed the face in the photograph. Add a few years, a blue baseball cap, and I was looking at the intruder who attacked Teresa and me.

CHAPTER SIXTEEN

Andrew Summerland-Hayes attacked Teresa, tried to take her jewelry box. Choked me. Andrew, son of Gregory, grandson of Albert, and great-grandson of Virginia and Harlan.

But why? The letters didn't belong to, or affect, him. Neither did the locket. The photos in the locket were connected to Esther Stiles. I was certain. One mystery would soon unravel, since Frankie and I had a date with her this afternoon.

Andrew and the jewelry box. There had to be another secret compartment concealing something Andrew wanted. That's the only explanation that made any sense. All this conjecture reminded me I must tell Deputy Rayburn I'd identified the intruder.

I gave the car keys to Tom. As we drove to Mike's house, four miles from the church, I called the sheriff's department.

"Deputy Rayburn, I can identify the man who attacked Teresa and me. It was Andrew Summerland-Hayes."

"Are you sure, ma'am?"

"Of course." Flipping pages of the yearbook, I found his photo. "I'm looking at his picture right now."

While I explained how I'd come to the conclusion it had to be one of the three Summerland-Hayes cousins and had compared their pictures, Tom parked along the curb of Mike's house. He tapped his watch.

I covered the phone with my hand and said to Tom, "I know we're late. You go on in. I'll be along in a minute."

Tom quietly closed the car door, and jogged to the house.

"Do you know where Andrew is now?" Rayburn asked.

"I believe he moved to Austin. That's according to Warren Howard. They all attended school together, and were friends. Warren is a friend of Andrew's brother, Conrad."

Rayburn cleared her throat. "We'll check your information. See if he has an alibi. What about your daughter-in-law? Did she also recognize his photograph?"

I'd shown the yearbook to Teresa before we'd left the church grounds.

"Yes, she did, although she's not as definite as I am."

"All right, Mrs. McDonough. We'll be in touch. Thank you." She didn't sound thoroughly convinced.

I dashed inside the house and apologized for being late. Rich, spicy aromas hit me the second I opened the door. Alma had prepared another five-star meal for lunch. *Posole*, a pork and hominy stew she had simmered all morning, and *bizcochitos*, anise flavored cookies for dessert, both items usually served at Christmas time.

After the meal, Teresa and Mike opened the array of gifts from Julia. They included toys, an elaborate highchair, an envelope, and a wide assortment of clothes in various sizes—we'd known for ages our grandchild was a boy.

Mike held the white legal-sized envelope, while Teresa examined the highchair and maneuvered it into different positions and heights. "This is fantastic, Julia! Thank you so much. Thank you for everything." Beaming, she settled next to Mike on the sofa.

Unable to contain my surprise at Julia's thoughtfulness, I lowered my head. Peeking at her while fiddling with my watch band, her undeniable pleasure amazed me. She'd obviously enjoyed selecting these generous gifts. They were practical, but tasteful. Just like Julia.

She slid to the edge of her seat like an impatient child. "Wait, there's one more thing. Go on, Mike, open the envelope."

Expecting a gift card, I glanced up.

With a curious smile, Mike removed a document from the envelope. His eyes moved back and forth, then his eyebrows shot up. "Wow! Grandmother, this is—"

"What?" we asked in unison.

"It's a college fund for Nate." Mike's voice trailed. "It's . . . it's more than I could have ever imagined, Grandmother. Thank you!"

Handing the page to Teresa, Mike stood and embraced Julia.

I knew she loved Mike, but the expression on her face reaffirmed his place in her heart. Recalling my antagonism toward her, I felt a flush infuse my cheeks. Thankfully, no one noticed. All eyes were on Mike and Julia.

A moment later, Mike returned to his seat and Julia said, "You know how much your Grandfather valued education. If he were here today, he'd rejoice that you have a college degree. And Joey and Teresa are working on theirs. He'd want the best for his number one great-grandson." Pointing to the gifts, she continued. "Those are from me, but the college fund is from Grandfather."

Julia's words swept over me like a spring storm. I was ready to adjust my opinion of her until she said *number one great-grandson*. How those words grated on my nerves. But I smiled, and helped carry the gifts back to the nursery.

Later, Joey called from the San Antonio airport. I chatted with him while sitting at the kitchen table.

"We made it back in one piece, Mama."

"Glad to hear it. When can I see you?"

Noises in the background indicated he was at the luggage carousel. "I'm riding back to my apartment with the group. But as soon as I get my car, I'll drive out to Brooder. Can't wait to see everyone. Wish my nephew was there, too."

And I couldn't wait to assess for myself the change in his attitude I'd gathered from his tone. If I hurried my business with Frankie, Tom and I could be home in time for Joey to stop by after his visit to his brother and sister-in-law. I was anxious to spend time with him and to hear more about his experiences.

Tom rode home with Julia. I drove to the nursing home to meet Frankie, locket and a score of questions ready.

Seated on a wooden bench in the shaded side garden, Frankie beckoned me. A shadow of caution darkened his gaze.

"Hi, Frankie!"

"Come sit a spell." He patted the space next to him. "I know we have to go in there." He jutted his chin toward the building. "But I . . . I don't want to."

Unable to keep the disappointment hidden, I arranged the folds of my yellow dress around my knees. "She won't talk to me if you don't come in."

Eyes focused on the branches above him, he swallowed. "I know, but I'm afraid she's gonna tell me something I don't want to hear."

"Like what?"

Frankie turned his thin body and looked right at me. "Esther had a son a few days before Ginny gave birth to John. I'm afraid of what she'll say when we go in there."

"Do you want to forget it and leave? We don't have to do this. I will try to live without the answers. Can you?"

His eyes glazed over and he bowed his head. "No. I need the truth. After all these years, I need the truth."

For a beat or two, we sat in silence, then I stood and offered him my hand. "Okay. Let's go."

Grunting, he pushed to a stand and took my hand. We entered the lobby, signed in, and passed several offices. The third door stood ajar. Was the Director of Nurses working on a Sunday?

I knocked on her door. "Excuse me. We're here to visit Esther Stiles. I brought her a bar of chocolate and want to make sure she's allowed to have it."

The plump, middle-aged woman smiled. "Thanks for asking. Let me check her file." She rolled her chair to the desk and punched half a dozen keys on the computer. "Um, Esther Stiles. Here she is. No dietary restrictions. She can have the candy."

"Thank you." Still holding hands, Frankie and I located Esther's hall. She sat in her wheelchair outside her room. Although she tracked our advance, she didn't move her chair.

"It's you again." Elbows propped on the arms of the chair, she eyed us with suspicion.

"We've come to ask those questions, Esther. Do you want to go into your room or use the lobby?"

She pointed to her room and entered. "Come in. My roommate's gone for the day."

Frankie sat on one of the beds, and I chose the lone chair next to Esther. With the plastic bag in hand, I waited as she fiddled with her hair, and adjusted the neckline of her blouse. She acted as if trying to delay the showdown.

"Esther, I brought you this." I placed a bar of Hershey's chocolate with almonds on her dresser. Her dark eyes widened, and she licked her lips. "But now I have something to show you." I displayed the handkerchief, the red initials visible.

Her hand flew to her mouth to cover her sharp intake of breath. "You found it."

Features somber, Frankie leaned forward. "Why was your handkerchief in Ginny's jewelry box?"

Esther's considerable body mass seemed to wither before us. She slumped in the chair and shook her head. She wasn't matching up to Frankie's description of a rattlesnake *or* a hornet. "So long ago, too many memories. What . . . what else did you find?"

Opening the linen square, I revealed the curl of hair and the gold locket. Esther reached for the items, but I moved my hand out of her grasp.

"We want answers, Esther. First, why did you insist that Frankie be here?"

Although muted light filled the corners of the room, nothing could conceal the turmoil ripping through her body. Muscles twitched along her jaw line, her eyes squinted closed, her hands fisted in her lap, but then a Niagara-sized sigh flooded from the depth of her past.

"It hurts so much to remember." A shudder shimmied across her shoulders, and she held up a shaky hand. "Okay. Okay. I'll tell you. The locket, as you know, Frankie, was Ginny's. The catch broke, and I fixed it for her one day. That's when I wrapped it in one of my handkerchiefs. Ginny was very ill, and I didn't think she'd ever open the secret drawer again."

"What about the curl of hair?" Frankie asked.

"Ginny had it in the jewelry box already. I put it with the locket."

"But whose hair is it?" The dark brown curl tickled my palm.

"It's . . . it's . . . Oh, Frankie. I don't know if I can tell you."

"You have to, Esther. You demanded I come, and you owe me the truth. Take your time, but I want to know and you have to tell me."

Esther's probable knowledge of the items I'd found in the second drawer spurred the cogs of my brain. Her reluctance to name the hair's donor signaled the possibility we might have to pry out information about the baby's photograph too. Did this mean she had a reason to keep the contents secret? Could the man who came to Norm's workshop be connected to Esther?

I studied the family portrait above her bed, then the headshot on her dresser—the one of the man I'd sort of recognized on my last visit. An idea struck me like a dozen lightning bolts. What if Esther had been behind one of the attempts to steal the jewelry box?

The quality of the faded picture on the dresser told me it was old. I stood and picked it up. "Who is this, Esther?"

She snatched the picture out of my hands and clutched it to her ample chest. "That's my . . . that's Stephen, my son." She peddled her feet and the wheelchair floated to the dresser. "This is his son, my grandson, James."

Esther removed a frame from the back which showed a tall, young man, again with familiar features, and handed it to me. I switched on the overhead light and studied the photo. He looked a lot like the second man who'd come to Norm's. I replaced the frame on the dresser.

"Did he try to take the jewelry box from me?"

She lowered her head. "I asked him to find it. I . . . I'd read about the estate sale in the newspaper. I was surprised to see the box listed. I thought it was long gone."

Frankie slid off the bed and paced the short distance to the window, impatience growing with every step. "Why? To get a handkerchief, a locket, and a strand of old hair?"

A feeble sob escaped Esther's throat. "Not the handkerchief, but the locket and hair."

"Why, Esther?" Frankie turned. "What don't you want people to know about the locket?"

I'm surprised Esther didn't burst into flames at the intensity of Frankie's eyes on her.

Hunching her shoulders, she stared at the frame in her crooked fingers. "It's the picture of the baby."

I opened the locket. "This one?"

She raised her head and nodded.

"The one that has the name Stephen written on the back but Frankie says is a picture of Johnny?"

"Yes. Yes, okay. That's why I wanted the jewelry box. To destroy my past. My mistakes."

"What mistakes?" Frankie perched on the edge of the bed like a hawk ready to strike.

"Frankie, please don't be mad at me. Promise you won't do anything crazy."

Frankie, eyes wide, scooted back and held up his hands. "I promise. I want to know the truth at last."

Esther inhaled and sunk lower in her chair. "Your sister and I had babies three days apart. I knew her mother was black, and each time Ginny gave birth, she was concerned about the baby's skin color. When Johnny was born, I could see he was darker than Mary Margaret and Albert had been." She laid Stephen's framed photo in her lap.

"My baby was light-skinned, and I was afraid my husband would find out I'd been . . . with . . . other men. I didn't even know who the father was. There were two or three white men . . ."

Esther concentrated on the far wall, but it may as well have been across the ocean. Memories kept her captive for several moments.

"What did you do, Esther?"

My words jerked her back to the present.

"I switched babies."

"No." The word exploded from Frankie's lips. "No, you didn't."

A tear trickled down her plump cheek. She managed a smile. "I'm sorry, but I did. The child you knew as Johnny was really my son." She studied the framed picture in her lap. "And the boy I took home, the darker skinned boy, was Ginny and Harlan's son."

"And Ginny never suspected?" I asked.

Esther closed her eyes. "No. You see she had a difficult time with the birth. Was real weak. She cuddled him for a few minutes but couldn't nurse her baby." Opening her eyes, she squinted at fingers laced over Stephen's face. "I nursed both babies, and when she wanted to see Johnny, I . . . I gave her my baby. No one knew."

"Not even Harlan?" I quirked an eyebrow at Esther. "He didn't know his own son?"

She hung her head again. "He . . . he saw him for a second or two, all wrapped up. He wasn't much into little babies and didn't notice any difference when he later held my boy."

"So, the picture in the locket is . . . who?" I stared at the tiny photo. "I'm confused."

Frankie's movements caught my attention. He clutched the bedspread, his dark face drawn, his lips quivering.

"It's the boy everyone thought was Ginny's son. My birth son."

Esther's answers bounced around my brain, clarifying most of the mess. "But why is the name Stephen on the back?"

Eyes downcast, she swayed back and forth. "When I repaired Ginny's locket, I examined the photograph and thought it would be my only chance to identify him. I pried it out and wrote *Stephen* on the back. I don't think anyone ever saw it."

"Until now." I snapped the locket closed. "So, this little boy is dead, but the son you raised is alive. And he, by blood, is a Summerland-Hayes."

"Yeah. I love the boy I raised, my Stephen." She tapped the glass-covered photo in her lap. "Just like I love all my other children." She pointed to various framed pictures on the dresser. "But Stephen don't know he's kin to them rich, white folk, and I want it to stay that way."

"Then why did you want the jewelry box?" I spread the handkerchief in my lap before wrapping it around the locket and curl of hair.

"Because I wanted to destroy those things." A shaky finger pointed to my hand. "Ginny was real good to me, but money changed her, and messed up her family. Right, Frankie?" She continued without waiting for his response. "Those

Summerland-Hayes people with their fancy name, ritzy houses and flashy cars, never were any happier than the rest of us." Shifting in her chair, she gained an inch or two in height.

"I never want my son Stephen or his son James to get wind of being kin to them fancy-schmancy folks on the hill. My kids have done okay. Don't need no highfalutin' name to be somebody in this world. No, sir. I don't want my sins visited on them."

I let her words settle in the air for a beat or two. "How did you convince James to try to steal the jewelry box?"

Guilt and shame clouded her face for a second. "I told him Ginny left something valuable in there for me, and no one else knew how to open it."

"What will you tell him now?"

Esther moved toward the dresser, but Frankie intercepted her, and took the frame from her.

"I'll tell him you found it and brought it to me. I'll convince him. I'll tell him it had sentimental value." Her eyes strayed to my hand. "Can . . . can I have my handkerchief?"

Seeing no reason to keep it, I removed the contents. "Sure."

"Thank you."

Frankie dropped onto the edge of the bed, studying the picture. "So this is Ginny's son." His fingers caressed the glass. "I can see her in his smile."

"You're right." Folding the handkerchief, Esther shifted in her chair. "I've often thought so, too."

Afternoon sunlight trickled through the blinds onto the floor tiles. A voice over the intercom announced Miss Patty was warming up the piano in the activity room for the sing-along.

Memories seemed to add a somber hue to the room.

After a while, Esther said, "I . . . I don't have anything else to say." She propelled her wheelchair backward. "I want to go to the sing-along. Frankie, put my picture of Stephen down now, please."

Hands trembling, Frankie stood and replaced the picture. "Yeah, it's time to go."

Snippets of our conversation ricocheted in my mind. Esther knew about one of the secret drawers. Maybe . . . "Esther, how many secret drawers are in the jewelry box?"

With the candy bar in hand, Esther propelled herself to the door. "Just the one where you found the locket." She turned left without a backward glance.

I shrugged. That idea didn't get very far.

Frankie and I turned right. I looped my arm through his, and we stopped in the lobby. His unsteady gait and shallow breathing concerned me.

"Let's sit a minute, Frankie." Leading him to a sofa, he plopped next to me. "So, what do you think about all she told us? Heavy isn't it?"

He only nodded.

"Do we have any legal obligation to tell the Summerland-Hayes family they have another branch of relatives? After all, sibling relationships can be proven with DNA. And Esther could face prosecution for switching—"

Frankie rested against my shoulder, head bowed.

"Frankie," I turned to him.

He raised a frail, shaking hand, and gasped, "I . . . I can't breathe."

His body slumped forward.

CHAPTER SEVENTEEN

"Do you want to come with me to visit Nate?" I tried to keep a positive tone as I approached Julia in the living room.

She patted her perfect chignon. "Sure. Any idea when he'll be allowed home?"

"Perhaps the doctor will have news today."

I entered the office and kissed Tom as he worked at the computer. He had to forgo the grandson visit to prepare for his presentations the following day in Austin.

During the hour-long drive, the tension in the car reached saturation point by the time I parked at the hospital. Julia never uttered a word of criticism on my driving, but her body language spoke a tome.

She did, however, criticize Joey for spending too little time with us. After he visited Mike and Teresa the previous day, he'd stayed with us an hour. I'd relished the sight of my youngest son gushing over his experience in San Salvador. He'd accepted the Lord as Savior as a young teen, but his week helping build and repair homes and a school, teaching Bible classes, and interacting with people in poverty, had profoundly affected him. I could see the change in his eyes. I could hear it in his voice. It shone out of his soul.

So when his grandmother whined about her number two grandson staying a little bitty hour, I wanted to throw her out the window. Or at least roll it down so the wind would dislodge her perfect platinum hair, and blow it all over her perfectly made-up face.

I clenched my jaw. *Your claws are showing*. The kudos Julia earned earlier by her generosity to Nate had long ceased to matter.

Wearing a dove gray pant suit accessorized by a double row of pearls, Julia slid her arm through mine as we waltzed down the hospital corridor. "Let's see if they've removed the wires from that baby. I want to see his face."

Colors of Deceit

We rode the elevator to the NICU in silence. I dusted imaginary lint off my blue jeans and tangerine T-shirt. Long ago, I gave up competing with Julia's style. Even if she condescended to don blue jeans—which I had never seen her wear in the twenty-five years I'd known her—she'd be exotic. If I wore a fashionable pant suit, I'd look as ridiculous as a dressed-up Brutus.

Student nurses were touring the NICU. Our ten-minute wait crawled by, each agonizing second longer than the last. When allowed in to see Nate, I visited first. He did have fewer wires and probes, and his little cap had been removed. Dark tufts of hair lay flattened on his tiny head. While I cooed in fascination, his eyelids fluttered open revealing chocolate irises. His skin tone was a good solid olive. I could just eat him up. Of course, Julia would be pleased. She'd shown great interest in his coloring, and now would be able to see more of his infant body.

Nate's little face was about the same as the last time I'd seen him. A good sign, I thought, indicating, to me at least, no increase in swelling. Questions to the nurse produced no definitive answer about his discharge date. My arms ached to hold my little grandson, but I forced myself to be content touching his cheek and stroking his shoulder.

While Julia took her turn, I stood by the window, ruminating on why she was concerned over Nate's hair color. I knew little about genetics, but it seemed obvious Mike and Teresa's child would have dark hair, and a good chance he'd have brown eyes. As for skin color, Teresa had olive tones like me, but Mike was lighter, almost as fair as Tom. What did it matter anyway?

I thought back to the births of Mike and Joey. Julia was overjoyed Mike had Tom's coloring, even the reddish tint to his brown hair, and his blue eyes. But then along came Joey. José. Little did we know when we named our sons that Tom would give the one who favored him his Scottish ancestry names, and I'd choose Hispanic names for the son who inherited my family's looks.

It could all be in my head, but I always thought Julia favored Mike over Joey. Mike, her *number one grandson*. Should being the number two grandson deserve second-class treatment?

Could Julia's obvious preference for Mike be because Joey resembled my ancestors? And now another generation would face the same fate.

This apparent favoritism bothered me all these years. I needed to end it now.

As Julia left the NICU, I wheeled around, determined to have a showdown.

She sauntered into the waiting room, a smile daring to crinkle the delicate skin at the corners of her eyes. "I spoke to the doctor."

Of course she did. There was no doctor in sight when I visited Nate.

"She says Nate may go home Wednesday."

"That's wonderful." Were my teeth clenched when I spoke?

"I can't wait to hold my number one great-grandson."

Blood thumped in my head as my blood pressure rose. It was now or never. "Julia, about that . . . that term you use."

"What term?"

"Number one—"

"Oh, that. Don't mind me."

"But I do mind. Come. Let's get some coffee." I punched the elevator button.

Peering at me from her lofty height advantage, even her voice sounded superior. "What is it? What have I done?"

The doors closed on the six passengers. I shook my head and refused to engage in conversation until we were alone.

Once secluded in a corner of the cafeteria with steaming lattes in front of us, I swallowed my anxiety and chose my words with care. "Please don't call Nate your number one great-grandson. You may not know it, but using number one and number two grandson for Mike and Joey is extremely upsetting to me. And I think . . . demeaning."

Julia gulped. "I beg your pardon? They've never said anything about their nicknames."

The boys had objected over the years, but Julia was right, they had never confronted her. Should I drop the subject to keep the peace? No.

"They have broached the subject with me, especially Joey."

"I didn't mean to offend. I thought it was kind of cute, that's all."

"That's not how it comes across." I'd taken the bull by the long, pointy horns and hadn't been gored yet. My courage expanded. I had to include another point of contention. "Especially when accompanied by outward signs of favoritism." I braced for the rampage.

Julia banged her cup on the table. Liquid sloshed out. She leaned back in the green plastic chair.

Here it comes.

"What do you mean by favoritism?"

Hands tightly gripping my cup, I opened the flood gates. Words gushed out. "Mike has received more expensive birthday and Christmas gifts than Joey. When we all lived in San Antonio, you attended many of Mike's Little League games, but often had an excuse when it came time for Joey's soccer games. While the kids were young, you'd hold Mike, but seldom Joey. You'd—"

"Joey was so fidgety."

Ignoring the nugget of truth in her last statement, I swirled the last of the coffee in my cup and swallowed it. On a roll, I couldn't stop. "I've thought long and hard on this topic since you first inquired about Nate's coloring. If you prefer Mike over Joey, that's fine, but please stop showing it. Please don't show your preference in front of Nate, either. If your opinion of my boys has something to do with the color of their skin, or what nationality they favor, then—"

Her jaw dropped open. "Maricella, how dare you insinuate I'm prejudiced!"

My eyebrows shot up, and I stared at her. Perfectly coiffed. Perfectly dressed. Perfectly outraged.

"Julia, you opened this can of worms, not me." Had I permanently offended my mother-in-law? I knew I should quit, but the anger bubbled up from deep within me and had to find release. "I won't allow you to perpetuate the same prejudice on another generation. I should have stood up earlier to defend my sons. Both my sons. Now I will defend Nate. He is ours—born of Hispanic mother, Hispanic-Scottish father. Accept him for what he is. Black, brown, white or . . . or purple-polka-dotted. He's our *first* grandson, our *oldest* grandson. Please don't call him *number one*."

Whew! After my rant, my chest heaved. Where was the relief I expected? Instead, I cringed as I recalled my words. And now I had to face the consequences of my foolhardy utterances.

Julia's peach-tinted lips formed a line so straight I envisioned an arrow tip on one end. She moved in the chair raising her eyes a fraction above mine. "I don't know what you're talking about. I . . . love both my grandsons the same. But Joey is . . . is different."

I couldn't argue that point. Their personalities were polar opposites. Mike was easy going and compliant, whereas Joey voiced his opinion at every turn. But that didn't excuse Julia's preferential treatment.

With her as my captive audience—at least she hadn't stormed out of the cafeteria—I continued with the suspicion that really bothered me. I deliberately softened my tone, hoping that I wouldn't come across as arrogant and overbearing. "What about when the boys were born? You were more curious about their skin color, hair color, eye color, than their health. And now the same thing with Nate. Why, Julia? I don't understand."

"I'm a little curious." One shoulder hiked slightly under the gray linen. "I want to know who he looks like. He is my num—my first great-grandson." Julia toyed with her cup. "That's the only reason."

Her gaze dropped under my scrutiny. What more could I say? She'd answered my questions and accusations. She knew my concerns, and she knew I was displeased with her treatment of my sons, deliberate or not.

As I evaluated the situation, I considered my attitude and behavior over the years. Had I been too thin-skinned, imagining criticisms where there were none? Taking offense when none was intended?

I knew I had to accept part of the blame, but in reaching this conclusion, Julia seemed to lose some of her hold over me. The formidable mother-in-law behind the Wizard of Oz's curtain was a woman like me after all. Not an unstained, faultless Christian, but a struggling woman, making mistakes.

I blinked. I had numerous faults, and had been forgiven much. I needed to work on forgiving her.

She raised her head. Frown lines marred her forehead.

Before facing Tom, I had to initiate a truce.

"Julia, I'm sorry if I offended you. I appreciate all you and Doug have done for us and don't want to damage our relationship. The things I said . . . they've been on my heart for a long time. I hope you understand why I had to say them." I lay my hand on the table, palm up. "Can we still be friends?"

Moving her cup aside, she drummed her pink acrylic nails on the table. The tap-tap-tap reverberated in my head like hammer blows on my coffin. Had I alienated her completely? How would I ever explain this to Tom?

But she silenced her fingers and took my hand. "Yes. Friends. I . . . I'll try to let Joey—"

"He loves you, you know. You're the only grandparent he has."

With a nod, she released my hand and retrieved her purse from the back of the chair. "I know. I'm sorry you thought those awful things about me."

The breath I'd been holding at bay escaped in a slow whoosh. I scooted the chair back. "Then, let's go home." My words squeaked out.

I couldn't believe I'd survived a confrontation with Julia.

My imagination ran in circles on the drive home. Julia initiated a benign topic of conversation. I participated, but expected the backlash. When it didn't come, I assumed Julia meant what she'd said in the hospital café. Or else she was waiting to tell Tom about my accusations.

But I didn't imagine the difference in her attitude toward me. Her tone held more respect, and her criticisms were minimal. If I'd stood up to her sooner, would it have improved my relationship with her long ago?

After parking in the garage, Julia entered the house, and my cell phone rang. *Great. Would she blab to Tom?* But I had to answer Frankie's call.

"Hi, Frankie. How are you this morning?"

"As fit as a fiddle. An old, worn out fiddle with sprung strings and a frayed bow, that is."

The image brought out a chuckle. "Did you stay long in the ER?"

The nursing home staff had attended to him immediately, and then I'd called his friends who transported him to the emergency room.

"No. About three hours. I was home by midnight. Doc concluded I was suffering from anxiety. Ha, ha. And I hadn't eaten all day 'cause I was worried about seeing Esther."

"That's understandable." Once inside the house, I headed to the bedroom.

"And silly me, I'd forgotten to take my medication."

"Silly indeed, but I'm glad to hear you're home—or at least not in the hospital."

I told him about visiting Nate, and shared some aspects of my conversation with Julia.

"I guess you and I have a different outlook. You know how this skin color thing affected my family," he said.

"Frankie, before you leave for Tennessee, do you want to meet any of Ginny's family? Her grandchildren, great-grandchildren?"

I dropped my purse on the dresser and sat on the bed while waiting for his answer. His silence spoke volumes.

He exhaled a long breath. "No. No. I've had enough of that family. Just like Esther said, I've done fine without 'em and I don't need 'em now."

"You sure?" Kicking off my shoes, I rested against the pillows. "This may be your last chance?"

"I'm sure. The last time I spoke to Ginny was two years before she died. I wanted to visit, but she wouldn't let me. Even after all those years, she wouldn't see me. And you know her sister Elisabeth deserted the family and moved to Houston." Frankie's pause emphasized his sorrow. "No, I don't want to meet the people who made Ginny feel like she had to forsake her brother."

"I understand."

Tom entered the bedroom and planted a kiss on my forehead. He sat next to me on the bed, and waited for me to conclude my conversation.

"Do you want the locket?"

A quivering sigh that sounded like a sob wafted to my ear. "Yes."

We made arrangement to meet next time I visited Kerrville, and I slipped the phone into my pocket.

Tom leaned closer. "Mama tells me Nate's coming home Wednesday."

My throat constricted with anxiety. I nodded. What else had Julia told him?

"You can be there when they arrive."

I worked Tuesdays and Thursdays for the Bandera School District and Spring Break was over. "Right. Alma, Lucia, and I can form a welcoming party."

"I have a surprise for you."

My husband's playful tone gave no indication he'd received an earful from his mother.

"What's that?"

"I made lunch." With a conspiratorial wink, he stood and offered me his hand. "Time to eat."

I'd been so focused on Frankie's call and worried over Julia's possible betrayal, I'd completely ignored the tantalizing aromas permeating the house.

Back in the kitchen, I set plates and silverware on the table. "Where's your mother?"

"I left her in the office."

I walked down the hall and called, "Julia, lunch is ready."

At the office door I halted in my tracks. Julia stood at the desk hunched over my notebook. "What are you doing?"

Bright pink infused her cheeks. "Nothing. Reading these notes. They're interesting." Quickly closing the notebook, she turned. "I'm starving." She brushed past me on her way to the kitchen.

My mouth gapped. Why had she been reading my notes on the jewelry box and the Summerland-Hayes family? I picked up the notebook and flipped through the pages. The book opened close to the front. Odd. Every time I flipped the book, it opened to the same spot. I lay the book flat on the desk. Why here?

Then I noticed the tell-tale jagged pieces of paper in the seam. A sheet had been ripped out. I studied the pages before and after. The family tree. The Summerland-Hayes family tree was missing.

Had Julia removed it?

CHAPTER EIGHTEEN

While munching on a piece of garlic toast, I stared at Julia across the table. Her toast, cut into bite-sized pieces, lay on her side plate. Tom seemed unaware of the undercurrent of hostility. He sat between us at the round kitchen table, chatting away.

Julia had torn the page from my notebook. She knew I knew. Her behavior gave it away.

With my eyes glued to her innocent expression, I lifted a forkful of lasagna to my mouth. She made a show of spearing lettuce, focusing on her salad bowl. Tom stood and carried his plate to the counter for a second helping.

I whispered, "Why'd you take that page?"

Julia kept eating.

"I know you removed it, Julia." I remembered her admonishing Tom to stop my research. "Why don't you want me to investigate the Summerland-Hayes family?"

Before answering, she arranged her fork carefully on the plate, and took a deliberate sip of iced tea. Her eyes did not meet mine. "I . . . I don't know what you're talking about." She wiped her mouth on her napkin. "Tom." This time her voice was loud and dripping saccharine sweetness.

"Yes, Mother?" Tom returned to the table.

"Did I tell you I'll be leaving in the morning?"

"So soon?" he asked, his expression genuine with disappointment.

Not soon enough. What happened to our truce forged at the hospital? Maybe I had been right about her all along. I lay my fork across my plate. Tension chugged up and down my throat, threatening to send my lasagna on a return visit.

I sloshed the tea in my glass while waiting for Tom to finish his second helping. Then we cleared the table. He stacked plates and silverware. Julia gathered glasses and napkins, and carried them to the counter.

"Here you go, Maricella. I can do the dishes."

Did I imagine the sugar coating on her words? "No, thank you, Julia. I'll have the dishwasher loaded in no time." Was this her way of apologizing?

"In that case I'll take a little nap." She planted a kiss on Tom's cheek and sauntered out of the kitchen.

"Good idea, Julia." Rinsing off a plate, I pursed my lips. With her safe in her room, I could chomp my anger into more manageable bits.

"I have a little more work to do." After topping off his glass of tea, Tom asked over his shoulder, "Do you need anything from the office, sweetheart?"

My mind in a whirl, I dried my hands and followed Tom down the hall. "Only this." I grabbed my notebook and turned, accidently kicking the trash can under the desk.

A wadded piece of lined note paper rolled out. I picked it up. Tom didn't use note paper. As I smoothed a corner, I recognized it—the Summerland-Hayes family tree.

"What's that?" Tom scooted the chair to the desk.

"It's a page from my notebook." I couldn't prove Julia had torn it out, and right now I didn't want to involve Tom in my suspicions.

Shoving the paper into my pocket, I returned to the sink and rinsed away tomato and cheese residue from the plates. But my mind wasn't on washing dishes. No. Over and over, I argued both sides of the precarious line between truth and not-truth. For years I'd lied to my family about my past, but I'd asked for and received their forgiveness.

Now Julia was lying to me. I hated how it made me feel inside, all worthless and angry. But I'd subjected Tom to my lies for over twenty years. He loved me anyway. Could I still love Julia although she lied about removing the page from my notebook? I'd always thought she and Doug were above reproach. Doug was, for sure.

I'm not saying that since I'd given my life to the Lord I was perfect, but I did work on the lying part. I tried to tell the truth. None of the Christian walk came naturally, but I learned how to trust in the Lord's grace for when I faltered.

But here was someone I'd admired in a larger-than-life sort of way and she lied to my face. When I had spiritual problems or questions, I'd present them to Tom, but how could I tell him his mother had torn a page out of my notebook and then lied about it?

With the dishwasher running, I carried my notebook outside to the back porch and smoothed out the scrunched up piece of paper. I copied the family tree onto a new sheet. March afternoon breezes ruffled hair across my face. I re-formed the ponytail to catch the errant strands, and gazed at the hills in the distance. The gurgling water splashing over the waterfall into the fishpond soothed the gnawing at my soul long enough for me to admit I had to forgive Julia.

Whatever reason she had for taking the page, and for trying to discourage my research into the Summerland-Hayes family, I needed to have a forgiving spirit. Remembering Daniel Ward's sermon on the four hundred-ninety spirit pricked my conscience. He based the lesson on a passage from the Gospel of Matthew, where Jesus said we must forgive seventy times seven, a symbolic number. I know the number of times I'd been forgiven was way up there. How could I stop at once or twice when someone wronged me?

But it was hard. *Please, Lord, help me to forgive Julia. Help me to understand her, to love and accept her.*

A thunder-clap jolted me from my silent communication with God. Gusts of damp wind swirled around me. I picked up Brutus and my notebook and hurried inside. Julia stood at the counter, head bowed over a mug of hot tea as if intentionally avoiding eye contact.

"Have a nice nap?" Brutus jumped out of my arms and skirted around Julia heading to his water bowl. I held the notebook to my chest.

Rubbing her temples, she closed her eyes for a second. "Yes, thanks, but I . . . I have a headache. I'll take my tea to the bedroom and stay a little longer in the quiet."

So you won't have to own up to the truth? I bit my lip. *Forgive. Let it go.*

"Sorry to hear that. Can I get you some Tylenol or something?"

"I have my prescription." Julia carried her tea mug to her room, turned, and a hint of a smile touched her lips. It even reached her eyes for a brief second. "Thanks anyway." The door closed behind her.

I collapsed against the counter. Electricity from the lightning outside seemed to have sparked between us. But fireworks hadn't erupted. *Thank you, Lord.*

A shudder fluttered through me. What just happened? Nothing I did. The Lord must have had a hand in softening the situation.

"Chella." Tom called from the office. "Can you come in here a sec?"

"What's wrong?" Entering the office, I gave Tom's shoulder a squeeze.

"Read over this section, please." He pointed to the computer screen. "It needs revising."

"Sure." We traded places and I worked on his presentation.

After a while, Julia emerged from her self-imposed exile, and offered to take us to supper in San Antonio. Since it was her last night she wanted to treat us.

We agreed to her suggestion, and enjoyed a meal at the Ranchlands Steak House. The Summerland-Hayes family and my notebook were never mentioned.

With Tom leaving at five o'clock the next morning for his Austin-and-beyond trip, Julia driving to Dallas, and me returning to work, we retired early.

During my lunch break at school the following day, I called Teresa. She reported no change in Nate's status. Her father and older sister, Alma Rose, had returned to Santa Fe, leaving her mother and Lucia to help with household chores, and spoiling the new mama. When I inquired after Mike and his work at the camp, Teresa's tone took on a reticent quality.

"He's fine. They had a big meeting yesterday and, um, his job description might change."

"Oh." I closed my lunch bag. "How exactly?"

"Not sure. The church leaders have another planning session this afternoon. I'm glad Mama and Lucia are here. I always thought my faith could sustain me through anything, but with Nate's uncertain medical condition, and now the doubt thrown at Mike's ability—"

"Doubt?"

"I shouldn't have mentioned it. I'm sorry. We don't want you to worry."

Too late. Mama bear didn't like criticism of her cub, but I swallowed the torrent of questions. "I know you and Mike can handle it. Perhaps we can talk tomorrow. I'll be there when you bring Nate home. Hope that's all right?"

"Of course. You don't have to ask. I'm looking forward to seeing you then."

I slid the phone into my pocket and cleaned off the table in the teacher's lounge. Forcing thoughts of Mike and his job to the back of my mind, I located the classroom for my next student, a second grader with spina bifida who also had severe hearing loss. I'd been learning sign language and how to finger spell in order to communicate with her and the other hearing impaired student on my caseload. After a brief conversation with her, I adjusted her leg braces, and we worked on adding a new set of exercises to her regime. Meetings with parents and staff filled up the rest of the school day.

On the way home, I stopped at Norm's. I hadn't heard from him since his phone call last week. Sylvester's bark greeted my approach to the workshop.

Raising his leathered face, Norm grinned. "Howdy. Long time, no see."

"Mother-in-law's been visiting." He knew of my tenuous relationship with her.

He grimaced. "And you survived?"

"The jury's still out. We had words." Tamping down memories of Julia and my notebook page, I removed my sunglasses. "But I have good news. Nate's coming home tomorrow. Is the jewelry box ready? I'd like to take it to Teresa."

After brushing sawdust off his blue jeans, Norm took the cigar out of his mouth. "Almost. I can have it ready by Thursday. This other job's taking longer than I thought."

"Thursday'll be fine. I'll stop by after school, but please keep it locked up. I'm not sure who's after it."

The cigar back between his teeth, he picked up a wood plane, and tested the blade. "Sure thing, Mrs. Mac. See you then."

With a good-bye nod to Norm, I patted Sylvester on the head and glanced in the corner. The shotgun stood amid the lumber. At least I knew Norm would keep the jewelry box safe. As I drove the last half-mile home, my mind traveled back to the intruder. He'd been quiet since the closet incident at the hospital. But I'd been surrounded by people the whole time. Maybe he couldn't get close. That is until now. I'd be alone tonight.

Goose bumps pin-pricked my arms. I drove into the garage and closed the door before leaving the safety of the car. Brutus bounded up and down like a kid on a trampoline. I picked him up and scurried inside. Alarm set, cell phone ready, but I still didn't feel safe. Could I call Norm and ask to borrow Sylvester? Or his shotgun?

My back glued to the wall, I closed my eyes and prayed. *Keep me safe, please, Lord. Keep me safe.*

Brutus pawing at my legs forced me to face reality. I had to feed him, find something in the refrigerator to eat. Most important of all, I had to breathe.

I dumped my purse and school bag on the counter, entered the office, and turned on the computer. Checking e-mail would divert my thoughts and unravel the knots in my gut. Settle the nerves.

Answering friends and colleagues diverted my mind in a positive direction. Responding to Joey put a song in my soul. I asked when he and I could meet during the week. Seems his brief visit Sunday hadn't satisfied my curiosity, especially when he mentioned Jade, a girl who'd been on the trip with him. Her name came up several times. Already, I wanted to meet this Jade.

Reading Mike's somber message, however, clouded the room. A man from Durban Street Church in Houston had voiced concerns about Mike's suitability for the job. He approved everything on paper, but after meeting Mike and Teresa Sunday before last, had changed his mind. The church in Brooder hired Mike, leaving the Houston man with no say in the decision, but he was a big cheese, and in the recent meeting had made his opinion known. Mike said the man's mean-spirited attitude spread like a cancer in the group, and others picked up on it.

Levelheaded Mike appeared to have handled himself maturely, but the hurt came through his written words. And his Mama was hopping mad. After a brief reply to Mike—lest I say something I'd regret—I stormed out of the office and with the intention of taking a shower.

My cell phone rang, and I tromped back to the kitchen to answer it.

"Hey, Joey. I just e-mailed you."

"Hi, Mama. I'll check that later, but right now I have a real big favor to ask. I know it's kinda late, but I need a research project from last semester that I have in the storeroom. It's for class tomorrow."

I pulled the phone from my ear and stared at it. What did he say? "Joey—"

"I know it's short notice, but we were only given the assignment today, and I've been stuck at work all afternoon."

Sinking into a kitchen chair, I clenched my teeth, and silently counted to ten.

"Mama, are you there?"

With deliberate calmness, I answered, "Yes, José."

"I know what you're going to say. I always put things off, but, seriously, Mama, this isn't my fault."

It never is, Joey. Joey, ever the procrastinator.

"What do you need?"

Relief seeped through his words as he described a project he'd completed the previous semester. He wanted to incorporate it into a current assignment. "I don't get off work until eight, and then I still have to complete the assignment." A long moment of silence. "Please, Mama."

Massaging my temples with thumb and index finger, I groaned. "Okay, *mijo*. Where will I find it?"

After describing the box, his voice took on a contrite tone. "Thanks, Mama. I'll meet you in the parking lot."

Reminded of the long hours Joey worked at the university bookstore, I felt a hint of remorse at my initial aggravation. "Sure. I'll text you when I arrive."

I deactivated the alarm and dashed out to the storeroom. The binder was exactly where Joey indicated. I returned to the house, collected my purse and a light jacket, and flipped on the outside floodlights before leaving.

The RV in front of me crawled along the two-lane country road that led to the interstate. The pavement which curved up and around the hills, offered scant opportunities to pass slow moving vehicles. A yellow sports car appeared in my rearview mirror, but kept its distance. Odd. Usually cars traveled close together behind a slow vehicle to take advantage of the infrequent passing lanes. Creepy little bugs of unease scurried across my scalp.

Once on the interstate into San Antonio, I deliberately stayed under the speed limit while keeping an eye on the sports car. Two wide black stripes ran up the middle of the hood. I could see them clearly because the car didn't fall back very far even when I sped up.

He was following me. Paranoia set in.

Adrenalin-heated blood filled my brain and shot through my body like electricity.

I switched lanes. So did he. He kept pace, but far enough away that I couldn't read a license plate number or identify the make of car.

My chest heaved as I sucked in air to ward off a faint. I had to do something. Stop for gasoline. That made sense.

Blinker on, I zoomed off at the next exit. If the yellow car exited, I'd know he was following me.

He didn't.

At the gas station, I pumped ten gallons while scanning the surroundings for a yellow sports car. None in sight.

Just as I inserted the key into the ignition, my phone jingled. I'd received a text. Joey explained he found a colleague to take over his shift, and suggested we meet at Carl's Diner, a restaurant halfway between the university and our house, now a few miles from my location.

Back on the interstate, I concentrated on the evening traffic in front of me, but my eyes darted back and forth, searching behind me every couple of seconds.

No yellow sports car. My fists relaxed on the steering wheel. Breathing returned to near normal.

A clump of vehicles ahead, red taillights, we all slowed.

Then I saw it. A yellow sports car with two black stripes up the hood.

Right behind me.

CHAPTER NINETEEN

How did it get there?

Knuckles ready to pop through my skin, I turned the steering wheel and veered into the next lane. The car followed. He echoed every move I made. No doubt now. I was being followed.

Should I meet Joey? Head to a police station? Overhead signs indicated I had two miles to my exit. Two miles to devise a plan.

Up ahead vehicles slowed behind a wide load carrier in the right lane. I zipped into the middle lane without using my blinker. The yellow car couldn't squeeze in behind me. I sped up and popped over into the left lane. This zigzag driving kept me on the edge of my seat. I veered around vehicles as if I'd never used a blinker before. How many traffic laws had I broken? Invincible, I ignored the nervous churning in my gut.

I kept changing lanes until I veered in front of the wide load carrier. A glance in the rearview mirror revealed the yellow car five or six vehicles behind me. I shot off at my exit which dipped down an incline, exceeding the speed limit, I'm sure, and tore along the access road.

Hurry, hurry. I swerved into the diner's parking lot and screeched to a stop next to a pickup truck which blocked the view of my car from the road. After I'd been there a minute or two without seeing the yellow sports car, my gorilla grip on the steering wheel eased.

I exhaled, and gnawed my bottom lip. Who would follow me and why? Did the relentless pursuit by the driver have something to do with the jewelry box?

Closing my eyes, I forced visions of yellow sports cars out of my head. If Tom had seen me moments ago, he would've thought I'd lost my mind.

I shrugged off the suspicions and picked up Joey's binder. Maybe it was my imagination. Why would a man follow me into San Antonio? With a quick glance over my shoulder, I hurried into the diner.

Joey greeted me with a hug and a profusion of gratitude.

Binder in hand, he said, "Thanks, Mama. You don't know how much I appreciate this." His words rang with sincerity as he pulled out the orange vinyl chair.

I removed my jacket before sitting. The public setting erased some of my jitters. "Okay, *mijo*. Reward me with a good grade on this project." Even to my ears my voice sounded tremulous.

His grin softened his angular features which stirred memories of his grandfather. Joey, taller than Mike by four inches, reminded me of my father as a young man. Before the murder.

My soul ached.

"I will." Joey removed menus from the stand to his left and slid one to me. "Mama, are you all right? You're kinda pale and—"

"Let's order then I'll tell you."

His dark wavy hair flopped over his forehead. Brushing it aside, he said, "Okay."

The waitress jotted down our order, and moments later brought glasses of iced tea.

Joey knew the gist of the jewelry box story. I filled in the gaps, ending with the possibility of a car following me.

I don't know how, but Joey's brown eyes took on a darker hue. Angry lines creased his brow. "Mama, this doesn't sound good. When did you first see the car?"

"Just a mile or two after I left home. I checked my rearview mirror frequently when the RV slowed me down."

With his frown frozen in place, Joey slipped off his black leather jacket, and then threw it over the back of the chair. "Do you know the make of the car?"

I squinted into my glass of tea trying to recall details from quick glimpses into the rearview mirror. "Wider than a Mustang, broad grill. And it had two black stripes up the hood. Possibly a Chevy Camaro."

When the boys were young, we had contests as we traveled to see who could identify the most cars. Sometimes I won. But since they no longer rode with me, my skills had deteriorated.

"Did it have the logo in the middle of the grill?"

Another memory check. "Um, yes, it did."

"Okay then, a Camaro."

My baby was so concerned, but what good would knowing the make of car do me? "Joey—"

"Mama, I don't like this."

"But . . . but he didn't take the exit when I did." I was beginning to regret telling Joey about the car.

"He could have doubled back."

Why did he have to say that?

The waitress set burgers, a basket of fries and onion rings, and extra napkins on the table. I could feel my arteries clogging as I looked over the food.

"Will there be anything else?" she asked.

We shook our heads.

"Y'all enjoy."

"Let's do as she says. Enjoy and forget the car. Okay?" I placed a napkin on my lap.

Joey chomped into his burger, but it took a while for the frown lines on his brow to clear.

Tables filled around us. We chatted about Nate, and Tom's possible promotion, but Joey couldn't leave the car alone.

"Are you going to tell Daddy about being followed?" He tore an onion ring apart, and stuffed half into his mouth.

"Yes. I promised I'd never lie again. He's not going to like it."

"Don't blame him. That jewelry box must be cursed." His white teeth flashed through his grin. "Sorry, I didn't mean that."

"Don't worry. I've thought the same thing."

"Do you still have it?"

After wiping my mouth, I wadded up the paper napkin. "No. Norm has it. He hasn't finished the repairs."

We continued to eat in silence, enjoying the music, but then Joey mentioned his earlier e-mail, and my ears perked up.

"This Jade, did you work with her in San Salvador?"

"Yeah. She's been there before."

"I see." Squirting ketchup onto a mound of fries, I eyed my son. "I'd like to meet her."

"Mama, we're not dating."

Oops. Had I read too much into his comments? "Sorry. Didn't mean to imply anything. Why don't you bring your mission group over for a meal? You can include her in the invite."

He wiped his mouth, then swallowed a long drink of tea. "I'll think about it." The waitress refilled his glass, and he stirred sugar into it. "But she goes by J."

"J-A-Y?"

"No, just J."

A girl named Jade who goes by J. I sat back nibbling fries while Joey finished his burger. He might not be dating J, but the way he said her name rang with a special affection, a serious note. He had girlfriends in the past. Some we approved of. Some we were glad to never see again. But I sensed a subtle difference in the way he talked about this one. I couldn't wait to meet her. Jade conjured up an exotic woman from the Far East. I pictured her tall, elegant, with straight black hair. Joey and J had a nice ring.

"Mama. Mama."

His touch on my hand returned me to Carl's. "Sorry, I was—"

"Be right back. There's a spot of ketchup on my shirt. I need to dab it with cold water before it stains." Joey pointed to his sleeve, and headed to the restroom.

Tingling from head to toe in anticipation of another daughter-in-law, I folded my arms. Aah, the joys of new love.

More Than a Memory by Garth Brooks pulsed the air, almost drowning out my thoughts of when Mike told us about Teresa. Humming, I glanced around the crowded diner and spotted a man hunched over his drink at the next table. Where had I seen shaggy, gray hair like that before? The wig on the man who stabbed A. J.? A shard of hot fear shot through me. Could this be the same man?

The image of a knife held to Connie's throat sent my hand to guard my own. *Joey, please hurry.* The man raised his head a fraction, but in the ambient light I couldn't see his face. My gaze dropped to his feet. Was he wearing cowboy boots? The muted shadows under the table hid his footwear from view.

Joey returned to the table. "Ready, Mama?"

I yanked him into his chair and whispered, "See that guy over there?" I pointed to my left. "I think he's the man who stabbed A. J."

As Joey stood, a scowl distorted his features.

"No, Joey. Don't."

He leaned over the table and lowered his voice. "But, Mama, if he is the murderer, we can have him arrested. If not, no harm done."

"Please don't do anything wild." I scooted back from the table. "Let's call the cops."

The music ended, and customer conversation intensified. The man extracted a bill from his wallet, deposited it next to his check, and then slid out of his chair.

Before I could stop Joey, he strode to the stranger's table. "Hey, mister. Can I—?"

The man shoved Joey and bolted for the door.

Without a backward glance, Joey charged after him.

The waitress hollered, "Wait, you haven't paid."

My eyes on the door, I opened my purse and threw three ten dollar bills on the table. "Keep the change." Hoping it was enough, I plucked our jackets off of the chairs and bolted outside.

Joey seemed to have the advantage as he chased the man through the crowded, parking lot. He almost caught up with him but then he tripped over something I couldn't see. By the time he scrambled up, his foe was scaling the chain-link fence at the end of the property. Joey clawed at the man's feet, but a well-placed kick to the face sent him reeling, and the stranger disappeared into a dark overgrown ditch beyond the fence.

My heart in my throat, I ran to Joey's side. "Are you okay?"

I examined his face.

"I'll be fine, Mama. I'll ice it at home."

"You sure?" I touched his cheek lightly. "Joey, Joey." Gathering him in my arms, I tried not to dwell on what could have happened.

His chin rested on the top of my head while he held me.

"Did you get a look at his face? Could you identify him?"

Joey took my arm, and we walked back to the parking lot. "Uh-uh. I was too angry. All I recall is shaggy gray hair. Weird. It didn't seem to match his young face."

"I'm sure it was a wig."

"Yeah, that makes sense. Up close, it didn't look real. He was tall. That's all I can remember."

"Did he say anything?"

"Nope."

Joey pointed to the diner. "I need my jacket."

"I have it, and I already paid the bill." I separated the jackets and handed him the black leather.

"Thanks."

As we headed to my vehicle, I searched the parking lot and surrounding area for a yellow sports car. If that man was the one who stabbed A. J., he could have followed me from Hanson Ridge. I swallowed over what felt like dry rocks in my throat and shivered as fear knotted in my stomach.

Joey must have sensed my unease. "Mama, what is it? You're all pale again." His arm acted like a security blanket draped across my shoulders.

"That man could have been in the yellow car."

I pressed the remote, and Joey opened my door.

"I'm going to follow you home. No arguing, okay?"

"I'd appreciate that."

The headlights of Joey's Mustang in my rearview mirror bolstered my confidence. I made it home without a case of indigestion. He offered to spend the night, but since he had an early class, I made him leave. After all, he still had to complete a project with the materials I gave him.

Safe in the house with the alarm set, I cuddled Brutus. "What would you say if we got a big dog?"

He looked at me with soft brown eyes and droopy ears as if to say he didn't like the idea at all. Although Brutus was small, I felt relatively safe. Having Joey see me home and check the house before leaving me alone helped a lot, too.

Swamped with exhaustion, I watched the evening TV news, with half my brain focused on everything but the war overseas. Later, I turned off the TV and headed to the office. One more e-mail check. Nothing of vital importance. The messages could wait until morning for replies.

As I passed the guest bedroom, I stopped and opened the door. Julia, the perfect guest, had stripped the bed and placed the used, folded linen on the chair. Propped on the dresser stood an envelope. Addressed to me.

CHAPTER TWENTY

Fear of being alone flew out the window. What could Julia possibly want to say to me? Nothing good, for sure.

I carried the cream envelope into the living room where I melted into my recliner and tucked my legs under my robe. Fingers shaking like leaves in a storm, I tore open the envelope, exposing a single sheet of embossed monogrammed paper. Who travels with personalized stationery?

Julia received an *A* in penmanship, no doubt. Perfectly formed loops and ovals covered the page.

Dear Maricella,

Words fail me. I don't know how I can explain my actions, so I won't even try. One day maybe I will be able to, but not now.

I tore the page from your book. I'm sorry I lied, but I couldn't talk about it in front of Thomas. Please understand that I am sorry.

As for Michael and José, I will do better. I've examined my heart and I think because Mike looked like his daddy did as a baby, I treated him differently. I didn't realize it showed, but obviously it did. You noticed. I'm sorry if I hurt Joey. I will apologize to him. I offer no excuses—there are none.

And I will be a good great-grandmother to Nathaniel. I will explain my actions. One day. I promise.

Regards,
Julia

The page fluttered out of my fingers to the floor. "Wow, Julia. Short and sweet, but it says so much."

Ready to delve between the lines, I picked up the letter and reread it. I puzzled over what possible explanation she could ever produce to justify interfering in my investigation of the Summerland-Hayes family. And Joey. He'd never discussed her attitude much, but occasionally in the past, a glint of resentment flared in his eyes when Grandmother couldn't attend a game, or sent a birthday card and gift but didn't come to his party. He acted tough and seemed to let minor insults run off his back like water off a slick raincoat. But a child, even a young teen, shouldn't have to make concessions for the behavior of his own grandmother.

Yes, Julia, you better apologize to José.

Brutus jumped onto my lap. I stroked his back, releasing pent up frustration in a long sigh. "Okay, poochy. Time for bed. But keep your ears open tonight."

After checking all the doors and windows again, I slid under the covers and forced visions of the intruder, ball caps, and yellow sports cars out of my mind. Eyes squeezed shut, I tried to concentrate on something pleasant and positive. Nate. Coming home tomorrow. I'd get to hold him. Cuddle him.

The shrill alarm clock penetrated my dream of being caught in the interwoven branches of an enormous tree labeled with names written in fancy calligraphy.

Rubbing my eyes, I giggled. "A family tree. I was in a family tree." Then a sobering thought crossed my mind. Would Julia send me that list of names?

Anticipation of the day's events spurred me to action. I swung my legs out of bed and opened the bedroom door. Brutus raised his head from his bean bag.

"So, we weren't disturbed by anyone. Thank you, God."

Wouldn't it be the best news ever if the intruder had given up his pursuit of the jewelry box?

Mike and Teresa didn't say what time they'd be home with Nate. I dressed and made an omelet for breakfast, talking to Joey on my cell phone between bites. He reported on the condition of his bruised cheek.

"I'm tough, Mama. Don't worry about me. Did you sleep okay?"

"Took a while, but yeah. Brutus kept me safe."

Joey's chuckle was music to my ears. "Big, mean Brutus. I'm picturing him keeping the bad guys away. Got to go. Class begins in fifteen minutes. *Adiós*."

I spent a half-hour tidying the house before setting off for Brooder, eyes peeled for yellow cars. I made it without seeing even one.

Lucia and Alma did not make the trip to San Antonio to pick up Nate. While waiting, Alma and I peeled vegetables, stirred sauces, and compared notes on the drama adult children brought to our lives.

At noon, Mike parked in the driveway. We hurried outside to welcome baby Nate. Mike extracted the carrier from the backseat, then opened the door for Teresa and offered her his hand. He escorted his family through the front door with a proud grin spread so wide he could have been auditioning for a toothpaste ad. Lucia and I deposited the bags in the living room.

Teresa settled on the sofa and removed the baby's blanket, holding him like a piece of the finest china ever produced. No wires or tubes obscured our view. His little hands fanned, then fisted, propping up his chin. A tiny bud of a mouth puckered, and his eyes fluttered, the left one able to open a mere fraction. He rooted to the right exposing the swollen, puffy side of his head, unchanged from what I remembered. The cyst must be about the same size.

"He's hungry," Teresa said.

"Can I feed him?" Holding out her hands, Lucia waited expectantly.

Mike picked up the baby bag from beside the sofa. "Better let us do it this first time. But you can hold him while Teresa and I prepare the formula."

Once Nate lay snug in Lucia's arms, she sat next to Alma. They showered him with oohs and aahs. I followed Mike and Teresa to the kitchen and observed the bottle preparation.

"Did I make the right decision not to breast feed, Chella?" Her voice caught, and she wiped a tear from her cheek.

"Mike and José survived on formula, as you can see."

"I know, but I—"

"Hush, my love. Don't second-guess yourself. You made the right decision for you." After kissing her cheek, Mike handed the warmed bottle to Teresa. "Come, let's feed our son."

Nate consumed his first meal at home with a rapt audience of two grandmothers, one aunt, Mama, and Papa. When he'd guzzled two-thirds of the bottle, we took turns burping him. What a sweet little bundle. Where did the newborn baby smell come from? It must be sent from heaven. Cuddling his little head on my shoulder, I bobbed up and down as I meandered through the living room, crooning a melody remembered from when I rocked my boys to sleep.

All too soon, I had to hand him back to Teresa. She changed his diaper and settled him in his crib while we reluctantly backed out of the room. We ate lunch almost in silence, with five pairs of ears trained for the faintest peep from the baby monitor.

Alma insisted on doing the dishes. Teresa and Lucia excused themselves and retreated to the bedroom. Seizing the opportunity, I motioned Mike to follow me outside with the intention of asking about his job. But he had other ideas.

"Mama, I'm worried."

Birds drinking from clear water in the birdbath scattered like bowling pins as we settled on the bench. "About your job?"

"No. Yes, but that's not what I need to talk to you about first. I'm worried about . . . the decisions I've made. About being a good provider. Do I have the strength to support Teresa as she adjusts to motherhood?" He rested his elbows on his knees, and covered his face with his hands. "I don't know if I can handle it all. I'm overwhelmed with guilt."

I slid my arm across his shoulders. "You've both been through some traumatic months. The roller coaster your emotions have ridden this past week alone would put Six Flags to shame."

His features somber, he straightened. "I know all of that in my head, but my heart doesn't agree."

"What are you feeling guilty about?"

One shoulder hiked a fraction. "Making this move. Changing jobs. Having a baby."

A lone mockingbird returned to the birdbath and eyed us as interlopers.

I lowered my voice so I wouldn't scare the bird away. "I know you, son. You are a man of strong faith. Didn't you and Teresa spend hours praying about these decisions? You both agreed that this is where God was leading you." I waited for his response, and when none came, continued. "Anxiety about being a new parent is nothing new. Ask your dad how he reacted after your birth. You will be a terrific father."

A lung-cleansing sigh escaped. Mike stretched his legs. "Thanks, Mama. I guess I needed to express my concerns out loud."

"You know Daddy and I will help in any way we can. Alma and Lucia will ease the day-to-day chores. But share your concerns with Teresa. She's a remarkable young woman. And keep praying."

"We will." He nodded, but his weak smile troubled me.

I leaned on his shoulder. "Now, tell me what else is troubling you. Teresa hinted your job description may change."

"Yeah." His head rested on mine. "It's the guy from Houston, the one I e-mailed you about, Stewart Casey. He's causing a lot of dissent."

The mockingbird plunged into the water, fluttered its wings, then flew away.

"What does Hank Trenton say?"

"Hank and the church leaders from Brooder have been working on this joint venture for almost a year. Hank said Stewart has been against it from the beginning, but he's in no position to object. He's not part of the Houston leadership. But he does have money."

"And money talks."

"I know, but so far the two churches have succeeded in their plans without Stewart's approval. That is until he came up here two weeks ago."

"Was that the first time you'd met him?"

"Yeah." Wriggling on the bench like a distracted child, Mike rubbed his thighs. "After you and Daddy left the Trentons that Sunday, we met at the church building later in the afternoon."

"You and Teresa?"

"Yes. She was tired and didn't stay long."

Arms folded, I worked my jaw from side to side.

"I know that look, Mama. What are you thinking?"

"I take it by his name Stewart is Anglo?"

"He is."

"I hate to say it, but in your e-mail you wrote his strongest objections came after meeting you. He agreed to everything on paper, he'd read your résumé. My conclusion is he thought Mike McDonough was a nice Anglo boy. Instead of being a nice boy of mixed parentage, married to a nice Hispanic girl."

"No, Mama. It can't be as black and white as that. Or should I say, as brown and white?"

"Why not?"

Scratching his head, Mike squinted. "Now that you mention it, Stewart did ask strange questions. He wanted to know how we met. If we had any friends who were Hispanic. He also made an innocuous statement about our ages." He pursed his lips. "I suppose you could be right."

My words of accusation sat heavy on my heart. I'd dealt with prejudice growing up, but Mike, looking more like his daddy, hadn't. He wasn't used to it. I couldn't shield him from it now either.

"Mama, you might be right. But we can handle it. I'll discuss this with Hank and the leadership. After all, they wanted Teresa and me *because* of our Hispanic connections and fluency in Spanish. And they are our bosses." He turned and kissed my cheek. "No, I have it wrong. We serve God and Him alone." This time his smile twinkled in his blue eyes as he stood and offered me his hand. His previous doubts seemed to have vanished. "Let's go inside."

The aroma of pecan pie and freshly brewed coffee greeted us as we entered the kitchen. How could anyone maintain a healthy weight eating Alma's delicious cooking?

Nate, now awake, rested in Teresa's arms, while the rest of the family ogled him between bites of pie and sips of decaf.

Thirty minutes later, Mike announced he needed to set off for the church office. I cuddled my grandson one last time, and then passed him back to Teresa, wishing we lived a little closer.

Another drive scanning the road for yellow cars. Another night alone.

I couldn't wait for Tom to call, so I punched in his speed dial number and curled up on the recliner. His phone rang and rang. Odd. He usually answered right away, especially in the evening. After leaving a message, I hunted for his itinerary and dialed the hotel room number in Odessa.

One, two, three rings. Then a husky female voice answered, "Hello."

My heart jerked to a stop. Couldn't be! I'd dialed the wrong number. "I . . . I'm sorry. I must have the wrong room."

"Who were you trying to reach, hun?"

Weighted into the chair, I couldn't think straight. I should have hung up, but I said, "Tom McDonough."

Giggles and a faint voice, like she held the phone away from her mouth. "Tommy, it's for you."

Tommy! No one called him Tommy.

Another muffled voice in the background, "Who is it?" Was that Tom?

"A woman."

"Oops. It's probably my wife."

More giggles.

Tom again. "Give me the phone." Pause. "Quit, Sally."

While I stared at the muted TV, the light in the living room seemed to flash red, orange, purple. My fingers ached from gripping the cell phone. *Relax. There must be a logical explanation.*

Tom's voice blasted in my ear. "Chella, is that you? Why'd you call my room phone?"

I could hardly breathe, let alone form a sentence.

"Chella, I know you're there. Please, listen. That was Sally. She and her boss came to my room . . ."

His explanation evaporated in my shock. Sure, Sally and her boss. Tom's words wafted in and out. Half of them registered, half disintegrated.

"Sweetheart, say something."

I drew in a lungful of air, and swallowed. The rage constricting my throat made me gag.

"Tom . . . I . . ." My mind went blank. I ended the call and closed my eyes.

My comfortable, predictable world rocked and rolled through the earthquake of suspicion. I'd never suspected Tom of being unfaithful to me—I'd never had reason to. Even with his frequent travels, I'd always known he was true to me. Was I wrong? Had this happened before?

Springing out of the chair, I stomped through the house, in disbelief, in anger, in tears. My cell phone rang. I stopped in the hall and whimpered. Silence, but then it rang again. It was probably Tom and I couldn't talk to him.

I tip-toed back to the living room—like I didn't want Tom to hear me—and located the phone wedged next to the recliner's arm.

Staring at it, I caved. "Tom—"

"Sweetheart, please don't hang up. Please."

Numbness had set in, but the thumping in my chest assured me I was alive.

"Maricella, did you hear what I said? Answer me."

"I . . . I did." My knees buckled, and I fell into the recliner.

"You do believe me, don't you? You can't . . . Maricella, you can't think Sally and I are, were—" A deep, low groan. "Sweetheart, say something."

"Why was she in your hotel room?"

"I told you. Sally and her boss, Wes, came to my room to pick up extra materials. She answered the phone because Wes and I were busy at the computer."

This time his words made their way into my consciousness, and I responded to Tom's sincerity. "I see." Now, feeling foolish for jumping to conclusions, I swiped tears from my face. "Tom, I'm sorry. I—"

"That's okay, Chella. You know I love you. Hey, listen. I have good news. Say hello to the new regional manager. I got the promotion."

I brushed aside all vestiges of residual doubt. "That's wonderful, Tom! When will the new job begin?"

"Sometime in April. I'll be based in San Antonio with limited travelling. But I'll be home most nights."

Were his gushing words a sign of guilt? He sure had changed the subject quickly.

"After twenty years, it'll be strange to have you home every night."

"Yeah, but I'm looking forward to the change. How about you?"

If he'd asked me ten minutes ago, I would have answered with enthusiasm. But now? "Sure, Tom. But it'll be an adjustment."

"Won't it." Tom's voice lowered to an intimate tone. "Have you made that list of chores for me? Since I'll be home more often, I'll have time for a lot more than chores, Chella."

I blushed at his meaning, but then giggles in the background brought Sally and Wes back into the picture. They were still in Tom's room while he flirted with me. Bristling with indignation, I frowned at my phone. How dare he? I'd have more than a list of chores waiting for him when he came home Friday evening.

"Tom, I have to go."

"Wait, sweetheart. Why did you call?"

Why had I called? Oh, yes. The yellow sports car. Might as well tell him.

"You're not going to like it."

I outlined the details about the car following me, and the wig-wearing man and Joey chasing him through the parking lot.

Tom's tone hardened. "Is he all right? Are you?"

"We're fine. Joey has a bruise on his cheek where the guy kicked him."

"I think it's time you stopped investigating the former jewelry box owners."

Brutus jumped onto my lap. I patted his head and tried to keep my voice even. "But I'm not investigating anymore. And after Norm repairs the box, I'm going to give it to Deputy Rayburn."

"Good idea. Let her investigate the Summerland-Hayes family."

"You remembered their name."

"Yeah. I told you the name rang a bell. One of the Kerrville hospital administrators is a Summerland-Hayes. Her first name begins with a *V*."

I nearly choked. Vivian, Gregory's wife. Andrew's mother. "Do you know her?"

"Met her once when I presented a workshop there. Why?"

"Just curious."

Although I'd vowed never to lie to Tom again, that didn't mean I had to share all my speculations with him, especially tonight when . . .

We talked a while longer, and then I remembered Tom's cell phone. "I did call you on your cell, but had to leave a message when you didn't answer."

"Blast it!" Tom seldom resorted to such exclamations. "I left it in my briefcase. Sorry, Chella. You know I turn it off during a presentation."

But you usually turn it back on right after, and here it is nearly nine o'clock. "Okay, Tom."

"I'll turn it on right now in case you need to call again."

His words faded like he moved away from the receiver. "There. It's on, but I have to go. Need to e-mail Kurt. See you Friday, my love."

My heart flip-flopped at his words of endearment, but right before he hung up, I'm sure I heard a voice in the distance say, "Hurry up, Tommy, we can't—"

Had my overworked imagination played a trick on me? I thought about calling Tom again, but changed my mind. He'd never given me cause to doubt his love or faithfulness. I had to trust his explanation now, until I could face him and read his eyes.

While checking the doors and windows one last time, I remembered I hadn't told Tom about Julia's letter. That information would keep. I snuggled under the covers and tried to read, but my conversation with Tom replayed over and over. My eyes jerked open when my cell phone rang. Who'd be calling after ten? Tom to explain further?

No. It was my neighbor. "Hey, Norm."

"Is Tom there?" His usual gravelly voice sounded weak.

"No, he's not. What's the matter?"

"I . . . I know it's late, but can you come over?"

At ten o'clock at night? By myself?

"What's wrong, Norm? Are you all right?"

"I need help. My dogs have been injured. I don't think Sylvester's going to make it."

CHAPTER TWENTY-ONE

"That's it, Norm. Slide in there. Careful now." I closed the pickup door and ran around to the driver's side.

"Thanks for driving. I . . . I couldn't."

"I know. We'll be at the clinic in no time."

Norm used the same animal clinic we did. Before leaving home, I'd snatched the veterinarian's business card off the refrigerator, and once I'd seen the extent of Sylvester's wounds, called the emergency number. Dr. Slaven said to bring the dogs in right away.

Norm's old stick shift truck lumbered down the driveway. I jumped out and opened the gate.

"Don't bother to close it," Norm said, hemmed in with Sylvester in his lap and Trixie at his feet.

The five mile drive to the clinic took forever. Sylvester's whimpers fueled my anger. Who could have done such a cruel thing to these animals?

The dogs' panting and whining punctuated the ten long minutes we waited for Dr. Slaven in the moonlit parking lot. Trixie rested her head on the seat between us. I stroked the bridge of her slender snout, and almost dissolved into tears at the pleading expression in her deep brown eyes.

At last, Dr. Slaven and her technician arrived and opened the clinic. They immediately led Sylvester to an examination room while Norm sank into a chair in the waiting room with Trixie huddled at his feet. Blood stains marred Norm's white shirt and khaki pants.

I settled next to him and rubbed his bowed shoulders. "Can you tell me what happened?"

He rested his elbows on his knees, twisting his hands together. "I'd fallen asleep in front of the TV like I do most nights. The dogs were outside. I don't like to have a light on, so whoever attacked the dogs must have seen a dark house and could have thought I was away or asleep. Next thing, I heard barking, growling and yelping, and then whining."

His voice faded.

"I'm sorry, Norm." If the jewelry box was the cause of this attack, I would never forgive myself. "Did you see who attacked Sylvester and Trixie?"

With fatigue and concern etched on his lined face, he straightened and shook his head. "When I heard the dogs, I grabbed the shotgun and ran to the back door. I turned on the outside lights and saw a figure jump the fence and disappear into the darkness. I . . . I couldn't do anything because that's when I noticed Sylvester lying in a pool of blood." He gritted his teeth and gazed at the ceiling.

"But you called me, and we're here now."

He removed his glasses and rubbed his eyes. Then he made a big show of cleaning the lenses on the hem of his shirt. After adjusting the frames on his face, he muttered, "Thanks, Mrs. Mac."

"Your dogs are in good hands." Tears filled my eyes as I patted Trixie's head.

She had a gash in her left side the rest of the blood on her fur was probably Sylvester's.

Dr. Slaven entered the waiting room. "Mr. Harrison, Sylvester has suffered numerous cuts. I'm assuming from a knife. First, I need to ascertain if he has any internal damage, then I'll suture the lacerations and give him IV fluids and antibiotics. We need to keep him at least a day to monitor his condition, watch for complications. My tech is preparing him for surgery. Bring Trixie through, please."

In silence, we followed Dr. Slaven to the examination room. Trixie loped behind until Norm lifted her onto the metal table.

With gloved hands, Dr. Slaven flattened the fur around Trixie's gash. "Ah, yes. Another knife wound. How did this happen?"

Norm again described what he'd seen and heard.

She continued her examination. "If it's any consolation, Mr. Harrison, your brave Sylvester had evidence in his mouth indicating he'd taken a bite out of his attacker. Bits of blue cloth and blood. I've saved the cloth for the sheriff."

"Good. Hope the man's in pain. If I ever get my hands on the—"

"Hey, Norm." I touched his arm. "Let's sit over here and give Dr. Slaven room to work on Trixie."

We settled on a small wooden bench, and kept our attention on the tech as he wiped the blood spatter off the dog's black and brown fur.

"I see just the one cut, but it's deep. She'll have to spend the night, too." Dr. Slaven scratched Trixie's ears. "She'll be fine. You can pick her up mid-afternoon. Call at noon. By then I will know more about Sylvester's condition, too."

Without a word, Norm bolted from the room. I stood and patted the panting dog.

Dr. Slaven, a tall, slender brunette, about my age, looked me in the eye. "You can take Mr. Harrison home now. He's had a shock. Can you stay with him a while?"

"Definitely." Sure, I'd stay with him. I dreaded going back to my empty house and facing another night alone. Tom's promotion couldn't come soon enough.

On the silent drive home, I thought about the jewelry box, but kept the question to myself. A little insensitive, considering the situation.

But as we neared Norm's property, he brought up the subject. "Do you think the guy who attacked my dogs was after your antique box?"

After turning onto the caliche driveway, I stopped. Norm climbed out, closed the gate and returned to the truck.

"Yes. Is . . . is it safe?"

"Uh-huh. It's locked up in the bottom of my gun cabinet. We'll check when we get inside."

Once in his house, that's the first thing he did. There, in the bottom compartment sat the jewelry box, safe and sound.

"I'm sorry, Norm. If you want, I can take it and have someone else repair it."

"No, no." The key grated as he relocked the cabinet. "I took the job and I'll finish it. Tomorrow. I have to fix the crack in the back which won't take long."

"Okay. Can I make you a cup of tea?"

Colors of Deceit

A rough chuckle bubbled up. "Nah, Mrs. Mac. Never touch the stuff. But you can put on a pot of coffee while I clean up."

His footsteps echoed down the hall while I searched in his kitchen cabinets for coffee. When the rich aroma of the brew filled the room, I poured a mug for Norm. I knew he liked it black. If I visited his workshop and he had a cup of coffee in hand, he always said if you added cream or sugar to your coffee, then you really didn't like coffee—you liked cream or sugar.

Intending to stay long enough for Norm's nerves to calm down, I declined his offer to share his midnight caffeine intake. I hoped to sleep a little in preparation for work the next day.

We chatted about his family. Two sons, Paul in Houston, Ben in Chicago, and his daughter Amy in Lubbock. Reminiscing about grandchildren and his expected first great-grandchild eased his anxiety. When Norm's mantel clock struck two, I distinctly heard my bed call me home. Crusty old Norm shooed me out.

He walked me to my car where he gave me a quick peck on the cheek. "Thanks, Mrs. Mac. I—"

I held up my hand, wanting to halt the flow of sentiment that threatened to spill over again. "No problem. Glad I knew how to drive a stick shift."

"Right." He cleared his throat. "Um, good night then. See you tomorrow."

"Ride with me to the gate."

"Good idea."

In my car, I gave him a gentle thump on his shoulder. "You be careful now. You don't have your dogs to warn you if the intruder comes back."

"No need to worry. I won't sleep much tonight, and I'll keep my shotgun close."

And I knew he would.

Norm closed the gate and waved.

Brutus welcomed me home while I checked doors and windows. Although weary, I knew I wouldn't be able to sleep right away. I propped pillows against the headboard and lay on the bed, clothed in the blue jeans and T-shirt I'd hastily thrown on when Norm called. Brutus joined me on the bed.

The jewelry box had caused too much trouble, but what could I do about it?

When Norm returned it, I'd try once more to locate another secret compartment. If I couldn't, I guess I could find Andrew's phone number, call him and tell him I'd found nothing else. If Andrew had hauled me into the closet at the hospital, then he already knew what I'd discovered in the box. Those items were of no value to him. I'd give him the box and be done with it. Surely, Teresa wouldn't mind. The box had hurt too many people—Andrew could have it. And if he was the intruder, then all this skullduggery would stop once he had the box.

Brutus's warm little body curled next to me, and I stroked his back. Poor Sylvester. Had his valiant effort protected a stupid old jewelry box? I closed my eyes.

Next thing I knew, the radio alarm buzzed me out of a dark dream.

I staggered to the bathroom, showered, and dressed. For breakfast, I ate a toasted bagel and downed a large mug of coffee. Then I called to check on Norm. He'd not slept at all—too wired, but he was raring to go and planned to repair the box in his house, not the workshop.

A full schedule of students kept me busy all day, elementary campus in the morning, and the high school in the afternoon, leaving me little time to dwell on my conversation with Tom. A quick dash to the grocery store on the way home, then I paid a visit to Norm. He had just returned with Trixie. Her shaved left flank revealed twelve stitches, and she wore a plastic halo collar so she couldn't lick her wound.

"They'll keep Sylvester at least one more day. He lost a lot of blood, but I stayed with him a while. He'll pull through. He's tough."

"Good to hear it. He's strong like you. Trixie doesn't look too happy with her collar."

"No." Norm chuckled. "She keeps trying to back out of it." Holding an unlit cigar in his hand, he motioned me inside. "Come. The box is finished."

The jewelry box perched on his kitchen table, shiny and whole. Looks were deceiving. The box hid a dangerous secret. I picked it up and rotated it, examining all sides. The areas Norm repaired were completely indiscernible.

"This is beautiful. Thanks. How much do I owe you?"

Norm slipped his glasses into the pocket of his tan T-shirt. "Nothing. What you did for me and my dogs last night is payment enough. I can't thank you—"

"Stop." I set the box down and took Norm's hand, his skin as rough as the sandpaper he used. "You'd do the same for me. So, hush."

Empathy swam across his face. He blinked, trying to keep his blue eyes clear.

I released his hand and slipped my arm around him. "I'll take this jewelry box out of your hair now, and if I were you, I'd put up a sign that says *Antique Jewelry Boxes Not Accepted Here*. Or something like that."

"Yeah. And you be careful, too." His voice strengthened with each word.

"I will." I tucked the box under my arm, and we walked to the front door. "I think I know who wants it. I've given his name to the Kerr county Sheriff's Department."

"Great. They can coordinate with our local guys. I called them this morning. A deputy already came out."

"I like the sound of that. What did he say?"

"He found where the dogs were attacked, and also located where my fence had been cut. They'll collect the blue cloth from Dr. Slaven. But there's not much more they can do right now. The rain early this morning washed away tracks and who knows what other evidence."

"Too bad." The sports car came vividly to mind. It would have left definite tracks. "I can ask Deputy Rayburn to check Andrew's alibi for last night."

"You do that."

Once we arrived at my car, Norm opened the door.

I slid in and deposited the jewelry box on the passenger seat. "Thanks again for repairing it. Let me know when Sylvester comes home."

He saluted. "Will do, Mrs. Mac."

Trixie, wearing her vinyl halo, trotted awkwardly next to Norm as he jogged down the driveway to open the gate. He held onto her while I drove through.

As I reached our gate, my cell phone rang.

"Mrs. McDonough, Deputy Rayburn. I have some news."

I almost swerved off the driveway. "Good or bad?" I couldn't tell by her tone.

"A bit of each. We received a report from the Austin Police Department.

Andrew has an alibi for the time of Teresa's attack. Rock solid. Therefore, he couldn't have been the man who came to her house that afternoon."

Not Andrew? I parked in the garage. "What about the attack on me?"

"For that night he has no alibi. He could have easily driven down from Austin."

By then I was in the house, sitting at the kitchen table. "And the incident at the hospital?"

"Again no solid alibi."

I drummed my fingers on the table, Brutus sitting at my feet, ears alert, wanting attention. "This doesn't make any sense. Teresa and I identified the man in the picture. Andrew. He attacked me—twice. But he didn't attack Teresa?"

"Allegedly, Mrs. McDonough. Just because he doesn't have an alibi doesn't mean he did it."

"But I can prove it. I can identify him."

"I know ma'am, but we'll need more evidence than that."

Bending to pat Brutus jogged my memory. Norm's dogs.

"What about a knife and bloody clothes?"

"I beg your pardon? What are you talking about?"

I described the attack on Norm's dogs. "If Andrew's car is searched, I'm sure you'll find blood somewhere. Sylvester lost a lot of blood and he bit his attacker. A Bandera County Deputy visited Norm today. He discovered the fence had been cut, and he will collect the evidence from the veterinarian's office."

Rayburn said the sheriffs' departments would coordinate efforts, but her flat tone dripped with doubt.

I mulled over her response. Why wouldn't she want all the evidence she could get? Enrapt in reflection, I jerked when my phone rang again. Joey. We chatted as I returned to the car to retrieve my school bag and the jewelry box—I couldn't believe I'd left it in an unlocked car. After closing the garage door, I set the alarm and resumed my conversation, safe inside my house cocoon.

Joey's enthusiasm for his newfound mission had not waned. He and three others from the original group planned to continue the work in El Salvador and were raising funds to return in June.

"Is J one of this group?"

"Yeah, Mama. And before you ask, yes, we've been on a date."

"Woohoo!" I couldn't help myself. "Sorry, *mijo*. You know I'm dying to meet her."

Silence.

"I promise I'll behave. I won't embarrass you. Or her."

"Okay." His voice wavered.

"How about lunch next Saturday? And . . . and if you don't want to do the official meet the parents deal, you can invite the others from the group, too."

Noises in the background muffled his words, then he said, "Okay. All five of us will come. Thanks, Mama. And please don't tease me."

"I won't. Promise. By the way, how's the face?"

"Healing. It's okay. Don't worry, Mama."

"Hmm. All right then, we'll see you a week from Saturday. Noon. Love you."

Bursting with pride at his resolve and twittering with excitement at meeting J, I fixed a pan of chicken fajitas, and ate my meal while making other phone calls. Mike reported Nate woke every two-and-a-half hours to feed, and no one got any sleep. They were working on a schedule to share nighttime feedings. Tom's call, although brief, sounded normal, routine, I was almost ready to wipe the previous conversation from the slate. Almost.

Showered and ready for bed, I sat in my recliner with my Bible in my lap. With all that had happened, I'd neglected my daily study. In fact, I hadn't opened the book since reviewing the passage on the armor of God in Ephesians. I turned to chapter six now. Shield of faith, belt of truth.

If only the Christian life was that easy. Go to a store and purchase your helmet, belt, breastplate, shield, and sword. Put them on and you'd never have to worry again. The evil one would never dare cross your path. You'd never doubt your husband's loyalty.

I closed my eyes and prayed for wisdom about using my figurative armor, and how to deal with the trials sent my way.

One of the more recent problems seemed to gloat from the coffee table. The jewelry box. Should I hide it? No way would I venture outside in the dark to hide it in the shed as I'd done before. I searched the house for a spot and chose the cedar chest in my bedroom. I'd already prodded and poked the wooded roses, hoping to find the other compartment, but the box refused to give up its secret.

With the antique hidden, I opened to the final chapter of my novel, but dropped the book when the house phone rang. Julia at ten-thirty? Norm again?

But neither of their numbers flashed on caller I. D.

Restricted.

A man answered. "Mrs. McDonough?"

"Yes."

"This is Warren Howard." His voice sounded muffled, different.

"What can I do for you, Warren?"

"Sorry to be calling so late." He coughed. "Forgive me, I have allergies. You know how it is this time of year."

"I do." A plausible explanation for his altered tone. "Warren, it's late—"

"Right. Mrs. McDonough, I'm curious. Have you had the jewelry box repaired yet?"

"Uh-huh. Picked it up today. It's perfect."

"I hope I'm not being too nosy, but what are you going to do with it now?"

I hesitated, unease growing at the direction of the conversation. "I'm going to give it back to Teresa. Let her decide what to do with it." The unease morphed into panic. "On second thought, since someone is still after it, there must be another secret drawer. I'm going to take it to the Kerr County Sheriff's Department. They can smash it open."

"I see. Okay, then. Like I said, I was curious. However, if Teresa no longer wants it, I might have a buyer. Let me know. Sorry to bother you."

He hung up, and I placed the receiver back on its charger stand. Throughout the conversation, something triggered my beware-meter. First, the late hour and his voice. But he explained he had allergies. If I didn't want it, he might have a buyer? But he knew it wasn't mine. Then—I couldn't quite put my finger on it.

I mentally replayed his part of the conversation. Mrs. McDonough. Mrs. McDonough.

Then it hit me. Warren called me Maricella.

What did I tell the man? That I had the box and would take it to Kerrville. I'd suggested the sheriff should smash the jewelry box to discover its secret.

A true antique dealer would have objected.

After considering all the information, I came to one conclusion.

Warren had not called me.

CHAPTER TWENTY-TWO

At nine the next morning, I set off for Kerrville. After the strange phone call the previous evening, I decided to deliver the jewelry box straight to the authorities.

Once on the country road, a quick glance in my rearview mirror showed clear pavement behind me. But when I checked again a minute later, a tan behemoth loomed on my tail hurtling closer and closer. Before I could react, the pickup rammed my Chevy Impala. I struggled to control the steering wheel, to turn the tires into the curve of the road, but the force of the blow rendered my efforts fruitless.

What should I do? A ravine at the side of the road flashed into my peripheral vision. My first instinct—to brake—met with too much resistance. The monster truck outmatched my sedan by a long shot. Accelerating, I spun the steering wheel with all my strength. May as well try to lasso a tornado for all the good it did. I clung to the steering wheel, gripping until my hands went numb, but it was like navigating a sailboat through a storm.

The ravine flashed by. Off the road now beyond the shoulder, the Chevy bumped along the rocky verge. My teeth chattered as if I were in a freezer. A grove of oaks stood a hundred yards away. Could I avoid them?

An engine roared. The none-too-gentle nudge from behind reminded me I had little say about my destiny. Tensed muscles hunched my shoulders over the steering wheel. Blood thundered in my head as sweat popped on my brow.

I turned the steering wheel again, attempting to maneuver the car back onto the road, but the pickup forced me sideways down the gully. The car lurched, two wheels leaving the ground, then thumped back down. Trees loomed closer.

With all remaining strength, I stamped on the brakes. My car shuddered to a stop. In the distant recesses of my foggy brain I heard a vehicle rumble away.

Listening. Waiting. Who had been in the pickup? Would he come back and bash in my window? I glanced around. But only the oak trees filled my vision. I peeled my fingers off the steering wheel one by one and craned my neck around again.

I was alone. Covering my face with trembling hands, I expelled the breath caught in my lungs and slumped over the wheel.

Roiling in my gut forced me to straighten. I opened my purse, suppressing an urge to throw up, and hunted for my phone.

Someone tapped on my window. I dropped the phone. *This is the end. He's here.* I looked up.

A young woman stood by the car, tugging on the door handle. I switched off the engine and opened the door.

"Are you all right? We saw that guy run you off the road. My boyfriend's calling the cops."

I ran a hand across my eyes. "I'm okay." After swinging my legs out of the car, I attempted to stand but my knees turned to jelly. "Whoa." I sank back into the car.

"You've had a shock. Better sit and wait for the cops."

"You're right." I gulped in air to settle the nausea. "Thanks for stopping. Did you . . . did you get his license number or . . . or see the driver?"

"I didn't. I don't think Jacob did either. We were driving the opposite direction." She shoved her hands into her pockets. "The pickup took off as we approached. That's when we turned around to check on you."

"Was a man driving?"

She kicked at the rocks with her booted heel. "Yeah."

My stomach tightened. "Excuse me." I scrambled to one of the trees and held onto the rough trunk while dry heaves convulsed through me. *Was it Andrew?*

After a few minutes, I returned to the car and inspected the damage to the rear and left side. Anything to keep from thinking what would have happened to me if Jacob and—

"What's your name?"

"I'm Shannon."

"Thanks again, Shannon. You and Jacob might have saved my life."

Distant sirens announced the imminent arrival of the authorities.

A young man in blue jeans and a western shirt tramped down the incline. "Hey, Shan. Cops are coming." He extended a can of beer and a bottle of water to me, both dripping with condensation. "Thought you'd like something to drink."

"Hi, Jacob. Thanks for helping. I'll take the water." After shaking his hand, I opened the bottle and sipped the cool liquid.

When the sirens stopped, Jacob climbed back to meet the officer. Shannon held my arm and almost dragged me up the steep grade.

LeBlanc, a young-looking deputy from the Bandera County Sheriff's Department, introduced himself, recorded our names, and then asked, "Mrs. McDonough, do you require medical attention?"

"No. I'm a little shaken, that's all."

He flipped a page in his notebook. "Usually an ambulance would also respond to a situation like this, but the one assigned to Hanson Ridge is assisting with a major wreck near Lakehills."

"I understand. No problem."

"You can wait in my patrol car while I question the Good Samaritans." LeBlanc opened the back door and I gratefully sat down.

He then wrote out Jacob's and Shannon's statements. They had an appointment in San Antonio, and were in a hurry to resume their journey.

I told LeBlanc all I could remember of the incident. As an afterthought, I included information on Andrew.

"Do you think he was in the pickup?"

Eyes closed, I tried to recreate the situation, but I couldn't recall any details of the driver. I shook my head. "I was focused on survival. Paid no attention to his face. But my gut tells me . . ."

If Andrew had called the previous night, he could have followed me. Before I left home I should have called for a police escort. I should have—

"I need facts, ma'am." The young deputy tipped his trooper hat back with his pen. "Have you tried to back out your vehicle?"

I shook off the *should haves*. "Sorry, what did you say?"

"Have you tried to move your vehicle? If it's stuck, I'll call a wrecker."

"No, I haven't. Can we try now?" Still shaken, I left the patrol car and headed down the incline. "Can I—?"

"Need a hand?"

"Yes, sir. Thanks." I grabbed his arm, glad to be wearing boots and jeans. I'd never have made it down the slope wobbling on heels. My rubbery legs could hardly support my weight even with the aid of a beefy young officer.

The engine turned over on the first try. Good old Chevy. My elation died when I stared at the floor where the jewelry box had landed in the melee. The base lay detached from the box, and the corner of a brown leather-bound book stuck out. I felt the blood drain from my face.

I dropped my purse onto the floor, covering the jewelry box. LeBlanc may be a deputy sheriff, but I wasn't taking any more chances. Whatever secrets that book concealed, they were the reason I'd been forced off the road. No one must know I had found the book.

LeBlanc leaned in the open window. "Before I let you drive, ma'am, I'll need to check the taillights."

He stepped to the rear of the vehicle and called out commands for brakes and signal indicators. All worked perfectly.

"I'm surprised all the lights are working. You can drive the car for now, ma'am, but have it checked out and repaired as soon as you can." He straightened and tore off a sheet from his clip board. "Here's your copy of the incident report. Are you going to be okay, ma'am? I can follow you into Bandera."

I filled my lungs with air. "I think so, but yes, please follow me. I'll drop my car off with a mechanic friend in Bandera."

After I reversed, the engine strained as I steered up the hill to the grassy shoulder. I think my Chevy and I were both happy to be out of that predicament.

The taupe Bandera Sheriff's vehicle behind me provided a layer of safety. No tan pickup would dare attack me again. Although I had an escort, my tense shoulder muscles and aching fingers only relaxed when I turned onto Main

Street in Bandera. The deputy stopped at the courthouse, and I drove to Roger Ward's body shop. He attended Hanson Ridge Community Church where his brother Daniel served as pastor.

Roger inspected the damage and estimated at least a week for repairs, but I didn't care because he gave me one of his loaner cars. Andrew, or whoever followed me, wouldn't know I had changed cars. I transferred the jewelry box and my purse, then hunted for my cell phone, which I'd dropped when Shannon knocked on the window.

After calling my insurance company and explaining the situation, Roger handed me the keys to a cream Ford Focus. Unnerved by the accident, I stopped at the OST restaurant. I checked my watch and noted I had at least two hours. My first babysitting gig would commence at one o'clock. Teresa needed to meet with her professor, and then wanted to take her mother and sister out for a thank you meal. Naturally, I'd accepted the opportunity to have Nate all to myself. But first, I had to discover the final—I hoped—secrets of the jewelry box before handing it over to Deputy Rayburn in Kerrville.

I gently picked up the box, hoping the fall hadn't damaged it again. I found no cracks or dings, although the base had detached. It had a metal spring clip on one end and a thin lip of wood on the other. Before attempting to reinsert it, I should figure out how to open it again.

Observing the mechanism in the base, I discovered that depressing the middle rose in the back while the box was upside-down, released the latch. To test this theory, I held it upside-down, inserted the base and snapped it closed. Then, I rubbed my hands together and pushed the middle rose. Ta-dah! The base popped open. How easy, once I knew the key. No leg twisted for this secret compartment. I placed the box on the floor, draped my jacket over it, and sauntered into the restaurant as if I had not a care in the world.

Intent on reading the leather-bound book now burning a hole in my purse, I chose a booth in the corner, with a clear view of the entrance. The waitress stopped at my table, and I ordered coffee and a chicken salad sandwich.

Anticipation swept up from my toes and made my fingers tingle. I opened the four by six inch book. The cover page said it all. *This journal belongs to Virginia Cora Summerland-Hayes. Book Five.* I thanked the waitress who delivered my sandwich and refilled my coffee mug. Virginia had four other journals. Where were they?

The handwritten pages blurred. What could she have to say that would make Andrew, her grandson—no, great-grandson—commit murder? The dated pages began in May 1990. I flipped through to the end. Several blank pages followed the last entry dated December 1993.

When did she die? I'd have to ask Franklin.

I read and read. Virginia wrote in detail about dinner parties, but then skimmed over an argument with Gregory. I'd have to search carefully for the nuggets making this little book so valuable—and dangerous.

Ten pages later, Emory's name caught my eye. I reviewed the family tree information I'd collected in my notebook. Emory disappeared in 1993. Virginia wrote this while he lived in Kerrville as part of the family.

August 3, 1990

Emory came by. Such a fine boy. Wish he'd marry that girl, but no one listens to me anymore. He brought me a diamond bracelet. I'm wearing it now. He knows how I love beautiful things. But I don't like how he and Gregory are always fighting. Today he said some downright awful things about Andrew. I think Emory's jealous because he doesn't have kids. Well, if he'd marry he could solve that little problem.

Emory didn't like his nephew, Andrew. Join the club.

I studied page after page, searching for names I recognized. Andrew's name surfaced again months later.

December 15, 1990

I told Gregory he and Vivian must control that oldest boy of theirs. Don't get me wrong. I love my great-grandchildren. Jacqui is a sweet girl, very funny and has a way with words. Marshall and Conrad are fine, but Andrew is a terror. When he was here last week I caught him going through my jewelry box. He said he was trying to open the secret drawer. And when I wouldn't show him how, he threw it down. Cracked the back and when I picked it up, the diamond bracelet Emory gave me was gone. I told Gregory and he said I must have misplaced it. But I know Andrew took it. That sneaky kid thinks he can pull one over on me. I'm going to keep an eye on him.

More confirmation. I chewed the last bite of sandwich and poured a packet of sweetener into my third mug of coffee. Andrew, the thief. Even as a child. What else had he done?

January 4, 1991

Gregory and Vivian came over with their kids today. I've got to admit Conrad is my favorite great-grandchild. I hope I don't show it because I'd hate for Andrew to hold it against him. They don't get along as it is. I don't want to add fuel to their sibling fire. Conrad reminds me of my Harlan. Andrew teases him and I can't stand it. Says he has funny hair, all curly. If only he knew.

So far, nothing Virginia wrote would convict anyone of a crime. I turned the page and nearly choked on my coffee.

January 19, 1991

Andrew tried to kill Gordon. I'm sure of it but no one believes me. Gordon came to see me at the big house. He went upstairs to get my sweater and I waited in the foyer. At the top of the stairs, I saw someone push him. I'm sure it was Andrew. He stared at me and motioned at the side of his head with his fingers like I was crazy. I know I saw him. Gordon broke his left arm, but it could have been worse. He told me Andrew has been phoning him and saying awful things to him. Why? Why is my family falling apart?

And then an entry tugged at my heart.

March 14, 1991

My Dear Frankie. Where are you? Happy Birthday. Why did I send you away? I could really do with your guidance and advice. You always were too smart for your own good. Where did you get your wisdom? I miss you so much, and after all I did to hide our parentage, it didn't matter in the end. They knew.

CHAPTER TWENTY-THREE

What did they know, Ginny? Did your family discover your racial background?

Should I let Frankie read this section? Would he want to know Ginny's family knew her secret before she died?

I gnawed my upper lip and turned pages until I found another entry of interest, this one again featuring Emory.

June 2, 1991

Emory has had problems with his arm. He's in constant pain, and the doctors can't explain why. He also doesn't believe me when I tell him I saw Andrew push him. He thinks he remembers a shove, but the fall knocked him out and he won't ask questions. He says it's water under the bridge. There's something else going on. When I mention Andrew's name, he changes the subject too quick. I know Emory and Gregory have been arguing a lot. Vivian tells me they fight all the time, mostly about Andrew. Why doesn't she do something to help her son?

Virginia didn't write for several months. Her next words in shaky script explained why.

October 13, 1991

It's good to be able to write again. I'm glad I'm home. I hate hospitals. Esther came to see me. That was a surprise. Haven't seen her since she retired five years ago. I miss her. She talked a lot about her children, specially her son. She was a good friend who kept my secrets. But she asked a strange question. She asked if I still had my wooden jewelry box with the carved roses and secret compartment. I told her I didn't use it anymore. (After Andrew fiddled with it that time I took out the jewelry and hid the box in my closet. I keep my journal in there now.) Esther was so funny. She said the jewelry box was the ugliest thing she'd ever seen. But I'll cherish it always. My Harlan gave it to me a long time ago. Seeing her again made me think of Frankie. All those letters she delivered. Frankie, hope you're happy.

Page after page detailed Virginia's life at the big house.

Early lunchtime customers filled the restaurant. I'd finished my sandwich and couldn't swallow another drop of coffee. Still, I wasn't ready to leave. Relinquishing my table, I toted my belongings to the seldom-used high counter, and sat in one of the seats covered by a real saddle. I wanted the refuge the restaurant provided, safe from prying eyes. After ordering a glass of iced tea, I continued reading.

February 26, 1992

I called Gordon yesterday. He said he'll visit me next weekend. I want the whole family over for lunch one day, but everyone's too busy. Mary Margaret says families today don't have time for such things. I said they should make time. In my day we had family meals all the time. How can that be bad?

Penciled in the margin were the words *I was right.* What had she been right about? Ginny's entry seven pages later in the journal described her reaction to Gordon's accident.

March 18, 1992

Gordon, my boy. May God bless you. Why did you drive late at night? I thought you had a driver. Poor, poor Albert and Bella. I know what it's like to bury a child. Parents shouldn't have to bury a child. Even if the child is not a boy but a man of 38. It shouldn't happen. And who else can I talk to about this horrible feeling that it wasn't an accident? I tried talking to the cops. They ignored my accusations. No one listens to me. They think I'm losing my marbles, but I'm quite sane. Too bad I don't have any proof that it wasn't an accident. Only thing I know is at the funeral Andrew was too smug, too happy, and he looked at me in that way again. Like he did when Emory fell. He motioned at the side of his head, making the crazy sign. But he stopped quick when his father looked at him.

I'm watching you, Andrew. I'm watching.

Ooh! Andrew again. I tore off a piece of napkin and marked the page. Most likely the journal documented more about Andrew. Enough to convict him of—what? Gordon's murder?

Virginia discussed a friend's birthday party she attended, an outing at the botanical gardens. On and on, but mention of core names dwindled to nothing. Then, close to the end of the journal, she penned incriminating words.

July 4, 1992

I finally had my family over for lunch. All except Gordon of course. And Frankie and Elizabeth—I wonder where they are? And Harlan and Johnny. We even had a fireworks display in the evening. I mean the kind you light up. But we had the other kind too. My bedroom is downstairs now. I can't climb all those stairs, so Mary Margaret made me a nice room in the back of the house. I went to take a nap after lunch but Andrew followed me. He said he wanted money. I opened my purse and he laughed. No Grams he said. I want money. Lots. He said he knew I was half-black and would tell everyone if I didn't give him money. I wrote him a check for $1,000, but before I gave it to him I told him I knew he'd killed Gordon. He didn't deny it. He pulled the check out of my hands saying I couldn't prove it. See, I knew he did it. Next time, and I'm sure there'll be a next time, I'm going to make him confess in writing because no one will take my word against his.

I sipped tea and checked my watch. An hour left. I kept reading. Virginia tried to tell various people of her suspicions, to no avail. She never wrote about making a police report, and I doubted she did.

November 9, 1992

I was in the hospital again. Emory came to see me. He doesn't look well. All pale and thin. What's happening to him? He told me I may hear bad things about him, and not to believe the stories. I didn't understand and he wouldn't explain. He almost cried when he left my room. When Mary Margaret brought me home I asked her what was wrong with her son, but she told me not to worry. Everyone tells me that. They all treat me like I'm too old to know what's going on, but I see things and I sense things. Something's wrong with Emory. I don't want to lose another grandchild.

November 12, 1992

I took a taxi to the family offices downtown. They were all surprised to see me. I demanded a meeting with Lawrence and Gregory. I asked deliberate questions about Emory but they hemmed and hawed. They hinted at problems with money, and I told them if I didn't get straight answers I'd change my will. That made their eyes pop. Gregory said he'd come by the house later in the week.

November 18, 1992

Gregory came at last. He says he has proof that Emory has been filing false reports and taking money from the company. I don't believe it. I told him I wanted to see proof. He said it was complicated. Here we go again. I'm not senile. Maybe I can't drive a car anymore, but I can still read and comprehend financial reports, and I can win at bridge more times than not. But he said the company accountant was handling it all. I better talk to Emory about this. Get his side of the story. He did warn me.

I made a quick trip to the restroom, then returned to my perch at the counter.

Ginny's entries were serious one minute, frivolous the next. I waded through the pages until I located more on the Emory thread early the following year.

January 7, 1993

   Some people are never grateful. Christmas was a grand affair at the big house, but then Andrew cornered me in my bedroom and demanded more money. (Like I knew he would.) And like the time before, I wrote him a check, but I asked for something first. I told him before I'd sign it, he had to tell me what he did to Gordon. He said he drove him out of San Antonio, drugged him, and pushed the car off the highway. I asked him why. But all he said was Gordon knew too much.

   I made him write it out and sign it. He said it would cost me. But he did it anyway. I ignored the arrogant smirk on his face. What good is money if it can't help my family? But then he said he knew Emory was special to me, and he was going down. Those are the words he used. Going down. I begged him not to hurt Emory and to come visit me next week. I promised to have something special for him. I want to know what he meant by Emory going down.

If Ginny made Andrew sign a confession, where was it? Now his attempts at stealing the jewelry box made sense. He wanted the confession. I flipped through the book again, but no loose pages fell out. Could it be in the box? I had to finish the last entries before leaving the restaurant. And then I'd check the box one more time for the confessions. Anxious to discover if Ginny persuaded Andrew to admit involvement in Emory's disappearance, I perused the final entries.

But an entry mentioning Frankie popped up before Emory's name appeared again.

January 9, 1993

   Frankie. Frankie. Wish I knew your address for sure. I need to tell you about Andrew and how he's blackmailing me. Seems every time he sees me he demands money. He's not just mean—he's evil. Such a shame because he has a look about him that reminds me of my Johnny. Why did I send you away? I'm sorry, Frankie. I miss you.

Did Ginny ever write that letter? I doubted it. Frankie would have mentioned such correspondence. Three days later, Ginny wrote more about Emory.

January 12, 1993

Emory came to see me late last night. He said he has to leave the country. The newspapers are going to print awful stories about him, but for me to remember they aren't true. I noticed the hurt in his eyes. I don't think he was lying. He hasn't before, so why would he now? He gave me an envelope to open after he got safely out of the country. He made me promise to wait three days, but he wouldn't tell me where he was going. Even when I begged. He said it was best if I didn't know. My dear, dear, Emory. What have you done?

January 13, 1993

I didn't wait three days. I couldn't. Emory's envelope contained a typed letter outlining all the money he gave Andrew to keep quiet. I don't understand why Emory didn't go to the police, but it seems Andrew knows something about him and has been blackmailing him for a couple of years. I know what that's like. Andrew, why are you so different from your brother and cousins?

January 16, 1993

The newspapers tell of a prominent Kerrville business man gone missing after allegedly embezzling thousands of dollars. They are wrong about my Emory. I called the police department and told them I had information about Emory's disappearance. They sent Detective Newman, a nice young man. I told him about Emory's visit and showed him the typed letter. He said because it wasn't handwritten, it wasn't proof, but he would question Andrew anyway. At last, some justice. I hate to say that about my own kin, but Andrew is a nasty piece of work. I wanted to give the detective the confession Andrew signed, but I couldn't find it. Maybe I am losing my marbles! Newman said he will keep in touch.

January 23, 1993

Another visit from Andrew. He was very angry. He said the police questioned him, and he blamed me. He demanded more money and I did like last time. I made him give me something first before I signed the check. I took out the paper Emory had typed. Andrew laughed. He said Uncle Emory sure kept accurate records. I asked Andrew what the payments were for.

He put his hands on my shoulders and bent over me—the first time I've ever really been afraid of him. I looked at his face, which used to be so sweet, always surrounded by his nice dark hair, but now I only saw hate. He said Uncle Emory helped him out of a jam. I demanded details.

He said he'd been with a girl and they'd used drugs. They were crossing the street and the girl was hit by a car and killed. The car left the scene. He'd called Emory for help. Said he couldn't call his own dad again, but knew ol' softy Emory would help. Emory drove there and picked up Andrew, and when the girl's body was found, Andrew was miles away.

The authorities never associated him with her death. He said Emory always felt bad about it, and Andrew took advantage of his guilty conscience.

I made Andrew sign the letter Emory typed. He asked why and I said if you want my money you'll do it. He said, Grams, you're such a tease. No one will believe you.

So now I have two confessions and I must hide them. (I did find the other one, and you'll never guess where. It must have slipped out of my journal and fallen behind a shoebox in my closet.)

I'll have to finish this later. I smell smoke.

That was the last word she wrote. Where did you hide the confessions, Ginny? And the smoke you smelled, was that from the fire that nearly destroyed the big house? I turned the remaining blank pages one by one. Not a single word. Nothing. I came to the back cover and left the book open, resting my chin on my hands.

Whew! Ginny, I admire your courage. I did a rough calculation and figured her to be about seventy-seven when she penned the final words. I knew little of her physical health, but mentally she sounded rational. But to discover one great-grandson had murdered a grandson and had been responsible for the exile of another must have been agony. She had no one to turn to. If Frankie had still been in her life, he'd have listened to her.

I rubbed the leather folded inside the back cover and almost fell off the stool. What was that? My fingers detected a slight ridge. Adrenaline-fueled blood heated my face. I scrutinized the area. There was a bulge under the leather. Flagging a passing waitress, I asked for a steak knife. When she delivered it, I pried up the leather and paper, careful not to destroy the old materials.

My painstaking surgery uncovered two folded papers—confessions of Gordon's murder and the signed payment statement from Emory.

These worn sheets were worth killing for.

CHAPTER TWENTY-FOUR

I paid my bill, and then ran down the street to the UPS store where I made copies of the confessions and relevant journal entries. Deputy Rayburn would need the complete journal but I wanted copies of certain sections, and surely Frankie would appreciate some, too.

The white-knuckled drive to Kerrville had me close to hysteria several times. I knew the anonymity of the loaner car granted me a smidgeon of protection, but every time a vehicle appeared in my rearview mirror, I tensed.

After I gave Deputy Rayburn the confessions and the journal with pertinent passages marked, I sped to Brooder. Since the jewelry box had divulged its last secret, I left it in the car. Teresa provided last minute instructions for Nate and reminded me they planned to return by six.

I checked on sleeping Nate, itching to pick him up, but squelched the desire and wandered through the quiet house, clearing my thoughts, relaxing. With Mike at Camp Alpha, I had Nate to myself at least for the afternoon. While he slept, I called Frankie and told him about Ginny's journal.

"And you've already given it to the cops?"

"I had to. Seems logical that Andrew was after the confessions. Don't know how they will stand up, but maybe they'll lead to his arrest. I need to feel safe, and if Teresa wants the jewelry box, she'd welcome that assurance, too."

A ragged sigh accompanied Frankie's words. "I understand, but—"

"I copied some entries for you. She missed you."

A thick silence followed.

"Can I get 'em now?"

"Sure. I'll be at Mike's house at least three hours. Come anytime." I gave him directions and hung up when Nate whimpered.

My week-old grandson had gained a little weight. His face and the left side of his head remained puffy, but his dark eyes sparkled. I picked him up and while covering his delicate cheeks with kisses, inhaled the intoxicatingly sweet newborn smell. After setting his prepared bottle in the warmer, I changed his diaper. Snuggling him into the crook of my neck, I carried him to the kitchen to retrieve the warmed formula.

Once settled in the armchair, I sang a favorite lullaby, *Caracolito*, about a little snail. Nate wolfed down the liquid, eyes on my face as if listening to every word of my song. The cyst hadn't interfered with his appetite. Mental images of holding Mike and Joey as infants swam before me. And now they were grown men. What adventures lay in Nate's future?

His little lips stilled. I removed the bottle and stood, transferring him to my shoulder. Patting his tiny back, I paced the living room. Through the large window I saw Frankie step onto the porch and opened the door before he rang the bell.

"Come in."

"Afternoon." Pointing to Nate, he whispered, "Sorry."

"He's not sleeping. In fact, I want him to stay awake a bit."

Frankie closed the door and stroked Nate's curls. "You forget how tiny a newborn is."

"I know. Would you like a drink? Tea, coffee?"

"No, thanks." He patted his middle. "Just had a big lunch."

I returned to the armchair and held the bottle for Nate. "Your copies are on the coffee table."

Papers in hand, Frankie dropped onto the sofa. He read each page, then set them aside and leaned back.

Nate slurped the formula. I adjusted the angle of the bottle. "What are you thinking, Frankie?"

Gaze fixed on the ceiling, Frankie rubbed his chin. "Mistakes. We all make mistakes and have to live with the consequences. I'm glad to hear Ginny thought about me, but our lives could have been vastly different. Family meals. Our kids growing up together. Sharing triumphs and tragedies."

I told him about her last entries where she indicated she would have confided in him if he'd been close by.

"Who knows? Could be her kids didn't take anything she said seriously. I know my oldest son objected to me making this trip. He'd have a conniption fit if he knew I was driving. And I'm a lot older than Ginny was when she wrote this." His hand rested on the papers next to him.

A car engine revved outside. I didn't investigate as Nate was almost asleep, and the noise soon ceased. "When did she die? The last entry was dated January 23, 1993."

"February of that year."

Nate's eyes closed and he stopped sucking. I placed the near empty bottle on the side table and adjusted him on my shoulder. "So, she must have hidden the journal in the jewelry box after writing on January 23, and then never opened the book again. What caused her death?"

"Heart. She had a weak heart."

Easing out of the chair, I swayed and gently patted Nate's back. Seems to be an automatic movement for me whenever I'm holding a baby. "I'm surprised Andrew didn't try to steal the box then. There must be a reason he waited all these years."

Frankie shifted to the edge of the cushion and, with a grunt, pushed up from the sofa. "I'm sure he has plenty of reasons, but no way we'll ever know." After staring at the journal pages again, he folded them. "Thanks for these. I'd better be going now. Oh, I brought something for you. Nearly forgot. Left it in the car."

"I'll come out with you."

The warm air of late March caressed us as we walked across the porch and down the driveway. With my attention on Nate and Frankie I only noticed the yellow car parked in front when we reached the curb.

My leg muscles seized. I stopped. Sandwiched between my Ford Focus and Frankie's gray pickup sat a yellow Camaro. Unable to move, I gawked at the vehicle as blood vacated my brain and a frigid hand gripped my heart.

The opening creak of Frankie's door echoed in the background. I gave the sports car another look. Two black stripes snaked up the middle of the hood.

Bile inched up my throat. Did someone in this neighborhood own such a fancy car? For a brief, insane second I thought of Joey. Joey loved cars. He would be wild with jealousy, or at least the old Joey would have been.

Was this the Camaro that had followed me? I couldn't help but peek inside. The dialed dashboard and two-tone leather seats spoke volumes as to its cost. But a flash of dark blue on the passenger seat caught my eye. I clutched Nate closer to my chest.

It was a royal-blue baseball cap.

My breath lodged in my throat and my heart raced. A blue baseball cap. What was attached to it? With my hand on Nate's back and neck, I moved closer to the glass. Dark curly hair surrounded the base of the cap. And next to it lay a shaggy gray wig.

I gasped. My knee joints turned to mush. A royal-blue baseball cap with dark curly hair attached, and a gray wig. In a yellow sports car parked outside Mike's house.

Frankie's truck door slammed and he approached me with a small gift bag in hand. I motioned him to hurry, knowing my mouth hung open and my eyes bugged out.

"Maricella, what's wrong?"

"Help me inside. Quick."

His free arm around me, he shepherded me to the porch, but we didn't move fast enough. A man charged from the side of the house, pointing a gun in our direction.

"No! Don't hurt my baby!" I cowered close to Frankie.

"We won't bother anyone if you do as you're told. Get inside." He jabbed the gun into my ribs.

Frankie stumbled on the steps and almost fell, but the man caught his arm and helped him up.

"Come on, old man. Don't want you sprawled all over the porch. Move faster."

"I'm trying." Frankie dropped the gift bag, and staggered across the porch.

"Open the door, Mrs. McDonough." He elongated the words as if we had all day.

With my hand on the doorknob, I froze for a second. The voice. I recognized the voice. The same gravely, smoker's rasp and Texas twang of the intruder who'd choked me, the man in the hospital closet. Shoving the door open, I shifted Nate to a safer position in the crook of my arm, and stopped in the center of the room. Frankie entered on my heels and perched on the edge of the sofa.

The man with the gun, who sort of looked like the yearbook picture of Andrew, closed the door and surveyed the living room. "Anyone else in the house?"

"No, but my son will be home any minute." Not quite a lie. "And my husband will be stopping by." Also not a lie. Tom planned on calling on his way home to see if I was still here.

Footsteps on the porch. Rescue already? The door opened and in walked Andrew's clone. Or at least that's what I thought at first glance.

The two men were the same height, the same build. One balding, one with short brown curly hair. They both looked like Andrew from the yearbook. They must be related. Shaking the brain freeze away, I sat in the armchair when Nate whimpered and wriggled.

Nestling him back on my shoulder, I scrutinized the two men standing at the front door, each brandishing a gun.

I followed a hunch. "What do you want, Andrew?"

The man who forced us into the house, the balding one, smirked. "So, you figured out who I am." He waved the gun around and moved in my direction. "Hooray for you." Then he aimed the weapon at Nate.

I'm sure my heart stopped as I stared into eyes as dark and cold as an arctic midnight. This was the man who stabbed A. J., who followed me, who ran away from Joey.

Where was Joey now?

"You must know what I want. That ridiculous little jewelry box. Where is it? I know you have it—"

"The phone call last night?" I tried to move Nate's little body away from the barrel of the gun, but Andrew slid onto the arm of the chair and wedged the black metal between Nate and me.

Colors of Deceit

"Please don't. Please. I'll tell you where it is. I'll give it to you." I lowered my arm and pushed the gun aside. "Please."

Andrew chuckled, a hollow sound lacking mirth. "Sure thing, Mrs. McDonough. You *will* give it to me. 'Cause right now I'm not too happy with you. Where is it?" He stood, aiming the gun at Nate.

"Young man." Frankie's hand trembled as he held is out. "You don't have to do that."

Nate must have sensed the tension or maybe I squeezed him too tightly, because he began to cry. I hushed him and patted his back.

Andrew sent Frankie a withering look then waved the gun in my face. "Don't play games with me, lady."

The other man stepped forward. "Andrew, don't—"

Andrew spun around. "I'm handling this. You keep watch like we planned." He turned back to me and raised his eyebrows, revealing eyes that seemed to shoot ice-daggers.

A shiver shimmied from head to toe. "It's in my car. Front seat," I said above Nate's wailing. Crooning to the baby, I eased out of the chair. "I have to change his diaper. He won't stop crying until I do." I moved toward the hall. "Please."

In one step, Andrew blocked my way. "I didn't see your Chevy out there. Isn't it road worthy?" He guffawed and slapped his knee.

Anger bubbled close to the surface when I recalled the ramming of my car just hours ago. It *was* Andrew. I swallowed the gall and clenched my teeth. "I have a loaner car. It's the cream Ford Focus." Turning sideways, I made sure Andrew's gun pointed at me, not at Nate.

"Ooh, smaller than what you're used to."

"How . . . how did you know I'd be here at my son's house?"

His shoulders rose and fell. "The phone call last night. You told me you were bringing the box to Kerrville, although you didn't say when. I took a chance it would be today. I patrolled the street in front of the Sheriff's Department while my . . . while he kept watch here." Andrew jutted his chin toward the other young man. "He told me your car wasn't here. I thought maybe you already stopped by and left the box. I was going to break in again. Got lucky when you came outside." Pointing to the sofa, he asked, "Who's your nosy friend?"

Frankie sat on the edge of the leather seat, his eyes darting back and forth. I knew he would help if he could, but his frail frame was no match for these two.

"His name is Frankie."

"Frankie, you better come with us. I'm not taking any chances."

Frankie eased off the sofa and joined me, giving me a sly wink.

Oh, Frankie, please don't try anything. I'd hate for you to get hurt.

I threw him a quick glance and moved my head in the briefest shake.

"Give me your keys." Andrew's hand waggled in my face.

Temporary amnesia. Where had I placed my purse? I patted Nate and tried to hush him while scanning the living room. Then I remembered I'd dumped my purse on the kitchen table.

"In there." Without waiting for permission, I entered the kitchen. A single key fastened on a large loop key chain poked out the side pouch. However, I used my body as a shield and slid my hand into the purse to locate my cell phone. With exaggerated movements, I shifted Nate from one shoulder to the other and managed to slip the phone into my jeans pocket. Then I removed the key.

"Here it is. The jewelry box is on the floor on the passenger side, under my jacket."

Snatching the key, Andrew motioned for the other man to leave his post at the door. "Go with her when she changes the baby."

The look-alike nodded and folded his arms, the gun poking from under his elbow. Without a backward glance, Andrew opened the front door and scampered across the porch. I carried Nate to his room and changed his diaper, speaking to him in Spanish. Frankie settled in the rocking chair, smiling in understanding.

"Hey, what you saying?" the man barked.

"I'm telling my grandson that he'll be clean and fresh in no time. And that you won't hurt him." I snapped the onesie and picked up Nate, soothing his whimpers. I blinked at the man as a flash of recognition from the yearbook crossed my mind. "You won't hurt him, will you Marshall?" His face resembled Andrew more now that he'd gained weight since the high school pictures were taken.

A bewildered frown wrinkled his brow when he backed up and leveled the gun at me. "How do you know who I am?"

Nate's body relaxed while I rocked back and forth. "Just a guess. I'm going to lay the baby in his bed, now. Okay?"

"Yeah. I guess."

Once in his bed, Nate's eyes fluttered for a second. I secured the sleeping sack around his waist and turned to Marshall. "You don't look comfortable doing this. That gun seems foreign in your hands. Why are you helping Andrew?"

After studying the weapon for a second, Marshall spread his arms. "He's my cousin. Used to be my best friend. We go way back—it's a long story."

I assisted Frankie out of the rocker, and then picked up the soiled diaper. "You okay, Frankie?"

He whispered, "I still know some moves."

With a squeeze on his arm, I hoped to deter him. "Let's leave Nate to sleep." I thought he'd be safer in a room by himself. "Marshall, I have information about Andrew that may get him arrested. He stabbed A. J. Howard. Do you want to be part of a murder investigation?"

Marshall frowned, but kept his mouth shut. Had I provided news about Andrew?

We traipsed down the hall, and after wrapping the diaper in a plastic bag, I threw it in the kitchen trashcan. "You could be the hero here. You could let me call the cops or—"

"No, ma'am. I have to do this."

So much for divide and conquer. For a moment, I thought I saw a softening around Marshall's eyes. What hold did Andrew have on him? The journal revealed nothing against Marshall or the other great-grandson, Conrad.

Once in the living room, Marshall ordered us to sit on the sofa. Andrew entered carrying the jewelry box, with frustration etched on his tanned face.

He threw the box in my lap. "I can't open it. Show me how."

With the box in my possession, I planned to use it to my advantage. I'd work slowly, demanding answers from Andrew before opening each compartment. I flexed my fingers, prodded roses and twisted a leg, and the front drawer popped open.

"See, it's empty. I told you when you pulled me into the closet in the hospital that there were letters in here addressed to your great-grandmother."

"Yeah, yeah. I remember."

One mystery answered. Andrew had forced me into the closet.

"Who'd you give the letters to?"

Frankie's elbow nudged my ribs. I tapped his knee. I wouldn't divulge his identity without his permission.

"I gave them to Virginia's brother."

Marshall, perched on the wide arm of the chair, asked, "She has a brother who's still alive? In Kerrville?"

"Yes."

"I didn't know that. Did you, Andrew?"

Andrew quit pacing beyond the coffee table and stopped directly in front of Frankie. He looked the old man up and down. "No, I didn't." With a flourish, he stuck the gun in his waistband. "Go on. Open another one."

I prodded and twisted, deliberately making wrong choices. "You've tried to steal this box before, haven't you?"

"So what if I did? Come on. What's taking so long?" Andrew paced again.

I made another choice. "I can't remember all the combinations." I exaggerated a frown and twisted the leg. "Did you break into the Howards' storeroom?"

A chuckle spewed from Andrew's mouth. "Yeah. A . . . a friend and I scuffled with Warren. Didn't know he broke his arm until I saw y'all in his office that day."

Swallowing a chunk of grief at his casual reference to A. J.'s last day on this earth, I jabbed at a rose. "Why did you come to Warren's office?"

"I . . . I couldn't hear anything in the courtyard. Had to get closer."

"I know you broke in here one night and choked me." Another rose prodded. "But who attacked my daughter-in-law that morning?"

"Suppose it can't hurt to tell you." With a grunt, he pointed. "It was Marshall."

Marshall threw up his hands.

Holding one of the legs, I kept myself from making the final twist, my brain cogs churning lickity-split. Marshall, Andrew. Looked alike physically. For a disguise all they'd need would be a baseball cap with hair attached.

"Wearing a baseball cap?"

"Told you it was a dumb idea." Sarcasm laced Marshall's words as he focused on his cousin.

"No, no. Great idea. It fooled her." Andrew propped a foot on the coffee table. "Didn't it? Quit stalling. Open that thing."

"Why'd you choose a cap from the company where Conrad worked?"

"Hey." Marshall stood. "You told me it was a cap you found. I didn't know it had a connection to your brother." He stormed off to the door and turned, his dark eyes blazing. "Andrew, you . . . you—"

As cool as an iceberg, Andrew glared at his cousin. "Shut up and sit." And then he aimed a finger at me. "Open it. *Now*."

His cold words tightened an icy band around my heart. After the third attempt, the back drawer opened.

"What was in there?"

I'd given the handkerchief to Esther and had taken the locket and hair out before giving the box to Norm, in case the sheriff might need the items some day for DNA testing.

"There was a locket in here that belonged to Virginia. I have it at home. It has a photo of her and your great-grandfather, and their child who died as an infant." Knowing Esther gave birth to the child who died, niggled at me, but I couldn't bring myself to tell Andrew and Marshall she had switched babies.

Sitting on the coffee table, Andrew's knees almost touched mine. He rubbed his left calf. "Keep it. That's not what I want. What else?" He tapped the domed lid. "Open another one."

With the box upside down, I pushed the middle rose at the back. The base popped off, revealing a cavity about the size of Ginny's journal. But taped to the underside of the base was a yellowed piece of paper. My eyes widened. Why hadn't I checked the box one more time? I have to admit, after locating the confessions, I thought the box had given up all its secrets.

Andrew jerked the box from my hands. "That's it. I bet that's what I need."

He picked at the tape which gave way easily, dumped the jewelry box on the table, and unfolded the single sheet of paper. He scanned it quickly and then threw it at me, cursing as he stood and towered over us.

"That's not what I want. That's my Gram's *precious* certificate. Stupid thing! The way she protected it you would think it was edged in gold."

CHAPTER TWENTY-FIVE

Frankie's body went rigid. I folded the certificate to keep the delicate paper intact. I hadn't told Frankie that Andrew knew of Virginia's mixed parentage and had blackmailed her. If Andrew knew, did others in the family also know? But Andrew didn't want the certificate. He drew the gun from his waistband and pointed it at my head.

"*Where is it?*" Each venom saturated word spat out in a staccato beat.

A sharp lump of fear lodged in my throat. I blinked and swallowed.

"Where is what?" Feigning ignorance came easy. Too easy.

"I know she kept it in there. Her journal. Where is it?"

I fixed my gaze on his face and shrugged. Even if I told him the sheriff had the book, he might harm us or worse. We could identify him. Doing everything I could to stall for time, I tried to keep my expression innocent. Wouldn't Mike be home soon? Or Tom? Or I could go to the bathroom and call the sheriff?

"I . . . I have something." Frankie shifted on the sofa and tugged the folded journal pages I'd copied for him from his back pocket.

"No, Frankie—"

"He means business. Here." Holding up the pages, he offered them to Andrew. "She copied these before giving the journal to the sheriff."

"Frankie!"

Andrew lowered the gun and snatched the pages. I knew he wouldn't find anything of value to him in the selections I'd chosen for Frankie. But with his interest diverted, Frankie grabbed a letter opener from under a book on the coffee table and slid it up his sleeve. I acknowledged his conspiratorial wink with a dip of my head.

"This is . . . this is junk." Andrew tossed the pages in the air. They floated down like goliath snowflakes.

Distracted by the falling pages, I didn't resist when Andrew yanked me up by my arm. "Why'd you give the journal to the sheriff? Now what am I supposed to do?" With the gun in his waistband again, he shook me, jostling loose a few brain cells, and possibly leaving bruises on my upper arms.

One kick at the coffee table moved it a mere six inches out of his way. Still gripping my arms, Andrew hauled me away from the sofa.

"What else did you find in the journal? Did she say stuff about me?"

Rubbing my stomach, willing the quivering to stop, I raised my eyes to Andrew's face now contorted with rage. "Please let me go. I . . . I can't think straight when you're squeezing my arm. I'll tell you what—"

"You'll tell me because hurting you is the least you have to worry about." His grip relaxed a tad. "The baby back there—"

"No!" I folded my hands as if in prayer. "Please. I'll tell you. Virginia wrote of many conversations with you. And she kept the confessions you signed."

"I knew it. Where are they?" Inching closer, he jerked the gun from his waistband and aimed it at my stomach.

"Wait a minute." Marshall stepped away from the door. "What confessions? Andrew, you never said—"

"I told you to shut up and stay by the door."

A frown creased his brow as Marshall backed up. "Hey, I agreed to help you out, but I didn't sign up for attacking people. I should have ignored your threats and stayed in Oregon."

With a slight shift of his arm, Andrew aimed the gun at his cousin. "Be quiet. You gotta keep up your end of the deal."

Marshall seemed to wither at Andrew's menacing tone.

The gun met my ribs again. "Where are they?"

"The sheriff has them." What good would it do to tell him I had copies in my notebook on the kitchen table?

From his observation post at the front door, Marshall shook his head. "It's too late, Drew. Let's leave."

"Not yet." Jerking my head backward by a hunk of hair, Andrew jammed the gun at my temple. "It's all her fault. From the moment she spent the night in this house she's been nothing but trouble."

Frankie, who'd risen quietly from the sofa, entered my peripheral vision. As much as I wanted rescuing, I failed to see how a man his age could provide it. I opened my mouth to protest, but he tapped Andrew on the shoulder.

Andrew jumped as if zapped by electricity. His hold on my hair relaxed enough for me to straighten.

"Get away, old man."

"But . . . but I have a solution. I know how you can fix what's in the journal."

"Hah! Sure you do." Lowering the gun, he glared at my friend. Contrary to his words, Andrew's eyes seemed to say he wanted Frankie's help.

I eased my hand up and released my hair from Andrew's grasp. "Listen to him. He might have something." I had no idea what Frankie had in mind, but would accept anything to calm Andrew's rage.

Doubt and hope flickered across Andrew's face. "Okay, but I don't trust you. Marshall, go get the baby."

"No! No!" I flung myself at Andrew, but he pushed me away.

"Lady, do you want to die? Bring that baby in here, now."

"Then let me. Please?"

A brief flicker of compassion touched Andrew's eyes. "All right. But go with her, Marsh."

With Marshall behind me, I hurried down the hall to Nate's room. At the door, I hesitated. "Um, Marshall, I need to use the restroom. Promise I'll be good. No monkey business." I held my palms out to him, and faked a sweet smile.

"Okay, but I'll be right outside the door."

I entered the bathroom, closed the door behind me and twisted the lock. Now was my chance. I slid my cell phone from my pocket and almost dropped it when Marshall pounded on the door.

"What's going on? I don't hear anything in there."

To keep up the pretense, I flushed the commode. After punching the number for Tom's speed dial, I cupped my free hand around the phone. When he answered, I whispered, "Just listen. Do not say anything."

After sliding the phone back into my pocket, I rinsed my hands. Would the sound hide Tom's voice if he questioned my instructions? *Please Tom, do as I ask.* I opened the door and said in a clear voice, "I hope Andrew won't use his gun on Nate."

Had Tom heard me? He knew who Andrew and Marshall were, and I hoped he would add two plus two and come up with help.

My conversation continued for Tom's benefit. "Marshall, why did you come here with Andrew?" I opened Nate's door and approached the crib. *Sorry, Nate.*

"See here, lady, I don't want to hurt you or the baby. I don't think Andrew will either."

"I have to change him." Waving my hand in the air, I held my nose. "Smell that?" I picked up the baby and cuddled him when he stirred. There was no odor, but I needed more time to convince Marshall to help us.

"Okay, but be quick."

I slipped off the sleeping sack, unsnapped the onesie and gently removed Nate's diaper. It was wet. I leaned in closer so Marshall couldn't see evidence of my deception, and put a clean diaper on the tiny body.

"Marshall," I thought if I used his name enough, I'd be able to touch a sensitive chord. Besides, I wanted to provide Tom as much information as possible. "Please. You don't want to be responsible for the deaths of three people—Frankie, the baby, me. Let us go. Tell Andrew to leave—"

"What's taking so long?" Andrew's voice echoed down the hall.

Stepping to the doorway, Marshall yelled, "She's changing him. Almost done."

I draped Nate over my shoulder and covered him with a thin blanket. "I'm ready, but Marshall, can I count on you? Your heart's not in this game, is it?"

With a quick rub on his forehead, he sighed. "Just go. I'll . . . I'll see what I can do."

My legs wobbled. Lunch churned in my gut as I carried Nate into the living room. Frankie sat on the edge of the sofa while Andrew paced by the front door.

"It's about time. Sit with him." Andrew pointed to Frankie. "He won't talk without you. Marsh, back here by the door." While Marshall resumed his post, Andrew moved to the coffee table and sat on it.

Using the gun as an extension of his arm, Andrew gestured to Frankie. "Talk now, old man. What's your solution?"

I shielded Nate with my arms. Frankie's expression begged me to go along with what he was about to say.

"Here's the deal. I know for sure Virginia was suffering from a rare brain disease—"

"What?" Andrew shot up, but sank down. "What disease and how would you know?"

"I know." He turned to me and winked, a sign meant for me. "See, she was my sister, my half-sister."

"No." Mouth agape, Andrew reared back.

"But you're black." Marshall deserted the door and strode to the sofa.

So much for other family members knowing of Ginny's heritage.

"Yes, Virginia was my half-sister. We had the same mother, but her father was the one with the brain disease. He passed it on to her."

"Wait, wait." Disbelief coated his words as Marshall raised his hand. "Forget the disease. You're black. That means Virginia was—"

"Half-black. Black mother. White father."

Slumping into the armchair, Marshall shook his head. "No, can't be. That means we're—Andrew it means we have . . ." His voice trailed, and his gaze darted from his cousin to Frankie.

Andrew's shoulders hiked in an exaggerated shrug. "Don't bother me none."

"That's because you've known a long time." A gentle kiss on Nate's head. "You blackmailed Virginia all those years ago. She wrote about it."

"So?" An I-don't-care frown creased Andrew's brow. "She had more money than she needed."

"How could you? Our own great-grandmother." With apparent disgust, Marshall tossed his gun on the side table. "How did you find out? Does anyone else know?"

Frankie whispered, "Is that true?"

I nodded.

After rubbing his calf again, Andrew stood. "Forget it. I want to hear what Great Uncle Frankie has to say. Tell me more about the brain thing. How can this help me?"

"Virginia and I have another sister in Houston. Elizabeth. She's still alive." Frankie nudged me into complicity. "She had the same father as Virginia, and inherited the brain disease, too. Made her as loony as all get out. She says and writes the craziest things. She's in a nursing home. Has to be." He laughed, a forced, vacant sound. "One time she told everyone President Reagan came by and made popcorn for everyone. No one takes her serious. She also keeps a journal. It's full of wonderful stories. I've read 'em and I wager they would shed doubt about the truth of the stories in Ginny's journal. Like her sister's, they are fantasies. Pure fantasy."

Andrew circled the coffee table and sat on it again. "Okaaaay. But what about the confessions?"

"They might be fabrications, too. Ginny had a wild imagination. I remember when we were kids—"

"But I signed 'em. I was young and stupid."

I studied Andrew's body language—the eager eyes, the jaw muscle twitches, the hunched shoulders. He wanted to believe this possibility. "How old were you when you signed them? Must have been many years ago." I knew it was 1993, but I wanted to keep up the illusion of support.

Andrew stared at the ceiling while counting on his fingers. "I was about eighteen, nineteen. Why?"

"Your signature's changed a lot since then, hasn't it? I bet they can't prove you actually signed them."

With a tap on my knee, Andrew grinned. "Good thinking, Mrs. McDonough. I like the way your mind works." His head bobbed as he squinted at us.

"And Andrew, you and Marshall have families, don't you?" I figured the men were in their late twenties, early thirties. "You must consider them."

"Yeah." Marshall sat forward, elbows on his knees. "What am I going to tell Emma and the girls?"

"You have daughters?" I asked.

"Taylor and Ally. If I go to jail—"

"No one's going to jail." Andrew's smirk contorted his face, but his eyes betrayed a hint of alarm.

I pounced on their uncertainty. "And you, Andrew. What about your family? Are you married? Do you have kids?" Warren had shared background on Andrew, but I wanted him to say the words.

Andrew scowled at the carpet, but when he spoke, his underlying anger emerged. "Yeah, I have a family. Or used to have one, before *she* had an affair. Now we're divorced. And I lost custody of my son because . . . because she—" He straightened. "Okay, enough of that." He spread his hand out into the room and held it up as if trying to halt the sentiment my words evoked.

My ploy may have backfired. I had no idea he harbored such anger.

His features hardened, his tone deepened. "Now, there's just one more thing. You two." He pointed to Frankie and me. "You've heard all this and know who we are. I can't trust you to be silent."

"We won't spill the beans." While rubbing Nate's back, I focused on Andrew's eyes, adding sugar to my words. "I'll . . . I'll change my description of the intruder, and I'll convince my neighbor to drop the investigation into the attack on his dogs."

A snicker blasted from Andrew, and he blushed for a brief second.

"Dogs? What did you do?" Marshall's accusing stare bored into his cousin.

Andrew hushed him with a hand motion. "Forget the dogs." Another rub to the bite on his calf. "Mrs. McDonough, I'm liking you more and more. But one thing you have to remember." After sliding next to me, Andrew placed his arm along the back of the sofa, the other hand casually pointing the gun at Nate's little curled up legs under the blanket. "I know where you live. I know you have a little dog." His smirk stretched wide. "But most of all, Grandma, I can see how much you love this little boy."

With his gun moving up and down Nate's back, Andrew kept his eyes on my face.

I froze, but managed a single nod. "I won't say anything else to incriminate you." If Tom heard our conversation, I wouldn't have to.

"Enough, Andrew. Let's go." Anxiety and a touch of disdain tinged Marshall's words as he stood.

"I've got one more question for Uncle Frankie." He turned. "Why haven't I seen you before? Did you ever visit the big house?"

Frankie, on the edge of the sofa, hiked a bony shoulder. "Ginny didn't want me around."

"I can see why," Marshall muttered, returning to the armchair. "You would have been hard to explain. Virginia's generation would have ostracized her. These days, attitudes and opinions are a little different. But Andrew, how did you know about her mixed parentage?"

"One day I visited Grams. I opened her bedroom door and saw her journal by her jewelry box. I was curious and flipped through it. It was an old one from the '70s. Her certificate fell out. It identifies the race of her parents."

"And you never told anyone else? Like your folks or mine?"

"Nope. It's been my little secret."

I remembered Ginny's words *but they knew anyway*. What did she mean? Nate stirred and whimpered. I soothed him with soft words, staring at the jewelry box. Virginia's treasure. How much pain and sorrow it had brought in its wake.

Suddenly, a thought bombarded my brain. "Andrew, I have a question for you. If you knew Virginia kept her journal and your confessions in her jewelry box, why didn't you destroy it before now? She's been gone a long time."

He gave the box a shove and chuckled. "Thought I had. Didn't know it survived the fire until I saw it on the estate sale inventory after the Howards bought it."

The house fire. Another crime to heap at Andrew's feet.

"You started the fire? That's it, Drew. I've had it. I'm leaving. Don't care what you do to me." Marshall stormed to the door, leaving his weapon on the side table. He grasped the knob but dropped his hand. "Someone's coming."

A shadow passed the windows, and then the doorbell rang.

CHAPTER TWENTY-SIX

Andrew's turbocharged leap to his feet sent the jewelry box tumbling onto Frankie's shoes. Frankie winced and placed the box back on the coffee table. During the commotion, Nate stirred again, turned his head, and slept on.

Andrew hissed, "Who is it, Marsh?"

Marshall stooped to peek through the peep hole, then turned and mouthed, "It's a young woman."

Who was it? Could I yell for help? But Andrew, standing inches from me, tightened his grip on the gun and aimed it at Nate. I couldn't risk it.

"Okay, okay." Andrew scanned the room. "We have to answer the door. Whoever it is knows people are in here. She probably heard us. Everyone be quiet. Let me think." He shifted his weight from foot to foot as he scratched his balding pate. "Marsh, take Frankie into the bedroom. And you." He pointed to me. "Get up." He hauled me up by one arm while Frankie and Marshall disappeared down the hall.

Marshall left his gun on the table. Could I get to it? Had Frankie seen it, too? With a hand on my shoulder, Andrew pushed me to the door, but as I touched the knob he reached for Nate.

"No, please!"

"Shut up and give him to me." After draping the baby over his forearm, holding him like a football, he aimed the gun at Nate's head. "Try anything. Anything and he's dead. Understand?"

"Yes." My heart twisted in my chest. Fear rooted me to the floor boards.

"Now, open the door. A foot or so."

The handle turned in my weak grip, and I pulled the door, forcing a smile. Andrew held Nate behind the door, a frightening reminder that I must follow his instructions exactly.

"Hello."

"Hi. Um, you're Mike's mother, right?" The blonde on the porch wore a purple tank top and black cut-off shorts. A scroll and rose tattoo spread across her shoulder.

"Uh-huh." My cheeks already ached from holding the phony smile in place.

"I'm Kathy Davis. From next door." Gum smacked with each word. "Your visitors are parked right in front of my house. They're blocking my sidewalk." Smack, smack. "I knew this would happen soon as your sort moved in."

My sort? Aha, now I had a pretty good idea who'd painted the racial slur on the door. Welcome to the neighborhood.

With that thought in mind, I had to force a pleasant tone. "Sorry about the inconvenience. They'll be leaving before long."

Kathy. Neighbor named Kathy. What had Teresa told me about her? Think. She had a son who was deaf. Right. Now, to make good use of my limited knowledge of sign language.

Releasing the doorknob, I rubbed my chin, then held both hands in front of my body out of Andrew's line of sight.

"When?" Kathy tapped her flip-flopped foot and stuck her hands on her curvy hips. "I want the gray truck moved by the time my husband gets home."

I made the sign for help by holding my right palm open at waist level, and fisting my left hand into it, raising it a fraction. I repeated the sign again and said, "Okay, that's my friend's truck. He'll be leaving soon." I smiled wide for Andrew's benefit but lowered my head, repeating the sign again and again.

Kathy stopped chewing the gum. Her blue-eyed gaze shot to my face. "What?"

I raised my voice a notch. "My friend will be leaving in a few minutes."

Next, I finger spelled G-U-N and darted my eyes to the right where Andrew stood with Nate. I spelled the word again to be sure she'd seen my awkward movements.

"I have to go now, Kathy. The baby needs to be fed."

"Sure." She backed away, and keeping her hand low, signed O-K, the letters flowing into each other, then spelled C-O-P-S. "Don't park in front of my sidewalk again." She nodded, vaulted off the porch and ran across the lawn.

Andrew closed the door with his foot. "Good. You did good." Nate whimpered. "Here, take your little brat."

Relief tears threatened to fall as I cradled Nate against my chest, hoping my wildly beating heart wouldn't keep him awake. Examining his head to see if Andrew's rough handling had interfered with the cyst, my amateur eye couldn't tell for sure, but Nate's breathing remained constant and his color looked good. *Thank you, Lord. Thank you for your protection.* I planted gentle kisses on his little curly tufts of hair.

Now, Kathy, be a good neighbor and call the sheriff. Tom, where are you? Have you also called the cops?

At Andrew's command Marshall and Frankie returned to the living room.

Rocking Nate in my arms, I approached Andrew. Loath to relinquish my hold on the baby, I still believed he'd be safer out of the room. "Andrew, please, since you have a way out of this . . . this predicament, please can I put Nate back in his bed? He has—"

"All right. Get him out of here. Marsh, go with her."

After laying Nate down, I crooned to him in Spanish. He'd slept through one dilemma after another, but would wake soon for another feeding. I hoped the uninvited guests would be long gone by then.

I sensed my escort behind me and turned. "Marshall, you must convince Andrew to leave before he hurts someone. You're made of better stuff than this." A gold crucifix hanging on a chain at his neck peeked through the opening of his blue shirt. "What would your mother say if she could see you now? How would you explain all this to Jesus?"

Backing away, eyes full of regret and mouth in a grim line, he dropped into the rocking chair. Head in his hands, he murmured, "Dear God, what have I done? What have I done?"

His unexpected reaction rendered me speechless for a second. "Marshall—"

"I'm sorry. I should never have agreed to do this." He bowed his head and swayed back and forth as he moaned.

Could I use his distraction to escape with Nate? But a faint scuffle from the living room commanded my attention. What were Andrew and Frankie up to? Marshall continued rocking and moaning, as if he hadn't heard.

I took advantage of his preoccupation and tiptoed out, and then hurried down the hall. Frankie and Andrew sprawled on the floor like wrestling adolescents.

How could I help Frankie? I seized Marshall's weapon from the side table and aimed it at the men, but when Marshall appeared in the hall, I pointed it at him instead. The cold steel wobbled in my two-fisted grip. Marshall and Andrew didn't know it, but I'd never fired a gun before. Never even held one. Slowing his steps, Marshall raised his hands in the universal sign of surrender.

"Sit over there, against the wall."

Marshall complied, resignation plastered across his face.

Meanwhile, Frankie and Andrew continued their tussle on the floor. With the gun aimed at Marshall—although I didn't think he'd put up any resistance—I watched the fracas. First Andrew was on top, then Frankie. The letter opener flashed in Frankie's hand. *Be careful, my friend.*

Then Andrew squealed like a baby, and his gun fired.

A searing hot pain spread through my left arm. My body slumped against the wall. Warm trickles ran down my arm into my hand. Blood. A gaping hole in the sleeve of my pink shirt soon disappeared in a sea of crimson.

Sliding onto the floor, I muttered, "Frankie, Frankie, I've been shot."

I'm not exactly sure what happened next, but Frankie hollered, "Hold on. I'm coming."

In the distance, wailing sirens sent relief washing over me. Help was just around the corner.

The back door squeaked open.

Now what? I couldn't think straight. Was Conrad also in on the deal with Andrew and Marshall?

It wasn't Conrad.

Tom's commanding physique materialized.

He seemed to absorb the scene in one glance and fell on the floor next to me.

"Dear God, Maricella. Where's Nate? Is he okay?"

I murmured something about him safe in his bed.

Although conscious, the next few minutes played out in a slow-motion fog. Tom eased the gun from my grip, and assessed my wound. He yelled at Frankie to pick up the gun at Andrew's side, then disappeared down the hall, returning with two towels.

He knelt beside me again. "Frankie, come get this towel for that . . . that jerk over there."

Gun in hand, Frankie snatched the towel from Tom.

"I heard bits and pieces of the conversation over the phone. Good plan. There's a huge wreck on the highway, but cops and an ambulance will be here soon. Right now, I'm going to stop the bleeding in your arm." He tore the sleeve off my shirt. "Looks like the bullet went right through."

Tom tended to my wound, then with the towel securely in place, he picked me up. The familiar scent of McGraw cologne and Tomness swept over me. I flung my right arm around his neck and burrowed against his chest. Safe at last.

The sirens were closing in. Tom laid me gently on the sofa and crouched at my side. I opened my eyes and tried to focus on the room.

Marshall, propped against the wall, with his knees bent, sat as if he already had handcuffs securing his wrists. Andrew glared at the gun barrel Frankie aimed at his heart. The man who'd terrorized us grabbed his head, blood oozing between his fingers. He wadded his makeshift bandage and held it over the gash in his temple. Had Frankie done that with a letter opener?

Sirens blared outside. Red and blue lights flashed into the room.

Tom, sidestepping Marshall, opened the front door wide. "Come in. We're okay."

I heard someone ask if people were hurt.

"Yes, deputy. My wife's been shot, and one of the criminals is bleeding."

The deputies stormed the house. Two rushed through the back door. Tom and Frankie surrendered the weapons to Rayburn.

While she slapped handcuffs around Marshall's wrists, paramedics attended to my arm and Andrew's gash.

Amidst the cacophony, Nate awoke. Tom took charge. I heard him in the kitchen crooning to the baby while he heated the formula.

Deputies escorted Andrew and Marshall outside, presumably to patrol cars. Tom joined me on the sofa where Nate slurped his formula, oblivious—thank the Lord—to all the chaos around him.

A dull ache joined the throbbing in my arm. The paramedic confirmed that the bullet tore through a chunk of muscle and would require stitches.

"Ma'am, we need to get you to the hospital." The EMT helped me stand. "Can you walk to the ambulance, or do you need the gurney?"

"I'll walk. See you later, Tom?"

"I've called Mike. As soon as he arrives, I'll head to the hospital." Tom's large hand covered half of Nate's body as he patted the tiny back.

Frankie halted his conversation with Rayburn, and quirked an eyebrow at me. "When I'm finished here, I'll come, too."

"One of my deputies will take your statement at the hospital." Rayburn turned her attention back to Frankie.

A muscle spasm rippled through my arm. I grimaced and hurried out with the EMTs.

The ten-mile ride to the hospital gave me time to process all that had happened. I couldn't believe we'd come out of the situation with only a flesh wound and a gash. Frankie could have been shot or stabbed. If I'd been standing a few inches to the right or left, the bullet would have entered my chest . . .

Closing my eyes, I allowed the tears free reign.

In the ER, a nurse cleaned my arm, and ascertained my tetanus shot was current. The doctor injected local anesthetic, and in no time, had stitched up the two wounds.

After nestling my arm in the sling, the nurse said, "Five stitches in front, six in back, Mrs. McDonough. Wound care instructions will be included in your discharge papers. I'll send in the deputy now."

A familiar young man entered. The deputy who'd questioned Teresa after her attack, but I couldn't recall his name.

"Afternoon, ma'am. I'm Deputy Wilson."

Ah, yes. "We have to stop meeting in the ER."

He chuckled as he slid a little recorder from his pocket. "I hope this is the last time, ma'am." He cleared his throat. "I'm ready for your statement."

I described everything from the moment I'd seen the blue baseball cap with attached curls and the wig in Andrew's car until the bullet ripped into my arm.

"We had two calls about this situation. Your husband and a Kathy Davis."

"The neighbor. Good. She picked up on my signs." Remembering her reason for coming to the house, I hoped Frankie was emotionally fit enough to drive the gray truck away. His friends weren't going to let him visit me again. Every time he did, a catastrophe seemed to follow.

Deputy Wilson turned off the recorder as Tom entered the room.

"Chella, sweetheart, are you all right?" With a kiss on my forehead, he held my free hand.

"Yeah. The wound doesn't bother me at all now. I'm still a little dazed, but glad to see you." I squeezed his hand.

Wilson backed away from the bed. "That'll be all for now, ma'am. I'll need you down at the station to sign your statement. Tomorrow morning, if possible."

"She'll be there. Thanks for everything." Shaking hands, Tom ushered Wilson out of the room.

Tom assured me Nate was none the worse for his ordeal, and he'd left him sleeping in Mike's arms. He added that Rayburn and two deputies were still at the house, but because Andrew and Marshall had confessed, the scene would soon be released.

While we chatted, Frankie knocked on the door. "Can I come in?"

I held out my hand. "Of course, dear friend. I want to hear all about your adventure. How did you manage to cut Andrew?"

Frankie settled in a chair close to the bed and described the events. "When you left the room with the baby and Marshall, I told Andrew he needed to reward me since we were related and I'd provided a way out of his dilemma. His face got all red and he paced the living room. When his back was to me I decided to act." Frankie closed his eyes for a second. "Oh, Lordy, I can't believe what I did. I stood and raised the letter opener to stab him. But he turned. The blade caught him in the head." Frankie touched his temple. "Right here. We struggled and next thing I know, his gun fired. I'm sorry, Maricella, I didn't know you were in the room." Deep furrows creased his brow. "I think the sight of his own blood scared Andrew more than anything, and by then we heard the sirens. He just plain gave up."

I winced moving my left arm into a more comfortable position in the sling. "But, Frankie, you could have been killed."

"My friend, I've lived enough years already. I had to do something."

"Dear Frankie." His fingers trembled in mine. What a brave man. Nate and I owed our lives to his quick thinking.

Before I could voice what was on my heart, the nurse returned with my discharge paperwork.

"That's my signal to leave." Frankie grunted as he stood. "I'll be in touch. You take it easy now, you hear." He kissed my cheek, patted Tom's shoulder, and shuffled out of the room.

Tom and I left the hospital with prescriptions for antibiotics and pain medication.

Returning to the house was gut-wrenching. No amount of pills could ease the pain. Andrew's yellow car still parked in front of my Ford seemed like an apparition from a nightmare. Tom parked behind it.

I averted my eyes as he guided me up the driveway. Once inside the living room, Tom shepherded me to the sofa.

"Want a cup of hot tea, Chella?"

Tea sounded good. "Please. Where's Mike?"

"Stay here while I go see."

He disappeared down the hall and returned seconds later. "He's in Nate's room. Let's leave them together for now. I'll make the tea."

As I lay on my side on the sofa, I spied a sheet of paper under the coffee table. Virginia's certificate. I rolled off the sofa onto my knees and picked it up. Clasping the page to my chest, I sat when Tom entered with two mugs of tea and the gift bag Frankie had dropped on the porch steps.

"I found this on the kitchen table. It has your name on it."

"Thanks. It's from Frankie." Someone must have brought it inside.

Tom placed the mugs and gift bag on the table.

"Honey, do me another favor, please. I'm kinda chilly. Could you fetch my jacket from the loaner car? Here's the key." Andrew had left it on the coffee table.

On the drive back from the hospital, I'd related the incident with my car. Tom expressed more concern and outrage, but since Andrew, the perpetrator had already been apprehended, we agreed to count our blessings.

"Sure, sweetheart. Be right back."

When he left the room, I opened the bag. A journal. Not leather-bound, but covered in a design of butterflies and bluebonnets, nevertheless a vivid connection to Virginia that stabbed at my heart. Frankie's inscription encouraged me to treasure every day, every family member, and to chronicle every little thing that mattered.

I set it aside and picked up the certificate, studying the page in earnest. Virginia's mother, Cora Ann Collier. Race, Negro. Father, Peter Robert O'Brien. Race, White. Date of birth, September 7, 1916.

All very interesting, but names and dates penciled lightly at the bottom of the yellowed page caught my eye. Virginia married Harlan in 1934, and in tiny print were the names and birth dates of their children. Mary Margaret 1935, Albert 1936, John 1940.

Franklin Jackson married Viola 1945, and I assumed the names of their children followed. Franklin 1946, Leon 1948, Velma 1952.

And the last one. Elizabeth married Charles Archer 1941. But their child's name, written at the edge of the paper, had suffered the wear and tear of time. All I could make out were two letters. *J* smudge, then *l*, and possibly an *i* following the *l*. Curiosity gnawed at me. What name could that be? Jali? Jeli? Joli? Juli? This name would make sense if I added another letter. An *e* or an *a*. Julie. Or Julia.

I folded the paper, and picked up my mug of tea. Frankie and Virginia and

Andrew, and the strange conversations we'd had in this room soared through my mind in colors of brown, black, tan.

Tom returned and joined me on the sofa, arranging my jacket around my shoulders. "There's a real bad odor near the yellow car. Smells like he parked over a sack of garbage or something. While I was out there I moved my van closer to the house." He placed my key on the table. "Okay now, sweetheart?"

"Thanks, but I have a question."

He picked up his mug and cocked his head. "As long as I don't have to get up again. What is it?"

Quickly, before I changed my mind, I asked, "What's your mother's maiden name?"

Tom turned sideways to look at me as if I'd finally lost my mind. "After a day like you've had, you want to know my mother's maiden name? Why?"

I cradled the mug with both hands and took a deep breath to bolster my courage, preparing for what I knew he would say. "Please, just indulge me. What's her maiden name?"

"You know she's secretive about her family and doesn't want me to tell anyone. Why don't you ask her yourself?"

"She's going to mail a list of names for a family tree. But I can't wait until then. Please tell me now."

"If she agreed to supply you with the names, then I guess it won't hurt. Archer. Julia Archer."

I chewed on my lip and mulled over his answer, which could explain Julia's hesitancy to provide me the list. "And what about your grandmother? What was her name?"

Eyebrows raised, Tom squinted at me over the rim of his mug. "She died when I was little. But I remember people called her Bessie."

CHAPTER TWENTY-SEVEN

No time to dwell on Tom's answer. Teresa, Alma, and Lucia's arrival at dusk meant I must explain what happened. With Mike holding Nate, I summarized the ordeal. Although I assured Teresa I'd done everything I could to protect Nate, she took him from Mike, and rocked him in his darkening room for a long time. My heart ached for her, overshadowing any residual shock or pain affecting me. Would I ever be trusted to babysit again?

Mike ordered pizza, and while Alma prepared a salad, I slipped down the hall to Nate's room. I heard him fussing, and poked my head around the door. "Teresa, *mija*, pizza will be here in a bit. Do you want to eat?"

The rocker creaked, Nate whimpered. Teresa remained silent.

I knelt by the chair, and placed my free hand on Teresa's knee. "I'm sorry Nate had to endure all this today. I'll understand if you never let me near him again. But please believe me, I would have given my life before letting them hurt him—"

"I know, and I wouldn't punish you or him by keeping you apart. It's . . . it's . . . I don't know what I'd do if anything happened—" Her words caught on a sob.

"I know, I know." On my feet, I enveloped her and the baby in a one-armed hug.

Against my middle, she blurted out, "He . . . he has the cyst and has to have surgery, and we don't know how it will affect him. I mean if he'll have brain damage. He's so tiny and I . . ."

Her voice faded into Nate's body.

I had no words of comfort or encouragement. How could I offer any to her when I'd brought these same concerns before God in my quest to discover why his servants were being treated unfairly? But I embraced her and Nate until her body relaxed. I turned as a sniffle broke the silence behind me. Peering into the gloom, I witnessed the rest of the family tip-toeing into the room. I moved close to Tom, while Mike bent over his wife and baby.

Tom whispered, "We need to call on the Lord. Let's gather around the chair." With a hand on Teresa's shoulder and the other on Nate's back, Tom bowed his head.

We closed in and laid hands on Teresa, Nate, and Mike. Tom opened the prayer, calling on the Savior to shower down His love and peace. In Spanish, Alma and Lucia asked for guidance. I asked for a special blessing of peace for Teresa. Mike closed with an offering of thanks for the protection the Lord had provided to everyone in the house that day.

The menace, hatred, and evil left behind by Andrew's actions seeped out the windows.

We ate pizza and salad, with Teresa feeding Nate part of the time. I ached to hold him again, but had to forgo the pleasure.

With Nate back in his crib, and the family seated in the living room, the antique box became the topic of discussion.

Mike pointed to it and turned to me. "So, you're certain there's nothing more in here to tempt anyone else to steal it?"

"All its secrets have been exposed." Sadness tweaked my heart as I thought of Virginia's certificate resting in my purse.

"Are you going to keep it?" Tom asked Teresa.

Snuggling next to Mike on the sofa, she shrugged. "I suppose. It is beautiful and unique. It sure will be an object of interest."

"Yeah." Lucia slid to the floor beside the coffee table and opened the box's domed lid. "Especially when that Andrew guy goes on trial and they say the evidence was found in his great-grandmother's jewelry box."

"Ooh, I didn't think of a trial." Displeasure clouded Teresa's face.

"The case may not go to court. While taking my statement at the hospital, Deputy Wilson said Andrew and Marshall had made full confessions."

We discussed the ins and outs of what this would mean to Andrew, Marshall, and the McDonough family. Eventually, the conversation turned to Teresa's meeting with her professor, and discussing her course schedule for completing her degree. With extensions given on assignments, she'd be able to finish in time and graduate in May.

By eight, Tom and I were ready to leave. Mike accompanied us outside. The neighbor's lights blazed from their front windows. Mike and Tom granted my plea and accompanied me to thank Kathy. I held my suspicion concerning the graffiti on the door for later.

Kathy answered my knock.

"Hi. Thank you for calling the cops. You saved our lives. The baby . . . We're very grateful." I extended my hand.

After a brief shake, she eyed us up and down. "Yeah. I saw 'em arrive and take two guys out in handcuffs. Glad it all worked out okay."

Tom and Mike offered their thanks, too.

A strand of blonde hair twirled between her fingers. "Was it drugs?"

"No, ma'am. They were holding my mother and baby at gun-point." Mike cleared his throat. "And in appreciation for your help we'd like to invite you and your family over for a barbeque tomorrow."

Kathy shuffled on bare feet. "I'll have to check with my hubby."

Mike slipped a business card from his shirt pocket. "Here's my card. Give us a call or come by sometime in the morning to let us know."

The door closed, and we traipsed across the lawn to the cars parked along the curb.

I looped my arm through Mike's. "Where'd that come from? A barbeque?"

"We've been meaning to have them over since moving in, but with Nate's early arrival, we never got around to it. Now is a perfect time. Alma and Lucia can help with preparations. Teresa can get to know our neighbors. This way we can show our appreciation with more than words." A shrug hiked his shoulders. "Spur of the moment plans are sometimes the best."

I hoped Teresa agreed. I'd never seen her in such a fragile emotional state, but then her baby's life had been threatened. Mike could be right. Getting to know the neighbors might be a tonic. And my suspicions linking them to the racial slur might be way off base. Or maybe they would decline the invitation. Would that give me an answer?

We reached Tom's van parked on the other side of Andrew's Camaro. "Hope it's okay to leave the loaner car, Mike. We'll come for it tomorrow."

"Sure, Mama. No problem."

The evening breeze wafted the garbage odor around us and up into the trees. Tom opened the passenger door and I slid inside, thankful to be rid of the jewelry box and its dangerous secrets. The remnants I had were the journal pages and confessions I'd copied, and Virginia's certificate. They were enough.

Mike asked, "You want to join us tomorrow?"

I peeked at Tom standing by my door and read his mind. "Not this time, *mijo*. Thanks anyway. Your dad's been gone four days, and I have a long list of chores for him."

Tom's deep chuckle sounded so good. "We'll come up tomorrow. See how Nate's doing and collect the car."

Mike kissed my cheek and then gave his dad a bear hug. With a wave, he returned to the house.

Tom climbed in and made his way to the highway. The drive back home gave me time to reflect on Tom's answer to my question. His mother's maiden name was Archer. Julia Archer. There had to be more than one person with that name, but they called his grandmother Bessie. Could that be a nickname for Elizabeth? Elizabeth from Houston. I nibbled my bottom lip.

If—a very big if—my mother-in-law *was* Julia Archer, daughter of Elizabeth, sister to Virginia, it might explain her obsession with skin color. Mike's, Joey's, and more recently, Nate's. Could she be worried her distant black ancestor's genes would be evident? At the back of my mind I always thought she objected to *my* color, to *my* heritage.

Tom parked next to the garage and switched off the ignition. If all of this proved true, how could I broach the subject with her? Should I even try?

◆◆◆

Norm called first thing the next morning to say he'd brought Sylvester home. I described the previous day's events and assured him Deputy Rayburn knew

Andrew had attacked his dogs.

"Mrs. Mac, if you weren't a lady, I'd use my favorite four letter words right now. I hope they throw the scoundrel so far in he don't see daylight for twenty years or more."

"He'll be convicted of murder for sure, and who knows what else." I filled in all the details I could.

"Hope your arm's as good as new real soon. If it's all the same to you, I don't want to see another one of them jewelry boxes for a long time."

"I don't blame you. Got to go, Norm. Tom's fixing brunch. I'll drop in to check on the dogs in a day or two."

Tom carried our meal to the back porch. Brutus bounded on the grass, chasing the birds away from the feeder next to the pond. Tom discussed his promotion in detail. I hadn't seen him this excited about his job in many years.

But concentrating on his exuberant words became harder and harder. In between bites of pancake and the occasional nod or verbal comment, my mind rehashed the restless night.

Woken by a sharp pain in my arm, I'd quietly left the bedroom for the kitchen where I swallowed another pain pill. Although my arm was the initial reason for getting up, it wasn't what kept me awake. The horrific events of the previous day played over and over like off-season re-runs on TV. Still able to send knots of delayed anxiety to my gut and sweat drops to my brow, they were, however, only one reason for my insomnia.

I hadn't yet found an opportunity to ask Tom about the woman in his room, or maybe I delayed the confrontation for fear of the outcome. Should I let it go? No. I couldn't ignore the nagging little seed of doubt. The nightmarish situation with Andrew and the aftermath had wiped it from my mind, and when I'd seen Tom as I sat on the floor bleeding, his possible indiscretion was the last thing I wanted to discuss. Also, Tom's possible connection to Virginia stuck at the back of my mind.

But I had a bigger problem to face—my inability to call on the Lord in one of the gravest situations of my life. In the midst of Andrew's siege, why hadn't I used the armor of God I'd studied about? Spying Marshall's gold crucifix spurred my mention of Jesus to him. Could I have circumvented the whole situation by invoking the armor as soon as Andrew entered the house?

Tom was my spiritual sounding board, but how could I discuss my dilemma with him when this Sally woman hovered between us? I had to ask him about her now, face to face, so I could gauge his reactions.

Holding my coffee mug, I squinted through the steam and summoned my courage.

With a forkful of food to his lips, Tom asked, "What's the matter? You're not eating much. Does your arm hurt? Do you need another pain pill?"

"No, no. The twinges are tolerable. I . . . I'm not hungry." I focused on his face and asked, "Tom, tell me again. Who is Sally and why was she in your room?"

His fork clattered to the table, food splattering on his shirt. A flush tinged his cheeks. "Oh, that. I told you—"

"Who is she?"

Brushing crumbs off his shirt, he kept his eyes averted. "She and Wes work for Surgical Matters." He paused for a second or two, then looked at me. "We presented a joint workshop. Had a follow-up report to compose and used my laptop."

Maybe medication hampered my body language reading skills, but Tom seemed to be telling the truth. Then why had he blushed when I mentioned her name?

"And that's all? Sally just happened to answer the phone?"

"Yeah. Like I told you, Wes and I were busy and she answered the phone." Telltale pink inched up his neck again.

"Tom, please. Give me some credit. I know it's more than that."

He made a low, pained sound. "Okay, but it's not what you think. Sally is . . . is a statuesque, well-proportioned, beautiful woman. Any red-blooded man would have to be half-dead not to notice her. I noticed." His hand went up to halt my comment. "But she's having an affair with Wes. She's a flirt, a tease. When she saw my Bible in my briefcase the first morning, she made a comment about corrupting the Bible banger."

"And did she?" I couldn't believe I asked the question. As soon as the words spewed out I wished I could haul them back.

"No, sweetheart. She tried, but I couldn't wait to say good-bye to that team and come home to you."

Ashamed, I bit my lip. "I'm sorry, Tom. I don't know what came over me."

"Hey, sweetheart, I understand. If I had my cell phone on, we wouldn't be having this conversation."

The coffee burned my mouth as I gulped down a bigger mouthful than I intended. Tom's answer, meant to reassure me—I think—had the opposite effect. If he'd answered his cell phone I wouldn't have known Sally was in his room. In all the years he traveled for his job, how often had a woman been in his room when I called?

I opened my mouth to throw another accusation at him, but he pushed his chair back and knelt in front of me.

"Wait, Chella, wait. That came out wrong. We need to have this conversation. You must know that I love only you. On our wedding day, I promised to be faithful, and I've kept that promise."

Adjusting the sling, I was the one who averted my eyes this time. When Tom signed the contract for his first sales rep job, we'd discussed the problem of being separated for days and nights. We'd vowed to be faithful to each other. How could I doubt Tom now?

He moved my chair so I faced him. "In the thousands of miles I've traveled for my job, I've seen many beautiful, desirable women. I'll admit at times I had to make a conscious effort to move out of temptation's path. But I'll swear on the Bible I always take with me, you are my heart's desire. You are the one I long for, the one I live for."

A gigantic lump of guilt slid down my throat as tears gathered in my eyes. "Tom," was all I managed to squeak out before he wrapped his arms around me.

My good arm circled his neck and I wept on his shoulder.

After a sobering moment, I raised my head. "Tom, forgive me for doubting you."

"Of course, sweetheart." With his arms around me, he studied my face.

"There's still something troubling you. What is it?" Returning to his chair, he grinned. "Compiling a list of chores for me since I'll be home more?"

After wiping my tears on a napkin, I said, "No, Tom. I need your help."

"For what?"

My concerns about not calling on the Lord came tumbling out. I don't know when it happened, but I ended up on Tom's lap, with the tear faucet working overtime. "I didn't use the armor yesterday. I'm not doing a good job at this Christian thing."

Squeezing me in a sideways hug, he kissed my forehead. "Yes, you are. You used God's armor without even knowing it. You—"

My cell phone rang. Caller I. D. displayed Mike. I showed Tom and clicked on the phone. "Hey, Mike."

"Hi, Mama. First, nothing major going on, but we won't be having a barbeque this evening. Kathy called. They have other plans and can't come."

He reported Nate and Teresa were fine, neither the worse for their experiences the previous day.

"Are you sure Teresa is okay?"

"Yeah. I'm keeping a close eye on her. But she's handling it okay, for now. The incident may have brought out the old Teresa's spunk."

"That's good news. We'll see you later." I turned off the phone and tapped the table. "And that's another thing."

"What?"

Slipping off his lap, I returned to my chair, explaining to Tom my suspicion Kathy or her husband had been responsible for the graffiti on Mike's front door.

He didn't agree with my assumption, but encouraged me to voice my concerns.

"I know the things that have happened to the kids are not earth-shattering, but it seems to me they're being punished for making a decision to serve in the ministry."

Tom squinted as if he hadn't heard me. "I don't understand. What do you mean?"

"The instant they made the decision, Teresa's diabetes and Nate's condition were diagnosed. And then the problems with the youth minister position, first with full-time pay changed to part-time—"

"But Mike's home computer business is almost up and running."

"I know, but everything is falling apart." I hiked a shoulder. "The man in Houston, Stewart somebody, who's causing trouble. I think it's because he thought Mike was Anglo. And now these other problems."

"You can't expect a perfect life for your children."

"But why are all these bad things happening when they're serving the Lord? They gave up so much. Why do they have to experience a Job thing?"

"A Job thing? Like in the book of Job?"

"Yeah. I've been trying to read it since I heard Hank Trenton's sermon."

After lacing his fingers, Tom tapped his thumbs together, a sure sign he was deep in thought. He tapped and tapped. "I'm not altogether sure I agree with you, but hear me out. We all face challenges and problems, sometimes because of the choices we make, sometimes not related to anything we've done. We can blame God, but ultimately we're responsible for our actions."

Leaning forward, he traced a pattern on the glass table top. "If I recall correctly, Job's wife told him to curse God and accept the consequences of death. Which he refused to do. The book is clear about how Satan caused Job's problems." Now focusing on me, he continued. "In our lives today we can't ignore the same adversary. I'm not saying Satan caused Nate's cysts or made the neighbors hate Hispanics, but there are things in this world over which we have no control. See where I'm going?"

"I think so. Like the passage on the armor of God where we're admonished to stand firm when the evil one comes."

"Right." Lifting his juice glass, he said, "In fact we can take a little from each scripture—the book of Job and Ephesians. The evil one, Satan, will do what he can to separate us from God. He's like a lion seeking to devour prey. We have to do all we can, using the armor we've already talked about, to fend him off and persevere." He drained his glass.

"So we're back to bad things happen to good people." I frowned into my near-empty mug of coffee.

"Yeah. Don't run out on God because you believe He's deserted our kids. He hasn't. He's right there, ready to bless their efforts. Ready to carry Nate through his surgery."

My cell phone rang again. Another call from Mike? Why? A chill tingled down my arm as I picked up the phone.

"Hello, son."

"Mama, the sheriff came with a wrecker to tow Andrew's car, and you'll never guess what they found."

"Don't keep me in suspense. Tell me."

"There was a disgusting stench emanating from the vehicle. They popped the trunk and found a body in there."

Closing my eyes, I asked, "Who?"

"A guy named Conrad Hayes. Do you know him?"

CHAPTER TWENTY-EIGHT

Late the following Friday afternoon, I stopped by Norm's workshop to check on him and the dogs, and to see if he could join us for the celebration of Nate's one month birthday party I was hosting in two weeks.

"Hey, Mrs. Mac. Long day?" He wiped dark stain on the leg of an ornate pedestal table.

"Yes. I had several meetings and wanted to submit my notes before I left school." I leaned against the bench. "How are the dogs?"

"Trixie is healing fine." Norm dipped his rag into the stain and smoothed it over the table top. "Sylvester, well, he's torn off one halo collar and insists on rolling in the dirt. I take him back to the clinic tomorrow to have his stitches removed—if he doesn't tug 'em out himself."

"I'm sure you'll both be happy about that."

"Yep." He eyed his handiwork. "That'll do." After closing the can of stain, he joined me at the bench.

"Will you be able to join us for Nate's party?" I asked.

"Sorry. I told you when you first asked that I might have to forgo the pleasure. Sure enough, my three kids are gathering in Houston for Paul's thirtieth birthday. I'm gonna spend a couple of days with them."

"I understand."

"What's happening with that family in Kerrville?"

Norm did not watch much TV news, and didn't like to read the newspapers. When I visited, I kept him up to date. "Last I heard neither Andrew nor Marshall will have a trial. They both confessed and accepted plea agreements."

"Do you know why Marshall aided his cousin?" Norm motioned me to follow him into the house.

"He committed minor crimes as a teen. Andrew used them as leverage, and, of course, he didn't give Marshall all the details of his plan to get the jewelry box."

We settled at the kitchen table.

"I guess once he was in on the game, it was too late to quit." Norm poured two glasses of iced tea, and handed one to me.

"Thanks. That's right. Marshall got in over his head."

"Anything else?"

"Plenty. A slew of articles about Virginia's journal and the confessions she hid in it. Emory Summerland-Hayes has been exonerated and returned to Kerrville. Remember, he was falsely accused of embezzling company funds. Andrew's confession included his part in stealing from the family business by using his father's security codes. He funneled funds to a secret account, but left a trail which implicated Emory. I sure wanted to be a little bird in the city to see what kind of reception Emory received. I hope there is a place for him in the family business."

"What about Andrew's brother? Didn't you say he was also a casualty?"

"Yes. Conrad's murder was motivated by pure jealousy and a lifetime of sibling hatred. Andrew had asked to borrow Conrad's truck. He refused. Apparently, years before, Conrad had disassociated himself from the family, especially his brother, hence dropping the Summerland part of his name." I sipped the sweet tea. "Andrew demanded the truck anyway, and when Conrad intervened, Andrew clobbered him over the head. When Andrew realized he'd hit too hard, he stuffed the body in the trunk of his Camaro. Then he drove Conrad's tan pickup to Hanson Ridge to await my departure for Kerrville. Andrew used the truck to run me off the road. Later, he ditched it in a back alley and drove his car, with his brother's body in the trunk, to Mike's house."

I shuddered at the memory of those terrorizing hours.

"You okay, Mrs. Mac?" Norm patted my arm, concern pouring out of his gaze.

It took me a moment to focus on the present. I gulped a swig of tea before replying, "Yes, thanks. It's hard to forget that awful afternoon."

"I imagine so. We can continue this conversation another time."

"I'm okay. Besides, there's plenty more to tell. Warren says all kinds of

Summerland-Hayes family laundry is being aired. Andrew's crimes and his connection to the journal brought to light Virginia's heritage. Mary Margaret and Albert had known, and had told Gregory and Rachael. So, Virginia's entry in the journal was partly right. Some of her family knew."

Norm poured more tea into his glass. "Want a refill?"

I shook my head and continued. "Andrew also divulged Frankie's connection to the Summerland-Hayes name. He declined an interview, but his branch of the family has added a new element for the media's exploitation." No one had discussed Elizabeth's relationship yet. If Frankie didn't talk about her, I certainly wouldn't.

"What about the woman in the nursing home you visited?"

After finishing my tea, I stared at the ice. "When the authorities questioned Esther Stiles, she slipped into a deep state of depression. Deputy Rayburn launched an investigation into the allegations of child swapping. It will be interesting to see if the Summerland-Hayes family welcome Stephen as a blood relative."

Norm's eyebrows arched. "Don't know what I would do if I learned I had another brother."

We sat in silence while Norm drained his tea glass.

"Last week I read Esther Stiles' obituary. I was sorry to hear of her passing. The article mentioned her children, Stephen included. What an emotional mess." I stood and carried my empty glass to the sink. "It's time I went home."

Norm escorted me to my car and waved as I drove away.

Of all the stories I'd read, the one that haunted me the most involved Conrad. A photo of his widow and three children displayed in the newspaper tore at my heart.

What could I have done differently to change the outcome? I'd spent many sleepless nights crushed by guilt. If only I'd surrendered the jewelry box to Andrew at the first hint he was the intruder. If only . . .

◆ ◆ ◆

We gathered at our house for Nate's celebration. Guests included Alma, Lucia, Mike, Teresa, Tom, and me. Joey and Jade hadn't arrived yet.

Surprise, surprise. Julia accepted. Two visits in one year. What next—snow in June?

When she drove up yesterday, she explained, "I want to be here for Nate's surgery. Hope you don't mind if I stay until Tuesday."

That would be four nights. Julia had never spent four nights in a row with us. She misread my slowness to respond.

"I could go to a motel. I should—"

"No, Julia. You're welcome to stay all week." What was I saying?

"Are you sure? Is your arm okay now?"

"It has healed nicely, thanks. I'm almost back to normal."

We'd engaged in our usual routine about the room being perfect—wasn't it the same room she'd used four weeks ago? And she wasn't any bother, was she?

As I displayed a plate of olives and pickles on the table, I squirmed at the memory of our discussion. *Get a grip. Forgive and forget.* Forgive. The forgiving part would come in time, but I knew the forgetting wouldn't be easy, although I did see a subtle change in Julia, a softening. Her words lacked the usual sharp bite of criticism, and her eyes didn't scan the furniture for dust. How could she find any when I'd spent hours cleaning?

No matter the change in her, the letter she wrote to me on her last visit sat as a reminder on my dresser. All the forgiving in the world couldn't erase the fact that she owed me an explanation. And I had questions about her past.

Pouring tea into glasses, I checked my watch. Joey was late. Had he changed his mind about bringing Jade to meet the family? Obviously, we'd cancelled the luncheon with Joey's mission group and this would be our first encounter. But then Brutus darted out the pet door, alerting me of an arrival.

I threw off my orange and yellow striped apron, checked my reflection in the mirror, and exited the back door. What would J look like? Would she be quiet and shy, or out-going? I waited on the caliche driveway, hoping my welcome—

Joey opened the passenger door of his Mustang. Out stepped a short, petite blonde. Or partial blonde. What happened to my tall, exotic vision?

"Mama, this is J."

My smile morphed to a gape. I snapped my mouth shut. That'll serve me right for speculating on her appearance. I smiled again and held out my hand. "Hi, J. Welcome!"

"Hey, Maricella." She shook my hand and glanced around. "Nice place." Her genuine words warmed her green eyes.

"Thanks! Come inside. We're pleased you could join us."

Joey led the way. The real J contrasted with my expectation to such a degree, I had to give myself a mental shake. Her short hair, dyed blonde at the front, stood up in spikes. The black hair in back lay close to her head. She wore a hot pink T-shirt and a knee-length denim skirt, and as she turned to follow Joey, a series of little butterfly tattoos on her inner claves above her ankles caught my eye. No one in my family had tattoos. At least, I didn't think my boys did.

Okay, don't judge. Don't be a hypocrite.

Joey introduced her to the family. Good thing I hadn't shared my vision of J with Tom. He accepted her as he'd done with many of Joey's friends, with genuine pleasure. Even Julia surprised me and asked the origin of her name. Too engrossed in my own speculation, I missed her reply. Joey seemed at ease in J's company, and she engaged Teresa in conversation right from the start. Her oldest sister had a baby, and J shared tales of her niece's antics.

Observations throughout the visit forced me to drastically adjust my opinion. Who needed a tall, exotic Jade, when this young lady enthralled us all with her wit and intelligence?

We assembled around the table, and Tom gave the blessing. I'd prepared roast lamb, with potatoes, carrots, and squash. Nate slept while we ate, giving us time to enjoy our meal together. With his surgery scheduled for the following Monday, Mike and Teresa were edgy, but I hoped they could relax, surrounded by family.

While helping with the dishes, Alma shared her plans. "Lucia and I will stay a week or so after the surgery. And then we must go back home."

I rinsed a delicate china bowl and placed it on the drying rack. "I know Teresa has enjoyed having you here. You've been a great help, I'm sure."

"*Sí*, and of course we loved spending time with her and Michael and *el bebé*." Alma wiped the bowl. "My Teresa is doing better now. She had a hard time at first with a little bit of the *depresión*." After placing the bowl on the counter, she fiddled with the rings on her fingers.

The saucepan I scoured now gleamed. "Did she tell her doctor?" Obviously, with Alma here, Teresa and I hadn't shared many intimate moments.

"*Sí*." Alma's black curls bounced as she bobbed her head. "She was embarrassed to admit it."

"Why?"

"You know her." She shrugged. "Teresa is stubborn. But I told her it happened to me, too. They did not have a big name for it then. We all helped out. Helped each other, you know. *Familia*." Alma began drying the saucepan.

A wave of regret washed over me. How I wished I'd had a big family when I was young and when the boys were born. "Teresa is strong. She'll make it. Many people are praying for her."

"*Sí*."

Continuing in silence, we completed the chore, then joined the others on the back porch enjoying the warm spring weather. I caught my breath when Julia invited Joey to sit beside her. A snarky comment came to mind, but I instantly shut it off. How could I continue to harbor ill-feelings toward her when she seemed to be thawing toward Joey?

Mike held Nate against his chest, facing out. The baby's dark eyes flickered from one adult to another, his little lips puckering as he gnawed on a tiny fist. All adult eyes focused on him. A giant eagle could have swooped by, and we wouldn't have flinched.

But when my cell phone rang, I shook off the grandmother trance and checked caller I. D. Frankie. I excused myself and skipped down the stairs to the lawn. "Hi, Frankie!"

"My flight to Tennessee leaves in the morning. I happen to be in the neighborhood. Are you home?"

"Uh-huh."

"Can I come by and pick up Ginny's certificate and her locket?"

"Sure." I ambled to the pond. "We're celebrating Nate's one month birthday."

"I don't want to intrude. You can mail them to me."

"No, no. I want to say good-bye in person, and you can meet my family." *And maybe some of yours?* I gave him directions and our gate code. After explaining to the group, I returned inside to wait for him.

The envelope holding Virginia's certificate and locket lay on the kitchen table. I thought about the penciled names at the bottom. Frankie would know for sure if Elizabeth's child was Juli, Julie or Julia. My mother-in-law never did give me the list she promised.

Crunching tires on the caliche announced his arrival. I opened the kitchen door. He eased out of a white Toyota Tacoma pickup truck and limped toward me. I'd seen him once since the Andrew incident, and that was by chance at the grocery store in Kerrville, and he'd lost weight since then.

"What's up, Frankie? New vehicle?"

"It's the arthritis. Been acting up since I tussled with Andrew. This truck's smaller, easier to get in and out of. Borrowing from friends, you know."

"And you're not eating."

He removed his clip-on sunglasses. "I know, I know. But I'm going home. My daughter-in-law will fatten me up."

I couldn't resist hugging him. "Good. Come inside."

We entered the house and he stopped in front of the windows overlooking the porch. "That view is as fine as cream gravy."

I chuckled. "You say the funniest things."

"I'd rather be remembered for witty words than off-color ones. It's just as easy to use humor as it is to use cuss words. Makes a better impression, too."

The hills and valleys in the distance created a delightful panorama.

"You must enjoy sitting out there."

"I do. That's where I write in the journal you gave me."

His grin added more crinkles to his cheeks. He draped an arm around me. "Glad you liked my gift. Now, before we go out, tell me who everyone is."

"Okay." I moved to the next window. "I'll start here on the right. That's Alma, Teresa's mother, then Lucia, her sister. And Tom—"

"But . . . but why is Elizabeth here?" He swayed against me.

I braced myself and held onto him "What? There's no Elizabeth—"

"Then who's that next to Tom?"

"That's Julia, his mother."

Julia Archer. Elizabeth. Bessie. I'd been right.

Confusion covered Frankie's face as he moved to an armchair and sat. "I don't understand. She sure looks like Elizabeth."

The envelope containing Virginia's certificate lay on the side table. I picked it up. "Frankie, I think I have an explanation. But tell me one thing." I slid the page out and unfolded it. "What name is written here by Elizabeth and Charles Archer?"

Adjusting his glasses, he studied the paper. "Julia. Their daughter's name was Julia."

My knees gave way, and I sat in the chair next to him. "I think my mother-in-law is Elizabeth's daughter."

He raised watery eyes to mine. "Is that right?"

After a brief mental debate weighing the consequences, I asked, "Want to prove it?"

"Do you?"

I searched his face. His eyes softened in anticipation. I eyeballed Julia outside. Did I want to prove it to hurt her, to satisfy something vile in me?

Next thing I knew, I was pacing to the sofa and back. Could I do it? Should I?

Frankie turned and stared out the window. "Yes, I want to know for sure. Lookee here. Virginia and Elizabeth are gone. The Kerrville kin are not for me. My sister didn't believe they would accept me. What if Julia is different?"

Oh, Frankie, you don't know Julia. But I opened the back door, swallowing the joy the confrontation at first elicited, and motioned for Julia to come inside.

"Me," she mouthed.

"Please."

Holding the door for her, I gulped as she entered. "Julia, this is my friend,

Franklin Jackson. You may know him."

He rose from his chair the same time she sank into one. Julia's hand covered her pink tinted lips, and her eyes grew as wide as dinner plates.

"I . . . you're my niece, Julia. If your parents were Elizabeth and Charles Archer of Houston, then—"

She held up her hand, fending off further details. "Don't say anymore." With head bowed, she produced a tissue from the jacket pocket of her rose-pink linen suit and dabbed at her eyes and upper lip. "I . . . I am their daughter. Are you Virginia and Elizabeth's half-brother?"

Frankie melted into the chair. "Yes. We lost touch with Elizabeth long ago."

Locating another tissue, Julia sniffed into it. "My mother never spoke of her past when I was young. She did, however, in the years before she died. I never knew anything about you or Virginia or the Summerland-Hayes family until then."

The tension in the room bounced between us. I sat on the sofa facing Frankie and Julia. All my bluster vanished. I felt acutely sorry for Frankie. If he wanted a relationship with Julia, I knew it wouldn't come easily. But then, if he was related to Julia, he was related to Tom, and by marriage, to me.

With a grunt, he pushed up. "I'd better go. On account of all the packing. My friends are taking me to the airport tomorrow. I . . . I need . . ."

I stood, too, and slid my arm around his shoulders. "Please stay and meet the family. After all, you are our Great Uncle."

"Hey, that's right." White teeth gleamed in his broad smile. "Tom's my great-nephew, and you are now my favorite niece." But his grin disappeared. His lips quivered and tears gathered in his eyes.

"I'll understand if you can't stay. But you're welcome anytime." Releasing his arm, I slid the certificate back into the envelope.

Frankie, now standing in front of Julia, shuffled uncertainly, looking at his feet. "I'm sorry for the shock this must be to you, but weren't you ever curious about your kin in Kerrville?" He drew a handkerchief from his back pocket and swiped at his eyes.

Julia's head sank lower. "No, I . . . I wasn't. After my mother told me about her mother, I was already married and established, and it was the '60s. Not a good time to acknowledge black family members." Her head rose a tad. "I'm sorry. I hoped to never hear from them again."

I recalled her conversation with Tom about my research into the Summerland-Hayes family. No wonder it bothered her.

Julia patted her neat chignon as she stood. With a nod to Frankie, she walked to her room and closed the door.

Why'd she leave so suddenly? Did Frankie's presence remind her too much of her battle with her past?

Frankie frowned at the closed door for a second and then heaved a soulful sigh. "Got to go. I'll meet the rest of the family another time. I . . . I can't handle any more emotional drama right now. And I'm tired." His eyes misted again. "Come out with me. Please."

With my arm looped through his, we walked through the kitchen to the garage and the driveway.

"Frankie, what can I say?"

"Nothing, my friend. Nothing I haven't heard before, and believe me, I've heard it all." He placed his hands on my shoulders. "But there's hope. There's always hope for a future where a person's color won't matter. Where what's in his heart will matter more."

"And your heart is pure gold, Frankie." I kissed his weathered cheek. "Please write, and keep in touch."

"I will. God bless."

"*Adiós.*"

He grunted as he climbed into the truck, and then meandered down the driveway. I waved until he disappeared around the curve.

When I returned to the living room, I glanced out the windows. Julia wasn't outside. I listened by her door and knocked. "Julia, can I come in?"

She opened the door and ushered me in. After settling in the chair, she motioned me to sit on the bed.

Words failed me. All the accusations I'd rehearsed sounded petty and juvenile, but I wanted answers. Why had she literally walked out on Frankie? Why had she made me feel like a second class citizen in my own family?

She crossed her legs, and leaned back in the chair. I focused on her tan pumps, expecting smooth excuses to flow from her lips.

"Has Frankie gone? I'm a coward. I couldn't face him." She continued before I could respond. "I owe you an explanation and an apology. And I have to beg for your forgiveness."

My head jerked up in surprise, and I blinked in confusion. Red-rimmed eyes seemed out of place in her usual perfect face.

Uncertain as to what was going to happen, I swallowed. "I'm listening."

Head lowered, she smoothed her flawless linen pants. "I'm ashamed of my behavior, and until our discussion a month ago, I was unaware of how much I'd allowed my heritage to influence how I treated people. Not just you and Joey. Many people in my years of ignoring, betraying my . . . my family. I've done a lot of soul searching these past weeks. A lot of praying."

She ripped out several tissues from the box on the dresser and dabbed at her eyes. "I became a snob. A racial snob, and treated people of color as . . . as, well, I'm not proud of my actions. And to know I treated you that way, too . . . I'm sorry. I don't know what else to say. It doesn't matter how long a person has been a Christian, there is always more to learn. And I've learned a lot from you." She raised her eyes to mine. "Can you forgive me?"

Twisting my hands together, I stared at my fingers. My mind reeled at her genuine words. She apologized to *me*? A battle waged. Recalling Julia's barbs and snide comments of past years still hurt. I knew I had to offer forgiveness, but her previous treatment of Joey jabbed at my heart. She had more amends to make.

"Of course, Julia, I forgive you. We all make mistakes, but we're family, a multi-colored family." A smile touched my lips for a second, then slipped away. "I do forgive you, but you must also talk to Joey." I slid off the bed and moved to the door. "And later on, I hope you will contact Frankie. He's a fine man."

After rising from the chair, she brushed imaginary specks of debris off her suit.

"Thank you, my dear. Talking of good people, you're a fine wife and mother."

I halted at the door and turned. She had never complimented me before.

Julia stepped closer and opened her arms. Hesitating, a thousand reasons for not hugging her shot through my head, but then one truth found its way to my heart. *Familia.*

Once in her embrace, we stood together brief seconds as years of distrust and deceit melted away.

We eased apart.

Inches above me, Julia beamed. "Maybe you're right. While I'm here, I might visit Kerrville. Go see the kin there. Get to know them."

Back stepping to the door, I rested against it to prevent my knees buckling. "Julia, are you serious?"

"Yes. I do want to meet them. And where did you say Frankie was going? Tennessee? I've never been to Tennessee."

I clapped a hand over my mouth and chuckled at the transformation. Not just her words. Her face radiated a new confidence, a peace that had not been there before.

"One more thing, when you go back outside, please ask Joey to come see me. He and I have a lot to talk about. Not only do I have mistakes to correct, I want to do something positive for the future, too. I believe he's raising money for a summer project?"

As I viewed the new Julia, a reality hit me broadside. Some of my perceived clashes with her had been of my own making. I had always been hypersensitive to her words. Maybe at least half the problems had been caused by my reacting to her.

My guilt hung heavy on my heart. How much had I contributed to the situation? The realization sent a wave of heat up my neck. How could I have been so blind?

I returned to my mother-in-law and wrapped my arms around her. "I have misjudged you. Forgive me for being hard to love, Julia."

She nodded and patted my shoulder.

We clung together for a few seconds, and then I headed to the back porch to find Joey. The peace forgiveness proffered filled my soul.

"Joey, Grandmother wants to see you."

I sat next to Tom and held his hand. His answering smile seemed to say it all. He could read me so well. He knew his mother and I had resolved our issues.

He squeezed my hand. "Are you okay?"

"Yes. All is right in my world."

TWENTY-NINE

Nate's surgery lasted three hours. Huddled in the waiting room, we thumbed through magazines, stared out the window, talked in low tones.

Mike never left Teresa's side.

When Dr. Janiskowski entered the room, they swarmed to meet her.

"How's Nate, Doctor?" Mike asked the question we all needed answered.

She ran her fingers through her hair and smiled. "He's doing fine. I drained the cyst and then inserted a shunt designed to constantly drain fluid away from his brain to be absorbed into his body."

By now, we all stood around the doctor, Lucia in Alma's embrace, Tom's arm around my shoulders, and Julia holding Joey's hand. My heart sang at her gesture.

Doctor Jan continued. "Long-term effects will be monitored by Nate's pediatrician. It's too early to tell if he suffered brain damage from the pressure of the fluid. His developmental milestones must be measured closely."

"When can we see him?" Teresa asked, her voice reedy and high-pitched.

"He's in recovery right now. Probably in an hour or so."

After the doctor left the room, we joined hands and thanked the Lord for Nate's successful surgery.

The tone in the waiting room brightened as we passed the hour in jovial conversation.

Mike and Teresa saw Nate first, followed by Alma and Lucia, and then Julia and Joey.

By the time Tom and I visited, Nate's head and face had almost returned to normal proportions. The little shaved area and two-inch scar reminded me of the fragility of life. I marveled at the visible shunt under his skin. What other advances in medical science would Nate see in his lifetime?

"He's going to be all right, sweetheart." Tom gathered me close.

"I know. We're all going to be fine. Like Job, we will survive and surpass anything we could have planned for ourselves." I snuggled against his chest. "Remember when you told me to study about the amour of God in Ephesians?"

"Sure."

"Well, I read the whole book and memorized verse twenty from chapter three. 'Now to Him who is able to do immeasurably more than all we ask or imagine . . .'" I touched Nate's tiny hand and his fingers curled around my pinkie.

"It's a hard concept to grasp, that our plans are puny compared to God's. Wonder what He has in store for the McDonough family?"

After I eased my pinkie out of Nate's grasp, I gave his cheek a final pat, and then looped my arm through Tom's. "With you by my side, I can't wait to find out."

Hand in hand, Tom and I tip-toed out of the room.

EPILOGUE

Andrew remains in prison, waiting to hear the sentence after his conviction for three murders and a variety of other crimes. Marshall will also serve jail time, although he provided evidence against Andrew. Warren told me Emory resumed running the family business. With his organizational expertise, he should be able to turn a profit in the next year or two. Virginia would be proud.

Warren and Connie are engaged and plan an August wedding. The Trentons and the Howards tried to convince Leah to move back to Brooder, but she wants to stay in San Antonio until after her baby is born and the older children complete their school year.

Teresa is keeping the jewelry box, but asked me not to show her how to open the secret compartments. She never wants anything concealed in there again. After her mother and sister returned to New Mexico, she adjusted quickly to school work, taking care of Nate, and household chores. Her emotional state improved, especially after the success of Nate's surgery. Naturally, Mike helps all he can, and on days I'm not at school, I spend time in Brooder, too.

The first group of students arrived from Houston. Camp Alpha is hopping with enthusiastic kids, and Mike's days are filled with solving problems. He is in his element. Although Stewart Casey from Houston still causes occasional problems, the church leaders have committed to the program and to Mike playing an integral part. With an infusion of funds from Buck and Lexi Ballard's foundation, Mike's position and salary have been increased to full-time status.

Joey and J visit us often. My impression of her changes constantly. She has deep spiritual beliefs and challenges Joey at every turn. He must stay on his toes to keep up with her. I want to know more about her. One of these days, she and I will have a heart-to-heart conversation—when I think the time is right.

Sylvester and Trixie have healed and keep Norm company when he works in his shop. He now has an electric gate, and the last time I stopped by, the shotgun was nowhere in sight.

Tom's new position with the company allows him to be home most evenings. What an adjustment that's been. We eat together almost every night and even share the cooking. I've had to relinquish some lone decision making, but I'm beginning to understand what a blessing it is having him here consistently. The incident with Sally has been resolved, but I've learned not to take Tom's fidelity for granted. I thank the Lord for him daily.

In our Bible studies we've had further discussions on the problem of Job, or rather my problem of viewing Mike and Teresa's circumstances as a punishment. In my understanding of the situation I'm not where Tom is yet, but I'm getting there. I still think they're being treated unfairly, but Tom reminds me life is not fair. God didn't promise us fairness. He promised us faithfulness.

For our twenty-sixth wedding anniversary, Tom gave me an antique jewelry box—with no secret compartments! His note inside reminded me how many people love me. I also realized I didn't need ancestors to have a family dynasty. Tom and I could begin our own. After all, we're off to a great start with Mike, Teresa, and Joey. And Nate. Who knows how many other children will join that little boy. Then there are Joey and J . . .

I've spent hours learning sign language at school, not only for my work with the students, but since the episode with Kathy when Andrew held a gun to Nate's head, the skill has taken a hold in my heart, and I see other practical applications.

Last weekend while visiting with Mike, Teresa, and Nate, Kathy's four-year-old son Chuck played on the greening lawn. I carried Nate outside where Chuck and I had a lengthy conversation in sign. He understood my stilted phrases and words, and taught me a few new signs. Kathy observed from her porch. Later, she joined us and asked if Teresa and I would like to come for coffee.

It might not be much, but it's a beginning.

Apricot and Ice-cream Torte

1 cup sliced almonds
1 teaspoon almond extract
18 oz jar apricot preserves
3 tablespoons butter
1 box Vanilla Wafer cookies
1½ quart container of vanilla ice-cream (rectangular container works best)

1. Toast almonds in the butter.
2. Place cookies in a zip-top plastic bag and pound with a mallet until crumbly.
3. Mix crumbs with almonds and almond extract.
4. Slice ice-cream into ½ inch slabs.
5. In a 9 x 13 inch dish, layer crumb mixture, ice-cream slabs, and apricot preserves. Repeat. Top with crumb mixture.
6. Freeze for several hours before serving. Serves 12.

Maricella received this recipe from her good friend Louise Larsen, Hondo, Texas.

Maricella's Carne Asada

3 pounds flank steak
1/3 cup lime juice
4 cloves garlic, minced
1 teaspoon salt
½ cup chopped fresh cilantro
1 tablespoon paprika
1 tablespoon chili powder

½ cup olive oil
2 tablespoons white vinegar
½ teaspoon sugar
1 teaspoon black pepper
1 teaspoon dried oregano
1 tablespoon ground cumin
1 minced jalapeño pepper, seeded

1. Mix all ingredients, **except the steak and olive oil** in a large glass or ceramic bowl. Slowly whisk in the olive oil until marinade is well combined. Remove 1 cup of the marinade, cover with plastic wrap and refrigerate for later use.
2. Place the flank steak between two sheets of plastic on a solid surface. Pound the steak with a meat mallet to a thickness of ¼ inch. Then poke the surface of the meat with a fork. Add the meat to the marinade in the large bowl, cover, and refrigerate for at least 4 hours.
3. Preheat outdoor grill for medium high heat, lightly oil the grate. (Can also use a cast iron grill pan on high heat for stove top cooking.) Remove meat from marinade and grill for 5 minutes per side. Discard used marinade.
4. Slice the meat across the grain. Pour the saved marinade over the hot meat and serve immediately. Serve with warmed tortillas, Pico de Gallo (fresh tomato salsa), and guacamole or sliced avocados. Six to eight servings.

Alma's Bizcochitos*, Anise Cookies

1 cup butter or lard

¾ cup white sugar

1 ½ teaspoons anise seeds

1 egg

3 cups all-purpose flour

1 teaspoon baking powder

½ teaspoon salt

1 to 2 tablespoons water or white wine

Topping:

½ cup white sugar

1 teaspoon cinnamon

1. Cream the butter or lard with ¾ cup sugar until light and fluffy. Crush the anise seeds in a mortar and pestle or use a spice grinder.
2. Add crushed anise seed and egg to sugar mixture. Mix thoroughly. Add the flour, baking powder, and salt. Stir to combine. If dough is too dry, gradually add a little water or wine.
3. Divide the dough in half. Pat each piece into a 1 inch thick disk. Wrap each disk in plastic and chill for at least 30 minutes.
4. In a wide, shallow bowl combine ½ cup sugar and cinnamon. Set aside.
5. Preheat oven to 325°F. Generously grease a baking sheet, or line it with parchment paper.
6. Use one disk at a time – keep the other one refrigerated. Flour a pastry board and roll out the dough to ¼ inch thickness. Use cookie cutters to form cookies. The traditional shape is fleur-de-lis. (The dough gets sticky and soft as soon as it warms up. Handle as little as possible. If it gets too sticky, refrigerate until firm again.)

7. Dip each cookie in the cinnamon sugar mixture, and place on cookie sheet. Or sprinkle mixture over cookies once on the sheet.
8. Bake for 12 to 15 minutes, until fluffy and barely tanned on edges. Transfer to a rack to cool. Be careful as the cookies are fragile.
9. Allow to cool. Store in a sealed container. Makes about 4 dozen cookies.

*Can also be spelled Biscochitos.

Alma's Posole

Cooking time: 2 ½ to 3 hours Serves 6

2 pounds pork shoulder or butt, cut into 1 inch chunks
3 dried New Mexico chilies, stems and seeds removed, finely chopped (can also use ancho chilies)
3 garlic cloves, chopped
2 teaspoons salt
6 cups cooked hominy (canned works fine)
2 teaspoons dried Mexican oregano
2 bay leaves
1 teaspoon ground cumin

Garnishes:
½ head shredded cabbage, seasoned with juice of 1 lime
½ cup chopped cilantro
1 sliced avocado
1 cup chopped green onions
½ cup shredded radishes
tortillas or tostado chips
(Tom likes to add sour cream and grated cheese)

1. Brown the meat in a pan with a little olive oil. Do it in batches so each piece gets good color.
2. Transfer meat to a large pot and cover with water. (Add a little water to pan used for browning and scrape out bits. Add to pot.)
3. Add garlic, chilies, salt, and bay leaves. Bring to a boil. Reduce heat to a steady simmer, cover, and cook until pork is fork tender, about 1 ½ hours.

4. Add drained hominy, oregano, and cumin. Continue cooking for another hour. Add additional water as necessary to keep ingredients covered. (Stew needs a lot of liquid.)
5. Taste and add more salt if necessary.
6. Serve in deep bowls.
7. Arrange garnishes in separate containers so guests can make their own selections.

Other Books

by Valerie Massey Goree

Visit http://www.parsonplacepress.com/store for more titles by Parson Place Press

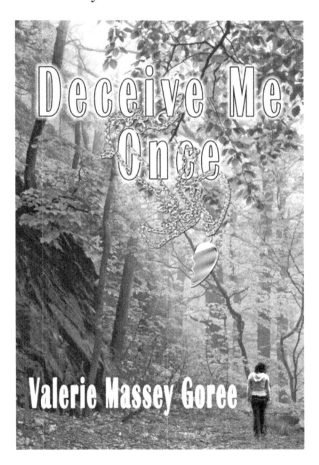

CPSIA information can be obtained at www.ICGtesting.com
Printed in the USA
LVOW03s0007060614

388881LV00001B/1/P